Cranberry Wine

Cranberry Wine

R.C. Bruce

Dedication and Prologue

Very often in the beginning of a romance or relationship we see small hints of personalities that we think to ourselves, it is okay, I can fix that. When and if it ends badly you think back and realize, I couldn't fix that. How do we reach the level of happiness we desire and what lengths are we willing to go to get out of a messy choice?

Yet, we gravitate to the next love hoping this time it will be that wonderful partnership we crave to last a lifetime.

This is dedicated to all the men and women who felt they made mistakes or wrong choices. Mistakes that sent a ripple into the universe. It will get better. Never give up your dreams for anyone. Never regret trying, just keep trying to get it right. I often wonder, how did I survive the ripples that were started by mistake or on purpose? I never gave up. I was not afraid to try again.

I want to thank my Husband most of all who always encourages me and has my back in everything. My three daughters who still love to come to my house for family dinners and my mother who made a fantastic chocolate cake and did not shy away from constructive criticism.

"All Wine is beautiful and unique, you can just choose one, or try them all. Some wine is tart, and some can be sweet. Ironically, the same can be said for a good book and most relationships" ~RCB

Contents

Foreword

This is the third book I have edited and published for Rebecca Conaty Bruce. It is completely different than the other two and will hold your interest to the end. In fact, there were times during the editing process where I had to remind myself that I was supposed to be editing – not getting drawn into the story.

We all make choices in life and each of them has an outcome, good or bad. Some choices lead to happiness while others result in abject sadness and a feeling of being boxed in with no way out. Rebecca has managed to capture the full range of emotions associated with diametrically opposed choices in "Cranberry Wine."

"Cranberry Wine" has been over a year in preparation as Rebecca started, stopped, and started again – and I know there was at least one time where she was ready to throw in the towel and abandon the project entirely. I am certainly glad she didn't: the result is, in my not-so-humble opinion, the best of her works that I have been a part of.

Through Rebeca's words, we get the compelling story of the life choices made by the protagonist, Antonia, an only child who was brought up in an idyllic setting on a ranch in Texas. The choices she makes after leaving the ranch affect not only the rest of her life, but the lives of many other people.

As Eleanor Roosevelt said, "In the long run, we shape our lives, and we shape ourselves. The process never ends until we die. And the choices we make are ultimately our own responsibility."

Michael Paul Hurd
Author/Editor/Publisher
Lineage Independent Publishing

Lineage Independent Publishing
Marriottsville, MD

https://lineage-indypub.com

Chapter 1: Cranberry Lane

We are all sailing out on a voyage of discovery, not knowing what will guide us or throw us off track along the way. We are only one decision away from a totally different life. A tragic event in your life has a ripple effect. An event happens, then it spreads like ripples on the water after you throw in a rock. A ripple effect starts and before you know it, the ones on the outside circle of ripples begin to suffer and drop away. You start to question yourself. Then fear sets in. Fear of not fitting in. Fear causes physiological changes that may produce behavioral reactions such as aggression. That is what the ripples do, they float and spread. If you do not protect yourself, the hurt you encounter from the ripples will fester and grow. This will create your story. You never know where you will be when the ripple finally reaches you and the things that make you who you are, begin.

Often the ripples are of your own making, and some are formed by a simple mistake or words that should not have been spoken. Often when you leave the house you turn to your dog and say, *"I will be right back"* but what if you don't return? When I left for college, I said those words to my mother as I often did. It was our thing. However, I never really returned home soon enough.

I remember a bright moonlight washed over a village I was visiting, illuminating the people wandering around the square. That is when I knew the ripples had finally reached me. There was no escaping it. The break-up had caused real damage. I see that now. I gave in to the hurt and released my urges from the chains I had neatly locked them in. I turned inward briefly, then the rage exploded inside me one day. I was never caught but I felt the guilt. Guilt creates a ripple.

The next steps in my life journey are what changed me forever. Everyone has a story. That is my story. My journey. My reaction to the ripples.

Some journeys remain etched in our soul because they caused us pain or led us to hurt those we once loved. A trained therapist can trace back to adverse childhood experiences and trauma, that if not dealt with and processed, can be the biggest contributor to mental issues and criminal activity in one's future. Basically, your life when the ripple hit you: why you did the things you do in life.

I despised looking at my life in the rear-view mirror. I did not care what others thought, I had good grades, good parents and I was skilled at riding horses. Most girls can shove their way through the pre-teen tide pool flawlessly and I was no different. I just put on a brave face, always, because being cowardly is not cute. I also had a boyfriend. I didn't think my life was normal because what is normal anyway? No, I was optimistic and thought my life was superbly planned and special. Things happen even if there is no reason behind it.

I was impulsive and overly confident maybe, but I did not become who I am from some kid in school tossing out doses of low self esteem. I was strong until I wasn't. I paid attention to the way people reacted to my boundaries, discovering the edge where their respect for me ended. The hurt that I suffered started slowly and unnoticeably. It is not an excuse.

In my case, I had urges. Urges to have the highest score in the class as well as urges to reach out and grab a tormentor by the throat. I even pictured it in my mind a few times but never acted on it. I was self controlled. My head on straight. Never gave my parents reason to scold me. Urges are dangerous if you are guided by them, but equally as dangerous to ignore them. I had urges, but I controlled them…until now.

Ironically, my life began on Cranberry Lane. It was a strange name for the dusty dirt road leading to our sixty-acre ranch near San Antonio, Texas, but mother insisted on it. Mother was born in Montana where it gets bitterly cold in the winter and where wild cranberries grew. Daddy was a cowboy, roping cattle and living in a bunk house. They met at a rodeo and momma loved the way he looked in the saddle. He was a tall man with a dream of owning a horse ranch in warmer climates. Mother agreed to move and give up her career as an accountant after they married but only if she could name the ranch. After much debate, Daddy caved and made a compromise allowing her to name the road leading to the ranch but not the ranch. "No respectable cowboy would name their sixty-acre ranch *Cranberry*," he would say shaking his head, "that is something you name a horse or a pie, not a working horse ranch in Texas!"

Daddy always compromised. He never expected mother to just obey. He respected her and valued her needs and opinions. Mother said "obey" was a poor choice of words and refused to have them in her wedding vows. So, the story goes that the road leading to the ranch was legally named Cranberry Lane. They named the ranch Antonia Ranch. A twist on the name of the town and their first and only child. Me. Now I am stuck with it. Good thing I turned out to be a girl.

I had no siblings; Mother said one was enough. She cared a lot about her appearance and couldn't risk not losing that poundage after the birth, so she said. "Not even a rock tumbler could smooth my edges after another baby," she would say.

Fortunately, I did have a best friend, Cara, who became like a sister to me. Her parents worked on the ranch, so we saw each other often. I told her all my secrets and she told me hers. We had a unique bond.

Cara was teased for her braces and pigtails, and I was teased for my initials, APE. Antonia Penelope Edwards. Kids will find anything to tease about, so when our teacher put our initials on the lockers and cubbies, the roar of the teasing girls was loud and instant: I don't know how many times I heard monkey noises in the hall behind my back. Cara said if she ever died, she would want to come back as a skunk: "I would have a cute face, no braces, and black and white fur instead of pig tails. I would attract girls who like to tease us into petting, then bam! I would just turn around, aim and fire! My butt would be my superpower and my sweet revenge."

"They would smell the stench of instant regret," I laughed. I knew she was only trying to make me feel better about the teasing. I personally thought it was all childish. Teasing could be the root cause for all our future choices. Teasing leads to unresolved anger issues. Cara's round face and pigtails wouldn't be so bad if it wasn't for the blunt cut bangs. However, she did not deserve the teasing and neither did I just because my initials spelled out the name for a giant furry animal. I would hate to think being teased for my initials may be what caused it all.

Constantly practicing restraint caused me anger and anger is a primal urge. It is not a negative emotion. Anger bubbles up if you hold back too long. I am sure my mother never gave it a second thought when she named me after my grandmother, Penelope. Mothers are unaware of the things they do without a thought that it could be the source of their child's future mental health issues. Mothers can cause a ripple.

Cara and I grew up spending every summer together, starting with kindergarten. Childhood summers are where you develop many things. A personality, courage, bravery and learn to kiss on the back of your hand. We pretended to be princesses, cowgirls and warriors. We became blood sisters with a rusty pocket knife under a tree in the far pasture. We recited a made-up oath with elaborate promises that always ended when school started again. The final summer before we were seniors in high school was the summer Cara stopped wearing her famous pig tails, got her braces removed, and went to live with her grandmother in Colorado. Mother packed us two large pieces of her chocolate cake and we headed for our spot in the far pasture. Cara and I cried under the same tree where we became blood sisters and I never saw her again. Losing touch with a childhood friend and summertime life lessons create a ripple of doubt. You doubt you will ever find another friend.

I also grew up with rowdy cowboys and ranchers for neighbors and playmates. I took pleasure in defying conventional fads and never wore dresses. I wore blue jeans, made the usual childhood mud pies, wore cowboy boots and rode my favorite horse, Julius. I heard whispers about being a tomboy or how I was not feminine enough. I understood it must be an ugly and loathsome thing to not be prissy like the other girls, but I preferred to think of myself as a nerd who had a plan. I simply saw them as shallow and brushed it off.

At times I would turn quickly to face the ones who whispered behind my back and watched them scurry like cockroaches. I saw it as funny, though I wondered if deep inside it tore at my self esteem. The urge to scare them became a pleasure. Bullies create a ripple.

My life consisted of Texas dust, rodeos and flirting with one particular ranch hand named Rick. If I wasn't in the barn trying to impress the man I dreamed I would marry one day, then I had my nose in a book. Some girls strived to have the perfect hair and they would have achieved success, others the right home or husband.

I thought college would be my goal for success. I wanted to be a surgeon. The sight of blood did not seem to bother me at all. I watched many times when a cowboy received a gash on his head and got stitched up. In addition to the dream of being a surgeon, I wanted to marry a cowboy. I wanted a tight jean wearing, rough and rowdy, but still sexy cowboy for a husband. That was the plan. College and a cowboy. I thought it was a perfect combo like peas and carrots. The children would come later. I wanted a passel of children.

Some people have a "Plan B" just in case their first plan does not come into fruition. I never had doubts. As a matter of fact, I was convinced if I thought it and wanted it bad enough it would just come true. I was not one for studying all summer. Education came easy for me. I spent my summers riding Julius and tagging along when my daddy took the ranch to the rodeo. I didn't go for the roping competition or the bull riding. I went for the tight-ass jeans on the cowboys. A few of us teens would sit on the fence watching as the parade of young men would be grooming their horse or practicing their roping behind the stadium.

I never wore make-up or fell into any fads. Having naturally long dark eyelashes and a perfect complexion, I saw no need. I did get my fair share of whistles from the cowboys while wearing *my* tight jeans. When we got back to the ranch late at night after a rodeo I would go to the barn pretending to brush Julius just so I could watch the muscles flex on the ranch hands as they put away the horses and saddles.

By the time I hit puberty, I would say I was a pretty frustrated girl. Just once I would have killed to be in the hay with a sexy cowboy. The closest I ever got was playing spin the bottle. Nothing against today's standards but I am pretty sure the lack of teenage experimentation may have been the reason I made the mistake of thinking attraction was love in my college years. I was so naïve.

Respect for my parents was foremost in my thoughts and actions. I may have dreamed about kissing in the hay but my daddy, William Alexander Edwards, would have banished me with a ticket to the train station if he ever heard of anything improper. My mother was an accountant before she became the wife of a rancher. She was organized and precise in everything down to her famous chocolate cake. The two-layer piece of chocolate heaven was cut into exactly twelve slices, and she counted them daily to see if I was sneaking cake before dinner. My parents were stiff, but they fit well together.

Our ranch house was built by my daddy as my mother counted the money and managed the time. We stayed in a small RV until the building was complete; I barely remember those days. Momma insisted on a wrap-around porch and daddy said that was fine as long as he could build a large stone fireplace in the center of our living room.

Sitting around the fire, we were a close family with daddy telling stories of his early days being a bull riding cowboy. Momma would say she worried he would have brain damage before they ever got to the wedding chapel. I listened to the stories with enchantment as though I was listening to a play unfold. Several times there would be music accompanying the stories and other cowboys would join in if we were outside sitting by the fire. I saw love and I felt love as well as a sense of community. That is definitely where my confidence came from. My parents always compromised and gave me an idea of what I expected a marriage to be. Life was good. I never lived in a plastic bubble, but my childhood was good, I thought. I was fearless, not bothered by idle gossip or bullies.

Before I left for college, my cowboy crush who was only a few years older, took me on a horseback ride to the farthest pasture. Rick packed a picnic lunch, and we sat under the only few trees on the ranch. After eating he took out his pocketknife and carved our initials in a tree.

"Antonia, this is my promise to love you forever. When you get back from college, we are going to get married and have lots of babies. When you walk across that stage at graduation, I will be in the front row. When you finish medical school, I will take you out to a fancy dinner to celebrate. I will be right here on the ranch waiting for you while you fulfill your dreams of becoming a surgeon. Just remember to come back to me, always."

"If you mean that, then kiss me right here on this blanket, Rick Reynolds!"

And he did. We kissed and kissed. We even kissed while riding our horses and he almost fell off leaning over too far. Even then I never thought it would come true. I thought it was just being silly to get a kiss or a hand up my blouse. I had no clue what it meant to love someone and make a lifelong promise to marry. I left for college the next day. Up to this point I thought my life was set, well planned and on track. I did not plan for all the forks in the road that appeared unexpectedly. I certainly never planned to commit a crime. Not me.

The first year of college whizzed by with no tribulations. Daddy bought me a Pontiac Firebird so I could come home to visit and look good while driving on campus. It was bright yellow so anyone with eyes could see me coming a mile away. It was so bright it hurt my eyes. Daddy called it "the Yellow Rose of Texas." I called it embarrassing.

Once a month I drove my Yellow Rose of Texas home to visit the ranch, my parents and Rick. Momma would have chocolate cake waiting for me and Rick would have my horse, Julius, all brushed and looking good. Rick always thought I was coming home to see him when actually Julius and Momma's chocolate cake were my priority. Daddy would check the oil in Yellow Rose and brag about how he picked her off the car lot just for me. By the second year of college, I rarely visited home. In my later years I would regret that. As I returned to college, I would always say, "I will be right back," as I waved from the window of the Yellow Rose.

I caught myself slacking in my studies because the basic classes were easy. So, I doubled up, taking two extra classes a semester and looking forward to starting pre-med and taking my MCATS earlier than predicted. I set a goal. My college roommate and I joined a study group. I was busy and focused. I forgot to visit home and almost forgot about Rick.

This was the beginning. I questioned everything looking back. Everyone enters a relationship whether it is friendship, romance or a business agreement noticing little hints of conflict and tell ourselves: *I can fix that. It will be fine.* When it ends badly, we look back and tell ourselves: *I couldn't fix that. It was not okay.*

Eventually I even questioned my relationship with wine, romance, and my uncontrollable urges. But it is not the beginning or the middle that keeps you looking for the right landing on the shore. The beginning is very important, I am told. Because how you start life and the lessons learned can greatly affect the rest of your life and what happens in the end. How you survive when the ripple hits you.

Chapter 2: One Spilled Drink

I set my eyes on Texas A&M University then on to Baylor College of Medicine in Houston. While attending Texas A&M, I was invited to attend many college parties. Most of the time, I turned down the invitations, preferring to stay home and read my anatomy books. Booze, loud music and dancing were foreign to me. The closest thing to a party on the ranch was a cookout or campfire singing with an acoustic guitar. I had no time for parties. But as they say, every rule has an exception and every college student gives in to peer pressure. It happens. A frat house was having their annual end of the term party. I agreed to go because I was hounded by my college roommate. She begged, actually, because she wanted to be with the popular students and wear her new dress.

Her name was Jill, a sweet girl who moved to the United States from the United Kingdom. Jill was a great roommate and best friend. She loved her studies and did not play loud music, both wonderful qualities to have in a roommate. She was an avid reader who fell asleep every night reading a romance novel or a 300-page dissertation on the importance of learning historical facts in Biblical times. Jill was a history major and talking to her was like talking to an encyclopedia. Jill successfully convinced me with her cute twiggy haircut and sweet voice to give at least one party a chance. There may have been some batting of the eye lashes and pouty face as well. So, I agreed. I should regret it, but everything happens for a reason.

"Accept whatever life offers you, Antonia," Jill would say.

"Am I supposed to believe that life is offering me a college frat party?" I asked.

"Yes. We both have studied hard; we deserve a break. Accept the gift."

The social party on campus was as much loud music as it was shoulder to shoulder students. The frat house was a two-story brick colonial with white columns in the front looking very grand except for the frat flags and loud music shaking the walls. I rolled my eyes as I managed to squeeze my way into the door.

Rubbing up against unfamiliar body parts was quite the new experience for me. I was tempted to turn around and just weave my way back out of this tuna fish can, Jill motivated me to keep moving on. I say motivated but seriously she gave me a big shove and I was finally through the wads of bodies.

Then everything changed. I popped through like a can of biscuits right into the chest of a handsome Architect student named Wade. He spilled some awful smelling liquid libation all over me. It looked like a deep burgundy wine, or someone had seriously bled to death all over my favorite shirt.

When I looked up at his six-foot-tall frame and our eyes met, I had that warm fuzzy feeling I heard other girls talk about during late night study groups. There I stood staring into the eyes of a dream; his broad shoulders made him seem larger than life. He was a perfect stranger but there was a spark, a sense of familiarity as deep as my soul.

They say your first love sets the tone for all the relationships in your future. Whoever "they" are, they got this one right. You can blow off the ripples from the mean kid in school who made you cry. You can scoff at the high school cheerleaders who made fun of the quality of your ponytail. You can give a hall pass to those with little or no imagination when trying to mock you simply because your initials are funny, but love is a whole different ball game.

Your legs become weak, your heart does this strange flutter and your throat's so dry you squeak when you try to talk. It took ten hard swallows before I gained the ability to form words that Wade could understand.

Technically it wasn't my first love: I did have a crush on a cowboy, but this felt like grown up feelings. The kind you read about in romance novels. I took it as a sign. A nudge from the love fairy. I thought had my path planned out all the way through to my internship. However, in my head I whispered, *"I think this journey to medical school is about to take an unexpected turn."*

"My name is Wade, I am so sorry about your…your…is that a pearl button cowboy shirt?" he stammered.

He didn't apologize for spilling the wine or the comment; instead his eyes grew a little more curious. He took a step back and looked me up and down, rubbing his smooth whisker free chin and making a grunting sound I was not familiar with. Half chuckle and half flirtatious.

"Uh-huh," I managed to squeak out. "I mean, yes, it is."

"Wow, I don't think I've seen a shirt like that on a college student before. You wear clothes like that all the time?" He grinned. "I mean, you have a pretty face and all, but this isn't a hoe-down, sweetie. You might be at the wrong party," he laughed.

That should have been my first sign. I should have told him it is not the clothes that matter. I should have walked away from his rude comments. Instead, I dove right into those shark-infested waters of attraction and never looked away.

We often believe what we think we see: I saw penetrating eyes and a kind face. Wade had said those magical words all women want to hear, *"You have a pretty face."* Wade had a mop of dark wavy hair, and the longest eye lashes I had ever seen on a man. He was smartly dressed in blue jeans that were obviously ironed and a white button-up shirt. His shoes were so shiny I could see my reflection. He wasn't a cowboy, but he was sexy.

Wade instantly had a unique leverage. Give me a compliment, I will follow you anywhere. I was sucked into his aroma, better than freshly cut hay on a good day at the ranch. A bubble that I could not bust my way out of. All intelligence left me at that moment. I babbled and smiled. I even let out a small giggle when he asked if I wanted to take off my shirt.

"I would take off anything for you," I thought.

Thank goodness for Jill, my college mate or that night would have gone down in infamy as the night I lost my virginity. She tapped me hard on the shoulder several times.

"Ouch" I shouted. "What is up with you tonight, Jill? Can't you see I am talking to someone?"

"I have been calling your name but apparently your ears have been affected by this goon spilling a drink on you."

Turning to acknowledge her at my shoulder, I said, "I'm absolutely fine, Jill. This is an old shirt, and I don't feel the wetness at all. As a matter of fact, it is keeping me cool on such a hot night. Didn't you say Texas weather takes something to get used to?"

One eyebrow was raised and her lip curled at the corner like she was looking at someone she just met. I stuck my tongue out at her to break up her worried look.

"His name is Wade, and I am just fine." I tried to give her the *leave me alone I just fell in love* look but she did not catch my hint.

"You don't sound fine, Antonia. You are talking funny, babbling like a drunk person. Let's go back to the dorm," said Jill, tugging on my arm. "We should not have come. There are so many people and I think someone touched my butt!"

"Relax, Jill. I am just looking. A girl can look, can't she?"

"Well, what would Rick think?" snapped Jill.

Rick was my childhood crush and the cowboy I thought would sweep me off my feet one day and we would elope on the back of my horse Julius. We had only shared one kiss. When I left for college, he left for the rodeo circuit. I had known him for years, yet I was still stunned by his rugged good looks when I visited home. My daddy loved him like the son he never had.

Shrugging, I looked back at Wade, noticing his eyes taking the liberty to peek down my blouse and for some unexplained reason, I found it endearing. Wade was interested in me. This was real. Not at all like playing spin the bottle in the barn with ranch hand Rick.

Am I the lucky one to be standing here with this dreamy guy?

Looking up at Wade, I searched for a sign in his eyes, hoping he felt the same bolt of electricity running down his spine as I did. Wade smiled the whitest set of teeth I had ever seen. Growing up on the ranch was all I knew, and I knew cowboys had tobacco breath or the belief that teeth were optional. Wade was certainly no cowboy. A warm feeling swept over me. A feeling I had never felt before, but it felt good. So I questioned myself.

"Is this what love feels like?"

Jill disappeared into the crowd. I was sure she would be fine. She was the most responsible and smartest girl I knew. It didn't matter at the time because all my focus was on Wade. We talked for hours. At least he talked for hours; I swooned, nodding 'yes' occasionally.

We ended up exchanging numbers that night. Wade was ahead of me in his studies for two years and for those two years Wade and I were inseparable. All I could think about was the next date with Wade and still passing my anatomy class. Love is not something you prepare for; it is something you give in to. Wade taught me how he liked me to dress, wear my hair and strongly encouraged me to throw away my favorite pair of cowboy boots.

"The only thing I like about country music is when I can change the channel. Your way of dressing is like country music. After all, I know what is best and how I want my future wife to look like and dress," he said. My face turned flush as the words "future wife" was on repeat in my head. I was smitten.

I still had two more years at Baylor when Wade graduated from Texas A&M. Wade planned a nice dinner at a high end *Brenner's on the Bayou.* A beautiful blue sequined dress was delivered to my dorm that he wanted me to wear that night, with matching heels. My heart fluttered joyously as I unwrapped the white box tied with a blue satin bow. Jill rolled her eyes at first, then happily agreed to help me get ready. When I arrived at the restaurant, Wade was dressed in a sleek black suit looking like he came out of GQ magazine.

"I took the liberty of ordering for you, Antonia"

"Okay, Wade, I guess that is fine"

"Do you trust me?" he asked. "I have to know I have your complete trust, or there is no us."

"Yes, Wade, I understand," I said as he pulled out my chair. He was being so sweet it gave me goose bumps. His voice was deep, just above a whisper. Wade reached for my hand. "It is just what I need in my life, Antonia." Wade continued, "You have to be disciplined to get anywhere in this world. I am going to build great things, do great things, and I can't have a wife that does not live up to my standards on my arm. Is it a surprise to you that I am giving you such instructions to live by?"

I am surprised but not stupid. I seem to notice the imperfections last.

I managed a smile, but his words did not go unforgotten. I did not really understand. I just agreed. I was confused and bewildered by his choice of words. I filed them away somewhere in the deep reaches of my mind to avoid any inappropriate urges rearing their ugly head. I started smoothing the tablecloth, trying to hide my concern. Wade controlled me. I knew it and so did my closest friends, but I loved him so much I felt I could handle it.

"Sometimes you just need to compromise to have nice things," Wade explained. "And you want nice things, don't you, Antonia?"

I have already dipped my toes in the water, no turning back now.

I shrugged it all off mildly pretending it did not matter in the grand scheme of things. I was country and he was mister high class with a beautiful future planned. I was uneasy. I rubbed the back of my neck trying to ease the stress headache from rearing its ugly head. Wade was good for me. I wanted to be a surgeon, that was my priority, until Wade came into my life, introducing me to fancy cars, beautiful dresses and fine dining. I can be a surgeon living in a high rise with a rich husband or stay here in Texas where I was born, hoping to be married to a cowboy. Either choice is a good one, but only one choice will give me Wade.

Obviously, there is a crack in everything good and the crack lets the light in. Watching what I expected to be a proposal turn into a lecture, was a crack in the plan. I saw the light but chose to ignore it. It was Wade's special night and I wanted to make it all about him.

When our dinner arrived, Wade clapped his hands excitedly, he loved a good steak. I preferred a salad. After several glasses of wine and leaving not even a crumb on his plate, Wade wiped his mouth with his napkin and reached for my hand again. His very touch made my heart skip a beat in anticipation. My body betrayed me. I couldn't resist his charms nor his touch. This fancy restaurant, the sequin and chiffon dress all added up to a proposal about to happen. I just knew it. I could feel it like the wind at the beach brushing your skin with light feathery strokes giving me goose bumps. I folded my napkin and checked my teeth with my tongue. *Can't have a proposal in a public restaurant with bits of salad in my teeth.*

Wade leaned in, looking right into my eyes. "I have something to tell you and according to how you react, it might lead to an important decision on your part," he began.

My pulse was racing. I placed my left hand elegantly on the table. My nails were perfect. The anticipation of seeing the ring was making me giddy. I smiled at him hoping he understood how much I adored him. Wade shifted his weight in his chair so he could lean over the table and get closer.

"We have talked about a future together and I have expressed a desire to take you on a lavish vacation in Italy. To get there, certain things must occur," he began. Leaning in as if he was about to tell me a deep secret. "I have been offered a job," he said softly.

Thinking I didn't hear him correctly but not wanting to interrupt or spoil the moment. I leaned in across the table as well.

"What? Did you say a job?" I asked.

"Yes, I was offered a job today. It was unexpected but I am very excited about it."

Hope this job offer comes with a proposal.

Wade excitedly explained the details of a new job offer in Chicago. I froze. Wade was smiling and he had an extraordinary sparkle in his eyes I had never seen before. When he spoke about starting the career he had dreamed about his entire life, my heart sank a little. Sitting there speechless I watched the way his lips moved while forming words. I went silent when I understood he was not preparing a proposal. His arms danced around, describing in excruciating detail his job plans and my mind went blank with disappointment. My heart began rhythmically beating faster and faster like it was pounding to the beat of a rap song.

No one knows the song in your heart unless you let them hear it. I thought Wade heard my heart song and it was all about our future. I felt he was grooming me to be his wife but left out my future and my career. I should be ecstatic, but it felt more like rolling waves struggling against the tide. I was disappointed there was no proposal tonight. Wade promised me the world if I did as he told me to do. To obey him. So, when I decided to drop out of medical school and move with him to Chicago, I truly believed it was the right choice. Wade was the choice for my future now and everyone had to accept it. I did.

Chapter 3: One Glass of Wine...

Wade and I started our life together in Chicago moving from our first small apartment to a two bedroom then a rental house. Always the next big thing or an upgrade, he called it. Always packing and unpacking and constantly keeping our home up to Wade's standards.

I was determined to make Chicago work even though I missed Texas and medical school. It was a painful goodbye when Wade came to collect me from my parents house. I left most of my clothes behind and only brought the clothes Wade had either purchased or picked out.

"I am against this but just know I will put all your things in the attic and keep them for you," my mother sniffled.

"I am going to be fine, Mother. Wade will take care of me. I will be right back."

I could eat those words right now.

Rick showed up briefly and gave me a long hug. I could see the disappointment in his face, but he never said a word. I watched him walk away hoping I wouldn't lose his friendship and our long talks late at night. He will always be my first best friend.

Sometimes at night in the darkest hour when my thoughts of home and happiness come forward and stand naked before me, I secretly weep. But during the day I can push it out of my mind and ignore it if I keep myself busy. I was busy as I sought out the best in Wade. A teacher once told me, "Everything valuable in the world is covered up. You only find them if you seek it out. Diamonds are deep in the ground; pearls are deep in the ocean."

She might have been subtly telling the girls to cover up their valuable body parts, but I took it as a much deeper philosophy. There had to be good deep down in Wade, covered up by his harsh criticisms. Chicago was both beautiful and intimidating at the same time. Famous for deep dish pizza, architecture, museums, and Wrigley Field but we never visited any thing. Wade would never eat pizza, and I always accepted that it was inevitable. There will be time later for discovering Chicago secrets, for now I had to be courageous and avoid confrontation to keep Wade happy. Chicago was not Texas with its open plains and horse ranches. Things change, no matter what the situation. Everything always changes. Remember that.

Wade moved up quickly in the company getting promotion after promotion. His work was recognized and every Sunday was spent driving around as Wade pointed out the buildings he was responsible for remodeling or building. It was impressive. I tried very hard to be supportive of his accomplishments but deep down I was thinking of my lost career. Would I one day boast of my career as a surgeon?

There were galas, ceremonies and ribbon-cutting ceremonies that we attended. Lavish food, dancing and drinks. More than my eyes had ever seen. It was almost vulgar to think of the money spent on these social gatherings with fully stocked alcohol and lobster tails. For every event, I had to wear a new dress chosen by Wade.

What should be every girl's dream to wear pretty dresses and be pampered, had become a loss of my own choices. I had my hair colored and trimmed at the finest salons, as well as my fingers and toes polished to the exact color to match my dress and shoes. I didn't mind the salon time, only because it gave me time to breathe for a few short hours without Wade hovering over me.

"You don't know how to be elegant, Antonia, so you need me to tell you how to dress" he said. "Think of me as your consultant."

"I dressed myself, all by myself, before I met you," I snapped.

Wade stopped abruptly, turning toward me slowly. "Do you want to go back to wearing cowboy boots and blue jeans, Antonia? I mean you could go back to your old life. I would think you would be more appreciative of this new life I have given you. I work hard to give you all the gowns and jewelry you want, don't I?"

I recognized the sternness in his face. I brushed the hair from my face and stared at him warily. I felt a challenging night ahead of us but could not stop the urges to lash out and defend myself yet again. "Yes, Wade, I know how hard you work. It is just that we don't have any time for fun." Shaking my head, I stood up and stared at the floor with my hand to my head. "Maybe…just maybe I am just missing home and my parents."

My parents and long talks with Rick – but that ship has sailed.

"Well, I have good news I was going to share with you at dinner tonight but since you are so sad with your life, I will share it with you now," he said sarcastically. "I have purchased a new home for us. I have drawn up the plans to have it remodeled completely, of course, but it should be finished in about a month and once we are all settled in, I thought you could invite your parents up for a visit so they can see how well you are living," he said.

"A house? Why didn't we talk about this? I mean I will have to pack everything again and get boxes." I kicked off my shoes and started to pace barefoot. Wade always hated me being barefoot. I saw his disapproving look out of the corner of my eye, but I ignored it. "Seeing my parents will be wonderful but this is our fourth move in two years, Wade!"

"What do you want, Antonia?"

"I want to settle down, have roots and feel purposeful. You could hire a maid or an assistant to do all this for you. I gave up a medical career because you said I was your future wife, for God's sake!"

As usual Wade walked over to me and put his big arms around me pulling me close to his chest. I felt like a child he was comforting after a tantrum. Holding me so I could not run until I calmed down. It was degrading but I would smell his cologne and cave, melting into his arms every time. Wade knew what worked on me.

"There, there, Antonia. This will be the last move. It will be our dream home, designed by me. The foyer alone is wide enough to park a car. It came on the market and I had to jump on it fast or lose it. Some very prominent people once lived there. It was meant to be my house."

I pulled away from Wade and crossed my arms staring up at him. "Do you promise this will be the last move? I mean you have promised me babies and marriage and that never happened, so why should I believe you now?"

"I don't like your unappreciative tone, Antonia. Would you rather go back to Texas and marry a rodeo king or me, the Chicago king? I am giving you a beautiful home where you can invite your parents and be proud." Wade smoothed his hair then stuffed his hands in his pocket. I recognized the tension in his face. "Why do you have to upset me, Antonia? I told you babies and marriage will come when you act like proper wife material. I am setting you up to be the queen of my castle. Isn't that enough for you?"

Softening my tone, I began to shuffle my feet. "I don't want to be queen Wade. I just want to be your wife and have a family. I want to see my family, my parents, and friends. But I also want my career. I am doing the best I can here, Wade. Isn't that enough for *you*?"

I felt the tears starting to sting my eyes, but I shook my head and fought them back. Wade was now the one shifting his weight and wiping his brow. I hated the silence. The not knowing if this will be the last straw to end it all feeling. "Please tell me you didn't buy a castle, did you?" Trying to remove some of the tension between us, I giggled and reached out to get a hug. Wade stepped back and put his hands up, then turned to walk away.

"Wait! Wade, don't run away! Stay and talk!" I pleaded.

"I am going to look over the final plans before we go to dinner. I need about an hour so be ready and please, for the love of heaven, put on some shoes or house slippers or something."

Then just as he was turning away, he stopped and put his hands on his hips. "When we move into the big house, I will hire a housekeeper. That way you can have more free time to do what ever it is you do when I am not around."

And that was it. Wade disappeared into the spare room that he converted into an office space so he could work from home occasionally. It was his man cave. He had the room painted and wallpapered before we even moved in. For a rental house it looked like a museum. Expensive art on the walls and he even had marble floors installed in his private bathroom. Wade wanted everything he touched to be perfect and special. Even me. I won't act surprised if he adds a gold toilet in the new house he is calling his castle. Every castle needs a throne for the royal ass.

I started to put on my shoes then changed my mind and kicked them across the floor. A moment of defiance always feels good. I hate arguing. Wade and I had not been intimate since we moved into this rental house. Every time I tried to snuggle with him, he pulled away. Sometimes Wade would leave our bed entirely and sleep in his office. I never felt so alone.

In college, I had my roommate, Jill. We would sit up talking for hours. She even made the best chocolate chip cookies in our dorm room toaster oven when we both needed to pull an all-night study session. Jill never had a cross word to say about anyone -- until she met Wade. She was not too fond of my choice to leave medical school and Rick, for that matter. She loved tagging along to rodeos during term breaks. We would both cheer Rick on as he won trophy after trophy and drool over all the rugged cowboys. If she saw me now, she would just shake her head.

I leaned back and sighed staring up at his recent art purchase hanging over the fireplace. Wade used to be romantic, buying flowers and having fancy dinner parties. Jill and I giggled on the phone about it for hours when we talked. Wade would hold my hand everywhere we went.

Lovemaking was frequent. I called it take-my-breath-away amazing. We made love with candlelight, essential oil rubs and flowers everywhere. He was every virgin's dream. It would be hard to top his skills. I felt very pampered and spoiled the first year we were together. Wade was either very much in love with me, or he knew exactly what it took to keep me here. After any heated conversation I could look forward to a phenomenal all night lovemaking session. Recently, it was only heated with no make-up session.

I was determined to try my best and not irritate the situation. I put on the special light blue chiffon dress, heels and necklace. I needed to be on time for dinner. I even wore the fake eyelashes he insisted would make me sexier. I imagine they take getting used to because I felt like a butterfly was sitting on my eye lids.

Determined to put Wade in a better mood, I walked into the living room and did a small twirl hoping to put a smile on his face. The skirt flared out slightly giving a slight peek at the black panties underneath. Wade looked at his watch and grunted. "You are two minutes late. I hope we make our reservations"

"Aren't you going to compliment me on the dress, Wade?"

"I picked it out and paid for it. I don't need to compliment myself for having good taste"

Wade and I struggled through dinner with bland conversation. He waved for the waiter, then ordered a bottle of expensive wine and two glasses. Wade poured my glass and then his.

"I don't care for wine, thank you," I said.

The waiter left the glass never acknowledging me. I looked over at Wade who was obviously disappointed. Wade sat back in his chair and stared at me raising his eyebrows. There was visible tension in his face and neck. "I take you to fine ribbon cutting ceremonies for buildings I designed. I escort you to galas celebrating my accomplishments, where it is expected to have a glass of wine or champagne. You should start trying to fit in more."

"Fit in more?" I glared at him then reached for the wine glass. "Fine. I will drink the damn wine, but just one glass."

"I ordered it special just for you. It is cranberry wine. I thought you would enjoy it," Wade snipped. "It might even improve your mood."

Of course, I felt like I had let him down. My shoulders hunched and I pulled at the collar on my dress. "Cranberry wine? I didn't know they made such a thing. You did this for me, Wade?"

Wade crumpled his napkin and tossed it on the table. "Yes, and as usual you have made me feel like my efforts have been wasted."

"Oh Wade, I am so sorry. I love the wine." I was gritting my teeth into a permanent fake smile in between sips of the wine. I reached out to touch his hand and he flinched pulling away. *Why am I always apologizing?*

After dinner, Wade had the driver wait while he helped me to the door. "One glass of wine and you are tipsy. That is normal until you get used to drinking. Get undressed and go straight to bed, Antonia"

"Aren't you coming to bed with me?"

"No, I am heading into the city. I have work to catch up on," said Wade.

I turned to watch as Wade was slowly starting to close the door. "No, wait. Where are you going?" It was really a last-minute effort. I actually did not care if he left. Sometimes you have to at least pretend you care just to have peace.

Wade did not respond; he just glanced at me and closed the door. Feeling slightly tipsy from one glass of wine, I shrugged it off, kicked off my shoes and headed upstairs to the bedroom and crawled into bed. *Wine makes me a little warm and fuzzy and a tiny bit horny. I like it.*

"I don't know what kind of childhood trauma he experienced but it is very rude to encourage one to drink then leave them on their own. Now I am talking to myself. The possibilities are endless after one glass of wine."

I safely fell asleep still in the blue chiffon dress with a slight bit of drool appearing on the pillow. It was about an hour later when the phone ringing woke me up. Thinking it was Wade, I answered with a sarcastic hello. It was Jill, my old college roommate whom I had not talked to in over a year.

"Antonia, it's Jill. Were you sleeping? You sound funny"

"No, I thought it was Wade. He had to go into the office in the city again. Makes me wonder if he has a mistress. Anyway, how are you, Jill? I am so glad you called. I had my first sip of wine tonight and boy it left me sleepy. How is your new teaching job?"

"Antonia, this is not a catch up on old times call, I have bad news."

"Bad news?"

"Yes, remember those times when you asked me to check up on your parents from time to time?"

I sat up straight in bed. "Yes, of course. They treat you like one of the family. Why are you telling me this?"

"Well, when you moved to Chicago your parents asked me to be their contact number in case of an emergency. There has been an emergency, Antonia. Rick asked me to be the one to call you. He is at the hospital. Your parents were in an accident"

"I don't understand. Are they alright?"

"Your father was driving, hauling a horse trailer. They decided to sponsor a rodeo here on the ranch. They hit a soft shoulder and the trailer jack-knifed and it flipped the truck. The hospital called me, and your mother was pronounced dead at the scene. Your father is in critical condition from the gearshift. It went into his chest, nicking an artery or something. It doesn't look good. Do you think Wade will allow you to come to Antonia Ranch?"

"Allow me?" those words reverberated in my head and I dropped the phone. I am not on the bank account. I am not on the rental agreement for this house. Wade made me sell my car. *Allow me* really hit me hard tonight. I slid to sit up on the side of the bed bursting into tears. "I have nothing. I am his prisoner!" I shouted.

Suddenly, I could hear Jill's coice: "Hello? Hello? Antonia, are you there?"

Scrambling to find the phone, I answered her. "I'm here, Jill. I don't know what to do. If I can't get in touch with Wade, will you buy me a ticket to fly to the ranch? I can pack and leave tonight. I will have to call a cab to get to the airport. Oh Jill, I feel so hopeless!"

"You are rambling. Slow down. I just told you some very bad news and you immediately went to Wade. Seriously, Antonia, get yourself together!" Jill yelled.

Jill agreed to make arrangements to get me to the Antonia Ranch, my childhood home. I had not visited in two years. My body shook. I bit my nails. Jill said she would call me back with the arrangements. I tried to call my father but it went straight to the answering machine. Dad had a cell phone, but mother never wanted to have one. "The home phone is enough for me," she would say. I paced for a few minutes; the muscles in my neck began to tense before I slumped to the floor.

Out of frustration, I grabbed at my chiffon skirt and started ripping it to shreds. My legs felt weak, so I crawled to the bathroom and used the sink to pull myself up. I stared at the face in the mirror as I bit my lip.

"Who have you become?" I yelled. I splashed cold water on my face, then an idea hit me. I ran to the spare room Wade had turned into his office and began scrounging through the drawers looking for cash or anything. At this point I was not sure what I was looking for. It was nervous energy. There was a safe but no key anywhere.

"I guess I have no choice but to call Wade. He will be furious that I disturbed him," I whispered. I felt a heaviness in my stomach like I was about to hurl. I started pacing again, practicing what I would say to Wade. Over and over, I paced then paused to think and practiced saying the words aloud. I was punching myself in the thighs with my fists. My mind was clearly distracted. Wade just announced he bought a house and now I need money to fly home. There was no use in putting it off any longer. Taking a deep breath I picked up the phone to dial Wade, when the phone rang an incoming call. It was Jill.

"The best I can do is get you a flight late tonight. Can you be packed and ready because the car will pick you up to take you to the airport in forty-five minutes."

"Yes, I will be ready and Jill…"

"Yes?"

"Thank you."

"Rick paid for the ticket; I made arrangements for the cab."

"Please tell Rick thank you and I appreciate him being there at the hospital with my parents."

"You can tell him yourself in person when you get here. He is very upset. He loves you and your parents, you know. I will tell him you are on the way."

I love him too.

Hanging up from Jill, I again put off calling Wade and threw the phone in my purse. I needed to put my head down and close my eyes trying to process.

I have no clue why I fear telling him, but the fear is real.

My mind raced trying to remember everything about my childhood while I furiously packed. I wanted to remember everything. My memories may be all I have left. Mother's Sunday dinners, Daddy coming in with rodeo dust and the chocolate cake my momma made. Just another traumatic event sent out a ripple and caught me. I felt like I was drowning. How much more hurt can I endure.

If only I had a life partner who spontaneously cared about my needs without prompting I would not feel so alone when facing emotional crisis. Wade would not be sympathetic, not if I have to return to Texas, just annoyed. His big fault that I hoped would change when I gave up my life to follow him. Wade tends to appear annoyed when I need comfort from him. Now I find myself avoiding any outward appearance of needing. Needing a hug when I am lonely or needing a pat on the back or a word of praise for going out of my way to keep the house clean and organized.

My needs are often met now with a gallon of rocky road ice cream while sitting in bed alone.

Bags packed, I was about ready to head toward the door when I looked down at my phone again. I was visibly sweating and my hand was shaking.

"What am I afraid of?"

Knowing I did not have the strength to listen to unsolicited advice from Wade, I slipped my phone back into my purse.

"I will just write him a note: 'I will be right back.'"

Chapter 4: Spilled Wine

My father was in critical condition and never regained consciousness. I leaned in, whispering in his ear and hoping the last words he would hear were mine. I apologized many times for leaving him and mother and the ranch. Ranch hands drifted in and out to visit for five minutes or so and gave me many words of encouragement. I was surrounded by warm-hearted people who loved me and my parents. Jill came every day and brought me food even though I ate very little.

"You have to eat and keep up your strength, Antonia. This could be a long ride," said Jill.

"I just don't feel like eating, Jill. My stomach is telling me one thing and my head another. The doctor doesn't give me much hope and I have no idea what to do anymore."

"You were always so confident, Antonia. What has happened to you?" Jill tried to smile as she rubbed my back, but I knew she saw the changes in me. I even started seeing how weak and vulnerable I was becoming. Wade did everything for me. I lost my self in a canopy of Wade's charisma and empty promises, always trying to do the right thing and be the right person so Wade would finally put a ring on my finger.

"I don't know what to do with the ranch if my parents die. We never spoke about it. I thought Daddy would live forever."

"Well, you don't have to decide anything now, Antonia. By the way, what did Wade say when you told him?"

"I left him a note."

"A note?"

"Yes, and I have not heard from him since I left. I basically expect nothing but the unexpected when it comes to Wade. He does not have a sympathetic bone in his body."

I could tell Jill was disappointed and suspicious, but I take it she has never had the urge to pee on someone's toothbrush. I can't handle Wade and his disrespect right now. Jill had no idea. Being my friend should come with a warning label. Jill, always being supportive, gave me a big squeeze and rested her head on my shoulder. I did not want to think about Wade right now. I assume he was angry. He may even be wondering if I left for good to come back to Texas and my pearl button shirts.

"Listen, Antonia. I know the real you, remember? All this pretending to be exactly what Wade wants for a wife has got to be exhausting. What matters right now is your parents and the ranch. How about we take a break out in the waiting room and have a cup of tea? There are many of your friends waiting to offer support. Rick, too. He has been asking about you."

The very thought of Rick made my heart flutter; I hadn't seen him since I left for Chicago. "I will be out in a minute, Jill. You go ahead."

Sitting down in the small chair next to my father's hospital bed I took a deep breath and pulled out my phone. Not one text or call from Wade appeared. I dialed his number then quickly hung up. Everyone has shadows in their past, they follow you around. I needed to face up to Wade. If I was waiting for it to get easier, that train has left the station. Wade will ask questions I have no answers to. Time to live brave, pull up the brave panties and make the call. He answered on the second ring.

"Hello, Antonia?"

"Yes, Wade, it's me. Who else would be calling you from this number?" I knew sarcasm was not the way to go and I found myself smacking my forehead with the palm of my hand. "I am sorry about that. Umm… I am at the hospital with my father. They say he is not doing well. My mother's body is waiting for my funeral arrangements in the morgue. I know you never got close to my parents, but this is something I just had to take care of. I hope you are not too upset with me leaving you a note"

There was a long silence before he spoke. "I understand, Antonia. Take as much time as you need and call me when you are ready to talk about coming back to Chicago. I don't have much time to talk right now but you take care of yourself. I hope I can trust you; I don't like not knowing what you are doing. You always give me trouble."

"Trouble and I are fully acquainted, Wade. I do miss your gorgeous face, but I really have to be here. I was afraid you wouldn't understand, and I don't know exactly how to deal with everything." I stood to look out the window of my father's hospital room and sighed. "I have to decide what to do with the ranch and make funeral arrangements. I wish you were here to help me. You do have a large supply of organizational skills floating around in your head,"

"I am not coming to Texas, Antonia. My life is here in Chicago. I find your lack of respect unsettling. Sell the ranch for all I care. I have to go. I am training the new housekeeper."

Shocked to hear those words, I stared, not focusing on anything except the yellow drapes that strangely reminded me of my car, the Yellow Rose of Texas. *Sell the ranch?*

I have always accepted that there would be a day my parents would pass away but their timing is lousy. I feel lost. I am supposed to have my parents for a lot longer. A part of me is trying to accept it, but part of me is also reluctant to disregard the veil of an only child needing her parents. I didn't expect Wade to understand. His parents died when he was young, and it made him stronger. He is the definition of a self-made man. The fear of bearing my soul for examination because I had parents and he didn't, seems a bit unfair. I assumed my adult life would be fulfilled before they left me alone. What I need is guidance and compassion. Wade was not forthcoming with even so much as condolences.

I did not finish medical school and there are so many things left undone in my life. My parents did not live long enough for me to make them proud. If I failed in my relationship with Wade, I always thought my parents would be here to welcome me back home. I had that comfort and now it is lost. I won't give up the ranch. It is my back-up plan.

Miserable and tired, I shuffled out to the waiting room and looked around for Jill and the cowboys. I must have had my feelings showing on my face because Jill stood up and crossed the room to meet me. All the ranch hands were staring at me. I avoided their eyes as if I was unsure where to look. Taking me by the shoulders, Jill guided me toward the table of food the ranch hands had put together.

"Why do you have the blank stare, dear Antonia? They are all here for you, and I am here for you. I take it your talk with Wade did not go well?" asked Jill discreetly as possible.

"I think I have uncovered long-suppressed resentments seething below the surface. He told me to sell the ranch. On the bright side he did not tell me I couldn't come home. So that is positive. Oh, and he hired a housekeeper," I said quietly.

"I don't care. You just come over here and get some food. Everyone in the whole state practically has sent over food. Your parents were truly loved and so are you."

Jill gave me a quick hug, placing her arm on my back and a slight push. A fairly good-sized crowd was forming around the table of food. "There is so much to choose from, Antonia. Have a salad or maybe a taco. You need to eat," she continued.

I glanced at the makeshift buffet of everything from pies to casseroles and it made me smile. "Is there any wine? I think I need to calm my nerves a little. Rum, Whiskey, hell I don't care if there is moonshine. I need a drink," I said. Jill frowned then shook her head disapprovingly.

The waiting room was bursting at the seams with cowboys from all around Texas. A beautiful sight to see, I must say. Someone started playing music on a guitar in the corner. Someone handed me a glass of wine with a friendly pat on the shoulder. As I continued to push through the crowd of blue jeans and boots, I noticed a familiar face. My father's ranch foreman, Rick, approached me with a sad but sympathetic smile.

"Hello Antonia. Sorry… if it is too loud we will cut it out. The guys just want to let your dad know and hear that we are here for him."

My father trusted Rick like a son. He was only about three years older than me when he came to live in the bunk house with his father. We promised to stay in touch but after a few late-night calls and Wade, communication stopped. Of course, I had a big schoolgirl crush on him. We even shared a first kiss in back of the barn after a thrilling game of spin the bottle.

Rick was my best friend. His masculinity lit up a room and caused women to wonder if there was more than just kindness behind those brown eyes. Sun kissed skin and a patch of thick chest hair came into view from his low buttoned shirt that appeared tight on his broad shoulders. I watched him swagger toward me and I met his grin with a warm smile. I smiled when I was in his presence as if he had magic powers in his pheromones causing me to blush.

Funny I never noticed how nice he wore his blue jeans.

"You have sure grown into a beautiful lady," said Rick in his familiar deep voice.

"I feel honored that you noticed, Rick. I remember stomping around in my daddy's boots and you telling me I would grow into them one day. Well, here I am all grown up."

Putting his hands on his hips to drink in a long top-to-bottom look at me, I began to pull my shoulders back so I measured up. Trying not to be awkward but secretly wanting to throw my arms around his beautiful neck and feel safe, I blushed like a schoolgirl.

"I believe the last time I saw you was when you left for Chicago with that yuppie boy. You are still a pretty pony," Rick said. Then looking down at the floor as though he was holding back emotions, he took a step closer. "Niceties aside. I am so sorry about your parents, Antonia. They have always been so good to me, and your momma made the best chocolate cake I have ever eaten." Pausing to pretend to lick his lips made me giggle. Rick stepped even closer and put his hands on my shoulder. His eyes were so sincere I felt the urge to reach for him. I craved the familiarity of him.

"Don't worry about anything back at the ranch, I am taking care of everything and keeping my prayers for your daddy."

"I expected nothing less from you Rick. I wasn't worried about the ranch at all. My father trusted you, so I trust you. He talked of you often when I called home."

"So you asked about me?"

"Yes, I did, Rick. Always."

Stepping even closer and leaning in until I felt his cheek brush mine, he whispered in my ear. "Listen, Antonia, everything we are and have been to each other will never die. I want you to know that. I am always here for you."

"I worry about that, Rick. I never want us to be strangers or so uncomfortable we can't talk. One thing you need to know: I have no plans to sell the ranch or make any fast decisions. You have nothing to worry about from me, either."

I clasped my hands behind my back like a schoolgirl as he again stepped closer into my personal space. I stood unwavering, enjoying the aroma of his cologne. Life can be a gift or a nightmare. Losing my parents was a nightmare but right now, it was a gift having Rick so close.

Rick cleared his throat then continued, his face only inches away, "Well, me and the guys feel the same about you and your parents. Well, I feel the same about you, the guys well…you know what I mean. We took the day off and gathered up here playing his favorite music to show him some love. I confess I hoped to see you more than anyone."

I felt my cheeks flush slightly with Rick standing so close. With his warm charm and nice comments, I felt the tears burning in my eyes. Rick held his arms open and I nodded my head that it was permitted. He quickly swooped in and wrapped me up in such a tight embrace, my feet left the ground. I breathed him in, throwing my arms around his neck and spilling my wine on the hospital waiting room carpet. It didn't matter. I hugged him back and neither of us wanted to let go. I needed the human closeness. My body ached for compassion and understanding. I let the tears flow as Rick held me in his arms. No one bothered us. I needed my best friend. I nuzzled my way into the warmth of his neck as he whispered. "I am right here, Antonia. I am right here."

The moment was only interrupted by the music suddenly stopping. I heard a woman's voice as I slowly let go and turned. Immediately, Jill was at my side grabbing my hand. Rick stood beside me taking my other hand in his. My father's nurse approached me slowly and I could tell by the look on her face that my worst fear of being alone was about to come to pass.

"Miss Antonia, I am afraid you might want to sit down."

"She is fine. Just say what you have to say. We got her," Rick said boldly.

"I am afraid your father just passed on. We are disconnecting all the machines now. You can come in anytime. I am so very sorry for your loss. He fought hard."

I swayed slightly as though my knees were letting me down. I felt Rick's arm around my waist and he and Jill held me up until one of the ranch hands scooted a chair over for me to sit down. I looked up at Jill and Rick hoping they knew how much I appreciated their love then drew my knees up to my chin, put my head in my hands, and began to cry. Rick knelt beside me and wrapped me in his arms. The staff kindly waited for me to sort out my feelings before I went in to say my final good-byes. Rick never left my side.

My father died on a Tuesday afternoon and was buried that Friday. Mother had passed away the week before, so the funeral director encouraged me to begin the process right away. I experienced human emotions that most people try to avoid. Losing my parents made me feel alone, even in a room full of people. I felt like I was next in line to die. They would never meet my children or be proud of me for becoming a surgeon.

Rick escorted me back to the ranch and spent the night in the guest room. He never left me alone. He came to check on me and I reached for him. Rick held me while I cried. Curled up in my childhood bed, I nestled my face in Rick's shoulder as he rubbed my back.

My father's lawyer contacted me with details of the will: Daddy left it all to me, the only daughter of a Texas rancher. I was numb, removed from any emotions except grief. Rick and Jill guided me through all the paperwork, and I placed the ranch and its responsibilities in Rick's capable hands.

Every day I sat on the bed in my parents' room. Running my hands on the quilt my mother made, I cherished the simplest memories: A coffee cup left in the sink, Momma's robe hanging on the back of the door. Memories floating around like the leaves of a tree in the wind. Our lives are like that breeze. As you pass by others, it touches them in some way and creates memories in a special place in your heart.

I have faith in my parent's final destiny even if I am not confident in my future. My parents did not know that morning when they left the ranch that they would not be coming home. I did not know when I left for Chicago with Wade that I would never see my parents again. Now I can't help but wonder when I look into Rick's eyes if I will ever see him again if I return to Chicago.

Rick was by my side every day, holding my hand and supplying medicinal hugs when needed. When the right person hugs you, it is like medicine. It heels, soothes and warms your heart. Rick warmed my heart. We spent nights talking by the huge fireplace my father built stone by stone. We took long rides on horseback until the sun went down. We stared at the stars while cuddling on a blanket. Even Jill came to a cookout and bonfire, a cowboy tribute to my parents. Rick made his famous brisket, ribs and baked beans on the grill.

After the funeral, I called Wade and made arrangements to fly home. It felt like chewing taffy, words getting caught in my teeth. For now, it was a chance to have no regrets or unfinished business, so I had to return. I told Jill first and after seeing the disappointment in her eyes I knew it was going to be dreadful telling Rick that I had to return to Chicago.

Jill was so kind and gave me the best friend hug and pat on the back. She sucked in a deep breath and wiped the tears from her eyes and mine. "You know I wish you would stay and never return to Chicago. However, I do understand the need for closure. I was actually hoping you would ask me to go back with you. Then after a brisk tour around the city hitting all the best places to eat, looking at architecture and catching a show, I would help you gather your belongings and return home. Is that still a possibility?" Jill asked.

"Jill, I am confused. My parents brought me up to not be a quitter, but to follow through with whatever you start. Do it to the best of your ability. If they are looking down on me from heaven, will they be shaking their head?"

"Well, on the other hand if you lay it all out there, they loved Rick and thought you would end up with him and give them grandchildren. Either way I think they would not shake their head. They would respect your need to follow through," said Jill.

Being my last night in Texas for an undetermined time, I decided to make dinner for Rick. Just the two of us in my ranch house. My childhood home. I pulled out one of Momma's fancy tablecloths and lit a candle. Rick came in the door after putting away the horses and knew right away. His first reaction was disappointment, shaking his head as he put his hat on the hook by the kitchen door.

"Rick, please let me explain. I just want to talk and have a nice dinner, please."

Looking down at the floor, Rick shook his head. "Do you want me to get my stuff and stay in the bunkhouse tonight so you can pack?"

"Rick, the main house will always be your home no matter where I am. It is going to be alright."

"No, it is not going to be alright, Antonia." Rick paused with his back turned toward me and his hands on his hips. I felt hopeless that Rick would ever understand. After a deep sigh he shook his head looking up at the ceiling.

"Since you went to the trouble to make dinner, I guess I can get in the shower and eat dinner with you. But only if we don't talk about Chicago or the turd that lives there!" said Rick.

"Okay."

I paced the hallway wringing my hands, listening to the shower run. I paused and placed my hand on the bathroom door. Something stirred inside me. It might be my last chance, my last night with Rick... forever. I laid my cheek on the door and closed my eyes, picturing Rick on the other side, naked.

The shower stopped and my heart starting beating faster. For a second I thought about running away, yet I stood there waiting. Rick opened the door with a towel wrapped around his waist. Our eyes met briefly. I wanted him to hold me and tell me everything was going to be alright.

With no hesitation Rick leaned down to kiss me. Releasing the towel, Rick picked me up. Wrapping my arms around his neck still wet from the shower, I breathed in the clean smell of soap. Years of wanting and desire burst into lust as I wrapped my legs around his waist. I gave in to my need for comfort and compassion as Rick carried me into his room and laid me gently on his bed. Knowing that Rick cared about me unconditionally was a driving force. Thoughts of betraying Wade never entered my mind. I needed someone to touch me like I was the most important woman in the room. My heart was breaking and Rick understood that. Wade would only tell me to pick myself up and go fix my make-up.

Rick allowed me to cry as he held me, kissing away all my tears. Choices had been made with no regrets. We needed each other's comfort, even if it was for one night. We never got to eat dinner at the dining room table, but we did snack on each other late into the night.

Perhaps it is because I realize more than ever that I will always have a place to come home to. An alternate destiny if I choose. Being here was not like a visit; it felt like a self-examination of where my life could have gone. A cleansing of anxiety and self doubt. I need closure with Wade, but I will always love Rick. I will always have the ranch, my memories and people who love me in Texas. I can face anything now.

Chapter 5: Shattered Bottle of Wine

Wade sent a car to pick me up at the airport. He didn't even come to pick me up in person. It felt cold and curious. He had explained to me that all my belongings had been moved to the new house. Not completely finished but enough was in place to stop the lease on the rental home and make it work. He bragged on how efficient and helpful the new housekeeper was at helping to ensure the move went smooth as silk. Her name is Marisa, he exclaimed while mentioning her attributes of organizing and coordinating the movers. In Wade's abrupt and to-the-point attitude he hinted that my coming back home was on a trial basis.

"There will be no more nonsense about the ranch or Texas in our lives, Antonia. You are either here to be and act like arm candy for a prestigious architect or you can decide to disappoint me. I hope you didn't bring any of that country clothing or knick knacks in your suitcase, either. I won't be home on the day you arrive until the late evening. Marisa and I will be choosing draperies for the guest room which is where I will be sleeping until you have proven yourself to me."

"I agreed to return because we have history and I do want to give it a chance," I sniffled.

"You agreed because you have nowhere else to go. Listen, just take a long bath and get acquainted with the new house, Antonia. You have two days to unpack and get acquainted with Marisa and the way things are now. I have a big night coming up. I pray you will be at your best"

"What is the big night?" I asked.

"There is a big celebration in my honor, proving that I have finally made a name for myself in this town. A lot has happened since you abruptly left me with only a note, Antonia, and I do not have time to explain it all"

"I said I was sorry, Wade. Don't worry, I will be ready"

"Good, because I feel like I might be booking that celebration trip to Italy if this big project does well"

Sitting at the airport while Wade spewed the rules to me made me nauseous. He always promised a trip when he made it big. Good thing he could not see me rolling my eyes. Occasionally I let myself think about Rick and Jill, the ranch and my childhood home. I chose to go back, but Wade believes he allowed me. However, I dutifully agreed and came across with the right tasteful words to impress on him. I am willing to try.

Wade was the first man I had known in the Biblical way and I am sure my parents would have expected me to honor that by giving it a chance.

"Try until you cannot try anymore before you give up," as my father would say. "I never gave up when breaking a young bronco," Daddy would point out.

I was not a quitter. Wade and I do have history. We met in college and fell in love. No one is perfect. He has his quirks and strange obsessions with clothing and presentation, but he is a handsome, successful architect. With that comes reputation and class. Strangely, I am the young bronco and Wade is breaking me. If he is not willing to quit, then neither am I. We can fix this relationship.

As the driver took the scenic route through downtown, the pavement was busy with tourists and businessmen. I always marveled at the complexity of the city. The smell of bread fresh out of the oven filled the air from the bake shop on the corner. The smell of the street merchants selling sausages competing with the smells coming from the coffee shop and the pizza parlor. The sun glinting off the stain glass window of a church with the backdrop of tall buildings. All were built by architects not so different than Wade. Yes, this was Chicago and it started to feel like home.

The driver pulled into the circular driveway of our new home and my eyes opened wide. I never got the chance to see it or the plans before I left for Texas. It was a gorgeous two-story home with white pillars standing tall at the front entry. Something I pictured similar to what you see in Rome. Wade and I talked often of a trip to Italy after he made it big in architecture and this house represented him making it big. High walls surrounded three sides of the house like a compound, a wrought-iron gate at the front.

Opening the front double doors, I immediately noticed the largeness of the grand entry foyer and the beautiful marble tile. It hit me that I was going to actually live here. *I could get used to this.* I put my suitcase down and did a twirl in the foyer that was big enough to park a car in. I ran through the first floor taking note of the gold faucets in the kitchen and bath. A crystal chandelier was hanging in the dining room as well as vaulted ceilings in every room. Crisp white walls were freshly painted throughout the house that almost made the rooms look sterile.

Over the marble fireplace hung a portrait of Wade. I had almost forgotten how handsome he was, if that was possible. I was humbled by the details in every room. New furniture and expensive oriental rugs were lavishly placed everywhere. It was a far cry from the ranch with its hardwood floors and farmhouse sink that I bathed in as a child.

I decided to check out the upstairs, so I grabbed my bags and slowly ascended the spiral staircase drinking in all the beauty. Locating my room was easy, it had Wade written all over it. I didn't mind, I couldn't wait for a hot foaming bath. White walls, white bedding and even white plush carpet. It was beautiful and clean but lacking any color or personality.

Not what I would have picked at all, but Wade always knows what is stylish and elegant.

The large claw-foot bathtub was calling my name, so I stripped down and started the hot water. Wade was right: I needed a hot luxurious bath right now to wash away all the emotional baggage from Texas. Stretching out in the bathtub, I relaxed and tried to persuade my self to be in a good mood for when Wade arrives home. My mind wandered back to Texas no matter what I tried. Rick and those strong arms holding me would not leave my memories. When I thought about the double funeral of my parents I started to cry, and I didn't want puffy eyes when I finally got to see Wade. I thought of butterflies, Jill, college days and even Italy, but nothing brought me peace. Imagining how Wade would be excited to see me led me to remembering our long lovemaking sessions. I squirmed my legs and considered touching myself but decided against it to save myself for Wade.

Relaxing and finally drifting away in thoughts, I heard a noise coming from downstairs. Assuming it was Wade I hurried out of the tub and threw on the bathrobe behind the door. It was also white. Soft cotton and white. Again, just go with it. At the bottom of the stairs, I could see Wade and a brunette woman chatting in very close proximity to each other, so close I felt a small jolt in my chest. I gave myself a moment to regain my composure and smoothed my wet hair back. *I am sure it means nothing. He is probably telling her to prepare a fancy dinner for me.*

Excited to see his dark curly hair and his pressed three-piece suit, I stopped at the top for the stairs. "Wade, you are home!" I said loudly.

Glancing up at me, Wade managed a half smile then spoke something so softly to the young woman, I could not make it out. Feeling a bit awkward, I tugged at my bathrobe trying to decide if I should start down the stairs or turn and go back to my room.

Wade turned to look up at me again and gave a small wave. "I see you made it home safely and found the bath. I will talk to you at dinner, Antonia, when you are dressed."

I spoke no words, just turned and walked quickly back to my room. The coldness in the air was thick and I flopped on my bed clenching my fists. In my head I had imagined Wade and I running toward each other until we embraced with a hot steamy kiss, romantically unable to keep our hands off each other. Sort of like they do in romance novels. Instead, I got a wave. A wave? I had forgotten how much the sight of him tugged at my heart until I was away. I am back and this is our lovely house, one he remodeled just for us. Now there is talk of a romantic trip to Italy where there could possibly, finally, be a proposal. I wanted marriage and a family very badly; I just had to be patient. Wade promised me when he made it big all would be right. This house says he has definitely made it big.

Sitting up, I intended to make Wade remember how much we were meant to be together. I decided to get dressed in one of his favorite dresses for dinner. I did my makeup, swept my hair up on the side, placing a nice pearl brooch in my hair. I picked the blue dress with delicate silver beads around the neckline. The hand-sewn beads make the eyes draw upward to the low scoop of the neck, exposing an ever so slight peek of cleavage. I was determined and classy with a little sexy thrown in for good measure. Now I must go meet this housekeeper face-to-face and win back Wade's affection, no matter what it takes.

Wade and I ate dinner with very little conversation. He did manage a smooch, just on my cheek as he sat down. I had yet to see the housekeeper until she suddenly appeared with two plates of food. A stuffed lobster tail, risotto and asparagus. Much different from the barbecue ribs and brisket I took the pleasure of devouring back in Texas. I managed a smile, but Marisa made no eye contact with me.

Her focus was only on Wade as she leaned over him to fill his glass of wine. She was leaning to allow her breasts to press against his shoulder and I may have noticed a wink from Wade out of the corner of my eye. My cheeks flushed but I took a deep breath and immediately picked up my empty wine glass, holding it out to Marisa with a daring smile. I may be from the south, but I know a flirty cow when I see one: we grill 'em and eat 'em for dinner!

Don't mess with a Texas girl!

Glancing back to Wade and then over to me, Marisa stood staring with the bottle still in her hand. She glared back at me like she could read my mind.

"Oh, did you want wine as well? I was under the impression you did not drink" she snarled.

I didn't have a chance to respond before Wade spoke. "Yes, she will have wine. I introduced her to having a drink with dinner. You may pour, Marisa," he said.

As Marisa started to pour, I suddenly put my glass down and took the bottle from her hand. Looking at the label I grinned, reaching to put my hand on Wade's arm.

"This is the cranberry wine you special-ordered for me, Wade. How nice of you to remember, darling," I said softly.

I shot Marisa a look back, then began to fill my wine glass. Our beloved housekeeper turned quickly to walk away; as she did, she managed to run her hand erotically across Wade's back. She stopped at the doorway, narrowed her eyes staring at me. "It was nice to meet you Miss Tonia," then walked away.

"My name is *Antonia*," I corrected disdainfully.

"Whatever…" she snarled.

Sitting up to be closer to Wade at the head of the long dining room table, I gently smiled. As he was stuffing the buttery lobster tail in his mouth, he looked at me and huffed. He had caught on to the lobbing of snarky looks between me and Marisa but apparently loved it. Maybe he was turned on by the competition.

"I am not sure we need a housekeeper, Wade. I just wanted help with moving and packing," I said softly. "I am sure I can take care of things now that I am back."

"Don't start, Antonia. I had a busy day. You left me with a note, so what was I supposed to do? I am an architect, and a darn good one if you haven't noticed. What I am not is a dishwasher and cook. Marisa is here to stay and there will be no more talk about it," said Wade.

Even though I was disappointed in the welcome I received since returning to Chicago, I decided to make the best of it. Being cowardly was only cute in the Wizard of Oz. I knew just what to do. I slowly unfolded my napkin and placed it in my lap, smoothing my dress. I then leaned slightly toward Wade exposing my bosom. Wade began to tell me of all the buildings he has managed to build or make plans for as well as all the accolades he has received. I listened and nodded at the appropriate times encouraging him to continue. Again, I reached over to fondly rub Wade's arm hoping for a better response.

"The house is beautiful, Wade. You have a right to be proud of your work. I know we haven't talked about it, but it was very traumatic burying my parents, I was upset as you can imagine. However, I know it is best to keep my memories in my heart and move on. I am sorry about the note; I should have called you. I want to make it up to you. Will you be visiting my room tonight? I missed you very much."

Wade swallowed his last bite of food, wiped his mouth and put his napkin on his plate before looking at me. He stared deep into my eyes like he did the day we met. Then leaning into me he took my hand.

"Did you miss me or my love making skills, Antonia? Did you miss me or what I can give you? I have questions and I do have needs" he said.

"Well, we always did have romantic nights. We are good together, Wade. I miss that so much. I will always miss my hometown, it's where I was born but I want you, Wade. All of you. Show me how much you missed me tonight. I will take care of all your needs."

As I leaned in for a kiss, we were interrupted by Marisa. "Here is the chocolate cake you wanted for dessert, Mr. Wade. Shall I leave it here on the table?"

I sat back in my chair and crossed my arms. "You have impeccable timing, Marisa"

Wade let out a sly giggle, then never taking his eyes off of me, he dismissed the housekeeper.

"Yes, leave it on the table," he answered, "We don't know if we are going to eat it or roll around in it. We won't be needing anything else from you tonight, Marisa. You can take the evening off, go to town or do what you want. I will see you in the morning."

Wade was acting passionate similar to when we first met in college. Maybe he is changing and my absence turned his annoyance into desire for me once again. Anyone can change if they really want to. Wade can build tall buildings so a little development of compassion and empathy should be easy for him. Settling into the new house and rekindling our love was something I wanted to see when I looked into his eyes. His devious smile was sending me good vibes that I had a long night of passion to look forward to.

Glancing up at the housekeeper I couldn't help but grin seeing the look of shock on Marisa's face. I reached out and touched the icing then sucked it off my finger as Wade watched. "Chocolate cake is my favorite food group," I laughed.

As Wade took my hand to lead me upstairs, we heard glass shattering. Wade called out to Marisa, who nastily replied with an edge to her voice, "It is okay, I accidentally broke the bottle of cranberry wine. It just slipped out of my hand. Oopsie!"

I swore I heard mumbling coming from the kitchen. "So sad it broke," mumbled Marisa sarcastically. I just laughed it off and pulled on Wade's arm. Nothing else needed to be said.

I have so many questions, but I don't care to know any of the answers. Self-respect is everything.

Chapter 6: Special Wine

Over the next several days, I stayed in bed as long as possible when Wade went to work. I was tired. We made up for lost time by having long lovemaking sessions late into the night though I was still exhausted from the gut-wrenching emotions of the past week. Many parties and gatherings celebrating the work of Wade and his company in and out of the city had kept us busy. Every special dinner that was catered had several bottles of different wines and Wade made sure there was cranberry wine just for me. I had begun to enjoy my life again – and the wine. When the wine calmed me down, most of the past began to fade a little more. Wade kept the specially ordered wine in stock, and me on my back long into the night. Sleeping was comfort and much needed refueling.

Our housekeeper, Marisa, never seemed pleased doing anything for me. She mostly took orders from Wade and smiled while talking to him, then gave me the cold shoulder or a smirk. I never looked at it as a competition or something I should get into a heavy discussion over. I rather enjoyed not cleaning the kitchen as I had done in our previous apartments.

This was a different life and a different Wade. He seemed more attentive, more generous, making grand gestures with his gifts of jewelry and clothing items for me to wear. I had begun to feel spoiled and special. I needed that from him.

When Wade was gone, I called Rick to check in and chatted sometimes for hours until he convinced me the ranch or the horses needed him. Talking to Rick was easy and smooth. There were moments, just a few, when the talk turned to me coming home. I felt the tug on my heart but explained to Rick that I was committed.

I was laying on the bed sideways one morning, watching Wade come from the shower and begin to get dressed for work. Teasing him using my charms and naked body was an easy task. He was a man with little body fat, working out at the gym faithfully. A stray gray hair would start to show in the hair, but his body showed no wear and tear. He was simply gorgeous. I let my silk bathrobe fall open slightly and watched as his eyes darted from my face to my nether regions.

"No teasing me today, Antonia. Everything must be just right. I am the pillar of the community. Tonight is the big night. A specially planned night."

As he fussed with his tie, Wade explained to me that tonight was the final gala of the season where he was going to be awarded and honored as the architect and businessman of the year.

"All the county commissioners and Mayor Metcalf will be in attendance, Antonia"

"I suppose it is fair to say that you are pleased?" I asked.

"Yes, I can even say I am proud of myself. I asked Marisa to have my tuxedo picked up from the cleaners and lay out the dress for you to wear. I will be going straight from work to have cocktails before the ceremony with a few people from work. I will have a driver pick you up so please be on time,"

"I will be perfect just for you, Wade." I said, giving him one last look at my breasts.

Wade scoffed and rolled his eyes trying to avoid my distractions. As he was opening the bedroom door to leave, he turned back.

"I was going to tell you later, but it is a special day for me and I want you to feel special as well. I asked Marisa to check on booking a trip to Italy. We leave tomorrow afternoon. She has the tickets and all the details and will pack your suitcase. Tonight will be a night you will never forget." Wade threw me a wink and a chuckle like his devious secret plan had been revealed. "I will see you tonight. It will be special."

I rolled on to my back and kicked my feet in the air like a child. I felt I had made it back into the good graces and heart of Wade. Any problems we experienced before were now just flies in the ointment. I started dancing around the room singing, *"I am going to Italy!"* over and over until I was exhausted.

Any time a day started good, something seems to make the other shoe drop. Tonight had to be perfect. *"It will be a night I will never forget"* resonated in my head. I looked around and called out to Marisa but could not locate her anywhere in the house. I bathed and did my hair, sweeping it up into a loose bun placing a diamond pin at the side. When there was only a little less than an hour left until the driver arrived, I was worried. I still could not find Marisa nor the dress I was supposed to wear.

I decided to take matters in my own hands; I feared disappointing Wade and he was not answering his phone. Choosing the sleeveless silver sequin gown was my best choice. I had only worn it once when we first moved to Chicago.

The dress was form-fitting, floor length with a very interesting slit up one side revealing a nice show of just enough leg. The neck scooped low so I wanted to choose a necklace that would draw the eye to my cleavage. I quickly pulled out the jewelry case and dumped it on the bed. Most of my better pieces seemed to be missing.

Not wanting to be late, I put on small diamond studs and a tear drop pearl necklace. This complimented the plunging neckline nicely. I grabbed my small silver matching handbag and was out the door to meet the driver. Many thoughts ran through my head about the missing jewelry as well as the missing housekeeper, but I was not about to worry or spoil anything for Wade. Not tonight. I won't let anything ruin the trip to Italy in two days.

As I closed the door to the car, I looked up at the house and thought I saw a figure in an upstairs window. Hmmm… Was Marisa trying to ruin the night? *"I will be right back and deal with you later,"* I whispered, then told the driver to go.

*   *   *   *   *

Antonia tried to open her eyes, but her eyelashes were stuck together. Panicking, she rubbed her eyes, ripping off her fake lashes. She could feel the puffiness of her face. Her eyes finally opened just a slit, enough to feel the sting of the sun and its brightness blinding her. She tried to feel around reaching for something that felt familiar. *"Where am I?"*

Hot metal continued burning her arm as she pushed herself upright. Her eyes desperately tried to focus; looking over, she recognized the green metal of a trash bin. The smell of rotting rubbish burned her nostrils. Her mouth was dry and her tongue swollen. A sharp pain throbbed in her head as she tried to brush away her thick mop of hair that was sticking to her face.

"I must be in the alley behind our home, but how did I get here?" she thought to herself. Her medical training started to kick in and she tried to do an assessment of her injuries. Antonia discovered she was missing a stiletto, her

favorite pair. A sharp pain radiated in her side indicating a possible broken rib. Her lip was swollen and bleeding and her beautiful sequin dress was torn from the sleeve, exposing a breast. On further inspection she realized the worst yet: she was missing her undergarments and had possibly suffered a blow to the head and the sharp pain in her ankle indicated a sprain or possibly a fracture.

Groaning in pain, Antonia slowly forced her body to stand using the trash bin as support. Grimacing from touching the hot metal, she pushed herself upright and swayed until she felt partly stable enough to stand. Looking at where she was sitting on the ground, she discovered a broken bottle of wine beside her. 'Cranberry Wine' was on the label.

"I feel like I have been punched a thousand times. Wade must be worried sick about me. I am in a nightmare. Please, someone wake me up!" she shouted in the air as she glanced around for anyone who could help.

Antonia managed to move slowly, one painful step at a time. Limping badly with only one shoe and holding her side to stabilize the broken rib, she turned down the alley avoiding the occasional pop bottle and stray cat.

Reaching the corner, she turned to make the block holding onto the cool cement wall surrounding their compound. Stopping to rest only a few seconds to catch her breath and allowing the coolness of the wall to touch her face. Antonia prayed the house servant, Marisa, would immediately assist her when she rang the bell. Wade would have surely come looking for her so he must be at his office. Antonia looked around for her pocketbook or her phone but found nothing. It seemed like hours before she rounded the last corner and made it to the front gated entry way. The iron gates that she assumed were only for decoration were shut tight and locked. Antonia rang the bell on the intercom several times with rapid hurry.

"Marisa, I need help!" she shouted into the intercom. "Wade, are you there?" she screamed. After no immediate response, she rang the buzzer several times in desperation. "Marisa, please get Wade. Tell him I am hurt! Please open the gate, I don't have my pocketbook; it must have been stolen!"

Antonia, feeling weak and nauseous, slumped to the ground still clinging to the wrought iron gate in desperation. Tears burned her eyes. With enough medical training under her belt, she imagined her injuries could be life-threatening. Feeling as though she would lose consciousness from the pain, she tilted her head back on the gate. Antonia had no knowledge of how she got there or what happened to her. She could only assume she had been assaulted and wracked her brain trying to remember her last moments of clarity. Pain shot through her side like a bolt of lightning as she passed out still clinging to the gate.

The mind is a powerful thing but also very complex: she was in a dream-like state as her life flashed before her eyes. It was not a good sign, but she gave in to it hoping it would clear her fog. She pictured the ranch and her parents. She had a vision of Rick riding her horse, Julius, waving goodbye.

Antonia also dreamed of when she met Wade in college. He was the tall dark-haired architect student. His charming smile and body made her weak in the knees. The hectic week of ceremonies and grand openings seemed to swirl in her head. Bottles of wine and loud music became a distant memory.

As another pain shot through her head, Antonia gasped for breath. She reached up to feel the blood trickling only to pass out again. Images of the house Wade had built floated through her mind like a movie. A five-bedroom home with chandeliers, expensive carpets, imported tile and an Olympic size swimming pool. *Why five bedrooms if there were no plans of children?* Wade made sure she took her birth control every day and had reminders set on her phone. Now she might not survive long enough to even see a wedding ring.

"Why is this happening to me?" She moaned drifting in and out of consciousness.

Antonia was unaware of how long she lay at the gate in the sun, occasionally screaming out in pain as she tried to move. She felt hopeless, realizing that her ankle was badly sprained, swelling rapidly, and rendering her temporarily immobile.

A metal creaking noise startled her awake. Her throat was dry and her swollen eyes barely opened a slit. It appeared to be the wrought iron gate moving. Antonia tried to look up hoping to see Wade coming to her rescue like a knight saving his queen. Instead, Marisa came into focus carrying a leather overnight bag. Marisa tossed the bag just beyond the gate and stood with her hands on her hips. Her dark hair was not in the usual bun at the back of the neck. "Help me! I need water," she moaned.

"You need nothing from me. Take the bag and leave," The maid's voice was devoid of any feeling or sympathy.

"What are you doing, Marisa? You aren't wearing your uniform. I almost didn't recognize you," Antonia extended her arm toward Marisa for assistance, "I think I was mugged or assaulted."

"Miss Toni, I have been instructed to pack a few things in a bag for you and turn you out. I am sure Wade told you this yesterday morning before he left. I quote, 'Marisa will pack a bag for you.' Now you are no longer welcome in this house," Marisa said coldly.

"What? Where is Wade? You have no authority to do this to me. I will tell Wade to terminate your employment. We are leaving on a trip to Italy tonight and I must get cleaned up." Ignoring the pain, Antonia allowed the anger of the situation to rise up. She drew in a deep breath and used all her strength to try and stand.

"Listen, Toni. Go away!" barked Marisa.

"No one calls me Toni! My name is Antonia. How dare you talk to me like this!"

Closing the gate, Marisa stepped back. She was pointing her finger toward Antonia and grabbing her chest while laughing. "Don't you get it, Antonia? It was Mr. Wade that instructed me to do this. He said buy tickets for Italy and pack a bag for Antonia. Oh, and he did say it would be a night you would never forget, remember?"

"Tickets for *us* to go to Italy! Don't you walk away! How do you know what Wade said to me privately?" she shouted. "Was this his plan all along? He wouldn't. I couldn't have been wrong about him. No! You are a liar. Wade loves me!"

Antonia screamed in pain and embarrassment. Defeated and unable to challenge Marisa, Antonia closed her eyes, allowing the burning tears to roll down her cheeks. Sometime after midnight she was again startled awake not knowing how long she had been out cold.

Slowly regaining awareness for a moment she noticed it had turned dark. She could barely make out her surroundings only noticing the street lights. Someone kicked at her leg sending a shooting pain forcing her to open her eyes. Two police officers stood over her. They had been called to remove her from the front of the house – the house she thought she would be sharing with Wade.

"Ma'am, you cannot sleep here," they said.

Taking notice of her condition and the blood on her head, the officers called an ambulance to take her to the local hospital. Once there, she slept for two days. On the third day she woke up in a hospital gown lying in crisp white sheets.

"Don't try to get up too fast, you are still weak sweetie" a nurse in blue scrubs said.

"What day is it?" Antonia asked. "I only had one glass of wine. Why does my head hurt?"

"It is Thursday," the nurse replied as she opened the curtains letting in the bright sunlight. "Must have been a big glass of wine if it was only one," she snarled. The nurse made a miffing sound as though she had heard a lie or two before. "You lost consciousness due to the blow to your head. Do you remember what happened to you sweetie?" asked the nurse.

Sitting up suddenly, Antonia screamed. "Our trip to Italy! We were supposed to fly out tonight, Wade must be so angry and disappointed. He said Marisa has the tickets!"

Pushing my shoulders down gently the nurse pulled the covers up straightening the bed. "Shhh, now. I don't know who Wade is. You were brought here by ambulance. Picked up off the street, as a matter of fact. Do you remember what happened to you at all?" asked the nurse. "You have a nasty split lip and burns to your arms."

Anxious and rambling, Antonia tried to push up to rest on her elbows. "The last thing I remember is attending a grand opening of the new municipal building. Wade, my boyfriend, was nominated for 'Businessman of the Year'. I wore my silver dress with the slit up the side – not the dress I was *supposed* to be wearing at all.

"I had a glass of cranberry wine at the gala. Wade was upset about something I said and then that's it…I don't remember anything else. Why can't I remember anything else? What happened to me?"

Tilting her head, the nurse looked at her with a condescending smile. "Well, from that knot on your head it looked as though someone gave you a beating. You can tell me anything sweetie, it's all confidential. Did one of your calls go wrong?"

"What? No! Do you think I am a hooker?"

With one hand on her hip the nurse rolled her eyes then counted on her fingers all the reasons that did point suspiciously to an alternative story. It was the sort of thing the nurse had seen many times before. "Well, let's see… You had on a ripped sparkly dress, no panties, and only one very pretty stiletto. Only one. Some fancy earrings and pearls but you were passed out on the street. Oh, there also were some personal items. You had some belongings in an expensive leather bag with you. I will get it from the closet. Maybe that will make you remember something. If you are not a hooker, then how did you get on the street in front of a fancy mansion?"

"Because I live there!" Antonia screamed.

"Don't think on it too hard right now. You are here to rest. You just sit tight; breakfast is coming soon. You might get lucky and be released this afternoon now that you are awake." The nurse pulled the bag from the closet and placed it on the bed between Antonia's legs. "Is this yours, sweetie?" the nurse asked curiously.

Antonia recognized the bag. Wade always wanted her to have an overnight bag in case they decided to stay at a hotel after one of the parties. As she felt the soft leather and started to unzip it, she had a flashback of Marisa tossing it out of the gate before she passed out.

Antonia immediately noticed a note on top of what looked like old sweatpants. Setting it aside for now, she rummaged through the clothes. Packed neatly with the sweatpants were one pair of faded blue jeans, running shoes, three cotton shirts and an old purse. Examining the inside of the purse she found three dollars, her ID and passport. Throwing the purse to the side, she picked up the note to read it:

Antonia, it has been a fun ride, but all this must come to an end. Don't dare try to come back to the house or I will have you for trespassing. You were never the one for me, I have met someone new and I will be taking her on the trip to Italy. Regards, Wade.

Feeling defeated, Antonia crumpled the note, tore it into pieces and tossed it in the trash bin with as much angry force as her bruised body could muster. Missing the trash bin, the pieces fluttered and landed all around the small trash can like ash from a fire. All the memories of the last couple of days came flooding back like a wild river rapids rushing through mountains.

She realized it had been ridiculous trusting Wade again. She remembered the flirtations but had looked the other way. Slamming her fists on the bed, Antonia let it all out. "I buried my parents! Wade brushed it off. He even told me to sell the ranch! The new house, separate bedrooms, the clues were there. I was just too determined to not see. I had blinders on. I hoped he would change. Was he hoping I would die? No, death would have brought police, this was a planned humiliation. To get rid of me!"

Antonia understood all of it. Waking up next to the dumpster, waiting at the gate, Marisa not wearing her uniform, it all made sense. Wade repeating, *"A night I will never forget?"* "The 'special' cranberry wine he had delivered just for me. It was special alright, laced with sleeping pills," she seethed.

In her rage Antonia's brain struggled with the emotions like a boxing match in her head. Tired, angry and hurt, Antonia pulled the blanket up over her head then muffling the sound with a pillow she screamed, "I am so mad! I was drugged! If I bring charges, they will just say I was drunk and wandered off. But no, I know I was drugged by Wade and the *housekeeper*!"

As the nurse brought in the breakfast tray and placed it on the rolling bedside table, she noticed Antonia had been crying and offered a tissue. "Listen, girlie, I am sorry I assumed you were some kind of broken and beaten street girl. I didn't mean to hurt your feelings."

Lowering the pillow Antonia hugged it tight and looked at the nurse with red eyes.

"My feelings are irrelevant. Guilt is a wasted emotion, and any expression of feelings was always viewed as defiance by Wade. Now I must somehow find a way to pick myself up and I am unsure how to do that. I can't go back to Texas with just three dollars to my name."

The nurse sat on the edge of the bed. "You can conquer this. Women are built to handle rejection, hurt and pain. Suffering produces courage and perseverance. Perseverance builds character and renewed values. It is our fundamental values that get us through day to day."

"I thought I had values, a career path and abilities. Now I have absolutely nothing."

"Listen Antonia, you have that fancy pearl necklace. Looks real. Besides, the only way out of this labyrinth of a suffering pity party is to find your courage. I live by the three A's. Acceptance, Appreciation and Attitude. I accept people for who they are, I appreciate my life and my gifts, but mess with me and you will see the attitude"

Standing at the foot of the bed the nurse crossed her arms and put on a serious face. "If someone is evil, accept that, but have no part of them because you cannot change them. Appreciate that you have the strength and ability to do whatever you set your mind to. Now the attitude, that is up to you, and no one would blame you for being a thoroughly pissed off ex-girlfriend. So, start with that!"

Chapter 7: No More Wine

Antonia left the hospital with the clothes she found in her bag. They felt strangely comfortable after all the years wearing gowns and fancy clothes to impress Wade and his colleagues. Stopping at the trash receptacle outside the hospital, Antonia tossed the hospital bag with the torn sparkly gown and her one stiletto, symbolically saying good-bye to her former life. *"Some journeys begin with a suitcase in hand. Leaving everything behind can lead to a new future ahead,"* she thought. Antonia wanted desperately to leave everything behind. The sting of embarrassment was only beginning to fade.

"Perhaps one day, after many years and a successful career as a surgeon, I will possibly look back on this humiliating time in my life and laugh, or possibly cry. I just need to survive until I can figure my way out of my current uncertain situation. I know I must accept what happened and appreciate that I am set free to start again but my attitude is something entirely different. My attitude wants to hold Wade under water until the bubbles stop."

The sun was warming and almost cleansing as she looked around to access her options. The hospital being just outside of the main downtown area, there was less traffic and a few shops. Walking was helping her to stretch the kinks out of her legs from being in bed for three days, but her ankle was still in a supportive elastic wrap. Taking deep breaths and long strides felt good and Antonia could feel her head being less foggy. She was almost starting to feel happy as though she had just been released from a jail cell and not the hospital.

Knowing she should call home to Texas and ask Rick to have money sent by wire, she began to look in shop windows for a Western Union sign. Curious as a schoolgirl, Antonia made it to the corner and went into the convenience store. Only having three dollars, she decided to splurge on a 20-ounce soda and chocolate bar. Chocolate was definitely her weakness. Chocolate cake was her favorite, but any chocolate would do. *"I need to enjoy my so-called freedom at least a few hours before I have to explain myself to others and why I am returning home to Texas,"* she thought to herself.

"Your total is $1.85, ma'am. Would you like to buy a lotto ticket? Odds are good. Today is the drawing and it is up to three million now," said the clerk.

"Sure, I just got my freedom today, so I am feeling quite lucky perhaps. This is my last dollar," laughed Antonia. Pushing the dollar across the counter she smiled at the clerk. "I have no place to live, but hey! Let me just take a chance and spend my last dollar. It is a crazy move that Wade would not approve of and that makes it all more exciting because I have nothing else to lose. He took it all. I was hit on the head, left for dead after my wine was spiked and I literally have nothing and somehow it feels exhilarating," Antonia mumbled to the clerk.

"Okay, ma'am. I don't understand what you are talking about obviously, but heck, today could be your lucky day. I like your attitude," replied the store clerk.

"Yes, it is all about the attitude, and my attitude is that I did not die at the hands of my nemesis. Sorry I guess 'nemesis' is a little over the top, don't you think?"

Placing the ticket in her handbag, Antonia strolled to the park in the town square. Drinking her soda, swinging her legs and munching on the candy bar made her feel alive. A chance a for a new start. Thinking about her college days and her pre-med classes made her feel displaced. "I was so close to finishing I could kick myself," she whispered.

Her life had become all about Wade. She trusted him when she should have trusted her instincts. Now she was sitting on a park bench covered in bird poop with no money, no clothes, no Wade and no mansion. "But I did not die!" she shouted. "No matter how messy my life is right now, I am invigorated because I am alive."

Soon the new feelings of freedom started to wear off. Antonia had to keep adjusting her attitude. The setting sun was sending bright orange colors across the sky like fire. She was putting off calling Rick at the ranch and asking for money just to have a few more moments of solitude. "I guess now is time to be responsible and call Texas. I can't sleep on the street, or I might be mistaken for a hooker again, even in sweat pants without the stilettos."

Crossing the street to return to the store and call Rick collect, she tossed her candy wrapper in the bin and looked up to notice a crowd forming in front of the convenience store. She stayed in the back ground and listened. The store clerk had the television on and the people standing outside were cheering. News crews were pulling up and journalists were trying to push through the crowd. The mood appeared happy and celebratory, so she pushed in closer trying to determine what the fuss was about.

"The winning ticket was sold here at my little store!" the clerk was shouting and throwing his hands in the air. A woman shoved a microphone in his face and started asking questions. The store clerk was nearly out of breath as he explained how his humble little store had sold the winning ticket. His eyes met Antonia's and he began to wave at her. Antonia tried to shrink down and hide but the clerk was drawing attention to her and before she knew it the crowd pushed her forward.

"Hey lady, come check your ticket! Everyone else here has already scanned theirs; maybe it was you! Come try," the clerk shouted.

The crowd parted, allowing Antonia through to the front. She stepped timidly inside the store. "I am sure it wasn't me but if you insist, I will get my ticket out. I only bought it a few hours ago."

The cheering crowd hushed as Antonia inserted her ticket in the machine. The news reporter stood beside her like a lion ready to pounce, her microphone inches from Antonia. Time froze as Antonia slowly pushed in the paper ticket. She hesitated for a second and took a deep breath. Most of her life choices swirled in her head: Wade, being a doctor, the glass of wine, the Ranch, her parents death and of course the dumpster.

With the final push, the ticket clicked then just as fast the machine began to hum, then bells started chiming. Confetti swirled around her face and people were shouting and cheering, slapping her on the back. Her eyes saw it, but her mind could not comprehend and she felt faint. The clerk grabbed her arm and pulled her aside shaking her.

"Do you understand? You won, miss, you really won!"

"I won? No, it must be a mistake. Are you sure?"

"Yes, you won. What is the first thing you are going to do with the money?"

*　*　*　*　*

My eyes didn't seem to blink like they should have. I was staring at the reporter that approached me shoving the microphone in my face. I felt uncomfortable as though the whole world was watching. I began fidgeting with my clothes. I was regretting my rumpled appearance.

"It wasn't me. It couldn't have been me. You are mistaken."

"Just tell Chicago how you feel holding the winning ticket" she asked. "What will you do with the money?"

"I... I... guess find a motel room and oh, I will buy a chocolate cake. I love chocolate cake," I managed to say. *Boy of all the things I could have said.*

I started backing away. There were no familiar faces in the crowd and I wanted to run. My mouth was dry. The crowd of onlookers pushed in. I felt panicked. What if someone saw me on television? Worse yet, what if *Wade* saw me? My brain was scrambling to find a logical excuse to get away from the store. "Please, I need to go. Can everyone please let me through?"

"You have to think bigger, lady! You won three million dollars!" someone shouted.

I had always been told I could be a little too blunt for some folks. So, I tried to conjure up some sympathy for those only trying to do their job and get a story.

"Okay, I guess I will buy two chocolate cakes!"

The crowd burst into laughter as the news reporter started speaking into the microphone asking more questions. "Can you tell us your name?"

Looking down at the ground and my feet. I tried to cover my face with my hand. "Umm, I would rather not say," I whispered. I pulled some hair to cover one eye.

"Oh, I see you want to remain anonymous?" asked the reporter.

I had exhausted all usual politeness and wanted to run but the crowd pushed in like sharks to a fresh tuna. Suddenly out of nowhere, someone took hold of my arm and began to pull me away through the mass of people. When I looked over, it was the store clerk. I smiled acknowledging his efforts as he began to shout at the people to leave me alone and give me some privacy. He pulled me through the crowd and as we popped out near the door, I banged my elbow on the bricks. White lightning of pain shot through my eyes as he gave me one last shove into the store. He locked the door behind us to keep the crowd out, then turned the sign on the door to 'Closed'. Standing there with one arm holding the other at the elbow and clutching my empty purse. I slowly started rocking back and forth.

"Are you okay? This can be overwhelming, but you do have the winning ticket. You must be a lucky person."

A wave of nausea rolled over me. The clerk brought a soda from the cooler and handed it to me "Thank you for saving me from the crowd. I sure don't feel lucky. I have never been lucky. I just buried my parents; my boyfriend left me for dead behind a dumpster and someone hit me on the head. I don't have a place to live, and I am feeling very shaky right now. Is there some where I can sit down?"

"Wow! I think this win came at the right time for you. You are one stressed-out woman. Let's sit in the back of the store and let you breathe. You are safe here. I am Hank and my wife is called Chime," said the store clerk.

"Lovely to meet you both," was all I could think to say.

After regaining my composure I explained to the clerk and his wife that I had just gotten out of the hospital and had no where to stay. They were so kind to help me call and get a room for the night at the Holiday Inn close to the store. The clerk was only able to give me 15% of the winnings now but it was enough to get a room. The rest would be deposited where I choose, after taxes, in about a week.

Feeling more relaxed that the crowd of people had started to disperse, the clerk's wife loaned Antonia a scarf to cover her head and led her out the back of the store all the way to the front door of the motel. Getting her key, Antonia went up to her room and immediately ordered room service. She was starving after only having a candy bar earlier that day.

"A large cheeseburger, fries and an entire chocolate cake…. Yes, that is correct. Just bring the whole cake ‚please. I am celebrating," she said to the concierge.

Sitting in the middle of the king size bed, Antonia munched on her cake and pulled out a pad of paper and pen from the desk.

"If I do have the winning ticket and this is real, I do have to think bigger and make a list of things I want to do with the money. Let's see, a nice car, perhaps? Nah, too many choices. A big house, perhaps? Nah, I couldn't decide where to live anyway. I have had enough of big houses. I need simple and personal with furniture from a thrift store, maybe. Comfy and cozy with a wood burning fireplace. A big old quilt on the bed to keep me warm and rocking chairs on a wrap around porch."

Frustrated, she flopped back on the pillows and wiped the chocolate from her face. The absurdity was that she was mentally describing the ranch as her perfect home. Antonia decided one thing, and that was she didn't want to stay in Chicago and Texas felt like giving up and giving in. She let her mind wander to Wade, fantasizing about the day he might see her on the news or bump into her in town and realize not only was she alive and well but had won the lottery.

"He would say I am unworthy," she whispered.

Antonia drew her limbs close to her body and hugged herself. Confident Chicago was not a choice, this time she tried to imagine moving back home to the ranch. "I could go back to school, go shopping with Jill or hang out with the hunky Rick... Wait... I am not ready for another relationship. I just feel sad. Being sad is not a crime; neither is indecision."

Waking up to a brand-new day with a full night sleep, Antonia stretched and opened the curtains greeting the day: the sun was starting to rise behind the tall buildings of the city; rays from the early morning sun shot up like a crown of gold giving the city the glory of another day.

"I wasn't promised a new day but here I am. I will live my life how I want to from now on" she said firmly. Thinking aloud she looked in the mirror at the bandages on her head and gently removed them. "I must be careful with my choices and not be too spontaneous. Spontaneity will fizzle just like my desire to wear high heels that squeezed my toes. Wade always insisted that it would spice up our love life to wear high heels. And it did, for a while. Staying at hotels similar to this one was a treat that inspired role play. Wade would pull me into a closet or back room and ravage me, pulling on my panties so hard they would rip. We would leave them where they fell, a souvenir for housekeeping to find and blush when we were almost caught. That was the thrill of it. Once we did it on a pool table in a client's house with the bust of an elk's head staring at me. All those memories soon will fizzle away.

"Right now, it is all about me starting a new life. I have to survive this ripple Wade started. I will not be homeless and helpless. Looking at this woman in the mirror now I would say she is fine the way she is. I have curves where they are supposed to be, nice boobs, long chestnut hair and a killer smile thanks to my orthodontist in seventh grade. I like me and Lord knows, I need to stop talking to myself."

Antonia called and ordered a large breakfast of eggs, bacon and pancakes with a hot cup of tea with sugar. Next, she started making a list of things to do:

Call Texas and let them know I am alright.

 Buy a cell phone.

Take a long shower.

Go shopping for clothes.

Stop thinking about Wade!

Antonia double-underlined the last item on the list. A plan to call Texas included hoping Rick could wire her some money until she settled opening a bank account and contacting the state Lottery. Antonia had inherited the ranch and a life insurance payout from her parents. *"This will get me started until I decide what I want to do when I grow up,"* she giggled.

It took several rings for Rick to answer the phone. He was obviously hesitant not recognizing the number on the caller ID. "Rick, it is me, Antonia."

"Antonia, I didn't recognize the number, Is everything okay with you?"

"Rick, things have happened, but I am okay now. Please don't ask too many questions, I don't want to talk about it right now. How is the ranch?"

"Antonia, you know how I feel about you. The ranch is fine, practically runs itself. If you need me to come to that big city and carry you home kicking and screaming, I will."

Just hearing Rick's voice on the phone made her feel emotional. Rick was a comfortable connection, a familiar calm in the storm. She loved him once, but never acted on it fully or treated it seriously. Always waiting for that perfect connection that she assumed would be unplanned and spontaneous like she read in the romance books. Similar to when she bumped into Wade, she thought it was a sign.

Note to self, romance books are fictional characters in a fictional world!

Antonia did feel a spark when she heard Rick's deep manly voice. She was just not sure what that meant exactly.

"I know you would come, Rick, you are forever the hero. However, I am not ready for that just yet. I need some time."

The phone line was silent except for a big sigh.

I imagined Rick standing there shifting his feet in the barn. He was a tall burly cowboy. A real man in my eyes with his tight blue jeans and boots. I never wanted to hurt his feelings. Rick is an important part of my life. The only thing I have to offer him is time. After we listened and sensed the hurt in the silence through the phone, Rick asked what I knew he would ask.

"Did he hurt you, Antonia?"

Holding back the sniffles she stammered for the right words. Holding a shaky hand to her forehead she managed to whisper, "He tried, but I am unbreakable."

"Just say the word, Antonia. Just say the damn word and I will be there," said Rick. His voice getting louder, irritation was replacing his usual carefully controlled tone.

"I know, Rick, but I can't. I need to evaluate my life. I am in an emotional tornado. I love you to death, but I just can't. I need some time. I might be home soon. Texas is my home but it also has memories that will only shove me further into questioning the reason for my existence. There has to be more. There has to be another path or a fork in the road that I must have missed. I don't want to feel foolish I won't give up. I just can't."

"It is not foolish to come home when you have been hurt or made a wrong choice. It is your safe place, I am your safe place!" he said.

"Going home is my last choice. When I go home it means I have made the decision that it is the best decision."

"So are you saying that if nothing better comes along you will come home?"

"I am saying my first thought is that of revenge. There is hate in my heart for the choices I made trusting the people I should have been wary of. If anyone cannot accept your dreams then walk away, no run away because they longer you stay the more open you leave yourself to be hurt badly. I want to reassess my dreams and my future choices before I settle into my life again. I want to be sure of everything."

"I will try to understand Antonia, just be safe," said Rick.

" I do need you to wire me some money. I am staying in a hotel, and I am safe. I know I want to buy some clothes and I don't know, maybe take a trip or something to clear my head but I can't face you or anyone."

"Take a trip and come home to Texas, Antonia. Come home to me. I will take care of you and never hurt you. You know that. I know you feel the same way about me. After seeing you at your parents' funeral, I didn't want you to leave. Please come home," pleaded Rick.

"I will let you know where I am always Rick. Trust me, please. I am safe. I will be in touch soon. And Rick, I do feel the same way. I just have to find my way right now. I feel lost. I won't ask you to wait for me. I never have, I can't do that to you. It is a shame I let you get away in the first place but know that I do feel love for you. Goodbye."

I no longer fear failure but I am terrified of regret. I regret trusting Wade, I don't want to regret Rick.

Antonia was reluctant to have that conversation with Rick bringing up old feelings that she could not reciprocate. As teenagers they flirted and kissed in the barn. A crush. Feelings unexplored. Then off to college and meeting Wade who swept her away from Texas, family and Rick. All regrets that she could not take back or erase. Events happen, they get filed away but they do not define us forever.

Regrets can take a different shape, a life lesson or lead to a better future. All she had to do was clear the old cobwebs of hurt feelings and replace them with something purposeful and vindicating. She knew she could not love anyone if she did not love herself. Her whole self. Gently biting her lip as she tapped her fingers on the bedside table, Antonia had an idea..

"What if…could I possibly?…that is it! I will take the trip to Italy alone. I can do this! I can do this alone!" she said aloud as she jumped out of bed. "I must contact a travel agent. No schedule or time frame. I will let the rhythm of Italy dictate the pace. A professor once told me; Change your surroundings if you want to change your life!"

Antonia had looked at brochures for years and years and knew all the sights she wanted to see. Clapping her hands like a giddy child she reached for the phone to call Rick back not letting him talk or try and change her mind.

"Listen Rick I am taking a trip to Italy. Don't you worry. I will be right back, and I will be right as rain! I will experience many new things that the old hurt and disappointment from my bad choice of Wade will fly right out of my head like spraying bug spray on a wasp nest."

Crawling back in bed, Antonia looked again at her list and scratched out the car and house and started adding clothes, suitcases, hats, and sensible shoes. Antonia called down to order a light lunch and a car. Giddy with excitement she blurted out to the lady at the front desk. "I am going to ride a gondola in Venice so I can hear the sensuous sounds of water lapping against the boat!"

"Okay, I am very happy for you, ma'am" she responded. "Would you like that charged to your room?"

"What? Can you do that?"

"I mean your lunch, ma'am, not your trip to Venice."

"Oh yea, please charge it to my room. Thank you.

Chapter 8: Wine in Italy

Antonia got up early to see the sunrise for the last time over the Chicago skyline. Every day was now a blank page and the urgency to travel the world was intoxicating. The sky had faded from gloomy gray to light blue as the sun burned away the morning clouds. A new bank account was set up in her name and the large deposit was there from the winnings. She checked it three times just to be sure. Antonia spent the last week preparing for the trip while waiting on the funds transfer. That day had finally arrived.

"I can learn from my errors or be depressed. I choose to accept my life, appreciate the lessons and change my attitude. Then I will finish my medical school."

Discreetly, she ripped a page from the phone book listing a travel agent. Leaving ten dollars on the nightstand eased her guilt for vandalizing the book. Skipping breakfast she checked out of the hotel, caught a cab and headed to the shopping district, purchasing lovely outfits, scarves and comfortable flats. No more high heels for her. She next purchased suitcases to put all her treasures in. She didn't even remove the tags before heading to the travel agent listed in the phone book.

"I want to leave right away, just book me on the next flight to Italy before I change my mind. Make it First Class. I might have a unique request though, please arrange for me to have a personal travel guide."

"That is no problem, I will pick one from our listings," said the agent with a wink. "I have the perfect one for you."

"I don't want to walk around alone throwing a coin in the fountains then take a bus to Rome to see the Vatican. I will need a guide and a driver because… well, why not? So can you arrange that?" Antonia asked.

"I can arrange any travel plans you desire. My name is Bethany; here is my personal cell phone number, and email so if you decide to extend your stay or want to change hotels just let me know. You are going to love Italy."

Antonia handed the travel agent a check for a retainer in case there are any changes in cost or different extended stays. "I have one more request," said Antonia.

"What ever you need," Bethany replied.

"May I change in your restroom? I just bought the most beautiful outfit to travel in and I have already checked out of the hotel."

"Of course, you can. While you change, shall I call a cab to take you to O'Hare?"

"That would be lovely."

Antonia emerged from the restroom wearing soft black flared long slacks, velvet shoes to match, a creamy beige silk blouse and a bright multi-colored scarf around her neck. Antonia felt vibrant, animated and sparkly. She gave the travel agent a little fashion show when she came out fully dressed.

"You look amazing," Bethany commented, "Like a million lottery bucks. No pun intended."

"Thank you, and don't worry: my confident, independent 'big girl panties' are on underneath all this. I am ready. No offense to Chicago, but I am so ready to leave."

Antonia had purchased five casual slacks, a long skirt, blouses in every color and matching hats. She was joyful, thankful and ready for adventure. She only cried a little, once, when she saw the price of the Louis Vuitton luggage, then casually crumpled the receipt and tossed it in the trash bin on the way out of the store, her head held high with the luggage in tow. Her stride was confident but not too proud. *"Only the best for this girl"* she whispered to herself.

Arriving at O'Hare, Antonia was greeted by a porter who treated her like a visiting dignitary or possibly a princess. She certainly felt like royalty. With her Louis Vuitton carry on bag she entered the First Class lounge and ordered a red wine spritzer. There was no chance of eliminating the huge smile on her face as she glanced around then took a long sip. Making a face, she flagged down the attendant and changed her order to a cola. *Not ready for wine.*

On the plane and settled, Antonia leaned back listening to the roar of the engines. Flying First Class was the right choice;. Soon Antonia drifted in and out of sleep, dreaming of a floating cloud. The sensational dream was a sign that all her burdens had been removed with this one decision. Several hours later after an overnight flight, the pilot announced they were landing in Rome. It was hard to control the flutter in her belly.

"I cannot believe I am actually here I may need someone to pinch me!" she squealed softly in excitement. Antonia's first sight of the city from her small airplane window was enough to set her heart racing.

A hectic cab ride and nervously checking into a hotel all by herself, Antonia pushed away any fear or anxiety. A quick change of clothing was in order, then looking at her itinerary she set out for the lobby where she was to meet her travel guide. Plans were laid out that her first sightseeing adventure was the Coliseum. Looking around the lobby with her hat held in her hands in front of her she spotted a gentleman entering the door. A considerably attractive man with dark curly hair wearing dark pants and a crisp white shirt. Antonia knew staring at him was risky but she couldn't help herself. *"Hubba, hubba!"* she whispered as she placed one hand on her hip. *"I am loving Italy already."*

Brushing his hair to the side, the attractive man lifted a white sign from his side and held it up glancing around the room. His eyes met Antonia's causing her to suddenly stiffen up in amazement. The sign read ANTONIA in all caps. At first she fanned herself trying to hide the flush in her cheeks then slowly raised her hand and gave a subtle wave and smoothed her hair.

Antonia watched him cross the lobby as though he was walking in slow motion. He was tall, dark and exotic. *I asked for a tour guide but I never expected this gorgeous specimen.* Nervously she managed a smile and extended her hand to greet him.

"Hello, I am Luca, your tour guide. I take it that you are Antonia. Am I correct?" he said with his sexy Italian accent.

"Yes, yes, I am Antonia. So nice to meet you."

"Do you need any assistance with getting your luggage to your room?" asked Luca.

I could think of lots of things for you to assist me with…

"I mean… No, I already checked in and the luggage is safely in my room."

Antonia felt her face flush again as she closed her eyes attempting to regain her composure. "*He is just a tour guide, keep yourself together,*" she thought to herself. "*A freaking gorgeous tour guide.*"

"Okay then. I have your itinerary just here in my pocket."

What else is in your pocket, next to the rocket? Geez, just stop and keep it together, girl!

"The itinerary tells me our first stop is the Coliseum. If that is correct then we must be on our way. My car is just outside."

Luca stood with his hand extended to cup her elbow and escort her to the car. "Are you okay, ma'am? Are you hungry?"

Let's see… It's been months since I've had sex and twelve hours since food, so basically I am starving in all areas.

"Oh no. I am just fine. I just need to catch my breath and focus. The Coliseum, you say? I am so ready. Just really excited, I mean yes, lets go," she said stammering. Antonia stepped forward and allowed Luca to take her arm. His gentle touch was comforting. She felt safe and managed to take a deep breath and follow him to the car where he opened the door for her.

"First stop was the coliseum." she nodded. "I am looking forward to it."

The car was a black Mercedes with soft tan leather seats. There was no glass between the front and back seats, so it felt comfortable not awkward. Luca drove with ease and explained a little about himself making small talk until they arrived within a short walking distance to the Coliseum. Again, Luca took Antonia's elbow and walked beside her.

The historical sight intrigued her. Luca explained that over 400,000 people and animals died here. Most of it now in ruins, it is now owned by the Vatican and is still a sight to see; imagining the anguish that went on here and the crowds cheering left her feeling melancholy. Luca was informative and spirited as he explained with great ease and compassion the history of the Coliseum in Rome. The sky was a little gray and cloudy, but it didn't matter. She was living her dream. It didn't hurt that her tour guide was a dream as well. Eventually she became comfortable enough with Luca to be able to carry on mild conversations. She still felt the need to sneak a peek at his gorgeous eyes and smooth skin that sent a faint jolt down her spine. *One point for me, asking for a tour guide. I must send a tip to Bethay. She chose well.*

"The rest of the day is up to you, Antonia. You may be tired and want to rest up for tomorrow so I can return you to your hotel. If you need to eat, your hotel has a café. If you are adventurous, I know a lovely place away from the crowds and tourists. A quaint place, with authentic Italian food. It must be your choice to come with me"

Letting out a small sigh, Antonia placed a hand on her chest trying to slow her quickening heartbeat. "I am a little tired, but I think I should appreciate a chance to eat dinner and take you up on your offer. Will you be dining with me or will it be a drop off and you wait in the car? My treat, of course. I prefer to not dine alone my first time in the country. A girl has to eat!"

"You are no girl. You are a beautiful woman, *la donna*. I will be honored to dine with you," said Luca.

"Umm… What does that mean, '*la donna*'? That is not my name, so I am curious."

"A woman, female, queen or just in your case, a beautiful woman, Antonia," Luca replied.

Feeling brave and flattered, Antonia placed her arm in the crook of Luca's arm.

"Then I suggest you take this woman to eat. I am starving.".

Luca drove Antonia to a quaint place to eat in a small part of town not too far from their first destination. Some tourists were there but mostly locals chatting away in Italian. Luca took the lead, and ordered in Italian for both of them, then offered her a glass of wine.

The lights were dim and the tables small and intimate with checkered tablecloths. In the center of each table was a candle dripping their waxy contents down the side of a bottle in an array of colors, creating a wax masterpiece of art. Antonia was mesmerized by the ambience.

A tray of grapes and cheese appeared at the table as an appetizer. Luca felt so comfortable being her guide; Antonia wondered if he gets this familiar with all his clients. The how and why were not important to Antonia. She was simply marveled at the fact she was in Italy eating dinner with a lovely companion, enjoying grapes and wine. There was no room in her mind for comparison or doubt. Deciding to accept the situation she was in right now as it was meant to be, she stared openly at Luca across the table while the flickering of the candle danced between them. His perfect white teeth and beautiful smile relaxed her in ways she never imagined.

After a exhilarating night meeting Luca, visiting the coliseum then dinner in a authentic Italian eatery, Antonia was delightedly exhausted. Falling asleep for the first time without drama or trauma on her mind was mercifully easier than she expected. Waking up the next morning was almost as thrilling. Antonia felt giddy, a feeling she had not felt since college days.

I woke up in Italy! Nothing can upset me!

Antonia wanted to choose her outfit wisely, hoping to attract a little attention maybe, so she chose the long flowing skirt, blue silk blouse and boots with a low heel. After a quick breakfast in the hotel's dining room, she anxiously waited in the lobby for Luca to arrive. He was picking her up rather early for a scenic drive to Venice where she was booked to take a gondola ride. *I hope Bethany booked it so Luca will ride with me even if I have to change the schedule.*

Antonia noticed the flash of smile as Luca opened the door for her. Her flowing skirt caught some wind and flowed like a ball gown in a perfume commercial; the slit allowed a peek at her long beautiful legs. Luca noticed immediately and flashed an approving look. Once inside the car she removed her hat letting her hair fall past her shoulders. It was obvious Luca noticed as she caught him stealing glances in the rear-view mirror. Luca explained the route and turned on some light music for the ride to Venice.

"Gondola ride, in the romantic city of Venice. It should be most pleasant for you," Luca said.

Sitting next to you is romantic enough for me.

"I am super excited; I have seen so many pictures of it in the movies. I can't believe in a few short hours I will be floating along in a Gondola. Will you be riding with me, Luca?"

"Again, it is your choice. A personal tour guide can be at your side for everything if you wish or we can just drive you to your destination."

"Luca, hopefully I'm not sounding too needy, but I wish you to join me on every excursion. I just hope your wife or family doesn't mind me taking up all your time. I really enjoy the company."

Slipped that right in there, didn't I?

Luca laughed a healthy laugh and gave Antonia a look in the rear view.

"There is no wife. I have not chosen one yet. I am too busy traveling around Italy and when I am not traveling, I stay with my family. You are a sly one, Antonia," he chuckled, "I see what you did there. I enjoy your company as well."

Pleased with herself, Antonia turned to look out the window and enjoy the scenery. Venice was one of the sights Antonia was scheduled to see with Wade during their visit. She secretly hoped he lost a lot of money ditching the trip and ditching her. She was now uncertain if there was ever a trip planned or was it a ruse to keep her in line.

"Luca is the only man I see right now. They say your trauma makes you stronger and I am feeling strong, I am at my peak. I am no longer trying to be the extreme people pleaser keeping my feelings hidden in my gut. I will go after what I want," she thought to herself.

Everything was perfect on arriving in Venice. The city was surrounded by water and Antonia met every challenging experience with child-like enthusiasm. The gondola ride was no different; her handsome Italian guide extended his hand and she stepped daintily on to the boat. Antonia felt special, like all eyes were on her, her skirt fluttering just enough to draw attention.

She sat back on the cushions and closed her eyes for a minute, taking it all in. Her nerves were calm as she perceived another delightful experience was ahead of her. The minute she stepped on the Venetian gondola with its handmade wood and intricate metal adornments she felt like royalty. When Luca took the seat next to her, she felt the warmth of his body touching hers. The gondolier began pushing through the canals with ease, his muscles flexing with each stroke of his long oar. Luca delighted in giving Antonia a tour as well as explaining some of the history. She also noticed the way the gondolier glanced back at her like she was someone beautiful and famous. Chills ran down her spine. The good kind.

"It would have been a shame to take a romantic gondola ride by yourself, *la donna*," Luca commented. "You look beautiful and I am honored to be sitting here with you. You make everyone notice your beauty."

"I am just so happy to be here," replied Antonia, blushing. "Everything I have seen in Italy is beautiful, including you, Luca."

"We will be coming to a traditional spot on the water soon. Do you wish to have the full experience, Antonia?" asked Luca.

Luca placed his arm around her shoulders and looked into her eyes. Sitting there face to face, Antonia sensed tenderness, but in the most erotic way.

"I am willing to experience all of what you are offering, Luca."

Antonia noticed the gondolier looking back over his shoulder to make an announcement. "We are reaching the kissing bridge very soon. It is tradition to kiss while the Gondola passes under the bridge," he winked.

"Is this true, Luca?" Antonia asked.

I so hope it is true

"Yes. You heard the gondolier correctly. It is the kissing bridge up ahead."

Antonia turned in her seat to face him, staring into Luca's eyes, her lips parted in anticipation. "Will you kiss me, Luca? I don't want any bad luck from breaking traditions."

"We must be under the bridge. Only a few more seconds, beautiful one."

As the front of the gondola reached the bridge Antonia turned toward Luca. Without hesitation, Luca put his hand on Antonia's cheek and pressed his lips ever so softly to hers and lingered there until they had passed under the bridge to the other side. It was gentle intimacy. A perfectly mastered tease of a kiss. His lips were soft and warm, sending bolts of lightning to her thighs until they began to quiver.

Even if he did kiss her for the tradition, Antonia wanted more. Luca kept his arm around Antonia for the rest of the ride, as though they were a couple on a romantic holiday. She rested her head on his shoulder wishing it would never end. Returning finally to the dock area, Luca pulled away and sat up straightening his clothes.

"If you do not mind, Antonia, I will exit first so I can get the car. The gondolier will assist you exiting the boat. He is a friend of my family; you can trust him."

As the gondolier guided the boat to the spot on the dock, he turned and spoke to Antonia. "Where will you visit next?" he asked.

"I think it is Tivoli fountain, after we have dinner," she replied.

"It is beautiful at night. Be sure to throw in a coin for good luck," he said. "You must toss over your left shoulder."

Antonia leaned back and took a few deep breaths, enjoying the gondola's rhythmic movements. Gathering her things, she placed her hat back on, a perpetual smile plastered on her face. She touched her lips remembering the kiss and closed her eyes. When the gondolier exited then reached out his hand to assist Antonia, she saw him. At first she wasn't sure, then she heard his laugh. It was him!

"Wade came to Italy without me!"

Antonia blinked her eyes and shook her head hoping it was an illusion. Antonia never thought she would ever see Wade again; now he was exiting a gondola a few feet in front of her and starting to walk her way. Panic started to set in and she wobbled slightly. The gondolier grabbed for her arm and Antonia, acting on instinct, grabbed his arm putting him in front of her. "He mustn't see me," she whispered.

Thinking fast, Antonia pulled the brim down to hide her face and watched. Wade exited the gondola docked right in front of hers. He stopped and turned to take someone's hand. A woman.

"I must see her face. Who did he bring to Italy?"

Antonia as discreetly as possible leaned to the side trying to catch a glimpse. Just as the two were passing, she looked up to see Wade escorting Marisa the housekeeper. Arm and arm they laughed as they walked away. Anger and humiliation started to bubble up through Antonia's veins. She began to tremble as her legs wobbled.

Marisa did warn her, but she blew it off. It was all true. What she had suspected was true. Wade planned the trip with Marisa. Wade and Marisa planned. The words seem too evil. I guess even highly respected businessmen can commit unspeakable crimes against women.

"This is why I was drugged, beaten and thrown out by the trash?"

Antonia came on this trip to forget Wade and Chicago. Now he is here and with the housekeeper! Afraid her anxiety would show and ruin the night, she put on a brave face and willed her legs to cooperate as she exited the gondola. Her feet back firmly on the ground, she turned and thanked the gondolier.

Still holding his hands for stability, Antonia made an attempt at small talk giving Wade and Marisa time to walk ahead.

"So you and Luca are friends?" she asked.

"All of my life. Luca is a well-respected member of my extended family, you could say. You seem afraid, are you okay?"

"Oh yes, I thought I saw someone I knew that is all. I am fine. Thank you for the lovely rode in your gondola."

Chapter 9: The Wine of Love

As Antonia left the gondola, she pulled out a scarf and wrapped it around her head. Barely peeking out to watch, she walked toward the parked cars following Wade and Marisa from a distance. Emotions were having a tug of war in her heart. Confused, knowing she should feel angry, embarrassed or betrayed. Instead, she felt something different. Disgust and hate were making an appearance and rumbling in her gut. Purposely devoid of any kinder emotions, she repeated conversations in her head. "*…Night I will never forget… Marisa will pack a bag for you.*" Her eyebrows lowering, she had a compulsion to run up on the couple and push them in the water. Her back stiffened watching them.

I have no weapon, just my scarf and purse but I could lasso Wade with my scarf, pull him back and watch him fall down the steps.

Feeling slightly defeated and fighting back all urges, she shuffled her feet and looked down at the pavement to avoid any eye contact. Looking up only briefly, she noticed Luca was waving to get her attention. Antonia returned her eyes to the ground daring to glance around hoping to go unnoticed. Luca was sporting his contagious smile. Antonia managed a smile back. It was not Luca's fault that she discovered her whole relationship with Wade was a lie, so she decided to be polite. One never knows how toxic a person is until you have your freedom far away from their controlling bad behavior. For each trial, there comes the strength to carry on.

I will try my best to carry on, but the wound is deeper than I thought.

Antonia noticed Luca staring at her in the rear view as she got in the car and quickly looked away. His accent was gorgeous and so was he; it was hard to be sad with all that staring at her. His jet-black curls and beautiful sea blue eyes would usually cause any woman to swoon. Antonia found it hard to feel happiness right now, being so full of uncontrollable fury.

I have to stop allowing the damage to control my life.

Not even a beautiful Italian man staring at her made her feel happy. Instead, she felt nothing. So, she shrugged it off and stared out the window in silence. Luca pulled the car as close as he could to the Trevi fountain. "We will have to walk a short distance from here, Antonia."

"I think I might just go back to the hotel and skip the fountain. Please just drive on," murmured Antonia. She sighed and leaned her head back on the leather seat.

"No, no, the Trevi fountain is absolutely an outdoor masterpiece to enjoy. You will see the lights and the teal-colored water. You must not miss it. I will walk with you," said Luca as he exited the car and opened her door. He offered her his hand and Antonia reluctantly accepted.

"I don't understand what happened to change your mood, Antonia. If it was me going to get the car just know it was necessary"

Looking up at him, his kind smile and sincere eyes gave her a small boost. She hoped his company would help her shake off the vision of Wade as he left the gondola. "It is not you, Luca. You were perfect during the Gondola ride. I enjoyed your company tremendously."

"What ever the problem is, visiting the fountain will lift your spirits high."

"Okay, but just for a moment please," Antonia said.

"I will walk with you. You seem too sad to be on a holiday. Do you want me to tell you something about myself to make you laugh?"

"I doubt anything about you will make me laugh but go ahead and try."

"My name is Luca Romeo Vitalia."

Antonia stopped walking and suppressing a giggle she turned to face Luca. "Are you making that up just to get me to smile?" Antonia laughed.

"No, I wish I was but my mother, she was a romantic writer who loves Shakespeare, so I get stuck with Romeo for many reasons. You can still just call me Luca. I haven't told too many people that before, especially someone I just met. I felt like you needed to know so you can get your mind off of whatever bad thing you were thinking about. Did it work?"

"Luca, I am just feeling a little sad. Something can trigger a bad memory and it takes a while to shake it off. It takes a distraction. You are a great distraction, I might say."

"Relax. Once you see the fountain your eyes will sparkle with delight," said Luca, grinning. "I will be your tour guide by your side."

Right now, I wouldn't want anyone else by my side.

Luca took Antonia by the elbow, escorting her to the front of the fountain. He began to explain how the fountain sits minutes away from the Pantheon and how it was built on the site of an ancient Roman water source. Antonia listened, trying hard not to let her mind wander to Wade.

"I see you are not impressed with my history lesson, Antonia. Let us go sit on a bench and breathe in the night air. Perhaps you will tell me what is troubling you tonight. What happens in Rome stays in Rome. Or is that too American?"

"That phrase is usually for Las Vegas, but I understand your meaning."

The fountain did not disappoint. Antonia stood for a moment, turning with her arms outward as if she was hoping for a release of the hurt she felt. A slight breeze caught her hair. Lowering her eyes from the stars she took pleasure in the dark shifting silhouettes of the couples meandering in the square. Taking Luca's arm, they too became an intimate couple strolling in the fountain square, anonymous to everyone who passed by. It gave Antonia a sense of deviousness pretending to be a couple. No one knew if they were newlyweds or traveler and tour guide. This felt safe and real. Appearances can be deceiving.

Sitting on a marble bench in the fountain square listening to the sound of the water as it rose and fell in the fountain, Luca placed his hand on her thigh and turned his face toward hers.

"It is also a tradition to kiss at this famous fountain."

"I won't question your traditions, even if they are made up just to cheer me up."

Closing her eyes, Antonia leaned in for a kiss expecting the same warm lips she experienced on the gondola. Simple but flirtatious. Instead, Luca put his hand at the back of her neck and pulled her in for a deep passionate kiss. A lover's kiss, one that would send shivers all the way to your toes and cause clothes to be torn to make way for lovemaking. Antonia felt passion and she returned that passion by holding his face in her hands as they kissed while in the shadows listening to the splashing sounds of the fountain.

Luca kissed her cheeks then continued to the tender area of her neck, only stopping briefly to whisper in her ear, "I am so drawn to you, Antonia. Did I also tell you it is tradition to invite me back to your hotel so I can make mad love to you?"

"That sounds lovely, and I hate to break tradition, but can we just enjoy this moment? Right here, right now. In the shadows with you, I can ignore the troubles of the past that haunt me. I can be whoever I want to be with you until we must return to reality."

Taking Luca's hands in hers, Antonia cleared her throat then pulled his hand to place it on her heart. She could feel the warmth of his hand on her breast through her clothes. She watched as Luca's expression changed. Letting her guard down felt like a rush of naughty with a bit of curiosity. Antonia let Luca explore as she did the same, running her hands on his thighs trying to distract herself from her own mind and shut down the regrets of the past. Brushing her hair back, she took a deep breath then held Luca's hands again.

"I... I have been hurt, Luca. My feelings are in a conflict, and I thought this trip would help me heal. I want to be with you. Instead, I am doing the past relationship dance in my head, complete with resentment and bitterness as my dance partners. I don't know if I should keep looking over my shoulder or cha-cha forward. I know it is not what you want to hear and believe me, I don't want to miss out on being with you."

Swallowing hard, she lowered her chin to her chest. "This is no reflection on you or my attraction to you, I think you are the sexiest man I have ever met. Do you understand or am I just throwing out word salad on an Italian man who may not understand my situation?"

Scooting closer, Luca placed his arm gently around Antonia's shoulder and gave her a warm squeeze. Not too close or too hard, just enough for his body to touch hers. His hand brushed over her breast and rested around her waist. Pulling her body closer, he guided her head into the crook of his neck. He let his lips linger on her cheek and brushed her hair from her face.

"I, too, have been hurt before, my heart shattered into a million pieces. It took a long time for my heart to be whole again. Sometimes you don't know the weight of the burden you have been carrying, until you experience the release. I think we should continue your tour of Italy and I will ensure that you will have a wonderful time. Italy is beautiful, you are beautiful. I don't want to miss out on being with you either, but I will wait until you are ready. No worries, I will be a gentleman. I have been instructed to take you to *Ristorante De Palazzos* after the fountain. Shall we go or do you prefer to sit a bit longer?"

Wiping her face free of the newly formed small trail of tears, Antonia without hesitation kissed him gently on the cheek and stroked his face.

"Just being in your presence makes me feel important and cared for. That is all I ever wanted. I am ready to dine, only if you will dine with me as my guest."

Antonia turned to face Luca. His eyes were drawing her in, his crisp white shirt fit him as a glove with the buttons opened just enough to reveal a tuft of chest hair. She pushed her fingers in his shirt to give the hair a small tug, teasing him.

"If you don't dine with me then I will go back to my hotel. I may even eat an entire chocolate cake so you would be saving me from myself."

Luca took Antonia's hands in his. "I will do whatever you wish; now we must go."

Luca and Antonia dined on the finest food in Italy. Antonia insisted on ordering several entrées just so she could try them all. The two of them laughed and talked for what seemed like hours in the dimly lit *ristorante*. A single candle again burned on the table between them. The flickering light from the candle gave off the vision of how beautiful a man her dinner companion really was. His personality oozed charm and wholesomeness at the same time. He was complex and not shallow. Luca shared a little of his life story with Antonia and she listened as the rhythm of his voice made her start to swoon and her troubles began to fade. Luca was the prescription she needed to thwart the memories from the past.

Antonia feasted while Luca shared his stories and some history of his family. Luca was the second son in a family of four boys and one girl. Luca was born in Pico, a small medieval town about an hour away from Rome by car. His grandparents grew olives and some grapes for a personal collection of wine. Luca described Pico as a quiet countryside with the Apennine mountains to the east. His father inherited the olive business from his mother and Luca grew up harvesting the olives with his siblings.

"We are a many generations of olive growing family in a small community," said Luca.

"It sounds like a charming life in a beautiful small village. I am originally from Texas. Short story with no romantic history like yours. I am an only child, no siblings, I grew up on a sixty-acre ranch around horses and cattle. There were cowboys and rodeos. Your childhood sounds way more interesting, Luca. I would love to see the small village you are from one day. I scheduled only big cities and famous locations for this trip. Perhaps you can arrange some sort of side trip? I can pay extra."

"It is something you cannot feel unless you see it with your own eyes. To smell the olives and taste the oil that we make from them. Someday my older brother, Rico, will inherit. Harvesting usually begins in October after the olives ripen under the sun throughout the summer and early fall. I return to help every year," explained Luca.

"I love autumn, when the dark rains come and wash the summer away. I guess it is a good thing I came when I did; I might have missed meeting you," said Antonia.

"Yes, this is my last job for the season then I will return to Pico to start the harvest."

"Are all your brothers as handsome as you?"

Luca smiled, pushed the candle to one side and reached across the table taking both of Antonia's hands. There was a flicker of attraction in his eyes. "There is a family resemblance: we are Italians. I, too, love the fall when the sky gets dark and the wind whispers through the shimmering silver-green olive leaves as far as the eye can see. It will be a secret goal of mine to show you where I grew up and meet my family. As far as good looks, I am the only one for you."

Now he is just teasing me!

He paused, staring into her eyes, searching for her response, then pulled away sitting up straight. "I think we have an early morning schedule. Perhaps I should drop you off at your hotel," he said pulling out a small notebook. "In the morning we are scheduled to travel to Pisa and see the *torre pendente*... Leaning Tower... and gardens. Then we drive to look at some vineyards, late lunch while touring a winery, ending with dinner and back to the hotel," explained Luca as he read from his list.

Antonia stared at Luca lingering on the trace of his jaw line as he spoke. Even with a slightly crooked nose, she decided he was very handsome. She silently wondered if she could handle a random Italian fling, something she would never have thought of doing. Looks are not everything, but she hoped his skills matched the body.

Still, she always hoped to find a true love that accepted her faults and little quirks because they had plenty of their own. Wade would tell her that the world perceives handsome men and women as "better" than others because of their good looks.

Gazing at Luca across the dinner table made her realize that nothing Wade ever said was true. Attraction consists of many things, and Luca had all the right things.

Luca was very kind and respectful when he dropped Antonia at her hotel. Walking her to the elevator he stopped and kissed her gently on both cheeks then waited for her to enter and the door was closed before he left. Luca was the last image as she laid down to sleep, but her mind had other plans.

Antonia had a restless night. The images of Wade exiting his gondola with Marisa the housekeeper played repeatedly in her mind. Scrunching the pillows, burying her face did not shield her from the relentless feature films playing in her dreams with Wade as the star of the show.

"I need to get Wade out of my head!"

She sat up putting her head in her hands, straining to remember her dinner with Luca. His beautiful face, his kindness and those kisses by the fountain, but nothing helped. After the same vision looped several times, she subconsciously started to add additional scenes where she confronted Wade and violently punched and screamed at him. By five a.m., she convinced herself that sleep was not her friend. Regrets and unfinished business are no sleeping pill.

I should have confronted Wade or at least reported it to the police. Proving it all would be humiliating at the very least. I should have anticipated Wade would still take the trip. Assuming without me he would cancel was a laughing mistake. The anger I should have felt then is coming up now. He will not ruin my life. I love me. If I see him again, I vow to kick him where it hurts! Then maybe I will feel better.

Pacing and talking to herself helped only slightly. Her brain wandered to revenge and violence, so she took some wine from the mini bar and sat cross-legged on the bed.

Antonia desperately wanted to get back the joy she felt when she first arrived in Italy, the peace of doing it on her own and the excitement she felt when she first laid eyes on the gorgeous Luca. The thrill of learning history while touring the coliseum and Pisa. Creating a silly but simple plan to get her joy back, Antonia filled up the deep bathtub to soak and prepare for the day with Luca. Washing away her bad dreams as well as the smell of Italian food from her hair, Antonia willed her body to relax.

I will take pictures of Luca and plaster them above my bed if I have to.

Allowing images of Luca and the delicious kisses in her head as she spread the bubbles of soap over her most intimate parts delighted her. She would much rather visit and tour his hometown village than anything commercialized ,but the Tower of Pisa does have its history. Antonia decided, if the offer of coming to her hotel arises again, she will not say no. Cuddling all night with a lovely man would surely clear out the images of Wade.

Deciding to let her hair air dry in the Italian sun, Antonia dressed in coral colored linen pants, white sleeveless top and loose flowing white chiffon blouse that she left unbuttoned to flow in the warm breeze. Opting out of room service, Antonia grabbed her hat and headed to the outdoor café. She anxiously ordered Italian coffee, biscotti with jelly and cheese.

The sun was beginning to peek out behind some marshmallow clouds that quickly disappeared. The café was part of the hotel with awnings of yellow and white stripes. They allowed a little shade and flapped gently in the breeze. She chose a small table on the edge of the café next to planters full of flowers and the sun to her back. Somewhere nearby she heard a bee buzzing at a flower. Sometimes not having anyone to converse with can be valuable in allowing the mind to clear. Noticing the endless clear blue sky made her feel insignificant. A speck in the big universe.

It was absurd that Antonia was twenty-six, unmarried and still trying to decide what to do next in her life. Her choices were endless just like the sky is endless. Had she stayed on the ranch in Texas she would have settled down with a ranch hand and had a child or two by now.

Antonia thought about Rick and his offer to bring her home and let him take care of her. Rick was familiar and ruggedly handsome. Masculinity oozed out of every pore. The kind of man that women take a second look at, especially in those tight jeans.

They did have a flirtatious connection, but college was always her priority and returning to medical school was still an option someday. She was intelligent, managed straight A's and studied fiercely.

The relationship with Wade did have its perks of fine cars, designer clothes and jewelry. However future choices would be made with more realistic possibilities. She was here with Luca and that choice is for now.

Antonia took the last sip of her coffee when she again heard a familiar voice. This time it was Marisa, the former housekeeper. Marisa was a loud talker and Antonia recognized that shrill voice. Pulling her hat down, Antonia leaned on the table and held up her menu to form a shield. Peering around trying to locate the voice, she spotted her.

I must be a moron. Of course, they would come to the same hotel.

Antonia cupped her ear to hear the conversation. Hoping to hear they were checking out or at least not going to the same destination would be fantastic.

"My fiancé is feeling ill. I think there was something wrong with his breakfast! Do not send in the housekeeping to room 201, he does not want to be disturbed. However, call for a doctor to see him right away. Oh, and send some bottled water and chicken broth to our room asap! Do I make myself clear? Are you writing this down? I will be out doing a little shopping until this afternoon. When I get back, my fiancé better be okay!" Marisa growled at the café manager.

"This request would be better served by the front desk manager, ma'am – "

Shaking her head rudely, then pounding on the desk, it was obvious Marisa was frustrated as she interrupted, "Please just send the water and soup up to room 201." Marisa flipped her hair and strutted away; she had the strut down pat, throwing her hips side to side. Antonia watched as the café manager rolled her eyes and turned back to her staff.

Fiancée?

"I need to stay calm. It is not my concern anymore," She whispered into her plastic menu shield. "Don't be tempted, Antonia. Dang it, I might be nuts, but I am not letting this opportunity go. Luca will have to wait; I am going to that room!"

Chapter 10: No Wine Needed

Folding her hands in her lap, Antonia closed her eyes and turned her face up to the sun. She had been suppressing doubts about her own mental balance, taking the blame, accepting defeat and controlling her urges for revenge. *I just want to be like a sunflower so I can stand tall and find the sunlight, even on the darkest of days.*

Feeling this was an opportunity to do something, she began tapping her foot. The truth hurts but not always the correct person. Wade was the one that needed to hurt a little. Antonia fought the strong urge to see Wade and unleash the anxiety and anger plaguing her. She took several breaths trying to calm the beast that was telling her to go to the room.

Wade is all alone; it would be a perfect time.

The need to get Wade out of her head led to an uncontrollable urge. Antonia tried to ignore the urge and focus on the trip and Luca. In a moment of weakness or possibly craziness, she chose the urge to pay a visit to Wade while Marisa would be out of the way shopping. She overheard her plans to be away, and that Wade was alone up in the room. Nervous but seriously determined, she stood up glancing around. She did not see Marisa or which way she stormed off.

It's now or never.

Antonia pulled her hat to cover half her face as she approached the front desk inside and tapped the bell. A young clerk she did not remember seeing before approached the desk with a courteous smile ready to assist. Putting on her best Marisa impersonation Antonia straightened her spine.

"How can I help you?"

"Yes, I am in room 201 and my fiancé has accidentally locked me out. He has been feeling ill and I came down here to talk to the staff to arrange for a doctor. I seem to have left my key in the room; do you have a spare?"

"The name on the room?"

From the look on the clerk's face, Antonia knew she played it too sweetly. Pausing, she lifted her chin, slammed her hand on the counter and tried again.

"Marisa and Wade. I need that key now! My fiancé could be dying from the poison you fed him this morning in your raggedy little café!"

Appearing to recognize the anger mode, the clerk nodded her head, scrambled but a second, then handed over the key with an outstretched hand. Keeping with the act of sarcasm that Marisa hands out, Antonia snatched the key card from the clerk's hand and immediately had to suppress saying 'thank you'.

Marisa would never be polite. I will leave the clerk a tip as an apology later.

Wrapping the key card in her scarf so as to not leave fingerprints, Antonia headed toward the elevators in the middle of the grand foyer. Looking at the few people waiting on elevators she had second thoughts. After a quick evaluation, she chose the stairs instead.

Taking the stairs two at a time in the back hallway Antonia moved with stealthy determination. Yelling at the clerk felt strangely good and got her blood pumping. It was out of character but Antonia was allowing the sweet and polite to morph into determined and bitchy.

Antonia had never mastered being spontaneous. She planned her future meticulously. College, pre-med, internship and training to be a surgeon at Foundation Surgical Hospital of San Antonio. Plans change. Sometimes for the good and sometimes it is devastating but plans change. Antonia had no real plan now, but it didn't scare her.

I will just let my urges free then let the ripples go where they may. If I want Wade out of my head, then I have to let the crazy out.

As she reached the second floor, she threw open the stairwell door. On each side of the landing were statues. Marble statues of barely clothed men. One resembling Michael Angelo's statue of David.

This must be the VIP floor.

Luckily, she did not have to wander down the hallway too far. Wade and Marisa's room was the first door closest to the stairway. The corner suite. Her mind raced and her palms started to sweat as she paused to examine the hallway. Putting her ear to the door, she listened for any sounds. Trying to make as little noise as possible, Antonia gently slid the door key; hearing the click, she pushed the door slowly. Entering the room, she was met by a grand foyer of sorts with doors on each side. Directly in front she noticed a large window with a view of Rome. She peeked in the door to the right and examined a sitting room with gold fixtures, elegant sofas upholstered in a delicate floral print, a fireplace, and a well-stocked bar with crystal glassware.

Tiptoeing to the left she turned the gold handle gently. It was the master suite and on the king-size bed lay a body she was extremely familiar with. One hairy muscular leg hung out of the white sheets and she knew it was him.

Wade had his back to the door, snoring and purring gently like he always did. Sometimes it would lull Antonia to sleep and other times she wanted to cover his head with a pillow. In front of the large glass window looking out over the city was a small wooden dinette set where the room service dishes still lay; the food was half eaten. Instead of moving directly to the bed, Antonia sat at the small table deciding on her next move trying to slow her heartbeat.

Staring at Wade sent a shiver down her spine. On the table were three plates, two covered by stainless-steel domes and one with half eaten steak, eggs, potatoes and a scrap of bacon. Standing, Antonia lifted the metal dome from one of the other plates: it was almost empty aside from a few runny egg yolks. She continually glanced over at Wade, expecting him to be staring back at her. She didn't know why she was so curious. She chalked it up to nerves and a tiny bit of jealousy.

Room service must be nice.

Trying not to make a sound, she peeked under the third stainless steel dome. A whole chocolate cake had not been sliced or touched. Antonia did not know whether to be mad because they ordered her favorite, or just stick her hand in the middle of it for spite. She chose the latter and enjoyed licking her fingers after.

Next, she turned toward Wade. Antonia had no idea how long Marisa would be shopping, so it was time to complete the confrontation. Wade looked soft like a sleeping baby. Fighting the urge to crawl naked under the covers and surprise him, she reminded herself that this was not a social call.

This situation calls for hard-core yelling and shouting.

Antonia cautiously picked up the sharp steak knife in one hand. Keeping the stainless-steel dome from the cake in her other hand, she crept slowly toward the bed like a knight with a sword and shield ready for war.

"Bam! Bam! Bam! Antonia banged the lid with the knife, ringing it like a dinner bell. Startled, Wade turned on his back and pulled at the sheet to cover himself.

"Are you awake now?' Antonia laughed. "You don't really think that sheet is going to protect you, do you?" she nervously laughed again.

"Antonia? What the hell are you doing here?" Wade hissed.

"That is not your concern right now. We have bigger concerns, you and me. This was my vacation, remember? You stole it from me! Just like you stole my life!"

Antonia stood there with the steak knife in one hand and the domed plate cover in the other. Rage makes people do things they would not normally do. Antonia took a pause to assess her situation, tossed the dome cover to the floor, then placed one hand on her hip.

It is my intent to look brave, not like a cartoon character.

"You are insane, Antonia! Get out of here before I call for law enforcement! Where is Marisa?" said Wade, struggling to sit up.

"Now Wade, do you see Marisa anywhere? I locked her in the closet." Laughing, Antonia twisted her face into an evil smile. "Or did I stab her then put her body in the bathtub? All good ideas, Wade. You know when you hear about the wife stabbing her husband seventy-seven times and the police are left wondering why? Well, I KNOW WHY," she laughed as she stomped her foot emphasizing each word.

"You left me by a dumpster, Wade! That is not an easy thing to get over. Wearing a dress that doesn't match your shoes is an easy thing to get over. Attempted murder, spiking a drink, cheating: all that deserves revenge. You started this ripple treating me like trash. What did you think was going to happen when I woke up beside the dumpster?"

"That is absurd, you could never do anything so bold. You are a weak woman, Antonia. Now stop this nonsense and leave my room immediately!" he shouted as he held a hand to his head.

"Weak? I am not weak. You made me stop believing in ever after. I go to my parents funeral and you slide in Marisa. What could you possibly see in Marisa? She possesses only a rudimentary intelligence. She's weak in body and mind and I am practically a freaking surgeon!"

"I was not looking for intelligence. That type talks back, worries about the size of their thighs and can't make a late-night grilled cheese. The version of me you created in your mind, Antonia, and what I wanted from you is not my responsibility." Wade ran his hands through his disheveled hair and looked up at Antonia who was still holding the knife.

"Are you scared, Wade?" she asked sarcastically.

Wade rolled his eyes and placed his head in his hands. He did not appear scared; he seemed annoyed and hung-over. Antonia cracked her neck from side to side trying to look intimidating like she had seen in the movies when two people are about to fight. Inside, her nerves were jumping like fleas on a hot plate.

Antonia moved closer until she was staring down at Wade, her nostrils flaring. Her pulse was elevated and she could feel it pounding in her ears. The last bit of rage had exploded and she embraced it. The ripple of mistreatment by Wade finally reached her and it changed her emotionally. Wade looked flushed. He was sick and weak.

"You are not taking me seriously, Wade. Lay back down and listen to me. You do not get to tell me what to do. Your precious Marisa left you to go shopping. I did not kill her. I was just trying to see your reaction."

Too nice… Let him think I murdered his precious Marisa.

"I have some things to discuss with you. It would be best if you sat right there in your boxer briefs and listened because I have to get you out of my head," Antonia shouted.

"I am naked…"

"Well, it doesn't matter, I'm not going to get any lady wood seeing you naked, so just lay back. I have the knife and you have to listen. That is how this goes," she said confidently.

Moving closer, Antonia held out the steak knife. She had no plan to harm him, but it felt wise to have space and a weapon between them. Her eyes caught the glimmer of something shiny on his left hand. It was a gold ring.

Did he and Marisa get married?

"Just lay back on those fluffy white pillows, Wade. I am no longer weak, I am angry. In what universe did you think you could just throw me out like the trash and get away with it?"

"Didn't I get away with it? Are you going to stab me?" asked Wade.

Antonia clinched her jaw as she swayed slightly with the knife still in her hand.

"Yes, I will, so don't tempt me. Just shut your mouth."

Wade slapped his hands on his thighs as he tried to sit up straighter. His countenance was weak and his shoulders slumped. Antonia had a fleeting moment of concern but shook her head to clear the cobwebs of regret and shame.

"You are sneaky and that impresses me," he taunted. "How did you get in my room?"

"If you let me talk, then I will leave Wade! I am the one in control now!"

Antonia began to sway shifting her weight from one foot to the other. The confrontation was not going as she thought it would. She hoped to be in and out after just a few minutes of telling him off. Deciding she needed to be bolder and take back control of the situation, she took another step closer holding the knife in her shaking hand. Wade showed very little fear and frowned at her efforts to scare him.

"You could not kill a fly Antonia. What is all the fussing about anyway? Where is the loyalty? My suggestion to you is to move on. Just leave and be happy," he quipped.

"You don't break a person by giving hate, then expect loyalty. I am not fussing. I am mad. The blue floral wallpaper is the only real element of fussy in this room. Is it the honeymoon suite or something? Never mind, don't answer that" she said looking around the room.

"There is that jealousy Antonia. Have you been drinking?"

"No wine needed. I am fully aware of what you did to me. You were never planning on marrying me, I am not upset about that now. I wouldn't want to be the wife of a man with his hand in the cookie jar."

"You referring to Marisa as the cookie jar?" he laughed. "All your words fall flat. I gave you everything and you never changed from a little girl from Texas. Just put the knife down, say what you want and obey me by GETTING OUT OF MY ROOM!" he shouted.

"Now see, I think obey is a poor choice of words Wade. I will never obey any man."

Wade's eyes bulged with rage. Wade bolted to slap the knife from Antonia, dropping the sheet to reveal his naked body. Antonia darted to the side, but Wade still managed to grab her by one arm. His breath was hot on her shoulder as she tried to squirm away. His other arm circled her trying to pin her arms down to her side. She felt his nakedness on her thigh and cringed.

Scrambling to keep her footing, Antonia grabbed his wrist trying to steady herself. Rearing her free arm back that was holding the knife, avoiding his grasp. The moment she regained her balance was the same moment recall hit. This moment felt memorable like it happened before. Images came flooding back to the night she was attacked and left by the dumpster. As his hand grabbed her wrist it had the sting of familiarity.

Horror struck Antonia as memories became clear. She took a deep breath sucking up all the courage she could muster. It was Wade who had pinned her arms down in the same way that night. With all her strength, she pushed Wade, took a step back and kicked at his groin, landing a hit that sent Wade doubling over pain. Taking advantage of his weakness from being sick, she shoved him again, punching her fist in his shoulder area. Then, grabbing a handful of his curly locks of hair, she jerked his head back and looked into his eyes for a brief second before shoving him down.

Antonia held the knife in front of her as if it was a Roman sword. She was panting to catch her breath. Deliberately, she held her gallant sword in a threatening manner, her eyes wide open glaring at Wade who was on his knees. She had not planned to hurt him, just get him to confess that he mistreated her, just yell at him and get things off her chest, but the knife now became her only hope of fighting him off.

I will not let him grab me agai!

Wade attempted to stand, mumbling swear words under his breath. Antonia felt her face flush as the heat of anger overcame her body.

"It was you! You held me down while someone kicked me in the ribs that night! Marisa was the one who put something in my drink, wasn't she?" Tears stung her eyes but she refused to cry, shaking them away. Antonia began heaving, struggling to breathe.

"So what? You have no proof. I just wanted you out of my life," Wade shouted. "The rest was Marisa's idea."

"I didn't remember until now. I could have died, Wade! How could you do that to me? Why would you do that to me? You… you are a monster!" she screeched.

Wade stood, his hair in his face. One hand covered his junk and the other grabbed his chest. He finally managed to stand fully and put his hands up as if to surrender. He had a menacing grin on his face like he knew a secret. There was no shame or remorse.

"Do not come any closer to me, Wade, or I swear – "

"Swear what? That you will cut it off with that dull steak knife? I saw you look. You want some of this, don't you?" he taunted, thrusting his hips forward for emphasis.

I wonder if now is the time I should tell him I always faked it?

Mounting frustrations and fear left a sheen of sweat on her forehead. Antonia opened her mouth to speak, to yell, but nothing came out. Fear wracked her body as she stood there trembling, searching for the right words to let him know the horror she felt.

"How about a glass of wine, Wade? Are you thirsty? I heard you were ill. Of course, you don't know if I put something in there while I watched you sleeping, do you? Just like you put something in my wine that night! You bastard! My special wine laced with sleeping pills! Is that why you encouraged me to drink? You told me it was so I would fit in at your social parties. It was all part of the scheme you and Marisa came up with to get rid of me."

Wade laughed at her. She looked him up and down watching his every move, ready to defend herself. She straightened her back slightly trying to look fierce. Wanting it all to end so she could move on, she drummed up the last ounce of courage and blasted him with her words.

"I am not interested in your opinion or any excuse you may want to spit out of your mouth. Stop talking and listen to me for once!"

"Fine. Get on with it and leave my sight. You sicken me, Antonia!"

Antonia swallowed hard and straightened her back. "You have nothing I want, Wade. Nothing. I didn't want the dresses, the shoes or the big house. I wanted my own career and my own life and still have a relationship. You say you gave everything to me? You never gave me choices. I have value. Seriously, Wade, why not do the respectful, man-up thing and just break up with me? I would have taken a suitcase and a plane ticket back to Texas any day! You made a choice.

"I was trying so hard, but I was miserable inside. Yet you decided to drug me and humiliate me. Poor choice, Wade. How will your fellow architects feel when they hear that you left your fiancé by a dumpster, beaten and bruised? You are a coward, Wade."

Hoping to end with one last hurtful blow to his ego, Antonia wrinkled her mouth like she was disgusted. "You are not a man of virtue by any means. I will use the worst things you did to me as fuel for my greatest victories. I should have listened to my family and friends. They knew you were no good!"

Wade had had enough of the arrows lobbed at his self esteem. He clenched his fists as he caught her glancing down to his groin yet again and thought it was his opportunity. He lunged at Antonia again, but this time she was ready. She closed her eyes and stiffened her arm, putting one foot back and holding the knife out like a jousting spear.

The knife made contact with Wade's chest and plunged in deep, upward just under the sternum. It went in all the way to the edge of the wooden handle. Antonia continued holding the knife once she felt it slide in his skin. She twisted it slightly from the weight of his body falling toward her, then she let it go as Wade stumbled backwards.

Wade landed on the bed, lying on his side, the knife protruding from his chest in an upward angle as blood poured onto the white sheets. He opened his mouth to scream. A scream that didn't make it past his throat: it was more like a gurgle. Antonia watched in horror as Wade struggled to breathe and saw fear in his eyes for the first time. Big, strong, loudmouth Wade was dying.

"Wade, I didn't mean to… I will get a doctor!" Antonia put her hand to her mouth, shocked at what had just happened. "Marisa asked for a doctor to come see you so I should probably just leave."

Closing her eyes and leaning her head back trying to soothe herself, Antonia swayed and wrapped her own arms around her upper body. Calmer, she began to scold the dying man. "I was just going to threaten you, chastise you for treating me the way you did! Now look at you, you are dying. It was your fault. You should not have lunged at me!"

I can't believe I said that to a dying man!

Antonia paced, wringing her hands for a moment, not knowing what to do. Wade gurgled again and Antonia stood beside him, careful not to step in the blood now pooling on the floor. His eyes were half open. Not yet dead, but too late to be saved. Antonia stared at him. His perfect nose, beautiful lips and professionally coiffed hair all now seemed unimpressive.

The life slowly drained from Wade's face. Reaching over, she pushed his eyelids down, closing his eyes as she stared at his face turning pale and slightly blue. Antonia had only seen a dead body in medical school. They were cold cadavers; now she was witnessing death as it happened. Antonia smoothed her hair back and bit her fingernail. She turned away but could not resist watching the blood pour from his wound one more time. Realizing there was nothing she could do to take it all back, there was no action to save him. She was sure the knife had entered his heart, severing an artery and causing him to bleed out.

Antonia took a deep breath accepting her actions. There were no tears. She shook her hands trying to ease the beating of her heart. In silence ,she watched Wade take his last breath. She placed her hands over her face and stomped her foot holding back a scream. Finally, she approached his body, leaning over it to check for life. Antonia whispered toward Wade's ear. "You tried to kill me but you didn't. Instead, you made me stronger. I pulled the knife out of my own back and used it for revenge. I freed myself and it felt good. I am not weak, Wade, I do talk back, I love my thighs and in college I made awesome grilled cheese sandwiches!"

Picking up a napkin she boldly wiped the handle of the knife still sticking out of Wade's chest. She frantically wiped the chair, the table and the stainless-steel domes as well. Noticing the chocolate cake, Antonia cut herself a fat slice, wrapped it in the embroidered cloth napkin from the hotel, and stashed it in her purse.

This will be my revenge snack later tonight.

After looking around the room, she pulled on the small dining table for two and turned it over, spilling its contents on the floor. "Oops… There goes the rest of the chocolate cake," she snickered. Using her scarf to open the door, she whispered her final words for Wade: "I have no more tears for you ,Wade. I finished crying in the instant that you died."

Antonia picked up her hat, slipped the room key in her handbag, wiped the door handle inside and out with her scarf, then let the door slam. In the elevator she smoothed her clothes and brushed her hair from her face. When the doors opened to the lobby, she was startled by Luca standing there.

"I called your room but you did not answer," said Luca.

Antonia nodded, then bolted out of the elevator. "Yes, Luca. Shall we go? Let's go see Pisa, and on the way can we stop for a drink? For some reason I have an awful taste in my mouth."

"Of course. I know a little café along the way. By the way, you have a little something red at the corner of your mouth. Let me wipe it for you," Luca said, taking out his handkerchief.

Antonia waved his efforts away, instead taking a tissue from her own handbag.

"It's fine. Probably just the jelly I had on my pastry this morning."

Antonia had a gutted feeling when the image of Wade popped in her head. Hooking her arm in Luca's, Antonia started walking briskly toward the hotel door pulling on Luca. She stopped when she felt him tug back gently.

"We are not late. No need to rush, Antonia. Pisa has been there for many years; it is not going anywhere."

Antonia looked over at the front desk and all around the lobby. No one even knew there was a dead man in room 201. Not one person knew the unimaginable happened upstairs. No one knew what she had done except Wade, and he was not going to tell anyone.

I can just walk out the door and no one will know.

Feeling slightly flushed, Antonia lifted her chin then squeezed Luca's arm. Luca was worried but did not want to upset Antonia by pushing her for an explanation. Sucking in a deep breath Antonia faced Luca and began waving her hand trying to cool her face.

"I am ready now. Sorry, I was feeling flushed from too much coffee. I am better now, Luca."

"I am sensing some uneasiness. I want you to know you can trust me," whispered Luca.

"I am perfectly fine. It is just a bad day, not a bad rest of my life. I am just so excited to go and leave Rome. I will be contacting my travel agent to switch my hotel to somewhere near Pisa perhaps. I just want to stop at the front desk and give the clerk a little gift. Do you think a $50 tip is good?"

Luca waited by the door as Antonia removed her hat, flashed a large smile and handed the clerk a folded bill. Antonia then met Luca at the entry doors and fondly placed her arm in the crook of his elbow -- mostly for support as her legs felt like they may fail her any minute.

"Now why don't you start telling me the history of the leaning tower. Why was it built?"

Luca flashed a smile and took Antonia by the hand. "The tower of Pisa was a freestanding bell tower…" Luca began.

Chapter 11: Excessive Wine

Antonia leaned back against the soft leather of the back seat. Noticing her hands trembling, she shoved them behind her back and closed her eyes. She felt flushed, with sweat starting to stream down her back and in between her breasts. She removed her white linen scarf and began to fan herself. Outside, the sun threw heat down on the black car.

"Can you make it cooler in here please, Luca? I'm feeling rather warm."

"It is an unusually hot day; I will turn up the air conditioning," replied Luca. He smiled back at Antonia, his face shadowed with stubble that only highlighted his pearly smile. Antonia broke his stare and glared out the window hoping to find solace in nature. Never wanting Luca to catch on to her disgrace, she hid her face from the view of the rear-view mirror.

After the night she woke up next to the dumpster, Antonia started thinking of Wade as the monster. Now the tables turned and she had become the monster. No need to let Luca see her in such a harsh light. He was kind and sweet. There was no need for him to become aware that she was a killer. 'Killer' and 'sweet' do not pair well. Not even in a foreign country.

Laying her head back, face toward the window, she closed her eyes and without warning the vision of Wade lying on the bed, knife in his chest, played like a movie. She had only gone there to taunt him. *"It could be considered self defense"* she thought to herself.

Antonia wondered how it all went wrong. Wade drove the coolest car on campus, a '69 Mustang with a custom shiny chrome grille. Wade was all about being noticed on campus. In contrast, Antonia always considered herself simple and plain, with dark brown hair, green eyes and a sprinkling of freckles across her perfect nose. At least her nose was pretty. Wade made her cover the freckles with makeup. Wade married the housekeeper. She was not the housekeeper; it was all a plan to get me out of the picture.

If I could be a fly on the wall and see Marisa's face.

"Its not my fault, he pushed me," she muttered.

"Did you say something, Antonia?" Luca asked.

Startled, Antonia wiped her tears. "I said Italy is beautiful."

"Agree, This place is paradise. Wait until you see the gardens. We could rent a scooter and tour the gardens, letting the breeze blow your hair about."

Antonia welcomed the interruption from her thoughts. She sat up straight in her seat and shook her tingling hands that had slightly fallen asleep from sitting on them too long.

"Yes, yes, it is hot and as much as I would love to re-live the scene from a 1960's movie, I need a soft pass. I didn't sleep well last night so excuse me for dozing off a little. Are we almost to Pisa? I have to use the restroom," she explained..

"If you can wait a few more kilometers. we will stop at the café I told you about. Maybe have a lunch and a glass of wine?"

"That sounds wonderful. Yes, I can wait," she replied. She didn't really have to use the restroom; she simply used it as a ruse to be alone, freshen up and make a phone call.

Arriving for lunch, Antonia took Luca's hand as she exited the car and looked around. The café sat on a small hill. The valley filled with olives went on for miles. Gnarled trees cast shadows on the stucco walls outside the small café. Inside, there was the aesthetic appeal of true Italy. Colorful porcelain tile halfway up the wall in deep blues and bright orange. The Italian tile formed a story of a valley and the origin of the café. Small intimate tables for two were scattered in the modest dining area of the café that was fairly empty except for a few locals. Luca pointed toward the restroom and Antonia nodded. Once in the restroom, she placed a frantic call to her travel agent.

"Bethany, you have to get me a room near Pisa. Tonight. I cannot go back to Rome."

"Did you bring your luggage, or should I have it sent to you by courier?" the travel agent asked.

"Can you do that for me? Good. yes, have it sent."

"We can do whatever you want, Antonia. It will only take a phone call. May I ask why you want to leave your accommodation? That hotel comes with a high five stars."

"Ummm…, No, it was fine. I just felt uncomfortable making my driver bring me all the way back. Pisa is in central Italy and my next planned tour is Tuscany, so it will be easier. I think I want an extra day here as well. Plans change; please just change me to a different hotel, bed and breakfast or whatever and text me the address," asked Antonia.

"It will be no problem. Should I put the new charge on your bank card?"

"Yes, that is fine and don't worry about getting a refund; just strike it off as my loss. And Bethany, I would like to confirm that my locations while in Italy are confidential."

"Of course. Just like we discussed, Antonia."

"And all credit card charges as well."

"We are discreet, no worries. I hope the personal tour guide is to your satisfaction."

"Luca is a dream, such a gentleman. Just text me the address where I will be staying, and I will give it to Luca. Thank you."

Antonia reached for the door to the restroom then paused, looking back. The kitchen wall was just outside so she scooted back to one of the stalls and using her foot she flushed.

"Just in case someone was listening," she thought to herself. As she was leaving, she bumped into Luca who was exiting the men's bathroom, still working on his zipper. His face flushed at first then a huge grin spread across his face as he noticed Antonia dart her eyes from his zipper to his face.

Good thing I did the courtesy flush.

"Shall we take a seat? I took the liberty of ordering for you," smiled Luca.

Antonia blushed slightly, nodded, then looked down at her feet trying to gain her composure thinking that it was not discreet at all to let her eyes wander.

But it shows I am human.

Luca offered Antonia his arm and escorted her to the table. Being near Luca made bad thoughts start to melt away. His body wash smelled like coconuts.

"Excellent. We start with the finest cheese and olive tasting, then I ordered you a divine pasta dish as an entrée. It is called *fettuccine al pomodoro*."

"It sounds amazing. You can order as many entrees as you like. I am totally prepared to eat my way through Italy," she laughed. "And wine, lots of wine, please."

After tasting the fresh olives soaked in olive oil and spices, Antonia sat back and remembered why she chose to visit and tour Italy. It had nothing to do with Wade. It had all to do with being alive and experiencing new things. It was a dream to taste the food and experience the romance of what Italy had to offer. Her whole life had consisted of growing up on a ranch in Texas and living with Wade in Chicago. Now she found herself relaxing her shoulders, eating local cuisine in a lovely off-the-road place, staring across the table at the dreamiest dinner partner.

Italy and Luca for the win.

Sitting in that café, far from Wade's dead body, Antonia refused to waste any more time thinking about Wade.

From now on I let Italy engulf me. No limits. I will drink too much wine, see pretty things and taste everything. Perhaps even Luca...

After lunch and another trip to the restroom, this time for real personal use, Antonia and Luca began the drive to Pisa. Looking at her phone she saw the text from her travel agent,

Bethany Harper, and gave the name of the bed and breakfast to Luca.

"I know the place well. It will be no problem," replied Luca, smiling.

Once they arrived at the Leaning Tower of Pisa, Antonia took out the 35mm camera she had purchased for the trip and spent hours posing for pictures. Giving Luca a quick lesson on how to focus and where to point and shoot, he became her traveling photographer. A warm breeze fluttered, causing Antonia's hair and shirt to fly, making it a perfect scenario for romantic shots. There were the silly poses pretending to hold up the tower and the serious ones as she sat on the lawn, the tower behind her, her green eyes glistening in the evening sun. Luca had the café prepare a takeaway package of the left-over food and a bottle of wine. As the sun began to set, Antonia and Luca sat on the lawn of the gardens snacking on olives and cheese.

"Luca, let's ask someone to take a picture of the two of us together with the tower in the background."

"Fantastic idea. Then I have a surprise for you, Antonia."

"A surprise? Taking me to eat at that darling café was enough of a surprise."

"This is special. Trust me. I have a friend here who can let us in to climb the tower. It is usually closed to tourists these last couple of years. He is also from the same town as me and no longer wanted to pick olives for a living. Would you like to do that?"

"Only if you come with me and kiss me at the top," Antonia giggled.

Luca blushed and looked down at his feet for a brief second.

"You flatter me too much, Antonia. I am just a working man who picks olives in the summer and a travel guide in the off season. I am not so special. I would not want to cross any boundaries."

"Luca, if anything you have been an amazing tour guide. I feel so comfortable with you. You are very special. I thought we had a connection. You said you felt it too. What changed?"

"I have not changed, Antonia. You changed. I felt you were putting distance between us."

Embarrassed, Antonia put her hand on her forehead and shifted her weight from one side to the other. "Oh, I see. Well, Luca, I will just have to settle for the climb. It will be fun, and I am sorry if I embarrassed you. I suppose I got caught up in the excitement. Just forget about it. Let's go climb that tower! In Texas, if we climbed to the top of anything we would place a Texas flag."

Antonia turned away from Luca and faced the tower and put her hands on her hips, attempting to hide her own embarrassment.

Too pushy, Antonia, calm down, hide the crazy.

Luca shook his head in disappointment, thinking he had offended Antonia. He walked up behind her and put his arms around her waist, looping through her arms still positioned on her hips. Nuzzling her neck ever so slightly and smelling the scent of her shampoo, Luca slowly held up the camera in front of her and whispered in her ear.

"There is a connection, I am so attracted to you."

Antonia leaned into Luca as he held her waist. Luca kissed her neck gently as they mysteriously began to slightly sway. Antonia took his hands; pulling them, she turned to face him. Throwing her arms around his neck, she pressed her body closer to his. Luca ran his hands on her back pulling her in until he could feel her breasts pressing against him. They stood embracing in the middle of the tower gardens until Luca broke the trance.

"I just want to return this camera so you can put it away in your bag during the climb. I would like to have time to hold you again – after the climb, of course. We are on a time schedule and I am feeling slightly embarrassed about the way my slacks are starting to… umm... get tight, showing the world my excitement."

I felt it.

Antonia took the camera from his hand and turned to face him while trying to suppress a giggle.

"I understand. Thank you for everything Luca. You are the best travel guide ever. You have been amazing. I never expected to find you or your bulging pants on this trip."

Luca stepped forward and brushed some hair from Antonia's face and gently tucked it behind her ear. Staring into her eyes, his perfect lips just inches away from hers, he smiled.

"*Molte grazie*, a thousand thank-yous, Antonia. I was not embarrassed at all. I will promise one thing, that I will hold your hand at the top, and perhaps take you in my arms. Of course, just so you will not be afraid of heights. Some have reported feeling dizzy from climbing the spiral staircase at an incline, but it will only take about thirty minutes to arrive at the top and I think you will enjoy the beautiful view."

"It is the best deal I have had all day, Luca. Let's go!"

After climbing the 251 steps to the top of the tower, they were greeted with a magnificent view of the entire town of Pisa. Its red roofed buildings and the mountains in the distance were breathtaking. Antonia looked down, taking in all her surroundings including the stunning Cathedral Square. Brushing her hands on the well-worn stone railings, she took a deep breath. Raising her hands in the air she shouted "I am in Italy!"

Luca smiled and stepped closer, taking Antonia's hand. "I think that is enough tourist shouting, I cannot allow my best customer to fall now, can I?"

Turning to face Luca, Antonia took both of his hands in hers. "I am just so excited, Luca". Tugging, she pulled him closer and threw her arms around his neck. The powerful wind gusts caused them to sway slightly and Luca took Antonia by her shoulders to steady her. They stared at each other as though time stood still for just the two of them.

The world and beauty of Italy swirled around them. They were all alone at the top of the Leaning Tower of Pisa. A thrilling emotion. Antonia felt a peaceful release from the tension she experienced earlier that day. Luca leaned in and gently kissed Antonia on her lips. A kiss that was warm and sincere. Antonia leaned back, looked into his eyes then pulled him in.

Kissing passionately, Luca started at her neck. Antonia threw her head back as Luca continued, pulling at the buttons of her blouse until he reached her firm breasts. Wrapping his arm around her waist, he eased her to the floor. Antonia had never experienced such passion and heat before. She moaned slightly as Luca's hand began to roam up her skirt. Luca leaned up, tilting his head to one side and listened.

Standing, Luca extended a hand to Antonia. Facing the outside wall, with their back to the stairwell, Antonia fussed with the buttons of her blouse and smoothed her skirt. Laughing, she couldn't help but think how some journeys are marked by uncontrollable passion.

The two stood frozen as a young boy and his parents reached the top of the stairs behind them. Acutely aware of the encounter they almost had, and still feeling aroused, they kept their backs turned. Letting the breeze hit their faces, they slowly regained composure. Luca turned to Antonia first and let out a small giggle, covering his mouth with his hand. Antonia, hearing Luca break, began what could only be called a full-blown gut laugh, followed by several snorts. Trying hard to stop the battle of snickering, they finally turned and quickly began the descent down the stairs, still letting out the occasional chortle as they descended.

The trek down the tower was more foreboding as Antonia watched her footing, feeling a little less secure. A slight vertigo made her pause. It could have been from the heated passion taking her breath away or the incline, but she continued her descent to the bottom of the tower. There, she fell into Luca's arms before laughing, holding hands crossing the gardens, all the way to the car.

"I have had a wonderful full day, Luca. I think it is time you take me to my new accommodations so I can rest and reflect."

"It is all up to you. We can rest, or shower or order a bottle of wine," said Luca.

"Have I had too much wine, Luca? Because I feel a little tipsy," laughed Antonia.

As they drove to the hillside and found the bed and breakfast arranged by her travel agent, Antonia noticed the glances from Luca in the rear-view mirror. She brushed her hands across her lips remembering the kiss at the top of the tower and returned a smile toward Luca.

We almost got caught. What a rush!

Antonia and Luca visually teased each other most of the ride. Breaking the silence, Luca sent air kisses as he made the turn into the parking area of the Ariston Bed and Breakfast. Stacked neatly on the steps, Antonia could see her familiar Louis Vuitton luggage.

"It appears your luggage has arrived," Luca observed.

"Yes, I have changed my plans to stay here two nights, Luca."

"No trouble that will work out. Bethany has already informed me. The vineyard you are to tour is about an hour away."

"This wonderful day just gets better and better. I feel so hopeful and free."

"'Hopeful' is a strange description when talking of your travel arrangements, Antonia. You almost appear as though you are running away from something. A very bad something. I truly hope Italy will heal what ever wounds you are experiencing."

"I told you I was hurt badly, Luca. The relationship died, as did the man. I have always wanted to travel, so I did. That is all it is. Please just let it go," Antonia pleaded.

"As you wish, but I will see you in the morning at 10 a.m. sharp. This B & B is famous for their strong coffee and magnificent breakfast," he smiled. "You do not want to sleep in and miss Tuscany."

"It might make it easier to not be late if you stayed here with me to ensure I set my alarm," Antonia teased. She was afraid to be alone with her thoughts.

"I would love nothing more than to stay with you and do unspeakable things to your beautiful body, Antonia. Unfortunately, I have a small errand to run for my family. If you keep that thought and do not change your mind, I will give a rain check."

"So you are backing out on that shower we talked about?"

"No, I am being reasonable. I need to get in touch with my family. I will be here by 10 a.m."

"I will be ready. This place is beautiful and tt will be hard to leave. I am falling in love with Italy," she winked.

Antonia leaned in and kissed Luca on the cheek, holding his chin in her hands. As he drove away, Antonia waved goodbye at the front door then entered the Ariston B & B.

It is just a fling. Stay calm and don't look so needy.

The room assigned to her was on the second floor with a small private balcony. The bed was dressed in all-white linens that complimented the wallpaper of soft roses. White crown molding lined the ceiling, giving the room an elegant appeal. A bottle of chilled wine from the local vineyards, some grapes, a jar of special olives and cheese were left on the bedside table. The private bath had brass fixtures and claw foot tub.

Opening the French doors, she stepped out on to the balcony. The night breeze forced the white curtains to billow. Crickets gave life to the darkness and the stars hung in the night sky so close she could almost reach out and touch them. Antonia made herself comfortable on the queen size bed, fluffing the pillows. Grabbing her pocketbook, she pulled out the slice of chocolate cake she stashed from Wade's hotel room, opened the wine and switched on the television:

"Details are vague concerning the American found dead in a hotel room in Rome," the news anchor started. "The *Polizia di Stato*, the civil national police, are questioning his traveling companion. The gentleman was stabbed, piercing his heart. It appears no one heard anything."

Antonia's mouth dropped open as she listened to the broadcast. Impulsively she threw her hands in the air and squealed. "I may have just gotten away with murder and eaten some of his chocolate cake!"

Chapter 12: Wine Must Be Sipped Slowly

The Tuscany morning sun filtered in waking Antonia slowly. It was Saturday, the day after Wade's death, and she still felt void of guilt or shame.

If you hide in the shadows, you forget what the daylight can bring.

Stretching, Antonia slid half out of the bed and let the sheets go slack. After a shuffle to the bathroom, she put on a white terry cloth robe then stepped out onto the balcony in her bare feet to welcome the day. There was no need to fill the silence with words when birds chirped and the winds ruffled the trees. Antonia was beginning to feel supremely confident in her ability to commit accidental murder and get away with it.

It is better to be happy, even if for just a short while, than just be okay for a lifetime. I shall not worry about the future, not for now. No one knows I am in Italy except Wade, and I am pretty sure he will not tell anyone. Marisa, the housekeeper who took my place assumes I vanished. Now it appears they might possibly blame her! She has no idea I got back on my feet, booked a trip, and left the country. I know I should feel remorse, sadness, or possibly grief over killing Wade, but I feel nothing. The aftertaste of stabbing a human being should be bitter but it wasn't. I want to see what the daylight will bring.

Antonia heard the noise of dishes clattering and a light tap on the door. She opened the door to find a tray with hot water for tea, a baguette, butter, and jam with a bowl of fresh strawberries. Deciding to eat on the balcony, she set the tray on the small glass table and dipped her tea bag as she propped her feet on the second chair. She vowed to not think of Wade today.

I suppose bad things linger in your subconscious mind. Something triggers it bringing it all to the forefront like a bad dream you have over and over.

Visually, Antonia could still picture Wade's naked body lying cold on the bed with a steak knife through the heart, blood trickling from the gaping wound in a lovely river pattern. She did chuckle this time when thinking about Marisa finding his body.

Serves her right for thinking she could just take what was mine. I would have loved to have seen her face when she found him. The first things she probably did were take his watch and the cash from his wallet before calling the authorities.

Wade had demanded perfection and she had once loved him like the sun and the moon. Luca, on the other hand, was like a bright star. Antonia knew one could aim for perfection but in the end perfection was unattainable and she was not about collecting a whole solar system looking for that one true love.

Antonia switched on the telly hoping to catch more news while she laid items out on the bed needed for her day trip then returned to the patio. The news reporter didn't give many details, but Antonia felt sure of two things: Wade was dead and she was free to be whoever she wanted to be with no worries of ever being caught. Perhaps it was a good thing Wade was found so soon. Blowflies can smell death up to five miles away.

Antonia finished sipping her tea and began munching on the fruit and bread when she realized the time. Brushing the crumbs from her bathrobe, she paused. "Life is so fragile," she whispered. Determined to start thinking only of her trip she stood up and stretched.

Perhaps a fling is all I need. Today is all about Tuscany and Luca, my gorgeous driver.

After a quick shower, Antonia combed her hair up in a messy bun and threw on some casual black slacks and a bright pink shirt. Luca honked the horn right at ten a.m. sharp. Antonia tossed bottled water in her handbag before tossing it over her shoulder and hurried out the door. Luca was beaming when he saw Antonia exit the front door of the B & B and jumped out to open the door for her.

"*Buongiorno,* Antonia," said Luca giving a slight bow.

"*Buongiorno*, Luca. Isn't it just a beautiful day today?"

"It is quite beautiful but not as beautiful as you," he replied taking her hand.

"It is true what they say, Italian is the romantic language. I feel a slight twinge every time you speak Italian to me. In a place you can only imagine," she laughed.

As Luca took his seat in the front, he adjusted the rearview mirror and caught Antonia's gaze. "Are you ready for your wine tasting experience in the Tuscan countryside?"

"I feel so renewed, I am ready for anything, Luca," Antonia replied. "Although I must confess, I drank an entire bottle last night. You must tell me about the little wine doors scattered around Italy. I heard during prohibition or something you would knock on the little door, and they would give you wine?"

"I will include that in my tour today. I feel you had a good rest, and your accommodations were acceptable?" asked Luca

"I could stay here forever," giggled Antonia. "My television got really good reception."

Luca started the car and they were on their way winding through the valleys. Grape vines lined either side of the road as far as the eye could see. It was beautiful. Antonia rolled her window down to breathe the Tuscan scented air as Luca, always the tour guide, began to give the itinerary for the day then gave her some more history on the little wine doors.

"We are driving to Florence, the capital city of Tuscany and one of the most fascinating cities in the entire world, according to me. Tuscany has few rivals for beautiful scenery. No one plans a visit to Tuscany without planning a visit to Florence. Florence means "City of the Lily." It is a treasure of artistic and vitality. Very old art and young grapes."

"I want to buy a few souvenirs today, Luca. What do you recommend?" Antonia asked.

"Things to buy in Florence are the Florentine olive oil, if you are fond of natural oils and Tuscan wine, of course. We will allow time to shop while strolling in the markets today. Do you have family back home you wish to buy gifts for?"

Antonia looked out the window, breaking eye contact with Luca in the rear-view mirror. "No, I used to, but it is just me now. I have no one to go back home to."

"Don't be sad, *Bella*, I have a large family, and sometimes it is not what you call fun times. Everyone lives a different life just as everyone is born into a different family," Luca explained.

Antonia was silent for the next few miles. Memories of her parents crept up and even though she vowed to have a worry-free day and enjoy the rest of Italy, she couldn't help to think how empty her life would be back in the United States. She had no one, no family to return to. Only the ranch, dust, tumbleweeds and of course, Rick. Visiting Italy had changed everything. Being surrounded by such natural beauty made her want to stay and simply start over.

"Okay, my *Bella*, we are arriving at our first stop. The Florence Cathedral. It is perhaps the most iconic attraction in Florence. Then we will find shops as we walk along *Ponte Vecchio*. Good shops selling jewelry of gold and silver, also later we will shop the markets for oils and wine. Are you excited?"

Giving a slight shake of her head to clear the thoughts Antonia looked back at Luca in the rear-view mirror and smiled, "I am always ready for an adventure."

"*Fantastico*, we shall not spend too much time here. You have a lunch scheduled at the vineyards. I worry you are starting to have that look on your face again. With such beauty and history, how can you be sad?"

Gathering her handbag and placing her hand on the car doorknob, she winked at Luca. "That is the problem Luca. Italy is making me want to stay and never return home. Life here seems so different and meaningful. I am not sad; I am conflicted."

"I am supposed to return home soon to help the family with the olives. If you don't want to rush home, perhaps you will come to my hometown and see what real life here is all about."

"I would love that, Luca. I will call my travel agent, Bethany, and make arrangements to extend my stay. If you think your parents will agree to me coming with you for a few days, that is."

"My family will love you. But my momma will put you to work. I am sure of it."

"I don't mind getting my hands dirty. I grew up on a ranch."

"*Meraviglioso*, meaning wonderful, I was so hoping you would say that to me. My wish is for you to come with me to Pico."

"I am looking forward to it".

"Now stay by me today. I want you to be safe," said Luca.

"If I want to be safe, I will buy a gun. I want to be free and wild."

Luca frowned then shrugged his shoulders assuming this was usual talk for an American. News from America always talks about random shootings of schools, shopping malls, and crime. He offered Antonia his arm and she gladly looped her arm in his as they began to stroll toward the cathedral. Luca was proud of knowing all the history of Italy. He broke into his tour with ease telling Antonia the highlights. Luca was so casual, always holding her hand or putting his arm around her shoulders as they strolled. The flirtation between them was obvious. Antonia never felt safer.

"The Cathedral construction started in the year 1296. It has a rich history, but the bell tower is a free-standing structure within the church complex. It is something we don't want to miss. Shall we go there now?"

"Yes. I did a little research on the bell tower, each of the seven bells at the top have their own name. Am I correct?" said Antonia.

"Very correct. Each bell has a name. The largest bell is called *Campanone* and was created in 1705. A few bells were cast using the remains of damaged or old bells. They ring a beautiful sound across all of Florence. The outside of the bell tower has rich history, too, and carvings telling the stories of the creation of man and woman."

"It is so beautiful, Luca. Italy has so much history; everyone should have a visit like this on their bucket list. What are all the other carvings?"

Luca and Antonia stood staring at the masterpiece, stopping to look at each carving in detail. Antonia put her hand on the stone and was moved by the artistry. She imagined the stone carver sitting for hours, most likely on a small wooden stool in the heat of the day, concentrating on his craft, taking pride in every chip and chisel.

"I wonder, did they know or understand the magnitude of how hundreds of years later many people would put their hand on their work and feel the history of what they created with their bare hands?"

"Many records were kept, and every creator is remembered for their part in the creation of the bell tower."

Luca took a few steps over and pointed toward the wall. "There are also professions highlighted just here in the stone. Such as sheepherding, music, astrology, weaving and of course wine-making. Further down there are additional images of the then-seven known planets. If you look further up you see the seven sacraments, Kings of Israel, and patriarchs. It is the history of the world and of Italy."

"I have never seen anything more magnificent in my life. I want to remember it always, perhaps there is a gift shop nearby with a sketching, or painting of it I can buy," said Antonia.

"They believed history was important, similar to someone wanting to know their genealogy on paper; we have history carved in stone. Let me take you to the market to shop a little before we go to the winery tour," said Luca.

Taking Antonia's arm, Luca gently brushed the side of her breast then turned and smiled. "I can be more than just a history lesson Antonia,' he winked. "I am good at a lot of things."

Antonia gave Luca a playful shove and grabbed his hand a little tighter. Talking about the future, affectionate touches and meeting his family were all leading to something. She wasn't sure what would happen, but intimacy was definitely on her mind.

Luca escorted Antonia to the marketplace where she purchased Florentine oil, bottles of wine, a small replica of the bell tower and a few paintings. After she made arrangements to have the items delivered to her B & B, they took a casual stroll back to where Luca parked the car.

"This is what I came to Italy for, Luca. Thank you again for being my tour guide." Leaning in to give him a kiss, letting him know she was open to everything he had to offer. "I am starving – so when do we have that lunch?" asked Antonia.

"We will be heading there now, to *Castello di Ama*, a beautiful medieval hilltop town just to the north. You will have a view of the hilltop hamlets, rolling hills and the salty coastline. You will experience award winning wine, lovely bruschetta and made-to-order hand tossed pizza from their wood-fired oven."

"Wow, Luca! You should do a commercial for them."

"I have been there several times with my clients; I know the place well and the owners personally."

"Okay, I will follow your lead. Take me away, Mr. Tour Guide."

On the short car ride to the vineyard, neither spoke and Antonia avoided Luca and his eyes in the rear-view mirror. Knowing that Bethany the travel agent hand picked Luca started to place doubts in Antonia's mind: *Many clients, wow!.*

Antonia felt wonderful and fully invested while visiting the cathedral and bell tower, but something was making her feel snarky. Perhaps that he said he took all his clients here started making her feel less special. Fearing she had offended her only friend in Italy, she stared out the window and propped her chin on her palms as they drove through winding roads until they arrived at the vineyard. Antonia fiddled with her bag, giving Luca time to exit the car and open the door for her hoping he saw it as a gesture of letting him do what he does best.

"Listen, Luca, I didn't mean to get so touchy-feely back there. I just cannot resist a little flirting. I will understand if you look at me as just another client. I am a grown woman. Hope that doesn't sound ungrateful or anything. I am just hungry. I get cranky when I am hungry."

"I have noticed you are up sometimes and down sometimes. I try to be happy and give you history and a fun time; it is my job. I do think you are special. Antonia. I hope

I show that to you. Both wings are on the same bird, no need to worry."

"That is a strange way of putting it, but I like it. Now let's go eat."

"It means we are on the same page, but I *did* get hired to show you around Italy."

Antonia paused for a moment and took in the beautiful scenery and the gorgeous vineyard surrounding the café. "It is like a fairytale," she whispered.

Luca opened the door to the *Castello di Ama* café, allowing Antonia to walk in first. Antonia scanned the room and chose a seat at the large bar with the high stools.

"The tables are nice, but they don't have the candles like we saw in the other eateries. It seems cozy with the lit candles in old wine bottles. I love the way the wax melts down the side."

Pulling up on the stool, she left an empty seat on either side. A couple were also seated at the bar area and Antonia nodded at the woman who glanced her way. She couldn't help but notice the woman appeared to have been crying even though she put her hand up to her face trying to hide.

Luca excused himself to visit the restroom while Antonia took a small menu and waited for the server. She was able to get a better look at the young woman and smiled.

"What do you recommend ordering?" Antonia asked the woman.

"Oh, we are tourists, not locals. We had the bruschetta with mozzarella and tomatoes as an appetizer. That was delicious. Then we ordered a pizza; we haven't gotten that yet."

Turning back to the server, Antonia ordered the recommended bruschetta and a pizza with the same on top. Trying to mind her own business, Antonia faced forward and began looking over the wine list. Her nerves were starting to be on edge and the hair on the back of her neck stood up. She remembered that look, the look of despair. How many times she was upset and never wanted anyone to know how she really felt worthless inside. Antonia slammed the wine list down and turned on the stool to face the woman after the man left for the restroom and it was just the two of them.

"Hello, I am Antonia. I am visiting here also, you know, doing the whole tourist thing. I could not help but notice that you are upset. Are you okay?"

"Oh, I am fine. I am Claudia. We have been touring a few weeks now for a long vacation. It is just a squabble, getting on each other's nerves, I suppose."

"Sorry to butt in... I recently came out of an abusive relationship and something just hit me wrong seeing the red mark on your face. Again, I do apologize. A long vacation touring Italy sounds wonderful. Did you do the wine sampling? I could sure use a recommendation; there are so many to choose from," asked Antonia, trying to change the subject.

Luca returned from the restroom and took the seat on her right, leaving the empty stool between Antonia and the woman. Luca took the list of wines and began to explain some of the best choices when the gentleman returned. Antonia gave Claudia a nod, indicating thank you. She also wanted to let her know that women watch out for each other. Then she turned and snuggled Luca's arm, leaning her head on his shoulder.

Noticing the tension, Antonia again glanced toward the couple. The man who joined Claudia leaned forward, staring at Antonia with a look on his face that definitely portrayed an angry "mind your business" look. Antonia's kind smile turned to a stern "back at ya" look. Immediately the thin man with a beer belly frame, slammed his hand on the bar causing Claudia to jump. Antonia turned on her stool and looked him directly in the eye. No fear in her body, just staring. Claudia, trying to diffuse the situation, put her hand on his shoulder.

"This is Antonia; she introduced herself while you were in the restroom. She is a tourist, too," said Claudia.

Claudia looked at Antonia, pleading with her eyes to not start trouble. "She asked about the food. I told her we had the bruschetta. That's all."

Anger bubbling to the surface, Antonia became rigid. A flashback of Wade lying dead in the hotel flashed across her brain like a neon hotel sign in Vegas. Luca tugged on her sleeve, and she snapped her head to look at him. Luca, seeing the rage on her face, touched her shoulder. "I was in the restroom like ten minutes. What happened? Is this man bothering you?"

I need to let it go.

Antonia shook her head and leaned toward Luca and the wine list. "I need some wine. What should we choose?"

"I like to choose local wine from their family vineyard for the tasting. It is usually the best. Perhaps we will need two bottles to go if we like it. It will put you in a nice calm mood."

Antonia looked at Luca. His beautiful skin and blue eyes. He was nearly six feet tall with his muscular chest nearly popping the buttons on his shirt. It calmed her somehow. She couldn't get him involved in a bar scrabble thinking he was being protective.

"Everything is fine now that you are sitting next to me. You are the most handsome man in all of Italy, Luca," said Antonia.

I bet he looks even more handsome naked.

"I hope your eyes are not deceiving you. That is tall order to live up to and you haven't even met my family," he snickered.

"Luca, how about you just pick for me. I know nothing about wine, except once I had cranberry wine. I never cared for any alcohol until I tasted this fruit of the vine here in Italy."

"Seriously?"

"Yes, I am serious."

"Antonia, there are so many things I could teach you."

"Hey, I am in Italy at a wine tasting, so look how far I have come, right? Trying new things, meeting handsome men, who knows what I am capable of learning. Teach me everything, Luca. One thing I did learn is no matter how many times I go to bed and sleep, I will never wake up perfect. However, today is starting to feel that way."

Luca leaned in to Antonia, lifting her chin to stare into her green eyes. "I do not know who hurt you, my sweet, but I hope I never meet him. You are a beautiful vibrant woman. Live your life and do not let anything stand in your way. Promise me that."

"It is never easy to get over a traumatic past relationship, Luca, but this is me trying. It is beyond lucky that I am even sitting here right now."

Luca leaned in further and gently touched his lips to hers as if they were the only two people in the room. Suddenly the stool behind Antonia flipped over and crashed to the ground. She heard Claudia scream and when Antonia turned, she saw Claudia was lying on the ground of the café. Luca rose from the stool and stood face to face with the man Claudia was sitting with.

"She fell, why you care anyway, mind your own business, Mr. Italiano!"

"*Fermata, bruto!*" shouted Luca, meaning stop you Brute!

The tension was palpable. Antonia felt like a small boat cutting through a storm, unsure if she would be sucked in or stay afloat. Feeling weak in the knees but determined to help, she offered a hand to Claudia, pulling her to her feet.

"No need for all this," the man stuttered. "I am sorry, I just want to go back to our hotel."

Antonia looked over at Claudia. "Is that what you want to do?"

Claudia nodded.

Luca stepped closer to Antonia putting his arm around her waist. "No one dies today."

Antonia felt confused and turned to look at Luca wondering if he secretly knew something. "That is a funny choice of words. What do you mean, Luca?" Luca simply shook his head.

Returning to their seats, Antonia grabbed the first glass of wine and gulped it all down. Reaching for the second glass, Luca touched her arm. "Slow down, my sweet. Wine is meant to be sipped and romanced."

"I have no patience for romancing wine. I just don't want to feel anything right now"

"Oh, you will feel something if you continue to drink so fast!" said Luca.

Antonia threw Luca a snarky look. "I am feeling anxious right now. I am deeply committed to finishing the three glasses of wine. Is that okay with you, Luca?"

"Your choices are your own. Whatever you do or have done, I am sure there is a good reason. Let yesterday go and enjoy today," said Luca.

Antonia searched his eyes for a sign that he knew what she had done. That he knew she allegedly got the room key posing as Marisa. That she argued then stabbed Wade in the hotel.

The two of them stared without blinking. The silence was only broken by Luca taking Antonia in his arms, holding her until she stopped trembling. Antonia took a deep breath and pushed away from his embrace.

"I want to know what it feels like to be drunk on wine, Luca. I try to avoid the things that frighten me the most. Right now, I frighten myself."

"I understand," replied Luca, "something has triggered a bad memory. Don't let it control you. I am right here."

"Then if you understand, teach me how to get so drunk I forget all the things that haunt me."

Antonia clutched the second glass of wine and gulped it down, daring Luca to stop her. Luca left to get the car. Antonia followed. When she slid in the back seat, she noticed Luca staring straight ahead with both hands on the steering wheel. In a few short miles, Luca pulled up to the Bed and Breakfast and put the car in park. Turning to look at Antonia with his arm across the back of the seat.

"Would you like help to your room Antonia or are you still insisting on drunken independence?" asked Luca.

"We brought two bottles of wine back with us and the rest of our food," she replied.

"There have been mixed signals all day. We are adults. Just tell me what you want Antonia."

Antonia leaned forward and touched Luca's arm, rubbing it gently. Everything had been going so well until she was triggered. She knew the ripples Wade created finally reached her, so she reacted. Antonia didn't want the day to end and she did not want to be alone.

"I do not want to be alone tonight," she whispered. Without hesitation, Luca jumped out of the car and came around to open the door for Antonia. Offering his hand, Luca pulled Antonia up and grabbed her around the waist, kissing her hard.

"Wasn't it you who told me to slow down?" she laughed.

"I will go as slow as you want me to…"

Chapter 13: Happy Wine

Antonia woke before sunrise. A pool of soft light began peering in through the blinds leaving darkness still lingering in the room. The smell of Luca was still in the air, on the sheets and on her skin. When Luca suggested he should leave, she didn't argue' she let him leave.

It is better to be happy for a few minutes than be alone your whole life.

Memories of their lovemaking were fresh and her body a little sore. Very similar to waves crashing on the shore, Luca brought Antonia to the peak again and again. Luca had moves similar to a wild animal in the bedroom, yet a consummate professional by day. A very endearing trait. Everyone has their secrets.

Sitting cross-legged on the bed, Antonia reached to turn on the bedside lamp but changed her mind. Sitting quietly in the dark is something she used to do as a child. Not able to see her hand in front of her face, she would wonder if this was what it felt like to be blind or dead. So much of life is spent in sadness or stress. The darkness hides it all.

Reflecting back on her life, she tried to remember a time when she was truly happy. Right now, she felt happy. Having made love to Luca, she earned the happy badge. But she knew that happiness could change like the weather.

Growing up she had an uneventful childhood. She was happy riding horses and joyful when a new calf was born. But she was also happy to leave the ranch and start college. Always reaching for that ultimate happiness level in a changing world, can be confusing. Antonia knew that lasting happiness cannot be found in pursuit of any goal or achievement and resides only in the human heart and mind.

Antonia started clearing the empty wine bottles from the night before, while making a pot of coffee. She poured herself a steaming hot cup of Italian dark roast and sat on the balcony. Watching the sun come up and spread its rays across the Tuscan hills was definitely a delight.

Today she was previously scheduled to travel to France and continue her tour of Europe. A goal in life should be to avoid suffering and leaving Italy and Luca would feel like suffering. It was also a real risk staying too long in any one place. Anyone who watches crime shows knows that. At anytime there could be a knock on the door and she could be taken in for questioning. Antonia learned from watching crime shows as a teenager with her mother, that no forced entry means the victim knew their assailant and the finger would be pointed at Marisa. Let her be the number one suspect. Let the chips fall where they land. "I have to care about the broader canvas and paint myself as free, until I am not." She whispered.

If today was the day she got away with murder, she couldn't have asked for a better day. Birds were chirping and the sun was shining with a warm breeze. Fall was coming to Italy, and she could see the vines ripe with grapes. Hoping Luca would make good on his suggestion to travel to his hometown, she decided to call her travel agent and extend her stay.

"Hello, Bethany. I am not quite ready to leave Italy. I have been thinking about visiting a small town called Pico, where they grow and harvest olives. Can you find me a place to stay there for about three or four days, maybe longer if all goes well."

"I am familiar with the village of Pico. I am searching now but I only see a room to rent. It is sort of a bed and breakfast, but I do not think they supply food service. You will have to eat in local cafés, I suppose. How does that sound?"

"It sounds amazing, I have had great food at some out- of -the way cafés. Just text me the address so I can give it to Luca."

"Speaking of Luca, he is scheduled to be off for the fall. I may have to find you a new tour guide. Unless you know something I don't know…"

"It was Luca's suggestion, so I think I am good. If not, I will be calling you to get me on the next plane out of here."

"Where will you want to go next so I can start looking to make arrangements?"

"I don't know, I think I am in love with Italy."

"Italy – or Luca?"

"I will let you know. The jury is still out."

As Antonia hung up the phone, she could hear voices getting loud in the hallway. She stepped closer and put her ear up to the door to listen. A woman was shouting loudly that she did not want to go! Antonia felt her blood boil listening to the couple fighting. Her throat tightened as she heard the voices fading.

I will not let this spoil my day. Italians just talk loud, that is all.

Curious, she grabbed the door handle preparing to thrust open the door and break up the fight. She swallowed hard and forced herself to pause. Antonia took a deep breath and flung open the door, finding herself alone in the hallway. Laughing she poured another cup of coffee and headed out to the balcony. After making love for hours with Luca last night, Antonia was not going to risk anything removing that memory from her mind.

I might not even shower. I don't want to lose his smell from my body. I am just going to marinate in it a while.

Once she was settled on the balcony, her legs propped and a blanket covering her legs she allowed herself to bask in the cues and innuendos from Luca. Was this love? Or did Italian tour guides sleep with all their customers. All the signs were there. Butterflies in the stomach, sharing desires, losing track of time. Euphoria from love making.

Antonia felt this could be the life she was waiting for. Eventually there would be marriage and possibly babies. Oh, how she wanted babies! She allowed her imagination to roam, picturing how beautiful their children would be with Luca's blue eyes. It made her giggle like she was on a merry-go-round. She loved it when the Texas state fair would come into town. The merry-go-round was safe, all the other rides scared her. Her daddy would say, "A merry-go-round only goes in circles to no where. Expand your life and live brave like a bronco rider."

If only he could see me now.

Luca called and explained he would come to pick her up at noon, so she got up and splashed water on her face, carefully patting it dry. Knowing she was to meet his parents today, she decided to choose casual black pants and a pale pink blouse with flats. Gathering her two suitcases, overnight case, and her pocketbook she decided to wait downstairs in the lobby.

Antonia took a seat in a comfortable Italian leather chair facing the window to wait for Luca. She pulled out a burgundy lip gloss and began applying it. It would go nicely with the black pants and pink blouse. Antonia nodded at the front desk clerk as she dabbed her lips on a tissue. He was a tall burly man with a large mustache. He was also the husband of her hostess. Some would say that the first sign of civilization was a man being attracted to the female and Antonia was making sure she was noticed by Luca.

Soon Luca pulled up in his car and Antonia rose to meet him at the front door. The burly man with the mustache was at her side in a flash asking to help with her luggage. Antonia flashed him a smile and took a step back graciously and watched as he grabbed her bags and began to head toward the door. Luca rushed over and offered to take them and the burly man nodded and handed them over.

"*Grazie, Signore*, but I can take it from here," said Luca.

Seeing the sad look on the owner's face, Antonia stepped up to him getting a little too close to his personal space and thanked him for a lovely stay at his bed and breakfast. It was an excessive use of irony, but she was feeling full of herself and perhaps she wanted him to catch the aroma still lingering from her lovemaking. Luca finished putting her cases in the boot and opened the car door for Antonia. "Did you enjoy your stay here, Antonia?" Luca asked..

"It was very memorable."

"Memorable in what way?" asked Luca.

"All of Italy was a romantic and historical trip that I will remember always. It touched my heart like nothing else could. I loved the remarkable beauty of the land and people as well as the deep strength I never knew I had that came bubbling up from my very soul. Yes, Luca, it was memorable, but my memories of our night were the best so far"

"*Magnifico*, Antonia! So, this means you may return to our Italy some day?"

Antonia leaned her head back on the leather seats and closed her eyes as if to trap the memories behind them. "Let me say perhaps a second trip could possibly be in my future. If I ever decide to leave. This beautiful country holds memories for me now that I will never forget."

"Aw, that is good to hear. I hope I am included in those memories. I see you had some raspberry jam for breakfast again."

"Why do you say that?"

Luca closed the door and took his seat in the front of the car. Adjusting the rear-view mirror, he smiled his usual pearly white teeth back at Antonia. "There is a tiny red spot on your shirt."

Antonia sat up in the seat staring at the tiny drop of red just above her right breast. Thinking quickly, reaching in her large purse Antonia pulled out a flower covered silk scarf and arranged it looping around her neck to cover the spot. It had to be a spot of Wade's blood that escaped when she thrust in the knife to his bare chest.

After a few deep breaths she pulled the scarf to the side and discovered it really was raspberry jam. She had forgotten she had not worn this blouse yet on this trip. Annoyed, Antonia turned to avoid eye contact and looked out the window, taking in all the last-minute scenery of the Tuscan landscape as Luca drove. If Luca did know something he was not showing his hand.

It is just my imagination and paranoia.

"This guy is so observant it irritates me, but I am not exposing myself so he can walk all over my choices with his size twelve shoes and turn me in." she mumbled to herself.

After their sensual night together, Antonia once again allowed herself to picture living here, to continue the warm feelings she had experienced with Luca. Possibly visiting his family farm and helping with the olive harvest. Wearing Italian clothes, knee boots and walking through the vineyards as if she belonged here. Now she worried if everything would always bring back the bad memories of Wade. Maybe it was not a good idea to get close to anyone and just go home to Texas.

Antonia knew in her heart she could not possibly proclaim this as a win. The knife in her hand and the control and power she felt gave her a thrill like nothing she had ever experienced. Growing up, her father told her what to do and had the power. She met Wade and he took over her life down to when she brushed her teeth and what clothes she wore. Now she felt for the first time she had control over her life. She could love who she wanted to love. A relationship with Luca or anyone could not make her change her mind.

Antonia was quiet the rest of the ride to Pico. Occasionally she would glance up to catch Luca staring at her in the rear-view. He was such a handsome man, but she was not willing to give up her life for anyone. After a few minutes of self-pity, she asked Luca to roll down the window. Letting the wind blow in her face, she vowed to slow down the internal guilt and enjoy what was right in front of her. Forcing herself to perk-the-hell-up, she scooted to the center of the back seat and leaned forward to touch Luca on the shoulder.

"I had a moment of doubt, but I am better now. Here is the address of the room to rent that my travel agent found for me. Please take me there so I can freshen up before I meet your parents."

Looking at the address, Luca began to laugh. He pulled the car to the side of the road and got out, opening the door for Antonia.

"What is so funny? Do you know this place? I heard it had good reviews."

Luca got in the back seat with Antonia, scooting her over to make room. Turning to her, Luca held her face in his hands. Luca begins kissing Antonia from the top of her head, her face, neck and ears. In between every smooch he whispers. "I know- this- place well." Stifling a chuckle, he stuttered, "I –was- born- there. It- is–my- parents- house. They have a room to rent."

"Oh, no! We won't have any privacy. Your parents will see me in my bathrobe!"

"It will be fine. I am glad you will be nearby. However, you are right: we may not have a lot of privacy, so we should take care of business right now," he snickered.

Luca reached under her bottom and pulled her toward him, laying her back on the seat. Using his mouth and his swift hands he pulled at her clothing. Antonia moaned, throwing her head back, giving herself over to him completely. Taking his time to caress every inch of her body, Luca ravished her, sending wave after wave crashing to the shore. Her need for his body was intense. When he was finished, he slumped, his body resting on hers. Antonia began running her hands through his hair as he rested his head on her breasts.

"I have never felt like this before, Luca," she confessed.

"What, you never had sex in the back seat of a car before?"

"Actually, no, but that is not what I meant. I mean I feel so good. I feel loved. As far as the sex goes, that was the kind of sex you only see on cable. My body thanks you," she laughed.

Luca pushed himself up and assisted Antonia to the upright position. They sat their hands on each other's thighs, sweaty from lovemaking and just chilled. Luca moved first and rummaged on the floorboard for his clothes. Smoothing his hair back he then leaned over and kissed Antonia.

"You really don't have to worry, Antonia. The room is located on the back side of the house and has its own outside entrance."

"Then what was all this?"

"I was thinking about you all day since I left and just had to have you. I thought it would be romantic and erotic. You did like it, right?"

"Oh, I am not complaining. You know how to make my thighs jiggle, and that tongue of yours is amazing. Maybe we should take rides in the country more often. Make it an after-dinner routine or something. I would hop into the back seat with you anytime."

"I will make a note of that. But seriously you may want to smooth your hair a bit, it looks sort of like a bird made a nest," Luca teased.

Antonia gave him a love slap on the arm then pulled a hairbrush from her purse.

"Then you can get in the front seat with me. I told my parents and my whole family about you. They are excited to meet you," Luca said sweetly.

"When you say the whole family, what does that mean, exactly?"

"You will see. Italians have big families. My *Nona*… Grandmother… will be there, too," he said.

Arriving at Luca's family olive farm was breathtaking. The view from the front seat was even better. It wasn't the fancy house or special manicured lawns; it was all beautifully intoxicating. All around the house were black poplar trees that had to be around seventy feet tall.

Closer to the house was a cobblestone driveway and the two-story home was made of sand-colored stones with a terracotta roof. Large wooden shutters covered the downstairs windows and doors so they could be opened to let the breeze flow through the house. On one side of the house there was a covered breezeway that led to another small villa. Luca pointed out that the room Antonia would be staying in was there. No sooner than Luca retrieved the luggage from the trunk, all the family came out to greet them.

Antonia was introduced to brothers, aunts and uncles, parents and lastly his *Nona,* with her snowy white hair. She was hugged by all and made to feel very welcome. Luca did his best to introduce them all, rattling off their names like he was calling roll at school.

"My mother, *la madre,* is Carmella. Brothers here are Enrico, Mateo and Roberto is traveling. My little sister Isabella, will visit soon, and you will meet her. My father is called Armando and his brother, our uncle, is Ricardo. Everyone, meet Antonia!" Luca said, pointing to everyone. "Please, she does not speak Italian, so I ask you as my family to only speak English when you are around her." The entire family nodded their assent.

"I am not sure I will remember everyone's name, but I thank you for allowing me to stay on your beautiful olive farm," said Antonia.

The heartwarming welcome filled her heart with such love and a tiny bit of jealousy. Antonia, being an only child, had never witnessed such a large and loving family. Luca and his siblings played, punched and hugged all the way to the front door. It was wonderful to watch.

Once inside, Antonia marveled at the woodwork, Italian tile and beautiful décor. It had an eclectic mix of furniture and fabrics. She was escorted through the main house to a long wooden dining table in an outdoor courtyard. The table was set with bunches of olive leaves for centerpieces placed down the center of the table.

"You are just in time, please sit," said his mother, Carmella.

Luca pulled out her chair for her and sat her next to his Nona with his father sitting at the head of the table. Luca stood before sitting, explaining the family traditions.

"Olive season is upon us and just like the whole family gathers to help with the picking, we also gather for a special dinner to kick off the season and pray for a bountiful harvest. I will show Antonia the olive trees after dinner."

Plates of olives soaked in olive oil with sprigs of rosemary and thyme were set out. Also, a traditional dish made with toasted bread topped with tomatoes, basil and olive oil drizzled on top. Beautiful cheeses and pasta were set in big decorative bowls. Luca's father took over as Luca sat beside Antonia. Starting with his own glass, he poured wine, then passed the bottle to his wife, who then passed it on around the table. He spoke of family, history and, of course, olives.

"Across this countryside, families, friends and neighbors gather in each other's olive grove to help pluck the olives from the trees by hand. Olives are a part of our lives. Every household produces its own fine oil for use, and we do set aside the best olives for my occasional martini."

A prayer was said blessing the harvest before everyone started passing the bowls of delicious food. Looking over at Luca, Antonia felt happier than she ever had before. They ate and drank well into the night. Everything was exaggerated and there was much laughing, storytelling and wine. Antonia noticed the resemblance in his brothers. Enrico ,or Rico as they called him, had his wife, Aria and small baby boy named Ricardo after Luca's uncle. When it was time for Aria to put little Ricardo to bed, Antonia asked to tag along.

"This house and the family have been a beautiful experience for me," said Antonia.

"You do not have a big family?" Aria asked as she changed the baby.

"No. I am an only child and my parents are deceased."

"That is too sad to think about. I am sorry for your loss."

"That is the main reason I took this trip. I wanted to find myself. Maybe start over," Antonia replied. "I am glad I did. It has been perfect."

"Would you like to hold the baby while I prepare the bottle?"

"I would love that. I have never held a baby before," said Antonia.

Staring at Antonia as she cooed and gazed into the eyes of little Ricardo, Aria reached out to touch her shoulder. "I am glad Luca brought you tonight. It will be sad for him when you leave to return to the states. And possibly just as sad for you to leave."

Letting her words sink in, Antonia began to feel alone, even though she was surrounded by people. They were a family; she was the guest.

A new chapter in her life had begun and she wanted to let it play out. She had no family to go home to, no attachments except the ranch back home. This new freedom gave Antonia an unexplained euphoric tingle down to her bones. Antonia felt like she finally got off the safe merry-go-round and took a chance on the thrill of the roller coaster, not knowing how or when the ride would end.

Chapter 14: Making Wine

Harvest time for grapes as well as olives was traditionally a family affair with everyone pitching in, then sharing the bounty afterwards around a fire. Olive oil is particularly spicy when it has just been pressed and most wines are a special treat. Luca's family had many groves of olive trees but only enough grape vines to produce a few bottles for personal use.

The family woke early the next morning to start the yearly plucking of the olives. Neighbors came to join in, hoping to be given some of the liquid gold from the olives for their own household. Antonia awoke early, excited to experience a typical Italian day plucking olives with Luca and is family. She was used to special days on the ranch when all ranch hands rose early to brand the cows or herd them to a new pasture.

As she threw on her dark jeans she purchased in town, she heard a light knock on her door. Opening the door, she found Luca standing there holding a pair of old boots, a long sleeve shirt and a grin.

I wonder if he will be like this on Christmas morning...

"Good morning, Luca! Please come in. What kind of presents did you bring me on this crisp morning?"

"My mother sent you one of her old pair of boots. She didn't know if you had proper footwear. And you need to wear this old long sleeve shirt so you don't scratch up your lovely arms. Don't frown; my mother is just being nice."

"I am willing to put on these boots and the shirt just so I can fit in with the family," Antonia said with a smile. "Do we get to eat first?"

"Of course! There is cappuccino, strong coffee, bread, jam and *cornetto* waiting for you."

"That sounds good to me, what is *cornetto*? Sausage, bacon?"

Luca laughed then set the items down and gave Antonia a big morning hug. Fresh from the shower, Antonia breathed in his dreamy man smell.

"The typical Italian breakfast consists of sweet foods. A *cornetto* is basically an Italian version of the french croissant. No meat today, like you are used to. But there is coffee and plenty of it. Embrace the new day with an open mind and open mouth," Luca chuckled.

"Alright then, let me slip on my boots and shirt, then we can get some coffee. Plenty of it," Antonia laughed, "you have a beautiful smile when you laugh. I cannot resist."

After breakfast and meeting with the friends and family for coffee, everyone walked down the hill to the closest olive grove. The trees reminded Antonia of grumpy old trees sporting a bad hair day, like in a cartoon. However, there was something so beautiful about rows of olive trees.

Plucking the olives was a technique that took Antonia a while to catch on to. Luca would pass by her carrying another full basket, stopping for a quick smooch or a flirty slap on her bottom. A short break was taken to eat olives and cheese and occasionally some bruschetta. A full eight hours went by before anyone headed toward the house. Luca's mother Carmella was waiting for everyone with a table set with a variety of food, mostly pasta and bread with olives and cheese on the side. And of course, there was wine.

Luca escorted Antonia back to her small villa attached to the main house so she could shower. They sat at the small table in the corner and Luca opened a bottle of wine. The villa was a comfortable open room with pine walls. It had a full bed on one side and a small sitting area near the only window. A very small kitchenette with a small sink and tiny fridge was on one side across from the bed. There was a beautifully tiled ensuite, with a large shower and soaking tub.

"I am just curious. Does your family eat like this every night or is it just for the harvest?"

"I am not sure what you are asking. Did you not enjoy the supper, Antonia?"

"Oh, I am loving every minute of this experience. I just want to get to know your family traditions. For example, do you ever enjoy fried chicken and mashed potatoes with gravy poured all over?" asked Antonia gently. "One of my favorites my mother made. Or for Thanksgiving, I bet you bake a big turkey and stuffing with cranberry sauce, right?"

Luca looked confused. He sat down next to Antonia, finished his entire glass of wine then poured another. Antonia didn't know why she was asking these questions. Something inside of her was feeling out of place. Or homesick.

"Never mind, Luca. I am just tired and trying to make conversation. I had a great time today and I am so grateful your family let me be a part of it all," she said.

"Italians don't have Thanksgiving like in the United States, but we do have many festivals to celebrate harvests of local food. We celebrate *Festa di San Martino*, which is translated to St. Martin's Feast Day. That is a celebration of harvest and giving thanks for family and friends. I have eaten chicken with a pasta, just not all fried like you explained. Does that answer your questions, Antonia?"

"Absolutely. Now I am just going to hop in the shower, and we can sit and relax or perhaps explore each other," she said with a sly giggle.

Anything to change the subject!

Luca set his wine glass down and stood up blocking Antonia from the bathroom. He put his finger under her chin and lifted her lips to meet his. "I am going to join my family outside for crushing the grapes to make the new wine. It is a tradition. Why don't you shower and rest up, Antonia. I will see you again in the morning."

"Oh okay, I will be ready with my boots on!"

I am tired, but was hoping for a little recreational snuggle.

"I am glad you are here, Antonia," said Luca as he gently kissed her cheek.

"Don't worry about me, Luca. I probably should call home and check on the ranch anyway."

As Luca closed the door, Antonia let out a quiet sigh of relief. She imagined bottles of Italian wine, traveling around sightseeing the country on day trips and visiting local shops. Olive picking was a great experience, but it was work. She had never actually worked an eight-hour day. Long shifts as an intern in medical school did not include reaching and climbing a wooden ladder plucking olives. It was exciting to meet Luca's family and be a part of their world but she was actually thinking she would be more of a guest here.

When he asked me to come with him to his hometown and visit, I could almost hear my lady parts cheering, not sweating in the family olive grove.

Antonia imagined Luca visiting her villa every night, enjoying long nights under the stars and some occasional wild circus sex. She decided to stop over-thinking and take a shower, then call Rick at the ranch and check in. An early night might be the best to ease her sore muscles.

With a towel on her head, she propped up on the pillows and called Texas.

"Rick, I am calling to check in. How is everything going?"

"Antonia! I was just thinking about you. Are you still traveling?" asked Rick.

Hearing Rick's deep voice gave her heart a little flutter. Antonia had been so wrapped up in Luca's olive grove she forgot how much she enjoyed conversations with Rick.

"Well, I have been to Rome, Pisa, Venice, Tuscany and now I am in Pico. I may also be in the middle of a mid-life crisis. I plucked olives today for eight hours," said Antonia.

"Well, I do like olive oil but only if it is rubbed on my brisket or ribs. It makes a nice sizzle when they hit the grill," he laughed. "Is this just part of the tour you are on, or are you starting a new career?"

"Not a career choice, just helping out an Italian family I met. So, tell me something about Texas. Anything new?"

"Let's see… It is hot. We are keeping the troughs filled with extra water. Our hay delivery was late and, oh, I asked Becky out to dinner."

"The hay was late…wait…what? Becky who? You don't mean Becky the bull rider, do you?" Antonia laughed.

There was a pause. Antonia cleared her throat and put her hand to her chest. Her heart did a slight flip-flop and she didn't understand why. It was as though fear was trying to creep into her mind. His deep voice made her spine tingle as a chill came over her.

"Rick, are you still there?"

"Listen, Antonia, I have been meaning to tell you, just I don't know when you will call. My birthday is in a few months, and I will be thirty damn years old! I am a man. I want things. I have had brief encounters, sure, but I want a family. I want little baby Ricks running around so I can teach them how to ride a horse. It is painfully obvious that you do not remember what we said to each other when you left for college."

"I don't know what to say other than, I don't remember every little thing we said. What does that have to do with Becky the bull rider, anyway?" Antonia asked. "She is not your type."

"I promised you I would wait for you to finish college and your career before, you know, I moved on. I know we were young, but I loved you. You said you were not ready for a commitment and that you becoming a doctor was a priority. I understood. I waited. You made other choices. It is fine. We are all fine. Becky showed me some interest and I finally made a choice, too. I am going to take her out and see how it goes."

Oh my goodness, why did my heart jump up in my throat?

"I do remember Rick. I am sorry. I guess I was looking at it wrong, I didn't take you seriously. I have the attention span of a gnat. Becoming a doctor was my only priority back then. Life just happened. There is so much I wish I could tell you," she sniffled.

"You can tell me anything, Antonia. Always."

"Not this. I just can't, especially over the phone. I really miss those bear hugs from my one and only childhood crush. I could use one right now. I am so sorry, Rick. I probably won't make it to your birthday celebration. I assume there will be lots of brisket and ribs."

"And potato salad," he laughed.

"I miss your cooking more than you will ever know. I would kill for some of your baked beans, too. I just have too many burdens on my mind. You will always be special to me, Rick."

"Burdens? What kind of burdens? Are you in trouble, Antonia?"

"The heaviest burden we carry is guilt. I have guilt, Rick."

"I was glad to hear you left that prick Wade. Yes, Jill told me the whole story; don't be mad at her. You should also call her more often. She worries about you. Does it have something to do with *him*?"

"It is basically the things that I have done and the choices I have made. I should have never left medical school. However, I am trying to turn things around now. Listen, one day I will make it up to you for missing your birthday. Thank you for taking care of the ranch for me."

I need to get off the phone before I start bawling.

"When do you think you will come home, Antonia? You know if things change in my life, I will want my own home. I can't keep staying in the guest room of your parents' homestead. I will still take care of things for you."

"I know, Rick. I hope you have a nice date with Becky. I have to go now. It is time to stomp the grapes for wine. Good-bye."

I secretly hope Becky snores and farts in her sleep.

"I am glad we had this talk, Antonia. I am always here for you. Good-bye."

Tossing her cell phone on the end of the bed, Antonia turned to bury her face in the pillows to cry like a baby. She had not had a good ugly cry since her parents died. She didn't even cry over Wade. Nothing made sense for why she was crying now. She just cried until her eyes were tired.

After the sun set, there was a light tapping on the door. Antonia wiped her face on the towel she had her hair in and answered the door. It was Luca's Nona. She was a little stout but appeared to be strong for her age. Nona was obviously a handsome woman in her day with light gray/blue eyes, except now she had a craggy black mole with a coarse spiky hair peeking out through the middle.

Weirdly I have an impulse to touch it.

"Antonia, you did not come to the fire with the rest of the family, so I came to check on you and bring you something to eat," said Nona.

In a wooden bowl covered with a soft white tea towel were four biscuits and a small jar of blackberry jam. She entered, pushing past Antonia, and placed it on the table then took a seat crossing her arms.

"Nona, that is so sweet of you. I am just tired, so I decided it was best to shower and rest. But don't worry. I will be up and ready in the morning."

"I can tell by your eyes you have been crying a long time, maybe forever. A woman's goal in life should be avoiding suffering and discovering their true happiness. Do you think you have found happiness in my Luca?"

Wow! No sugar coating this conversation…

Antonia sat in the chair across from Nona and began to brush imaginary crumbs from the table, avoiding eye contact.

"Honestly, I am very happy with Luca, but I have no idea what it all means. I mean, we have had no discussions or made any plans. I do see our differences, but I also just want to enjoy him. And the family of course," Antonia explained.

"You have a home in the United States. Luca has a home here. He will not inherit this land, that goes to his brother Rico. Will you stay here with Luca or return home?"

"Wow, Nona, you get right to the point. What if I am not sure where home is?"

Never breaking a smile or missing a beat, Nona fired off the questions. "Who snatches up their life to make a roost in a foreign country?" asked Nona. "Could you?"

"I have not seriously thought about it. I am unsure what the future holds," replied Antonia.

Pulling a small pocketknife from her pocket, Nona pulled a biscuit from the bowl she brought and split it in half. She then spread it with the blackberry jam and handed half to Antonia.

"You eat. I am going to tell you a story... This house and olive grove belonged to my grandparents. I was born and raised here. I met my husband while he was here working. Love at first sight. We wanted to be together, but I was a young girl and my parents did not allow me to date. Enrico, my husband, was from Milan, a city in north Italy. My oldest grandson is named after him. So, the father of my two children, god rest his soul, gave up everything to move here to Pico just to marry me. He was seventeen and I was fifteen. We were married 49 years before he passed away. He never regretted marrying me, but not a day went by that he did not talk about how he missed Milan and his family. You see they did not approve of Enrico marrying me, so they stopped speaking to him for 30 years. They only spoke to his sister Alma. She kept in touch with us. Then one day he took a trip to Milan when his father, Mario, was dying. That is the story. If you cannot leave your family, then go home now. Do not break my Luca's heart. Eat your biscuits and sleep. I will see your eyes in the morning sun, I will know if you are happy."

And with that, Nona left Antonia to ponder. Antonia pulled her legs up in the chair hugging them with one arm while the other was putting the soft biscuits into her mouth. "I didn't get a chance to tell her I have no family to leave. Just a ranch. No family," she sniffled. "I know one thing for sure, I am going to get fat if I stay here. These biscuits are the bomb," she muttered.

Antonia had a restless night's sleep tossing and turning. She could not get the story Nona told her out of her head and when she tried, Rick popped up like a jack in the box to invade her dreams. She pictured him with Becky the bull rider by his side. Not a pretty dream.

Becky had short blonde hair with the tips died pink. Pink was her style. Pink cowboy boots and all. She got her reputation after taking a bet with some of the ranch hands that she could go longer than eight seconds on a mechanical bull. Becky was thin with no hips or butt to speak of, and her breasts were less than a handful.

The cowboys called her 'Toothpick' until the night they were all at a bar in Dallas. Becky made them swear to stop calling her 'Toothpick' if she rode the mechanical bull the longest. Well, that thin girl wrapped her long legs around that bull and rode it just shy of nine minutes. No one could beat her time. Seeing that they all had a few beers in their belly, they demanded a do-over. For three weekends in a row, Becky beat the cowboys. From then on she was officially known all over San Antonio as Becky the bull rider.

At least Rick would be dating someone famous.

As morning started to fill the small one-room villa with sunlight, Antonia crawled out of bed and put her unruly hair on top of her head and pinned it. Putting on the blue jeans, boots and shirt, she glanced in the mirror. She no longer recognized her reflection. For so long she had dressed in elegant clothes and beautiful jewelry. Now she looked worn and drab. Glancing over at her Louis Vuitton luggage, she slumped her shoulders. "I guess it doesn't matter what you have, but who you are with. I miss my beautiful clothes, but I am happy with Luca," she mumbled. "Plain and drab is where it is at for now."

Just about the time she was ready to go find the family for coffee and sweet breads, there was a knock on the villa door. Thinking it would be Luca, she flung open the door and was surprised to see Aria and her baby standing there; she waved them in. Before closing the door, she glanced outside looking for Luca. Aria caught on right away.

"Luca is not with me. He sent me and baby Ricky to escort you to breakfast," explained Aria. "I hope you do not mind. Ricky was fussy this morning so I thought a walk would help. Are you ready to go, Antonia?"

"I just need to grab my hat but first, can I snuggle with baby Ricky?" she said holding out her arms. "I didn't know you were calling him Ricky," said Antonia.

"Well, Rico's uncle Ricardo is who he is named after. With too many Ricos and Enricos, we felt like our baby needed some distinction. His own name for his own personality. Ricky just fits him, don't you think?"

We need a bunch of baby Ricks and Rick's running around.

"I think it is perfect, Aria. You are so lucky; he is a gorgeous baby. I hope to have a baby one day. More than one, actually. I would love a house full."

"You seem to be really good with babies, Antonia. A natural."

"Do you really think so, Aria? I have an idea: why don't Luca and I watch baby Ricky one night for you and Enrico so you can have a night out?"

"Oh, that would be nice, Antonia, but I don't think Luca would be keen on that idea. He has made it clear many times: he doesn't like babies. Says it ties you down. They are a handful, but I enjoy being a mom. We should go. Don't want to be late for olive plucking. Nona would freak out, show you her Italian temper."

Nona will freak out? How about I am freaking out right now!

And just like that Antonia's mind was sent into a episode of 'this is your life'. Luca not liking or wanting children is a very disappointing curve ball. Having given up so many things just to be with Wade in a previous relationship, Antonia had to wonder if she was possibly heading down another path of disappointment and pain. In her mind as in many minds of women there is a check list of things to achieve in life as well as things to never tolerate or give up on. Antonia had made this lest and remade this mental list several times. It was always college, career, a wonderful marriage and children. Many children.

The opposite can be true in a situation where the man wants to procreate and the wife has difficulty conceiving, is that a deal breaker?

At this moment Antonia is conflicted and decided to hold back any judgment and fight the fear of disappointment until she and Luca get more serious with a serious commitment.

Chapter 15: New Wine

Antonia's renewed smile and attitude after talking with Rick last night had turned into a concerning frown with the words Aria spoke. Returning the baby to his mother, she grabbed her hat and followed Aria out the door.

Luca stood up to pull out her chair when they arrived in the courtyard. Avoiding eye contact with Luca, Antonia immediately started loading her plate with one of everything. Luca poured her a cup of coffee then touched her shoulder. Not wanting to look him in the eye, she whispered. "I am just very hungry this morning."

The sky was turning a pewter shade of gray. Gray skies, the color without color, between black and white. A slight mist could be felt. Antonia was quiet, avoiding all conversations, stuffing as many croissants… *cornetti*… into her mouth as possible. If she was chewing, maybe no one would expect her to engage in casual conversation. Remembering what Nona said about looking into her eyes this morning, she avoided her as well. This time the group hopped in the back of trucks to ride to the furthest away olive groves. The plan was to finish the family's olives today so they could help a neighbor this afternoon and tomorrow.

Luca chattered explaining the oldest olive trees were the furthest from the home. "Some olive trees can live up to 2000 years," he said. Antonia knew what he was doing. He was trying to engage her in conversation so she would have to acknowledge him.

Nice try, but women have been avoiding conversations for years. We are pros.

Arriving at the grove of old olive trees, Luca helped Antonia set up her ladder and bucket then walked off to assist others. At the top of the ladder, she could peer over the top and see Luca talking to Mateo, his brother, two trees away. As Mateo continued to pluck olives, Luca talked. Using their arms expressively, the plucking came to a halt and soon the voices rose. Antonia observed quietly, wondering what the two brothers could be arguing about. She saw Luca suddenly smack the ladder hard making it wobble. Mateo jumped down from the ladder and the two men began shouting again in Italian.

Antonia could not make out all the words because of them going from Italian to English but a few words stood out in the heated exchange. "Did you tell her?" shouted the man.

Tell me friggin' what? Am I the 'her' in this conversation?

The rain began to fall harder. It was actually refreshing. Antonia came down her ladder quietly and tried to listen, but the rain was drowning out the conversation. Antonia moved closer, keeping a fat olive tree between her and the two men. Luca's stance was one of alertness, his face wearing the expression of fury. "No, I did not. Not yet!" Luca shouted back.

Mixed feelings were swirling in her brain. Should she step forward to break it up, defending Luca, or keep her distance? Antonia looked around hoping she was not the only witness to the shouting. Suddenly Rico, Luca's older brother appeared behind her and tapped her shoulder.

Busted.

"No worries, brothers argue sometimes. I will calm Mateo down," smiled Rico.

Luca, Mateo and Rico all continued to shout in Italian, until Rico points over his shoulder toward Antonia. The two men then stop and turn toward her with stern faces. Now anyone that knows anything knows that spending time in a foreign country you tend to pick up a few words or phrases. Antonia distinctly picked up on the fact that somehow, she was the topic of their conversation. Among other things, she picked up the word *segreta*. Repeated over and over with fervor, meaning secret.

Turning too quickly to avoid embarrassment for eavesdropping, Antonia decided to run in the pouring rain, through the olive trees and mud, which resulted in an even more embarrassing fall on her tushy as her feet wearing Nona's boots, could gain no traction. Flat on her aching bum, gravity forced her feet up in the air in a not-so-lady-like position. Turning to get on all fours, she made a feeble attempt to stand. Again, she lost footing like a gymnast wearing roller skates and did a swan dive face first in the mud. After the lovely face plant, she gave up and pretended the performance was meant to be for entertainment purposes and gave a small curtsy.

Oh, God!, I hope they didn't see me.

At first there were only intermittent snickers, then came the snorts and full-on belly laughs. Antonia closed her eyes to block any tears. She could not bear the shame of letting them see her cry. It was a sacrifice without expectation. Slowly she began to reach out for anything to grab and pull herself up. Slithering like a snake and grabbing handfuls of mud to pull herself forward, she managed to get close enough to the olive tree she had been plucking. Antonia grabbed a branch, then the wooden ladder to get to her knees, then finally stood upright. She began spitting and spewing the mud that had managed to enter her mouth when she fell face first. The men looming over her just watching in awe at her flexibility.

How lady like am I at this moment.

Numb with horror, Antonia brushed herself off as if it was just a crumb of mud, straightened her pony tail and took a deep breath. Holding her head high, she bolted. Like an awkward gazelle doing the high step, she ran. Over the first small hill, she followed the dirt road then slowed as the road sloped slightly, dodging puddles.

Damn these rolling hills in Italy.

Trying to picture herself in high school, running track for P.E. class, she kept telling herself to keep going. "I will make it back to the villa, pack my bags and leave. I just can't stay here," she sniffled. "I won't stay."

Her arms were flailing as she tried to find a rhythm in the pouring rain, concentrating on her high step, trying not to fall, and looking ahead with confidence. Suddenly, she felt someone grab her arm and stopped just shy of another nosedive. Luca had chased after her. Standing there facing him with his expression of distaste, like he was avoiding a dirty word you were never supposed to utter, Antonia tried to pull her arm away from his grasp, but he held on tight.

"What are you doing, Antonia? It is a long way back to the villa," he said. His deep voice boomed like thunder as the rain continued to soak them to the bone.

"What does it look like I am doing? I am going back to the villa. I am leaving. I cannot stay here, Luca. Tell me, am I your big secret or is there something I am missing?"

"Antonia, I don't understand you. There is no secret. Come back and I will take you in the truck to get cleaned up," said Luca.

Luca smoothed his hair back from his face. Trying to comfort Antonia, he stepped closer and took her hands in his. She pulled away.

As she wiped mud from her face she opened up and unleashed her anger. "Is it no secret that you have brought other women here to help with plucking the olives! It is no secret that you think long distance relationships don't work. And it is no longer a secret that... that you don't like babies!" Antonia paused, looking up letting the rain mix in with the tears on her face. "Well Luca, you keep your secrets, I have a secret too!"

"Antonia, this entire conversation is insane. I already know about your secret and everything else we can talk about," smiled Luca.

"What do you know? You don't know. You really don't know my secret, Luca!"

Antonia began to back away. She looked back toward the olive groves then back toward the villa. She did not know whether to run or act calmly and let Luca get the truck. She felt stuck and scared. Her clothes were soaked and she had left her phone in the villa, so she had little choice.

"Antonia, you sit here by this one-hundred-year-old cypress tree. I will get the truck. Everything will be fine; you will see. We can talk after a nice hot shower."

Antonia sat with her knees pulled up and her head resting on her arms. Small glitchy movies of the last few weeks played over in her mind. Many times, she suspected Luca knew she killed Wade, but how could he have known? Here she thought she was enjoying time with a beautiful man and falling in love. Someone she could trust. Someone who has beautiful lips she wanted to chew on. Shaking her head, she sat up straight trying to focus on the facts. She was in a serious predicament that could go very badly.

"I can run, but I would not make it to the villa before Luca gets here with the truck. It is a few miles on foot. There is a huge chance that Luca doesn't know, and he is bluffing." She stood and began to pace, talking aloud to herself hoping a suitable solution would magically appear in her head. "If he truly does know I killed a man then why hasn't he turned me in? Perhaps he brought me here to his family villa to hide me out and protect me. Nah, that is not likely. It sounds ridiculous just saying it out loud. I think the only reasonable solution is to leave Pico and get away from the villa… and Luca."

Antonia started walking toward the villa; she no longer felt the rain. If Luca caught up with a vehicle, she would allow him to drive her to the villa then make an excuse to be alone and secretly pack her things. Walking helped her think. One call to Bethany would get her out of town tonight. Trudging along with her head down, she soon heard the rumble of the family truck. As he stopped, she turned and hopped into the passenger seat. Avoiding any eye contact with Luca, she stared at her muddy feet.

Might as well make a clean break. If I look at his sexy smile, I may change my mind.

"You know, I always planned to visit Paris. I am thinking I may call my travel agent and have her get me a flight as soon as possible," Antonia said casually.

"I would have to drive you back to Rome to catch a plane. Are you sure that is what you want to do, Antonia?" asked Luca snickering. "I would think you would want to avoid going anywhere near Rome."

Oh shit! He does know.

"There are other airports in Italy, I am sure. I will just pick one," she stammered.

"Oh, sure. There is one in Milan, one in Florence. Just depends on where you are going." Luca said casually.

Looking straight ahead, Antonia could see the roof of the villa coming into view. Her plan was to jump out and rush into the villa claiming she needed a shower to clean off the mud. From there it depended on Bethany the travel agent. It wasn't the most supreme plan, but it was a start.

At the villa, Antonia reached for the door handle. Luca grabbed her arm and she turned fearfully to look at him.

Her father's words ran through her head: *"If the first step of the plan fails, the rest will surely fall apart."*

"Tonight is the night we drink the new wine made from the harvested grapes. It is in celebration of the olive season coming to an end. It is not much but they are from our small vineyard. If you leave, you will always wonder how it would have turned out," Luca said. His eyes were serious and piercing. Luca was not just talking about wine, and she knew it. Antonia began to tremble. She jerked her arm from his grip, opened the door and stepped back still facing him.

"I need a shower. I don't care about the new wine or how it all turns out."

Antonia knew everyone would still be down at the olive groves with only Nona at the main house. Once inside the small villa, she stripped off all her clothes and grabbed her phone from the bedside table. She called Bethany the travel agent, but there was no answer. She left a message, clicked on the radio and headed for the shower.

Turning the shower as hot as she could stand it, she stepped in letting the water just pour down her naked body. She accepted the cleansing feeling it gave her, hoping all her sins and feelings would be washed away. Antonia cried as she slapped her hands into the tile walls and stomped her feet purging all past emotions.

I am so tired of relationships ruining my life.

As Antonia reached for her body wash, she heard the door of the shower clink. Luca appeared behind her and took the bottle from her hand. As she turned to shout at him, he put his index finger to her lips shushing her. His naked body only inches from hers; her head swooned and she felt faint. Turning her sideways with her back against the cool tile, he kissed her passionately. He pressed his body hard against hers and, grabbing her wrists, he forced them above her head.

For a moment Antonia gave in to the passion, then opening her eyes she pushed him away.

"No, I can't do this, Luca. I am upset with you."

"I understand." Luca pressed his body harder against hers and allowed his hands to roam. Antonia let out a small squeal then pushed at him again.

"I am serious Luca, I… I… don't want to do this."

"I understand."

"Well, then… Are you going to leave?"

"I will rub soap all over your body. You know you will like it. Just turn around."

Grabbing Antonia by the waist, he gently turned her to face the wall. She no longer fought it and placed her hands on the wall as though she was being frisked at the airport. Luca pressed against her, teasing her as he began to sway to the music playing on the radio. Their bodies moved as one. He increased the intensity by kissing her neck fiercely with little love bites while whispering how good she tasted.

"You don't understand, Luca."

"I do understand. I will show you how much I understand."

Luca started with rubbing soap all over her back and worked his way down. Antonia arched her back enjoying the sensations. His touch was like fire heating her up with every nibble and caress. Just before the moment came to climax, he whispered in her ear. "Do you understand now? I love you, Antonia?"

I understand.

After the shower, Luca and Antonia moved to the bedroom, spooning for hours under the soft cotton sheets. Not wanting to spoil the moment, neither spoke. Luca stirred then stretched, taking up most of the bed. Antonia laughed.

"What is so funny?"

"We need a bigger bed," she snickered.

"But the shower was just the right size, was it not?"

"That shower…that shower was…"

"Perfetta?" he asked.

"Yes, it was perfect Luca. You are amazing and perfect in so many areas. I can easily fall in love, but will I regret it one day. Can you promise me that we will not have a messy break up and I will experience feelings of failure at yet another relationship?"

"Wow, you need not get so deep in your feelings Antonia. Love is simple. Either you love or you do not."

"Love is not simple Luca."

Chapter 16: Hidden Wine

Luca swept his legs from under the sheets and walked around the room to find his clothes; Antonia admired his beautiful buns as he entered the bathroom. The phone rang and Antonia recognized the number: it was Bethany, her travel agent. Antonia answered the phone as she wrapped the quilt around herself.

"Great timing, Bethany," she whispered.

"I can barely hear you, Antonia. Your message sounded desperate. Is everything okay?"

"Yes and no. I am unsure of what my next move should be."

"If you need to leave Pico in a hurry, I can find you a flight out of Florence later today. Are you still with Luca and his family?"

"Yes, but you say you can get me a flight today?"

Wondering if Luca could hear her conversation, she went to stand by the door and said things she hoped him to hear. Maybe it was a risky move, but after hearing that Rick was moving on, she needed to know Luca's intentions. "I was thinking of Paris next, Bethany. But umm… I will have to call you back and give you more details and confirm the date. I am loving the area, but I think it is time to leave and not overstay my welcome. I will be in touch. Gotta go. Bye."

"Antonia, wait – "

Antonia hung up the phone just as Luca came out of the bathroom. His expression was sad. He smoothed his hair back with his hand and approached her.

"I do not want you to leave and I think I showed you how much I care about you. I expressed my love for you."

"Luca, I don't know what to say. I care about you too," she explained. Then shuffling over to the bed, she sat down placing her hands in her lap. "Does everyone in your family know… I mean… about my secret?"

Luca chuckled slightly then sat beside her on the bed and began putting on his shoes. "The only family that knows are the ones who may be needed to help you. As far as the secret, the shouting at the grove today was about the secret I am keeping from you."

"I don't understand," Antonia said, furrowing her brows.

"My family is worried I am getting close to you. They see I have strong feelings, so they are concerned. And they have good reasons."

"What reasons?"

"Just promise me you won't run off to Paris or back to the states somewhere and I will explain it all. Now we have to go to dinner with the family and celebrate the harvest. It is important to me. Then if you are still uncomfortable and want to get away, I will take you to see another part of Italy. Maybe Milan, where my grandfather is from. My father's cousin Aldo lives there. He is my Godfather. Or maybe by the coast or perhaps Sicily. Just not another country. Not now. I want you to be with me forever, Antonia."

"Will I be safe?"

"You are always safe with me. We will take a long week, shut up in a beautiful villa overlooking the mountains or hotel if you prefer, and I will tell you everything. However, it goes both ways. You must tell me all about what happened in Rome. We will make a safe, intelligent plan after we have shared all our secrets," said Luca with a serious smile.

"A plan for our future?"

"If that is what we both want."

Antonia had lost hope of ever having a normal relationship. The definition of normal was only a fantasy that she conjured up as a child. Life was way harder than childhood dreams. What if the things she wanted in one relationship can come true in another? She did not want to regret the chances she never took. One bad choice or bad relationship should not jade her from trying again.

After a few glasses of wine with the family, Luca and Antonia returned to the villa and began making plans to get away and sort out their relationship. Hope was finally in the air and her face seemed to shine. Sitting cross-legged on the bed like she did in college, Antonia picked up her phone and paper, ready to make a plan.

"I can admit that I am looking forward to getting away with you, Luca. It is exciting. Once we decide where we are going, I will call Bethany and she can make us a reservation."

"No, Antonia, do not tell anyone. I want to be hidden from everyone. As a matter of fact you don't have to even bring your phone with you," said Luca.

"Well, I have to bring my phone. I mean, what if the ranch needs me. I don't feel comfortable leaving my phone. Where will we stay?"

"You are starting to think too much, Antonia. You need to rid yourself of this outsider mentality, like you do not deserve to be loved. I told you when you are with me, you are safe. I will take care of everything. Do you trust me?" asked Luca.

There is that word again, trust. I trusted Wade and was left by a dumpster.

Antonia got quiet. It is not as though she hadn't heard those exact words before. Luca sensed her hesitation and turned to her. "Bring whatever you want if that makes you comfortable. Now get some sleep; we are leaving at the crack of morning light before the rest of the family awakes. This is going to be fantastic and possibly epic."

"Epic?"

"Isn't that the word they use nowadays?"

"Maybe if they are talking about a Cat 5 hurricane," laughed Antonia.

Antonia did not sleep well. She felt like she was on the merry-go-round again, going in circles. In college she was independent. Wade had taken her down the rabbit hole into submission. She gained her freedom from Wade and set out to travel. Independent again. Now Luca was acting like he wanted to control her life. Does having a successful relationship have to mean losing your voice, giving up your own opinions and giving in to the man's desires?

Get off the merry-go-round, Antonia.

Antonia packed everything she brought on the trip and slipped her cell phone in her handbag. Luca brought the car around and put her bags in the trunk.

"I see you packed light. When I said bring whatever makes you comfortable, I didn't mean all your possessions," chuckled Luca, shaking his head.

"I am comfortable bringing it all. Everything I own fits in these two suitcases."

"Okay, I get it. Let's bring it all. Now I am no longer your official tour guide Antonia, I am your Italian lover, so get in the front seat," he demanded sensually. He playfully slapped her bum as she slipped by him and into the seat.

As Luca started the car, he reached over and squeezed Antonia's thigh just above the knee.

"First stop, Milan. There I have arranged to stay with family. And for your delight and love of history, we will visit the *Santa Maria delle Grazie* church and convent. Holy Mary of Grace Church is world known for housing the Last Supper Painting by Leonardo da Vinci."

"Oh Luca, that is wonderful! I always wanted to see it. We will be able to get close to it?"

"It covers an entire wall of the church, so yes you will see it and you can purchase a copy for a souvenir if you like. You Americans love your trinkets."

The drive up to northern Italy was thrilling, including the magnificent sunrise that met them halfway there. Luca decided to stop over at a small café for coffee and Antonia took advantage of the break for a restroom stop. After a few minutes alone in the bathroom, Antonia took out her phone and hesitantly sent a quick text to Bethany. Her thoughts were that someone should know. In her opinion, Luca skipped over a few steps while planning to take her away on a trip. Pole-vaulted, actually. "Why is it so dang hard to completely and unequivocally trust someone?" she whispered. As she tapped her foot and bit her lip, she sent the text:

Bethany, I am fine. Just wanted to keep you informed of my location. We are visiting Milan. I thought someone should know where I am. I trust you will keep it confidential unless...

Antonia hesitated then finished... *"Unless I need help."*

Feeling pleased with herself for making the decision, she slipped her phone back into her handbag and started to exit the bathroom. Pausing, she pulled out her phone again and without hesitation, she sent the same text to Rick at the ranch then walked out of the bathroom feeling confident.

I am no longer anyone's child, I have no parents to worry about where I am. At least someone will worry about me.

Heading back into the main dining area she received notification of a text back from Bethany.

"Milan, got it. If you need a way out I can help."

Once she was back in the dining room, Antonia noticed Luca talking to an older gentleman dressed in a black suit smoking a cigar. Thinking it was odd that he knew someone every where they went, she walked slowly as to not interrupt their conversation. Luca introduced the man as an old friend of the family. The man left with only a grin and nod towards Antonia.

Luca acted like it was a normal occurrence to not introduce someone by name and Antonia decided to let it go. There was no reason to challenge him as they were having such a lovely day; even so, she was subconsciously filing it all away in her brain, the human file cabinet.

The rest of the day was spent driving through the beautiful countryside avoiding major roads until they reached the city of Milan. Antonia pushed aside the worry of not having a reservation and decided to see how things pan out. The scenery in Italy was never horrid and took her mind to a happier place every time.

What could possibly happen?

Luca pulled the car into the driveway of a very nice two-story home. He stopped at the gate and pushed a few numbers on the keypad. Soon someone came over the speaker.

"It's Luca." Was all that was said and the gates opened with a clang. Luca pulled the car to a circular drive, stopping in front of massive, intricately ornate doors. On each side of the doors were tall cypress trees, native to Italy. As they exited the car, a robust man came out to greet them. He embraced Luca, patting him on the back and kissing his cheek.

Antonia waited and watched, admiring how friendly and physical Luca's family was. Her parents hugged her routinely, of course, but this was quite the expression of love she was witnessing. Antonia had met one aunt her whole life and that was her mother's sister. Aunt Connie was a stout woman who had a sweet disposition and a heart of gold. She sent Antonia gifts for Christmas every year until she passed away from emphysema when Antonia was a young teenager. Antonia's father grew up in a boys' home. He never knew if he had siblings or not and never sought to find out. Watching Luca with his family made Antonia smile.

Soon the man who greeted Luca turned toward Antonia and held his arms open. Antonia glanced at Luca then stepped in for the biggest welcoming hug ever.

"I am Aldo, the cousin to Armando who is Luca's father. I have heard about this pretty lady coming with Luca, but you are even more beautiful in person. Welcome to my home."

"Thank you, it is a beautiful home," said Antonia.

Antonia was in awe of the marble floors throughout the foyer with magnificent chandeliers and the artwork covering the walls. Luca escorted Antonia to the room they would be staying in upstairs. She ran her hand along the banister feeling the woodwork.

"This place is gorgeous, Luca. What do they do for a living?" she asked.

Luca never glanced at Antonia, he just kept climbing the stairs carrying her luggage until they reached the second floor. Luca stopped and snapped his head to look at her with a serious face, puzzling Antonia. "Don't ask questions like that. Do you think somehow they don't deserve nice things? Don't ask questions," said Luca.

"I was only making conversation, I didn't mean – "

Luca cut her short. "I know what you meant, Antonia, and my answer still stands. Don't ask."

Luca placed the luggage in the room at the foot of the bed then immediately went to the windows and pulled the curtains shut. Luca pulled out a suit jacket and began dressing, fiddling with his tie. Antonia sat on the king size bed gazing around the room at the opulence. The wallpaper had cherubs and there was gold crown molding all around the top of the high ceilings. She had the feeling of being in a palace.

As Luca fastened his cufflinks, he appeared nervous and anxious. "As long as we are staying here, the curtains remain closed. If you need light, turn on a lamp. Now, how do I look?"

"You look handsome, of course. Why are you so dressed up?"

"We are expected to dress for dinner, Antonia. Rest up then put on a nice evening dress and I will call you when dinner is served. I am going to visit a little while with our host in private."

Antonia crossed her legs and leaned back staring up at Luca. "Luca dear, I don't have a nice evening dress. I don't even own one anymore. I brought casual but classy clothes because I AM ON VACATION!" She managed to say while gritting her teeth. Antonia stood up in front of Luca and straightened his tie. "Besides, if you would have told me I needed a nice dress for dinner, I would have bought one before we arrived. Why does dinner have to be fancy, anyway?"

Luca looked down at the ground shifting his weight. There was clearly something he was not telling Antonia and she could sense it. "Okay, I might as well tell you. There will be a few important people at dinner, and I wanted to make a good impression. You are beautiful to me, and I want everyone to notice your beauty as well."

"Go on, there is more. I can see it in your eyes. Who are these important people, Luca?"

"There may be, possibly, or not... an ex-girlfriend of mine here tonight for dinner. She has remained a friend of the family, so they invited her. Her name is Simone."

"I see. Okay, with this big expensive house, I assume they have a housekeeper of some kind. So you send her up here, and don't worry darling, I will be show-off worthy."

With a quick kiss on the cheek, Luca was out the door. Antonia estimated she had two hours before dinner, so she started with hair and make up. She was determined to be as beautiful as possible. Picking up her hairbrush she started to work a hair miracle.

By the time Antonia was called down to dinner, she had on a beautiful dark blue satin dress, black high heels and had put on her best pearls. The pearls were a souvenir and yet a reminder from Wade that she could be strong in spite of any man who tried to control her – or throw her out by a dumpster. The housekeeper named Sierra not only found a dress in one of the guest bedrooms but gave her all the dirt on Simone, the ex-girlfriend, as they shared a bottle of wine from the hosts' wine cellar. As Antonia descended the marble stairs for dinner, the slit in the skirt of the dress revealed her beautiful legs and all eyes were on her. The smile on Luca's face let her know he was pleased. Simone was a beauty, but *she* had chosen to wear casual slacks, leaving Antonia's beauty room to shine.

Chapter 17: Stolen Wine

It was morning with only a slight sliver of light peering in from the curtains Luca had shut so tight. Waking up in a dark room gave the feeling of stormy weather. In Texas, it gets black as night when a storm rolls in. Antonia reached for the bedside lamp just as Luca entered the room.

"Did I miss breakfast?"

"Yes, but I brought some toast and coffee for you. After you are dressed, we can walk the grounds and see the gardens and statues," said Luca.

"Will we be staying here another night? I need to return the dress."

"Yes, but just one more night. Our hosts asked if I could do a favor for him and take a package to Salerno. You will like it there, very casual. It is a port city built on the ruins of a Roman temple. There we will meet another family member who will take the package on to Sicily," said Luca yawning. "That is what he wanted to talk to me in private about when we arrived. I do many trips, so it is something for you to get used to."

"So we are going to travel south?"

"Yes. I have to do this favor. You will like it, I told you. It has some sparkling beaches and sailboats. Is that a problem?"

"No, I just thought since we are so close to France and Austria here that maybe we could go out of Italy. Maybe see another country, or perhaps Paris?"

Luca was putting on his shoes with his back to Antonia, but she could sense some rolling of the eyes. "You are so stuck on Paris, Antonia. Yes, it is a nice romantic city but there is so much in Italy you have not seen yet. Get dressed; today we see the Last Supper and see all that Milan has to offer. We have one day then we will be traveling again."

Luca swiveled on the bed facing her. Putting his hands in his lap as though he was straining to keep calm. "I will tell you this much. If we were ever to marry, the family will have to approve of the marriage. Last night you passed the test beautifully. Now we need to prove our loyalty, so get dressed and please do as I say."

Shrugging her shoulders as she began to dress, there was a knock on the bedroom door. From the bathroom she could hear the host asking about a missing bottle of wine. Quickly she slipped over to the bedside table and grabbed the bottle of wine Sierra the housekeeper had brought to the room, the evening before. She quickly hid the empty bottle in the bedside table and crossed her legs casually. Antonia heard the voices getting louder. Then someone or something slammed against the door jam with a loud thud. Antonia crept closer to the door trying to hear the conversation. Luca had his back toward her.

"Godfather, I promise you we did not steal the wine. I will question Antonia, but I am sure it is just a misunderstanding. You will see."

Luca shut the door and turned, surprised to see Antonia standing there with her arms crossed. "Our host is your Godfather?"

"Luca took a deep breath and put his hands in his pockets.

"Yes, Italians have big families and yes everyone has a Godfather. I told you this. Don't read too much into it. Right now, I really need you to listen. Did you happen to take any wine? I have to ask."

Antonia walked to the bedside table and opened the drawer, pulling out the empty bottle.

"You mean this bottle?"

"Oh my God, Antonia! Did you take it from the wine cellar? I mean, when were you in the wine cellar?" Luca asked as he started to pace. "Don't you see his family name on the bottle?"

"I wasn't. Sierra brought it when she brought me the dress. We had some wine… well… a lot of wine since the bottle is empty. Actually, Sierra drank a lot of wine while I got dressed, now that I think about it. Why is this relevant?"

"Do I have to spell it out for you, Antonia?"

"Spell what out? What is the big deal? It is not like they can't afford it; there was wine flowing at dinner. They filled my glass three times."

"Get dressed now. Pack up everything you don't want to leave behind. We are leaving. Maybe if I do this favor, he will forget about it. Let's go. We are driving straight to Salerno."

"Luca, calm down. I will just go apologize. He won't be mad at me. He likes me. I mean he smiled so much at me last night I thought he was flirting with me," laughed Antonia.

"Hide the bottle and get packed now! It looks like we have to have that talk sooner than later. I can't believe you haven't picked up any clues yet. You met my uncle Ricardo, and now my Godfather? Never mind, we have to leave right now. Please just do it and don't say anything else about the wine."

Ricardo did wear a lot of gold rings, the man in the café smoking cigars and ...oh, my God!

Luca was frantically gathering clothes and throwing them in the suitcases as Antonia slowly lowered to the bed with her mouth gaping open. Her face turned ashen. She stared into space. "Do you mean what I think you mean Luca?"

Luca never stopped to look at her; he just kept packing. Beads of sweat appeared on his upper lip.

"Luca, talk to me, please."

"If I tell them it was Sierra, she could be fired or worse, punished maybe. It is forbidden to go in the wine cellar and she should have known that. Maybe they were setting you up. Maybe Sierra wanted you to look bad. Better if it was me or you who made the mistake of taking the wine. Can you please stop daydreaming and get your... *merda*... shit together?" Luca shouted.

Snapping out of her daze, Antonia began to put on her pants while stuffing her Louis Vuitton luggage with anything she could grab. Looking all around her, even glancing behind as though someone might be there. She sprinted to the bathroom and gathered her toothbrush and comb. She understood the seriousness. Zipping her luggage, she gave the room a final look.

"I am ready," she said in a low tone.

Luca glanced in her direction and gave a silent chuckle, putting his knuckles to his mouth.

"What is it now? This is not funny Luca; you are scaring me. I read books you know."

"You might want to put on a real shirt, not a very cute cotton jammie top." he smirked.

"Oh, I guess I am still digesting what you just hinted at. Forgive me for being nervous! I don't know if this is going to work, Luca. I mean I may not be cut out for this kind of life," she moaned. "I don't want to wake up next to the head of a horse for drinking someone's wine."

"Don't be pessimistic. We both have baggage we bring into the relationship."

"I am not pessimistic. I can handle your baggage, Luca, as long as you don't unpack it on me. Besides, I meant it won't work running out of the house. We should just explain," she frowned.

"The most important thing to this family is loyalty and trust. So trust me when I say we have to go, and by that, I mean right now," he said gritting his teeth. "When it is dark."

Luca and Antonia quietly made their exit from the house and sped off, leaving the beautiful mansion, the Godfather and the empty bottle of expensive wine behind. The orb suspended in the sky we familiarly call the full moon, *la luna piena* in Italian, was shining brightly as if it was showing them the way.

Getting an early start helped them get far enough away to finally relax and stop at a café for something to eat. The server addressed Luca by name, then Luca ordered several things on the menu, not only to allow Antonia to taste them all but also to try and cheer her up. Lastly, he asked if they had any chocolate cake. Antonia hadn't had any of her favorite dessert in a while, so he thought it would please her.

"Just for you Antonia," Luca smiled, reaching for her hand. "See, I remembered."

"Nice gesture, Luca, but the state my life is in right now, I don't even want chocolate cake. My favorite dessert evokes memories. Memories of my Momma, my childhood, celebrations, and pleasure. Right now, I feel sad. Sad that we left because we may be in danger. Sad that Sierra will possibly suffer and sad that I have fallen so deeply in love with you. I say sad because I feel you may be taking me down a rabbit hole. Perhaps It would be best if I just return to the states and my ranch," said Antonia with her voice wavering.

Luca, feeling the sting of rejection, brushed his hair back as he sat back in his chair. His lips pressed together in a slight grimace. In his mind he was weighing the pros and cons. Playing the *'what if?'* game in his head. He began playing with the salt and pepper shakers. Tapping them, pushing them around like toy soldiers.

"You caught me off guard, Antonia. I know it is a tough decision. Strictly from my point of view, I have never found a woman that I believed would understand and not judge. Then you came along looking so carefree and absolutely stunning. So, let's just put it out there: you got into a little trouble. So having a strong physical attraction to you, I let my self fall in love with you emotionally as well. I am sorry if I assumed you not only felt the same way, but would also accept that I got into a little trouble, too. My trouble being my family. We both have secrets."

Antonia leaned back and studied Luca. His handsome face hid an internal conflict. Recalling all the conversations with his family, about long distance relationships and babies, Antonia found an inability to focus. Drawing on her moral beliefs did not jive because she herself had committed a heinous crime. At least now she knew – or thought she knew -- Luca's secret and it could have been worse. The unfairness of the situation was that they both loved each other.

Will love be enough this time?

Sitting in silence gave Luca time to reflect and come up with a possible solution. They needed to talk and be honest. No more beating around the bush. He needed to tell Antonia the full story and hopefully she would explain the reason for what she did. Sitting up straight, Luca waved to the server.

"Can we possibly put all that food wrapped up to go?" asked Luca.

Antonia sat up straight, nodding her approval with a pleased expression. She picked up her handbag and threw it over her shoulder. "Let me use the restroom and I will meet you at the door. Let's get out of here. It's too stuffy."

In the restroom, Antonia phoned Bethany to inform her that she was no longer in Milan and that she would let her know her next stop. "I will need a hotel reservation, less than an hour away from my current location, and reserve it in a different name… Don't ask why… Make it under 'Antonia Romeo." Using Luca's middle name would ward off anyone looking for them. She gave permission for Bethany to keep Rick informed as well, then washed her hands and headed out the door to meet Luca. Again Bethany repeated the words of her last text. "If you need a way out I can help."

"I just need a hotel for now Bethany. We will talk later."

After driving a short distance, the couple spotted the local hotel that Bethany had texted and Luca pulled in. He grabbed the suitcases and Antonia carried all the food. After they were inside, curtains pulled and a chair jammed under the doorknob, they sat down on the bed and spread out all the food. It was a feast. Pasta dishes, olives, fish, bruschetta and… chocolate cake.

"We forgot the wine," Luca observed.

"After last night, I don't think I want wine. Just go buy a couple of sodas from the machine," laughed Antonia.

That night was a memorable late-into-the-night feasting, talking, and sometimes crying night. Antonia sampled all the food and at the same time she spilled her life story to Luca. He responded with a non-judgmental nod and even tissues to dry her tears. They laughed occasionally, too. Especially the part about Wade being naked when she stabbed him and how she believed Marisa would be blamed.

Luca applauded Antonia's courage to trust him with all the details. Antonia also gushed about college and her best friend Jill. She even told him about Rick the handsome ranch hand who was her first kiss at age fifteen.

My lips tingled for an hour after that kiss.

Antonia explained the excitement when she first met Wade and her disappointment in how he treated her, especially when her parents died. Wincing, Antonia explained her anguish of being drugged and waking up beside a dumpster. Luca sat up, looking serious. He punched the mattress aggressively, nearly spilling his soda.

"I would have killed him if you didn't!" Luca said loudly. "I am so sorry you went through all that, my love. I am here now. The second mouse gets the cheese, as they say. No more secrets. It is *finito.*"

"I am not following?"

"The first mouse is killed by the mouse trap but the second mouse comes in and swoops up the delicious cheese."

"Am I supposed to be the cheese in this scenario?"

Luca flashed a smile then stood starting to pace back and forth in front of the king size bed. Knowing that it was his turn next made his nerves jumpy. His shoulders were lowered and loose. He unbuttoned his shirt and let it flow free like a super hero cape as he paced. Clasping his hands behind his back, Luca started the story of the family he was born into.

"My Nona told you she fell in love with a boy from Milan and how his family did not approve of the marriage. Well here is a bit of history. Enrico, my grandfather who married Nona, came from an Italian family with connections to organized crime that originated in Sicily. Nona's father-in-law was named Mario Vitalia. Mario was born in Sicily; he married into another big family and had two children, Enrico and Alma. Mario was deep into the Italian mafia from both sides. In Italian, *Mario* means manly. He was very manly, trust me.

Enrico is who my oldest brother is named after: my grandfather, son of Mario, and why we call him Rico to keep them straight." Luca cleared his throat and took a long drink of his soda before continuing. "Alma, being a female could not run the family business, so it fell to Enrico, my grandfather who fell in love with a girl from Pico, my Nona. He wanted to stay in Pico and he did, taking a chance that love would win. So when the only son wanted to leave the family and marry my grandmother, Nona, it caused a shift in the family.

"A lot of meetings and threats later, love won and Enrico stayed in Pico and married the love of his life. The only way that was accepted was if Enrico promised to have sons and grandsons, and so forth. The family did not speak to my grandfather and he was abolished. However, it was decided that he must choose a son from every generation to "participate" in the family business when they came of age." Luca again paused to make sure Antonia was keeping up.

"I think I follow so far. Enrico and Nona had two sons. Your father, Armando, and Ricardo. I would guess that Ricardo joined the family business and Armando grows olives like his father-in-law," explained Antonia. Nona's parents gave them the olive grove to run.

"How did you know?" asked Luca.

"It was obvious. Ricardo never married. Spoke in Italian most of the time. Kind of creepy, sorry, not sorry, and he was quiet. He actually looked just like all the movies I have seen."

"It is okay. He is always very stiff. You really watch too many movies about the mafia. However, since Ricardo never had children and my father did, then one of my father's sons had to continue in the family business. Do you understand?"

"Oh my! Rico the oldest son becomes the olive farmer and you are the next son? Jesus, Luca! This is heavy. What does that make you do?" Antonia asked as she bit her lip.

Luca took a seat on the bed next to Antonia and pulled her in close. He kissed her forehead and rubbed her back. Pushing her hair behind her ear, Luca began gently kissing her neck. Whispering, he reluctantly gave more details.

"My parents had five children, knowing one of us would be joining the family business. I will be required to do many things. Some I cannot speak of and yes, some things dangerous. I can marry, but I choose to never have children. My uncle Ricardo never had children. It could be dangerous. Mario was murdered in front of his family. It will be little baby Ricky next in line, son of my brother Rico and Aria."

Antonia sighed, trying to comprehend everything Luca was saying. Her family tree looked like a straight line compared to his. When she was younger, Antonia would dream of many things in the future and what it would be like. She once joked with Rick about having many children. In her dreams, her parents would be wonderful grandparents watching the children while she worked as a surgeon. Mother would teach the children how to make quilts and bake a chocolate cake. Having children was never a plan, just expected. Luca made her see what horrifying responsibility would possibly be handed down to them as part of an Italian mafia family.

Family Tree

Mario Vitalia Family
Married Francesca Marrow, had 2 children.
Mario was ambushed at a festival in front of his family.
Francesca was killed a week later while leaving her husband's funeral
Alma Vitalia and **EnricoVitalia**

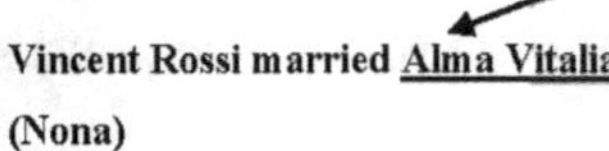

Vincent Rossi married <u>Alma Vitalia</u>   **<u>Enrico Vitalia</u> married Isabella**
(Nona)

Vincent killed at family festival   Enrico killed at family festival
Alma paralyzed by bullet to the spine   Nona lives on family olive farm

(They had 2 children)   (They had 2 children)
1 **Aldo Rossi** married Bonita Fuci   1 **Ricardo Vitalia**
   Lives in Milan, Italy   - never married
2 **Romeo Rossi** died age four   2 **Armando Vitalia**
   Killed by stray bullet   - married Carmella
   At the family festival   (had five children)
                          1 **Enrico Vitalia II** (Rico)
                             Married Aria Lutella
                         2 **Luca Vitalia**
                         3 **Mateo Vitalia**
                             married Rosa
                         4 **Isabella Vitalia**
                             Married Lorenzo Fuci
                         5 **Roberto** Vitalia

Chapter 18: Forbidden Wine

After a decent rest at the motel and feasting on their favorite foods, Luca retrieved some coffee from the hotel lobby. In an attempt to dissect the layers of his cryptic words from the night before, Antonia held back any reply until she could think on it overnight. She thought she was doing a good job hiding her emotions, but he noticed.

Of course, he noticed! He notices everything.

"Do they know?" she asked.

"Does who know what, Antonia?"

"Do Aria and Rico know that their beautiful baby boy will some day be forced into the family business… the mafia business?" asked Antonia.

"Yes, they know. It has never been a secret. Are you worried?"

"I am a bit concerned about you and me. If we…further pursue our relationship…I mean, you did say you loved me. So I assume I can never…, Oh never mind!"

"It is easier if you actually say what is on your mind, Antonia. Spit it out. Today I am an open book. You have no chance of changing my mind, so all decisions are yours to make about what you want. My mind will not change."

"I actually may just spit out this coffee. It is horrid," said Antonia.

"First sodas from a machine and now coffee. I feel so much like an American tourist," Luca teased.

"Very funny. We don't all drink sodas from a machine. Okay, so what would be expected of me, if I was ever to be married to someone in the family business?" she asked confidently.

After all the open spilling of secrets last night, she felt more at ease and safe to talk about anything with Luca. Luca took a sip of the watered down coffee and immediately made a face. "You are right: this is awful coffee. I have been spoiled by Nona and her coffee."

"Since you mention it, will you always live with Nona and have her cook for you?"

Luca's eyes got big and his cheeks slightly blushed. He stood, changing the subject. "We should pack up and head to our destination. However, I must emphasize this, it is a business. We are not the mobsters you see in movies and television. It is an organized business and perhaps not so legal, Import and export is the best way to describe it," said Luca.

Still curious, Antonia casually continued to ask a few questions hoping to learn more as she starting gathering her things. "Does it have anything to do with the olives?"

"Not at all. The small grove is my father and mother's business. Handed down to them from my Nona and grandfather on her side of the family. It is complicated but we work it out as a family. No olives are harmed. I know you are going to ask so, I can simply say some exports are electronic devices and some are weapons, perhaps. We never know what is in the packages we are delivering. Speaking of which, we need to get going to deliver the package we were trusted with. I am so extremely happy we can talk openly about this now."

"Sure, but one last question… Well, I can't really promise there will not be more, but for now I want to know if I... or we, especially me, actually, will be in any danger," Antonia asked.

"Not if we do as we are told," Luca replied. "Now let's get going."

Taking a glance around the room making sure they had everything, Antonia dropped the room key on the dresser and headed for the door. At the last minute she turned back and wiped the key with her shirt, then let it slip out of her shirt to the dresser.

Better get used to not leaving fingerprints anywhere.

Before getting too far down the road toward Salerno, they stopped for better coffee and grabbed a few sandwiches to go. The sandwiches were a surprising delight with salami, mozzarella cheese, pickled onions, and piles of thinly sliced capicola ham.

"Wow! This is the best thing I have eaten since I've been here. No offense meant for your Nona's beautiful pasta, but I *am* from Texas. I am kind of a meat lover."

"No offense taken. I pegged you for a meat lover when you asked about fried chicken," laughed Luca. "When we marry, you can cook anything you want. Until then, you are stuck with Nona's pasta. It is her house."

"About that: where will we live? The villa is small."

"I will be traveling very often. When I am gone, you will need to be with my family. We will live in the villa where you stayed. I will move some of my belongings there. Or we can stay in my room in the main house; your choice," replied Luca.

"Not much of a choice," chuckled Antonia.

Antonia and Luca drove with the windows down enjoying the fall weather as they devoured the yummy sandwiches. With about an hour left to go until they arrived at their drop off point, Luca pulled over to call ahead and verify the hand off. Luca stepped out of the car while making the call, claiming he needed to stretch his legs.

Antonia watched as he walked away then turned walking back before turning around to make the same route. A long stretching pace. A few times it appeared Luca raised his voice and the hand not holding the phone became animated. Worried something was wrong, she pulled out her own phone and sent a quick text to Bethany letting her know exactly where she was via GPS and where she was heading. Antonia used to think the world was safe, but that was a long time ago before college and before she met Luca. She knew that Bethany would forward the text to Rick at the ranch, like they previously discussed.

Satisfied that keeping in touch was the least she could do. Antonia put away her phone as Luca approached the car. Luca retrieved something from the trunk then proceeded to get back in the driver's seat. As he opened the door, Antonia noticed his jacket flap open slightly to reveal a gun in his waistband. His expression held no amusement with the conversation he just had. Antonia decided to let some steam evaporate from his demeanor before reaching over and touching his arm.

"Is everything okay, Luca?" asked Antonia in a calm soothing voice.

"Yes no worries. I just had to explain again about the wine, and it pissed me off. I told Aldo that night that you meant a lot to me. I think he knows how much now and I won't tolerate any mistreatment. Women and children are off limits. It is all good now, nothing to worry about."

"Are you concerned about the package exchange?"

"We are meeting a man they call *il Diavolo*, the devil. I just need to focus right now," he explained. "Put the wine incident behinds us, Antonia. It was his special stash, a forbidden wine. Illegal wine. It is now in the past. He won't retaliate or bring it up again."

"Retaliate? That is a bit impetuous, don't you think?"

"Let it go. You are always safe with me, Antonia. It is settled."

Would he have hurt us in retaliation for drinking a bottle of his forbidden wine?

Antonia felt uneasy even though Luca wanted to drop the subject. She thought the wine was all a mistake at best. Sierra offered the wine as a welcome gift. Still, Luca acting upset and carrying a concealed weapon did not sit well with her. At the ranch, Rick always holstered a gun and so did most of the ranch hands, including her Daddy. They were always prepared for a rattlesnake or coyote bothering the cattle. Antonia had seen, handled, and shot guns before, but this situation seemed extremely different. Carrying a gun to protect oneself from rattlesnakes, is not the same protection a gun means in the mafia.

Antonia tried to make herself relax, but after Luca explained they were meeting 'the devil,' it was sweaty palms and be attentive time. Not having this experience before,

Antonia put on a brave face for the rest of the trip and bit her bottom lip.

I have traded a controlling relationship for an illegal enterprise with no babies in my future.

At the exchange destination, Antonia stayed in the car as Luca got out, grabbed a box wrapped in brown paper from the trunk. Luca walked over to a black SUV and got in the back seat. Antonia felt her heart rate increase slightly and she was frozen staring at the car door, waiting for Luca to emerge. After a few short minutes, Luca opened the door and walked back to the car and they drove off. No lingering or adjusting the radio; he just put it in drive and off they went.

"Do you know what was in the package, Luca?"

"No I don't and it is best not to ask."

"It was certainly bigger than a bread box," Antonia chuckled.

"You will get used to all of this. Mostly I will be making the trips on my own and you will be safe at home with the family. Now let's focus on getting some lunch, okay?"

Antonia had so many questions floating around in her head. She glanced over at Luca thinking how much she adored him. He was a total snack, refined and gorgeous. She had started having deep feelings for him even before she learned of his family business. Still, communication was very important after the whole fiasco with Wade. This time, she wanted to clear the air.

"I do want to find a lovely out-of-the-way place for lunch, Luca, but I also want you and I to communicate. We can't have any secrets if this is going to work. I have questions," she said.

Be brave, ask and be sure.

Luca glanced over at Antonia and flashed a smile, one that made her heart melt. "Okay, how about you can ask all the questions you want until we get to the café, then no more questions until we are alone tonight. I just want to enjoy being with you the rest of the day. Deal?"

"Deal. First question, Is everything you do, or the family does, illegal?"

Luca laughed then straightened up to sit taller in the seat. "We have legal businesses. They are used as a public front for most of the family's wealth. Distribution is up to the head of the family. We have money, in case you are worried, my love. I know you love to shop like most women do. There will be no concerns if you want to buy ten pairs of shoes."

I have my own money, but he doesn't know that.

Luca reached over and gave Antonia a squeeze on the thigh. "My tour guide business is legitimate. Not to say that I don't deliver a package or two while driving all over Italy, but the business is legal. If you are worried about me or anyone going to prison, being in the family business is a prison, just a different type of prison," he laughed.

"Interesting way to think about it. Okay how much further to the café?" Antonia asked.

"Does that count as your next question?" Luca chuckled. "Not too far to the cafe."

"Not fair!" she laughed.

Antonia wiggled in the seat so she could face Luca. She wanted to see his face while asking questions. She reached over stroking his hair then followed the line of his jaw with her finger. Luca lowered his eyes while raising a brow. "Don't make me pull this car over and take you to the back seat. It has been a while."

Putting her hands in her lap Antonia continued. "Okay. When you used the word retaliation, what exactly do you mean?" she asked.

"I will tell you a story. A man was in front of a crowd of people attempting to cross the street in a busy downtown plaza. Let's just say Rome. Waiting for the light to change, he seems to step out in the traffic prematurely resulting in his head hitting the pavement. A truck runs over his head, popping it like a melon. Was he pushed or was it death by accident?"

"It depends on who was in the crowd behind him, I suppose."

"After the man is smashed by the truck tire, the crowd disperses. There are the few who would scream and make a scene, calling for ambulance services, creating a confusion. Bottom line, no witness means it will be called an unfortunate accident. In the movies there are drive-by shootings, blood pouring in the street, and slit throats. That is a rare occasion and reserved for severe cases of disrespect or mutiny. Here we are called *la famiglia*, because we are family. Blood related, generation to generation, or by marriage."

Luca slowed the car looking for his turn to find the small café. Determining he was turning on the correct road, he smiled and reached over to caress Antonia's cheek. Antonia faced forward trying to understand the meaning of his cryptic story. Ignorance can be bliss when it comes to having a family member in the mafia, but she had a quest to never be ignorant when it came to love, ever again.

Pulling in to the parking lot, Antonia suddenly recognized that the cars all seemed familiar. Most were black Mercedes. Some small expensive-looking sports cars were dotted in among the sedans and SUVs. The small off-the-beaten-path cafés that Luca frequently took her to appeared to have the same clientele with the occasional tourist sprinkled in. Luca always seemed to be familiar with the owners and there were customers as well that knew him everywhere.

Luca unfastened his seatbelt and leaned over to kiss Antonia. "Your brow is furrowed like your mind is busy buzzing away. Thinking too much, my love. You can ask more questions tonight if you must, but for now let's enjoy some wine that is not forbidden and magnificent food that is not take out."

Antonia managed a smile releasing the tension in her face. She grabbed at Luca's lapel pulling him closer for a lingering kiss, teasing him. "Just one last question before we go in?"

"You are killing me, acting so hot and sexy, but go ahead. I am an open book to you, Antonia, and only to you."

"I do not mean to tease, well, maybe a little, but I will make it up to you tonight with a long lovemaking session, I promise. I am just curious about all these little cafés you seem to take me to. Are they random? Or do you just know all the good places to eat in Italy?" she asked.

"You have incredible discernment, my love."

"I am not just a pretty face."

"What was it that tipped you off? The cars in the parking lot or the familiar greetings from all when we enter?" said Luca.

"Both."

"Let us just say you have noticed legal family businesses. All well-run by families, distant cousins by blood, or a family we have a connection to. Alliances through marriage are a part of our world. Plus they have the best home-cooked food in all of Italy in my opinion. Now let's go in and eat, I am famished." Luca paused, looking at Antonia with a lingering grin while winking one eye. "Unless of course you want to take me up on the offer to crawl into the back seat?"

"Food first, then we go home. The seat belt was poking me in my back side last time if I remember correctly," Antonia laughed. "I still have the bruise to prove it!"

"I will be grateful if you allow me to rub and kiss that bruise," Luca teased.

Antonia waved him off, shaking her head as she got out of the car. Luca took her hand as they entered the Café La Rosa. Everyone greeted Luca as soon as they walked in the door.

This is one big family.

Chapter 19: Family Wine

Antonia was excited to be greeted by most of the guests in the café. She likened it to a time when, after church in Texas, they had dinner on the grounds. Everyone had food and everyone talked to everyone. There were always a few church ladies who gathered in a corner to gossip, men standing around sneaking a cigarette, and children running helter-skelter oblivious to everything except playing and chasing each other.

After pulling a few tables together, the café owners brought out plenty of large pasta entrees and bottles of their family wine. Luca introduced her to several people, excluding a handful of men seated in the back booths. A few of the wives came and sat near Antonia while Luca visited the secretive men in the back to share a cigar. Children ran inside the café oblivious to the family business and lifestyle they were born into.

Funny how young children around the world begin life so innocent and unaware.

The food was delicious and the atmosphere was perfect. Almost too perfect. Antonia chatted and smiled while cooing over babies and complimenting the food. She got the impression that most of the wives had no career outside of the home. The older women almost appeared shocked that Antonia had nearly completed medical school. The younger wives were obviously envious and asked tons of questions about America and college. It was not that Italian women didn't go to college, it was the general consensus that mafia wives did not go to college and have a career outside of the home. This made Antonia a little uneasy. Luca had already made it clear he did not want children.

I will never be a stay at home mom, so what will I do?

After plenty of food and a few too many glasses of wine, Antonia began to look around for Luca. Ready to go home to the villa and have additional conversations, Antonia rose from her chair and started to wander to the back of the café where the men were gathered. As she walked past the door to the kitchen she felt an arm on her shoulder. Turning, she stopped and was surprised by Mateo, Luca's younger brother.

"Mateo, I did not know you were here also?"

"I have been sitting in the back with a few of the more experienced men. Women do not join the men at these gatherings. They usually visit with the other wives. It is tradition. Were you looking for Luca?" asked Mateo. "It is not wise to bother him."

Antonia and Mateo had not had the pleasure of too many conversations. Aside from introductions and short greetings during the plucking of the olives, Antonia had never stood this close, much less talked to Mateo or any of Luca's brothers. Mateo had the same hair and eyes as Luca but he was much taller and thinner. She assumed he had intelligence we recognize as most basic from the way he put his sentences together. Antonia tilted her head back to look up at him.

"Are you trying to tell me I don't dare to look for Luca as some kind of threat? Or is it forbidden to walk around on my own?" said Antonia.

Feeling quite liberal after her glasses of wine she stepped closer to Mateo, getting in his personal space. Challenging him. Recognizing Mateo as the brother that started yelled at Luca, asking questions about her in the olive grove. Placing her hands on her hips she stood up straight trying to appear taller.

"In America, women have just as many rights as men do. I don't need your approval. Are you aware of that, Mateo?"

With a straight face and never breaking his stare, Mateo answered abruptly. "I strongly suggest you stay right here. Sit down and have some coffee, or maybe even a breath mint, while I go and inform Luca you are ready to go home."

Mateo never smiled or even flinched as he stepped past Antonia and disappeared into the back of the café. Antonia put a hand up to her mouth trying to smell her breath. A little embarrassed by her own words to Mateo, she immediately regretted it. She was educated and, yes, in love with a mafia boss, but she was not a wimp. Furious, she stormed toward the restroom. As she entered a stall, someone entered the restroom behind her. Turning to see who followed her, It was Mateo's fiancé Rosa. Antonia had only met her at the family dinners. She was a dark haired beauty but very young. As Antonia exited the stall she straightened her shoulders trying to restrain herself from any further outburst.

"Hello Rosa. Tell me, is Rosa an Italian name?"

Rosa laughed and leaned back on a porcelain sink crossing her arms. "Hello to you as well, Antonia. I was named after the saint, Rosa de Lima. I assure you that I am all Italian. Unlike you, of course. Antonia is a Spanish name, is it not?" Rosa asked.

Sensing a little hostility, Antonia again regretted her words. "I am sorry, Rosa. I have had way too much wine. My words keep coming out of my mouth all bitchy. And no, it is a Texas name. I was named after the town our family ranch is in."

"I understand. Maybe you are feeling like you do not fit in to this family. But I assure you, that if Luca accepts you then we will all accept you, no worries."

"Accept me or tolerate me?" laughed Antonia as she washed her hands.

"I don't think you understand where Luca ranks in this family. I heard he has told you some things about the family, but I don't think he told you all of it. Luca is next in line.

Ricardo his uncle even takes orders from Luca. Even Aldo, his godfather, takes orders from Luca. Soon he will be the head of this family. I am here to give you some advice. Don't ask too many questions and perhaps put the American idea of where women stand out of your vocabulary," said Rosa.

Antonia stood there looking at her self in the mirror, then turned to face Rosa still leaning on the sink. "Rosa, you seem like a smart woman. What do you hope to do after you marry Mateo? Will you have babies and keep the house like a good wife?"

"Mateo wants us to have a big family. That is one thing I love about him. I heard your conversation with the other wives about college. I, too, planned on going to college and becoming a school teacher, until I met Mateo. I am not sad about it. It is what I want now," said Rosa.

She could have both a family and a career, in my opinion.

Antonia suddenly felt overwhelming sadness and did not quite understand why. She leaned on the sink and allowed the tears to flow watching each tear hit the white porcelain and enter the drain.

Down the proverbial drain, just like most of my dreams.

Rosa retrieved some tissue to wipe her eyes. "I hope I did not upset you, Antonia."

"No, it was nothing you said. I miss my parents. I miss college and I miss Texas. I have no siblings, no sisters to talk to and talking to you and all of the wives made me feel like I have a family again. But, I… I am expected to give up all my dreams for the future. Change everything about me. I want these to be happy tears, Rosa. But still I feel something is missing."

"Well when you and Luca marry, we will be sisters-in-law. We can talk and raise our children together. Let me give you a hug, sister. Welcome to *la famiglia*."

It was apparent to Antonia that Luca had never expressed to the entire family that he never wanted children of his own. There was no need dwelling on it any longer. After hugging it out, the two women exited the bathroom. Immediately Antonia spotted Luca, who came to be by her side. Taking his arm and pulling him close, she whispered asking him to please take her home. Luca raised a hand to wave good-bye and hurried to the door.

The beginning of the car ride back to the family olive farm was quiet. Luca loosened his tie and turned on the radio allowing Antonia time to be the one to start the conversation. Antonia turned toward the window and noticed the dark cloudless sky with only the moon shining brighter than the stars. The temperature was turning cooler as the days of fall would soon become winter in Italy. Most of the festivals and harvests had passed. The gatherings and celebrations at the villages and café's were a great deterrent from her inner thoughts filed away in the back of her mind. She had practically forgotten about stabbing Wade and even medical school. Only when she was alone with her thoughts did she revisit her dreams of being a surgeon. Luca, not being fond of the silence between them, turned off the radio and reached for Antonia's hand.

"I cannot fix any problems between us if you do not talk to me, Antonia."

Antonia struggled for the right words to say, hoping to not upset Luca. The chill in the air gave her an idea. "I do not have a winter coat and it is getting colder now. The weather is changing. Maybe I should go shopping tomorrow. Maybe take Aria or Rosa with me."

I lied, but it was for the best.

"Italy's winter is generally mild along the coasts and the south. Only cold and snowy inland especially in the northern mountains. We will make sure you have proper clothing, Antonia."

"I want to shop and choose the items I need. I just need some time to window shop or eat lunch at a random place I pick to eat. Is there a problem with just us girls shopping and having a day out?"

"I have to take a little trip tomorrow, Antonia. I think you may need a good night sleep and we shall discuss this in the morning," said Luca.

"I love you dearly, Luca, but I do have a drivers license and a passport that says I can rent a car and drive in Italy. I am getting closer to thirty than I care to think about. Much older than your brothers wives and girlfriends and my internal clock is ticking so loud it sounds like a barrage of cannon fire!"

Confused, Luca looked over at Antonia trying to understand. "What does that mean, Antonia? I don't understand what it is that you want. If you want a cannon, I will buy you a cannon."

And this is why I fell in love with this crazy Italian.

Antonia shook her had then buried her face in her hands and mumbled. "No, Luca, I don't want you to buy me a cannon. It means I want to go shopping. I just want to go shopping."

As they arrived at Luca's family home, Antonia headed straight for the villa and Luca excused himself to go talk to his parents. Antonia welcomed the time alone after spending most of the day surrounded by more of the family. Taking a hot shower made it easy to drift off to sleep once her head hit the pillow.

In the morning, Antonia was awakened by the light pouring into the room making her head throb. Opening the windows for fresh air, she heard the sound of birds chirping loudly from the trees surrounding the villa which is always a good sign that winter is approaching. In an attempt to stretch her tired muscles, she looked around for Luca, listening for the shower. The pillow next to her was empty and cold as if Luca had never come to bed. Antonia lumbered into the bathroom and splashed water on her face not wanting to look in the mirror. Puffiness around the eyes from crying and redness from too much wine was not an early-morning gift.

Standing in the middle of the villa, Antonia tried to envision spending the rest of her life living here. The cupboards were empty, the fridge was barren except for a half empty bottle of wine and there were no small appliances. No coffee pot or toaster. Nothing to allow any sort of independent living for a married couple.

"If I am to live here, there has to be changes. I am not tromping over to the main house every morning for a cup of coffee," she snorted.

Throwing on casual clothes and a heavily worn gray sweater she found in the closet, Antonia headed for the main house with her pocketbook over her shoulder. Cutting through the kitchen and out to the courtyard where she heard voices, Antonia was not surprised to see all the women sitting around the big wooden family table in the courtyard.

She felt a little uneasy standing there with her hands on her hips hoping nothing offensive popped out of her mouth.

I feel like I live in a group home.

Nona stood up greeting Antonia and offered coffee. She scooted a plate of assorted breads her way and waved for Antonia to have a seat joining the family.

"Listen, I understand the closeness of the family and don't get me wrong, I think it is lovely. However, I am having a hard time waking up, putting on clothes and trekking over to the main house just to have coffee in the morning. I mean there is not even a toaster in the villa," Antonia remarked. "Will anyone mind if I purchase a few small appliances and at least stock my fridge with juice and sandwich meat?"

Nona walked around the table and stood beside Antonia putting her hand on the small of her back. "Please sit down Antonia. There is coffee and juice on the table. No need to make a fuss."

Running her hands through her hair then down her face in frustration, Antonia turned toward Nona. "Thank you, Nona, but you don't understand what I am trying to say. I want to make my own coffee, in my own villa, in my own coffee pot. I guess what I am trying to say is I want to go to town and shop. I don't even know whose sweater I am wearing. So, who is coming with me?" Antonia said. She looked at Rosa who immediately looked down at her coffee cup. Then at

Aria who was bouncing baby Ricky up and down on her knee.

Ricky is so sweet looking he may be made of candy.

"No one wants to go?" she asked. Throwing her hands up in the air like she was giving up, Antonia pulled out a chair and sat down. Swiping a few tears away in frustration she finally poured herself a cup of coffee. Staring at the table and her cup of coffee she took a deep breath.

"Does anyone know where Luca is this morning, because I don't," she said gritting her teeth.

Rosa looked up from her coffee and met with Antonia's eyes. "Luca and Mateo left early this morning and before you ask, no, I do not know where. I don't bother asking anymore."

Antonia drank her coffee in silence as the women began to chat and baby Ricky babbled. When she finished, she stood up and looked at Nona.

"Is there a truck available that I can drive, I have a license."

"Well I should ask Armando, Luca's father. He is just outside in the garden," said Nona.

"Thank you, I will go look for him. I will also like to know if there is a library in Pico. I need to do some research on colleges in the area."

"Yes, *si*. Armando, Luca's father will tell you the way," smiled Nona.

Antonia found Armando near the first row of olive trees inspecting the branches.

"It is going to be a good crop next season. What brings you out to the groves this morning, Antonia?"

After Antonia started pouring out her need to have some independence, Armando put his arm around her and guided her to his truck. Opening the door for her he paused and offered her his handkerchief then went around to the drivers side.

"You no worry, I need something from town as well. Sometimes I drive into town just to have a little break from the olives and the family. Those women can just chirp, chirp, chirp like little birds. You come with me today," he said.

Antonia knew Armando, Luca's father, had offered to drive to town claiming that he needed something just to get her to calm down. They climbed into one of the trucks used during olive season and were on their way. Rolling down the window for a breeze, the smell of the olives still teased her senses. The cool air on her face felt invigorating. Antonia threw her hand out the window like she did as a child riding with her own dad, allowing the wind to catch it and toss it around as she struggled to keep her arm straight.

"Antonia, I am glad we get to spend a little time together. We haven't had a chance to talk just you and me."

"I am glad, also. Really, I am. I have felt so anxious lately. I mean, I love it here and I love Luca and the entire family so really I don't know why I feel so jittery," she started to ramble. "I feel out of place sometimes and I have to remind myself I am in a different country, a different experience with different people. I can learn to adjust, that is not the problem. The question is do I want to adjust and change?"

It is not always difficult to change. I changed my life to grow olives. I accept the fact that my wife stays tucked away in her office writing books. Change can be good or it can be too difficult," he explained.

"I can understand your point Armando. Some changes enhance your life adding things you had not thought about or experienced. I am having a hard time deciding if it is a life changing change I will regret or is it simply giving in just for the sake of being in love?"

"Your world is so big. You have done many things and tried many things. I think in your head you had a whole life planned. Am I right?"

"Yes, I did. I am sorry if it seems I am complaining," said Antonia.

"I do not fear complaining. I see in you a strong person trying to figure things out. Trying to make choices and changes that you may or may not be able to live with. My father before me had to make hard choices but he stood his ground. His family was very angry with his life choices. Has Luca told you enough to where you understand some of what I am telling you?"

"Oh yes, of course. We talked quite a bit about the family history. That is what has me perplexed. If only I had met him sooner or if he was born in a different line in *la famiglia*."

Looking over at Armando as they drove to town talking about choices, Antonia could see where the men in the family got their ruggedly handsome looks. Armando still had a head of hair with silver streaks beginning to take over the jet black hair of his youth. She noticed his hands were strong and rugged as he gripped the steering wheel. In his white bib overalls he could easily pass as a Texas farmer.

"I was where you are once, Antonia. I had to make choices and change my entire life, too. It made my family very angry but luckily my brother Ricardo helped me. I owe my life to him. Do you understand?"

"Yes, Luca explained. He looks up to you and his uncle Ricardo. That is why he doesn't want to have children of his own. He never wants them to have to make a choice."

"I am wise, Antonia. My brother, Ricardo, may have taken on the family business while I stay with the olives, but I knew what the cost was. That is why he is so close to my children and visits often. It is important to me that he feels close to us. Luca will feel close to his brother's children as well. It is an exchange. He won't be a father but he will be the best uncle."

Leaving the unpaved road, Armando turned on to the smooth road heading toward town. The old pick-up truck began purring along as he shifted the gears. Antonia could see the buildings of Pico come into view and she was excited to get away from the farm hoping to have a fresh outlook on her situation.

Sometimes a change of scenery is all you need to see things clearly.

Armando glanced over when he pulled up to the stop sign. "You are intelligent and you must not forget that you are important, too, Antonia." Armando cleared his throat and turned on his blinker to head toward the town square.

"I have never regretted my choice to marry Carmella and stay on to take care of my parents' olive farm. Ricardo has said he does not regret taking my place in the family business. It worked out how it was supposed to. It is rare in this family to be able to choose your life. What one does can always have an affect on someone else. It could bring the whole family down, so it is a delicate balance," said Armando.

"I completely understand the ripple effect," said Antonia. "What decisions I make here in Italy will affect my life forever and those I left behind in Texas."

"Just remember this, the most painful thing is losing yourself in the process of loving someone else. If you do not want this life, then leave Italy before you bring harm to the family or yourself."

Chapter 20: Picnic Wine

Luca's father continued to talk as he drove, pointing out different points of interest around Pico and occasionally throwing in a reference to the family business. He parked the truck in Pico's historic district and led Antonia down a cobblestone lane with arched passageways. Beautiful, colorful flowers were growing through craggy piles of stones and on the sides of the buildings in this medieval village. Armando explained how the piles of stones were still here where they fell after World War II bombing raids. Antonia loved the beauty as well as the history behind it all. After a short distance Armando guided her into a small village grocery where he purchased wine, cheese and bread.

"We will go to the castle at the peak and have a typical Italian lunch," said Armando.

"I didn't know there was a castle."

"Yes at the highest point. That is where Pico gets its name. From there you will see Liri valley and the surrounding hills, which are covered with olive trees and grape vines as far as the eye can see. This is our history and our culture. Not the family business that my brother and my son Luca are engaged with. Come, you will see," Armando said leading the way.

Reaching the peak, Antonia looked out at the mountains to the east and the valley below. It was breathtaking and indescribable. Antonia helped set out the small blanket on the grass as Armando broke off some bread and handed her a piece with a chunk of cheese.

"I often come here to enjoy the beauty surrounding my village and remember why my father, Enrico, decided to defy his family and marry my mother, Luca's Nona. When my father died, I vowed to stay on the land and harvest the olives as tradition. My brother Ricardo wanted more excitement in his life so he chose to join the family business."

"The Italian Mafia?"

"Well yes, but I prefer to just call it 'family business'. I am not ashamed of it, but the more I come here to think about it all, I am glad I made my choice," said Armando. "So is my wife Carmella, Luca's mother. Although she finds it fascinating to write about, she also loves our life and our olive trees."

"I don't see Carmella often. She has been at a few family dinners but she leaves before I get a chance to get to know her. I don't remember her at the olive harvest either. If she is to be my mother-in-law, I suppose I should at least have a few conversations with her," frowned Antonia.

"Oh, I see. Luca did not tell you? Carmella is a writer. She writes novels about the family business. Or as you say the mafia. Luca disagrees with her talent and they rarely speak. Ricardo, my brother, has no problem with it because he says it is mostly fiction but he does discourage her from using any family names," laughed Armando. "She stays to herself writing in her room."

They continued to enjoy the scenery and the breeze as they ate the bread and cheese while sharing a bottle of wine. It felt good to just enjoy and not think about anything.

"How does the family feel about you buying grocery store wine and not your family's wine?" Antonia asked.

Armando laughed as he threw his head back and finished the bottle. "They do not know. This is my secret and now it is our little secret. Besides, there is no bad wine in Italy."

"I really needed this today, Armando. Thank you for showing me your secret place."

"It is not too much of a secret, Pico has been here for hundreds of years back to the Roman times. However, we all forget sometimes to be still and delight in the beauty that surrounds us in the place we call home," said Armando.

"I miss my home sometimes, but it is not as pretty as Italy. Texas has a different beauty and people I love still live there. I think I understand what you are trying to tell me, I am not just marrying Luca, the future mafia boss, but I am marrying Italy, Pico, and his entire family."

"Yes, but you don't have to give up anything, just add to what you already have," he smiled.

"I understand, but unfortunately I have nothing. My parents are dead. I don't know what I need in my life to make me feel whole. I thought it was a career I needed. Speaking of which, I need or actually I want, to add a few things to the villa. Like a coffee pot for one and some linens perhaps. Can you take me somewhere to purchase all those things?"

"I know just the place. First we must soak in one last look at the view. Breathe the fresh air and smell the rich dirt that creates the best olives in the world," smiled Armando.

After a few minutes, Antonia and her future father-in-law gathered the empty wine bottle and blanket then made the trip back to the truck. Armando drove Antonia around to a few stores so she could purchase all the items she needed – and a few she didn't. After arriving back at the family home, Aria and Rosa came out to greet her and help her carry the parcels into the villa. Soon the three woman were cleaning, decorating and rearranging the villa to look more like a home.

"I love these blankets you bought, Antonia. They will make the bed look inviting as well as the flowers on the new curtains. Luca will think you are nesting," said Rosa laughing.

"I never really thought about what Luca would think, to be honest. I just want to make it comfortable and pretty. I guess I just wanted to make it my own. Is that a bad thing?"

"I think it is wonderful. We both live in the main home. I don't think I could change anything even if I wanted to. It is Nona's home; we just all live in it," commented Aria.

Rosa shrugged her shoulders. "I don't really care about pretty things. Mateo travels too much. It is like we are roommates. He wouldn't notice if I cut my hair."

"I never really asked permission. Luca told me that when we marry, the villa will be our home so I just assumed I can decorate it my own way," said Antonia.

Aria put little Ricky on the floor to crawl so she could help hang the new curtains. As she stood on the chair holding one end of the curtain rod waiting on Antonia, she came up with a plan. She was so excited she nearly lost her balance.

"Wait, so if Luca moves in here, then we can have his room in the main house to create a nursery for Ricky!" Aria shouted. "He needs room to learn to crawl and places for his toys"

Antonia shook her head at Aria's excitement. It was nice having other females to talk to. Sisters were a joy she never knew was missing in her life. She watched as Rosa was kind enough to put her hand up to help Aria so she would not fall.

When they had the curtains all hung the three of them stood back and admired them.

"Do you think Luca will love them?" asked Antonia.

"Well Luca loves you so I am sure he will love the curtains," laughed Rosa.

"They look so nice; it brightens the room. Now I want new curtains," laughed Aria.

"Well, curtains are nice but you have other things to buy before curtains Aria," Rosa said turning to Aria. The two girls giggled looking at each other. Aria put her hand over her mouth as though they had a secret between sisters.

"Let me in on this secret, I thought we were bonding?" Antonia smiled putting on a pouty face. "It is no fun being left out"

Rosa did the turn-the-key to lock her mouth gesture and took a step back. Aria's grin turned to a stone face tight lip. Then shrugging her shoulders she put her hands on her stomach and began to rub them in a circle.

"I am pregnant."

Antonia's mouth opened, then catching herself, she plastered on the biggest grin she could manage. Aria's words reverberated in Antonia's ears. Holding her arms out to embrace Aria she closed her eyes tight demanding them to hold back any tears.

People cry happy tears too, just fake it.

Aria was shorter than the three girls, with long thick wavy hair and a good-sized set of hips. Antonia wondered what it would feel like to have a baby growing inside her body as she hugged Aria so close she could smell her shampoo. She extended her arms to take a step back as if she was inspecting Aria's ability to have a child. Thinking she should have noticed the small bump forming, she couldn't stop staring. Rosa stepped forward and placed a gentle hand on Antonia, breaking the awkward moment.

"It has been fun helping you, Antonia, but we better be getting up to the main house to help Carmella and Nona with dinner. I think it is some sort of seafood pasta tonight. Yum. Will you and Luca be joining us for dinner tonight?" ask Rosa.

Antonia looked at Rosa, secretly glad she broke the silence. Folding her hands across her chest she quickly brushed a small tear that escaped and left a snail trail down her cheek.

"I will probably do that, yes. That sounds good. I am a little tired from a busy day and I planned on using my laptop to search for colleges, so we will see. I don't know when to expect Luca, so I may wait for him," Antonia stammered.

Rosa touched Antonia's arm and smiled. "You join us if you feel up to it. We are family."

Aria picked up her baby Ricky and had him pretend to blow a kiss and Antonia pretended to catch it. Then both women left the villa and shut the door, leaving Antonia to slump into another round of *what-the-hell-am-I-doing- here* while crying into her pillow. Just as she was drifting off to sleep, the phone rang. As she looked at the caller ID she noticed it was Rick from the ranch. She actually had him programmed in her phone as "Rick from the ranch". Through her teen years and up until the day she left college for Chicago, she had him listed in her phone as "My Crush". Antonia answered the phone excited to talk to a familiar voice.

"Rick! I am so happy to hear your voice. What's happening? How is the ranch?"

"Slow down, sweetie! I want to know how you are and why I haven't heard from you in a while," said Rick in his deepest Texas stud voice.

Antonia shivered hearing him being concerned. Rick always warmed her heart in the sweetest way. Mother would tease her that she treated Rick like an old comfortable pair of slippers.

Not wanting to sound too sullen and ill-tempered, Antonia sat cross legged on the bed and took a deep breath. "Oh, Rick! I am so sorry. We have done some more traveling around Italy and today I had a picnic lunch overlooking a beautiful valley of olive trees," she said.

"I am happy for you, Antonia. I bet that was beautiful. I suppose Italy is way prettier than dusty old Texas," Rick replied.

"To be perfectly honest, I miss 'dusty old Texas', Rick. I love it here. I love the people I am surrounded by and the beauty of Italy. I just can't shake the feeling that…"Antonia paused.

"What Antonia? The feeling that you are missing something or perhaps missing me?" laughed Rick. "I know you are not missing mucking out the stalls, are you?"

"No, I mean yes, sort of like I am missing something, but it's not just that. I can't put my finger on it. I want to tell you everything, Rick, but I am afraid to hurt you or have you feel different about me. I have feelings for Luca. Strong feelings. And don't get mad because I never told you about him. He became more than a tour guide to me, Rick," Antonia stammered.

"Antonia, if you are trying to tell me that you are in love with this dude and plan on staying in Italy, just spit it out. This hurts that you can't tell me these things -- in more ways than one! I mean, damn it, Antonia, are you ever coming back?" asked Rick loudly.

Antonia began to sniffle, holding back tears as much as possible. But it was Rick. Her best guy. Her childhood crush and the man she thought she would end up married to and having babies with. The one she confided in as a young girl. Antonia needed his comforting way of reminding her who she was. "Rick, I am confused. One day I am happy and the next day I am fighting back tears, loneliness and even a little fear."

"Fear? Fear should not be a word coming from your mouth, Antonia. I am pacing in the barn right now you got me so upset. Is he a big dude? Did he put his hands on you? What the hell are you afraid of, Antonia?" asked Rick desperately.

"No, he is kind to me, Rick. He is not as tall as you, but that is not important."

"Tell me what it is or I swear I am buying a plane ticket to Italy right now! This cowboy knows how to throw you over my shoulder and carry you home. Remember that!"

"It is his job, his career and worst of all, he doesn't want any children. There, I said it. I always thought I would have children," Antonia said starting to sob.

Rick listened to Antonia cry as he leaned up against the side of the barn. Closing his eyes, he pinched the bridge of his nose. He felt this way once before when Antonia left for college. He kicked the dirt with his boots feeling foolish and helpless. He once tried to move on and forget about Antonia, but every time hope reared its ugly head, he fell for her once again. Swallowing hard, Rick had to dig deep to find words of comfort and still be the friend Antonia needed.

"Antonia, please don't cry. I should have never let you go to Italy alone. It was too soon after you and that prick Wade broke up. You were vulnerable. I don't know what kind of career this dude has, but you should never be afraid. As far as babies are concerned, I don't know what to say except maybe I will tell you a memory I think about often." Swallowing hard, Rick continued. "Do you remember the time we carved our initials in the side of the new barn and your daddy got so mad?"

"Yes, he told you to paint over it."

"While we were painting, I told you I wanted to have five kids and you punched me in the gut and yelled at me. Do you remember what you said?"

"I said I want an even number and five wasn't an even number," Antonia laughed.

Rick took his hat off and smoothed his hair back. Trying not to choke up, he took a cleansing breath. "Antonia, you are not a tree with roots in the ground forever, you are free to move. All I can do is remind you that you are loved here in Texas. Come home. There is nothing to fear here. We don't even have to marry. We can just have babies or adopt a whole house full."

"What about Becky the bull rider?"

"That dang girl ran off with a rodeo clown after the last rodeo we had in Amarillo. She never came back to the ranch. No call, no show. Ain't that something?"

"That is sad," Antonia giggled.

"Nah, I couldn't shake the feeling of how odd it felt giving her a hug. I could practically wrap my arms around her twice," Rick chuckled. "So what is it that you started to tell me you cannot shake the feeling of?"

"I can't shake the feeling that… this place, this beautiful Italy, is not forever."

Chapter 21: Imported Wine

Antonia sat outside the front door to the villa in a simple woven chair, watching the sun setting. It was slowly disappearing over the mountains and leaving the last golden rays in the sky. Luca had still not returned home. At the main house she could faintly hear the talking and laughing of Luca's family enjoying dinner together. Going to eat with the family would have been the right thing to do and she knew it would make Luca happy. Instead, she folded her legs in the chair and munched on cheese and bread she had purchased earlier from the market.

After her long conversation with Rick, Antonia was unable to shut her brain off. Needing time to sort out her worries and choices for her future, she just sat staring at the sky until the stars began to appear. She was determined to begin to reason and to struggle with her choices instead of ignoring them. In the past, she had a tendency to go with the flow assuming any doubts would all work themselves out.

Having a plan and following through is way better and less complicated.

Antonia planned her life like so many young girls did: education, marriage, raise a family. That was it, no detours. Once a plan had been changed or broken, was there any hope of being satisfied? Some people plan to take a year off and travel, some plan to travel after retirement. Antonia never planned any further than being a surgeon and marrying Rick, her high school crush.

With every twist and turn of the plan she made for her life, Antonia embraced the possibilities assuming it would turn out even better than her outdated archaic childhood plan. If she acknowledged this future with Luca in Italy, and sees it come to fruition, then how will she know if it would have ever worked out with Rick? Maybe this here and now was the opportunity of a lifetime even though she would break one or the other's heart.

Antonia knew two things were true now in Italy and may never change: she had strong feelings of love for Luca, and Luca knew what she had done in Rome.

Allowing herself to imagine a life back in Texas, she also knew two things to be true: she had lifelong feelings of love for Rick and he would give her everything she wanted.

Finishing her bread and cheese, Antonia stood up and stretched. She heard a rustling of leaves coming from the path behind the villa. She froze trying to detect if it was a breeze blowing the leaves or if it was a person. As she turned to look behind her, Luca appeared from the side of the villa with a devious grin on his face. He stretched out his arms hoping for a hug.

"Did I scare you, Antonia?" he chuckled.

Putting her hand up to stop him from coming any closer, Antonia took a step back. "I think the question here is did you want to scare me and why?"

"Antonia, my love, it was a joke. I went to the main house and you were not there. My sister-in-law is preparing us a plate of food to bring over, so I came around the back to try and beat her here. I wanted to be the first to see you and get a welcome home kiss. That is all. Why are you so jumpy?" he asked.

Luca's face turned serious. He placed his hands on his hips, extended one leg, and stood there staring at Antonia. He could sense her annoyance and became disappointed with her reaction.

Antonia scanned his handsome physique and his luscious lips. Luca had also become familiar, but like a newer pair of slippers. He was handsome in his slim fitting black slacks and white crisp shirt. Antonia, feeling foolish, turned her eyes downward for a moment, then looked up at Luca, smiling as she threw herself into his arms. Luca wrapped his arms around Antonia tightly and she enjoyed the feeling of warmth and breathed in his aroma. All feelings of loneliness and doubt began to fade.

Love the one you're with?

Just as they were beginning to enjoy and explore each other's body, Rosa appeared with two nicely wrapped plates of food and a bottle of the family's wine. Rosa held out the plates for Luca and handed the bottle of wine to Antonia. Not wanting to interrupt the homecoming romance, she simply turned and waved a hand good-night. The couple laughed and headed inside to enjoy the food in private.

Luca and Antonia did what they did best: lay out the food and feast. Antonia chatted between bites how she had a picnic with Armando, Luca's father, and then went on a little shopping spree to spruce up the villa. Luca listened attentively, oohing and nodding appropriately as Antonia explained her adventures in detail.

"I haven't stopped talking. I should let you have a turn, Luca. What did you do that was exciting while you were away for so long?" Asked Antonia as she stuffed more pasta into her mouth.

Wiping his mouth and taking a sip of wine, Luca folded his napkin and leaned back on the pillows to unfasten his pants. "Antonia, you know basically what I do, so I don't think it is wise to give you any details that you don't need to know. It is safer for you."

"That is a little discouraging. What will we talk about when you get home from your 'job' every day? I can only talk about the new curtains so much before we are both bored to death."

Luca chuckled slightly and began clearing the dishes. "I like to hear about your day and what you and the ladies were up to. I mean, there will be times when we talk about my travels, maybe, but there will also be times when we don't have to talk at all, if you catch my drift," he snickered.

Feeling a little put out, Antonia handed Luca her plate. While he was starting to wash the dishes, Antonia pulled out her lap top from the bedside table. She googled medical universities in Italy and found quite a few popped up.

If he doesn't want to talk, then I will entertain myself.

Detecting the coolness in the air, Luca left the dishes in the sink and went to sit on the bed next to Antonia. Trying to break the silence, Luca began bouncing on the bed so the laptop jiggled and Antonia closed it to give him a stern look while trying not to laugh. Choosing his words wisely, Luca tried to create an interactive conversation to please Antonia as he leaned in to kiss her forehead.

"Antonia, my love, I am sorry I was gone for almost twenty-four hours and have not communicated with you enough. Would you please consider giving me the pleasure of conversation as well as forgiving me for the lack of attention I should be giving to a beautiful woman who shares a bed with me?"

"That was pretty good. I love the beautiful woman part," she smiled.

"I try."

"It was a very good try."

"Thank you."

Antonia returned the laptop to the bedside table and sat up and gently brushed her hand through Luca's hair. Luca was a handsome man and she knew she should feel lucky.

"I do not want to argue. I just want attention. Not just physical attention but I also crave intelligent conversation. You do remember that I have almost 7 years of college behind me? So, you can see how I can only discuss laundry soap, new curtains, and the cost of diapers for so long. I am struggling, Luca. Struggling with what I think you expect of me and what I actually need to be content. All while living in a villa surrounded by olive groves. Do you understand?"

Luca took off his shirt to get more comfortable then climbed on the bed so he could sit crossed legged facing Antonia. Taking her hands in his he stared into her eyes.

"I forget you are American sometimes. I know that may sound strange but I remind myself that you are not an Italian mafia wife. Staying here with my family while I work is not only to protect you but to learn our ways and become part of the family. What can I do to make you happy, Antonia? What do you need from me?" he asked softly. "I will not lose you."

Antonia caressed his cheek gently then reached around and tugged hard on his ear. He let out a howl and gave her a cross look as he rubbed his ear. Antonia sat up a little straighter and crossed her arms.

"First of all, Italian women go to college too! Not all stay at home taking care of children while their husband goes to work. Did you know that Rosa gave up a career as a school teacher to stay at home while Mateo learns the family business? Aria never finished school to stay at home raising baby Ricky and now she is pregnant again. They are two very nice girls, don't get me wrong." Antonia paused to take a breath. "Your youngest brother, Roberto, I have only seen once because, according to your father, he is riding his scooter all over Rome chasing girls with short skirts."

Luca threw his head back and let out a howl. Then releasing Antonia's hands, he began to clap as if he was listening to a comedy on the radio about Italian families.

"I know you want babies Antonia, but it is not my choice to simply deny you what you desire. I would give you the world. I do love being an uncle and you can be the smartest and greatest doting aunt there ever was. There are other choices. It is not one way or the highway."

"I know you are right. I can find happiness in other things. But do I want to – or am I forced to – by my Italian husband to be?" asked Antonia.

"Maybe you can learn to cook pasta with Nona or decorate. Lord knows, that main house could use some updating. I have sadly been sleeping in the same bed from my childhood," he snickered. "And possibly the same bedsheets and curtains. I don't wash them; they just appear on the bed. Perhaps you can make it a mission to find out who the laundry fairy is?"

"Okay, you go ahead and laugh Luca. I am telling you it will be hard to not have children of my own when and if we get married. I am trying to understand your reasoning. Woman can have a full life without children. I get that. So basically, I need something for me to be excited about. So I started looking up colleges here in Italy. I can transfer my transcripts and finish getting my medical degree. Pico only has one general practitioner. I checked," smiled Antonia.

Luca changed his position and scooted up to lay beside Antonia on the pillows. Taking her hand he kissed it softly then held it on his chest.

"First of all," he paused. " You see how I am using your words?" he smiled.

"Go ahead, I am listening."

"You used the words when or if we get married. We have talked about it often and I think it is a matter of when, not if. However, you gave me an idea. Why don't we set a date for a big wedding and you can stay busy planning it. No budget.

You can have handmade silk gowns and enough flowers to cover the entire olive grove and property if you wish. You can use the chickens as flower girls and have your fried chicken as the main meal. What ever you want, but it is a pass on going back to college in my eyes."

Luca squeezed her hand turning his head to look at her hoping she would now be content. Antonia turned on her side to face him. She began to play with the hair on his chest and gently caress a circle around his nipples teasing him. When Luca turned to face her with anticipation on his mind she quickly plucked a chest hair making him yelp.

Never underestimate the things I will do.

"There is no ring on my finger. You assured me that I would never be in danger. Now you say no children, no college, no career outside of the home! I love you madly, Luca, I really do, but I will not sacrifice my happiness for a relationship ever again. I can't," said Antonia. "It is like a dart aimed squarely at my heart, Luca.".

"I am gathering you like to play tough. I must change my approach during lovemaking," he laughed. "Don't pull my hair or tweak my ear again; it hurts! I have to be the man in this relationship. Also, I want to point out to you that it is not a matter of keeping you bored or shackled to the villa. I am well aware how strong of a woman you are, my love."

"Being a woman is my strength, not my weakness, Luca," she replied.

Luca sat up rubbing his nipple then his ear to make his point. Antonia rolled her eyes.

"It is simple, Antonia. Let me explain how I see things. If someone knows you leave the house to go to a job and they have a reason to retaliate or get vengeance on me or my family, they will show up at your job. I want you to feel at ease here at the villa. Safe, here, not at a job."

"Well, it will take a little more than a simple hobby or learning to cook pasta to make me feel at ease. I have quite a bit of education under my belt. I will regret not finishing medical school. I know I will regret it. I can make some changes but you are asking me to be something I am not."

Luca sat up and fluffed his pillows then offered to do the same for Antonia. After getting comfortable he folded his hands in his lap and took a nervous breath. "I guess I will tell you a little about my 'job' as you call it, so you will understand. But first, I love you madly, too, Antonia. I want you to know I think of forever when I look into your eyes. The ring will come."

Luca and Antonia spent the next few hours into the night talking about the life of a mafia family. At times, Luca paced the floor and other times Antonia paced while Luca lay naked on the bed. Luca explained how the mafia survived in the shadows for over a century in Sicily. The roots of the mafia were so strong that it took over a hundred years and a massacre to break the secrecy. The true face of the Sicilian mafia was exposed, Luca's great-grandfather, Mario, was involved and he eventually was murdered in cold blood in front of his family while attending a festival. Many knew that he and his family would be attending that festival for the olives as they always did in support of Nona and her husband. Mario's daughter, Alma, was paralyzed from a bullet to the spine. Alma's son and grandson to Mario, little Romeo, was killed by a stray bullet. He was only four years old.   Mario's wife Francesca was shot a week later while leaving her husband's funeral. It was a brutal blow to the Vitalia name and the family.

"Another reason why my middle name is Romeo," Luca frowned. "Romeo was the younger brother to my godfather, Aldo. The one we stayed with in Milan. This happened many years ago, of course, but Aldo had to grow up without his brother and his grandparents."

"No wonder he was so upset about a bottle of wine being taken. He has had so much taken from him and his family. It must have triggered something inside of him," Antonia said softly. "I am sorry for his loss."

Luca went on to explain that his family suffered great loss and to this day there are some who hold a grudge for the years of suffering at the hands of Mario Vitalia, his great-grandfather.

"Family alliances are important; it is as though we are a bigger stronger family and can expect stronger protection. Every family profits: there is no more stealing and keeping all the money. We have a chain of command and accountants. My sister, Isabella, is married and lives in Sicily. They are our connection there. It is complicated, but it works for now." Luca finished and rolled toward Antonia who was sitting next to him. "By the way, why am I the only one naked?" he asked.

"It is hot in here. But before we turn in for the night, one more question?" asked Antonia.

"Okay you have until I fall asleep to ask your question. I'm having another glass of wine."

"Again, not fair. But if you answer me, I will rub your back until you drift off. Is it a deal?" whispered Antonia teasing him.

"Antonia, my love, I am afraid if you rub my back, we won't be talking for very long. Want to ask me what I will do to you?" he joked.

"Not if that counts as my question."

"You are killing me, Antonia. I am slowly dying from lack of passionate kissing."

"It's a two part question."

"Oh, joy… I cannot wait to hear this. I think you are just stalling until I am too tired to make love. Go ahead, I am listening, you *donna che prende in giro*, teasing woman," he grinned.

"I want to know what you did in the last twenty hours that kept you away from me and why couldn't you simply call me and check in. I was worried. What if something happened to you like what happened to your great-grandfather? Where does that leave me?" asked Antonia.

Luca opened his eyes wide and propped his head on his elbow to look at Antonia. "I believe, if I can count correctly, that is more than two questions."

"If I am to trust you, then you trust me. Tell me what you do when you are away. You know my deepest, darkest secret, Luca so it is only fair, don't you think?" asked Antonia.

Blackmail is not one sided.

"Okay, if you must know something before you let me sleep, I was delivering imported wine to family cafés."

Antonia tilted her head looking confused. "Imported wine?"

Luca nodded his head confirming it was a perplexing thing to say. "Now think about that for a minute. We produce the finest wine in all the world. Why would we import wine from a foreign country? Don't answer; it will save time if I just tell you. The wine is in a crate that is clearly stamped as imported wine. But that is just the top layer if you open the crate to inspect. Underneath the wine of Columbia, Africa or some other fake place, is a false chamber full of guns. Very bad guns, but worth a lot of money to many people."

"This is sounding like a clandestine gun running enterprise," Antonia gasped. "So I am gathering that the cafés are the legal family business that covers for the illegal guns. Who needs the guns? Do you sell them?"

Luca sat up on the side of the bed and stretched his neck side to side making a loud pop. Standing up with his back to Antonia, he placed his hands on his hips. Antonia admired the view for a moment, then sensing a coldness in the room, she got out of bed and walked around to face him. Slight fear gripped her and she didn't understand why.

"Luca, I just want you to know that I feel so special right now. You trusted me and that means the world to me. I want to know all my options and what will happen if I choose to stay," said Antonia. "No one has ever trusted me enough to open up the way you have here tonight. I want to trust and be trusted. I want to forget everything from the past and allow happiness and love in my heart again. You mean everything to me, Luca. I want this to work. I am done looking, I want you and only you. Just help me make that choice. I can't give up every part of me or there will be nothing left for us to build on."

Even though Luca stood stiff, Antonia began to kiss him, hoping for a response. She threw her arms around him and leaped into his arms. Wrapping herself around him like a spider monkey. Antonia licked his ear then kissed his neck as she moaned like a kitten in heat. It didn't take long for Luca to give in and began to return the affections. Putting her down on her own two feet again, he began pulling at Antonia's shirt. Smiling like she won the war, Antonia raised her arms, allowing him to undress her. As Luca got the shirt just to her elbows he stopped, twisting the shirt to restrain her as if he had handcuffs. He stared into her eyes. Antonia squealed as if it was an exciting game he was playing. Then Luca pulled her closer and whispered in her ear.

"It is over, you know all that I am going to ever tell you. I cannot bear some of the memories you are dredging up; it is not something to talk about. No more questions, Antonia or we are over. *Capisci?* Do you understand?"

Antonia squirmed as her face began to flush. Slight panic set in just before Luca let loose and removed the shirt from her arms. Immediately he grabbed Antonia lowering her hard to the bed pinning her arms above her head. Antonia started to protest. Quickly Luca put his finger to her lips. "Not one word," he whispered.

Luca struggled to remove her panties with one hand, ripping them slightly, as the other hand held both wrists above her head. Antonia was experiencing fear and pleasure simultaneously. She closed her eyes, submitting to him she wrapped her legs around his waist. Luca ravished her body sending wave after wave crashing against the shore well into the night. Their bodies wet from sweaty love making, the couple fell asleep entangled.

Chapter 22: Pleasure of Old Wine

Antonia woke stiff and sore. She gently lifted Luca's arm from around her waist and scooted his right leg from under her thigh. Sitting up on the side of the bed to brush the sweaty hair from her face, she noticed the afternoon sun spilling in the windows from the edge of the curtains. Staring at herself in the bathroom mirror, she got a chill.

That was the best sleep I had in months, but the fear has planted itself deep inside of me.

When she returned from the bathroom, Luca was just starting to stir. Antonia began filling the new coffee machine she bought, feeling satisfied with her purchase. Pulling two coffee mugs from the cabinet above the sink, Antonia sat down at the small table crossing her legs as Luca struggled to get out of bed. Watching his beautiful body as he strolled to the bathroom made her squirm a little remembering the warm pleasure of last evening. She could hear him wash his face before he came out to sit across from her at the table. Antonia couldn't help but be all smiles.

"This is paradise to me, Luca. Sitting naked at our dining table, just the two of us, and brewing our own coffee. Wouldn't you agree?"

"I will admit it is nice, especially to not have to get dressed. Drinking coffee naked, now that is a happy discovery. My life now has been irrevocably changed," said

Luca raising his cup. "However, the best part and most special is being with a beautiful woman that I have fallen deeply in love with. You do understand that someone has made coffee for me my whole life, so that is not so special," Luca laughed.

"Don't make fun, Luca. It is serendipity, making happy discoveries by accident," remarked Antonia. "Drinking coffee naked is a happy discovery."

"You force me to be the man you want me to be, Antonia. That is no accident. That makes me a little bit nervous and beyond happy. You can never leave me. But I might leave you, just for a few moments, to go see what is left from the family breakfast and I will bring it back here so we can continue being naked and eat. I am starving," laughed Luca.

"You are so slick with your words and quite a teaser. I guess you worked up an appetite last night. I will wait right here drinking my coffee while you go forage for food, my cave man," Antonia laughed.

It took a little longer than Antonia expected. Assuming his Nona would wonder why he didn't show up for breakfast, Antonia naturally assumed Luca was appeasing her instead of rushing away. It was sweet and peaceful in the villa with the sun shining through the new curtains.

Having a little time on her hands, Antonia decided to take out her laptop. She was determined to continue looking up universities that would accept her transfer from the states but got interrupted by an email notification. Curiosity got the best of her so she had sent an inquiry to Texas A&M asking for a recommendation. Opening her email she found a reply stating that the University of Milan was the best university for clinical medicine. It was ranked number 55 in the world. Excited, she stood and clapped her hands as though she was applauding her own good luck.

I don't think I will tell Luca right away. He will warm up to the idea eventually, I won't give him a choice.

Antonia closed the laptop as she heard Luca coming in the door. In his hands were a straw basket of goodies. "Nona sent a little of everything. We can stay closed up in here all day if we wanted to and not starve," he laughed.

"Not starving is good. I figured Nona would hold you up asking why we are secluding ourselves."

"Not just that, I mean she did ask but, Roberto, my little brother is home from his travels. Rosa and Mateo are going to plan their wedding and Rico announced the pregnancy of Aria. Everyone was toasting and laughing."

As Luca laid out the breads, cheese, jams and *cornetti,* Antonia looked at him for signs of regret. Wanting a little cozy hideaway so they can be alone meant Luca had to be without his family gatherings, something he had experienced since birth.

We were raised so differently.

Luca went on to happily chat about his little brother, Roberto, being home from his visit to Rome and Sicily. Antonia watched his face light up as he talked. Luca couldn't wait to sit and talk to his brother after being gone for three months. As he stuffed a piece of cheese in his mouth, he began to tell her how Mateo's wedding will be such a big celebration with food and really old wine the family saves for special occasions.

Antonia could see the excitement in Luca's face. He had an overall visage that glowed. His arms were flailing in big oversized movements as he described his anticipation of the wedding celebration and the family's old wine kept just for the occasion. There were even a few fist pumps in the air. Antonia understood the excitement in her own way. In Texas if someone did well at a rodeo there were bonfires and shooting guns in the air. Back slapping and chest bumps were not at all odd but a celebratory prevalence. Holidays and special occasions will always be different no matter where you are. Just like the stars are ever steady, always there but different wherever the place you are gazing up at them happens to be. Antonia wanted family, no matter how it came to her; she wanted family and friends to enjoy special moments with. Being an only child was her reference. It was a good life but there was always the feeling that she was alone. Determined to be a part of Luca's family, Antonia put away the laptop, deciding to keep it to herself for now. She reached over and touched Luca's hand and lovingly smiled at him.

"Let's get dressed and go join the family, Luca. I want to hear all about your brother's travels and then I hope Rosa will allow me to help her plan that wedding! I have loads of ideas to share with her."

"Are you sure? I thought you wanted to be just the two of us today?" asked Luca.

"Luca, we have the rest of our lives to be alone. Today is special and I want to do whatever makes you happy," said Antonia.

"Now you are speaking the language of love," he smiled.

"You go ahead. I need a few minutes to spruce up."

Seeing how happy it made Luca as he grabbed a jacket and kissed her good-bye made Antonia put her hand to her chest. Changes in plans should be spur of the moment and carefree with no feeling of dread or regret. Antonia knew this special time with his family was important to Luca so she could easily make the exception and join in.

Wasn't it Walt Whitman who said "Be curious, not judgmental"?

Antonia found herself very curious. Life seemed to have offered her a second chance after Wade. She had taken chances before on relationships. This time she wanted to be sure before she committed, even if the questions were causing a huge rift. So, yet again she found herself jumping in with both feet, throwing caution to the wind.

Grabbing the gray wool sweater she found in the closet, she put it on the bed to wear after her shower and smiled with satisfaction. It was starting to feel like a *welcome to the family* gift. Her cell phone rang just as she got to the door. It was Rick. Her first thought was to ignore it and call him back but something nagged at her to answer.

"Rick, I was just about to leave the villa. Is everything alright at the ranch?"

"Hello, sweetie. My first problem is that you are not here, Antonia. That will always be a problem in my eyes, anyway. Second problem is we found some fencing down and a few cattle wandered, so it will take a little chunk of money to run that fence line again. I will have to hire a few locals to get it done fast. I wanted to let you know ahead of time in case you see the bank account dip a little," said Rick. "I am doing the best I can."

"Oh, Rick! It's okay and honestly I haven't even looked at the finances for the ranch. I assume you will take care of everything," replied Antonia. "Listen, if the ranch needs extra money to pay for things, I have money and I will wire it to you."

When Rick did not respond right away, it made her feel uncomfortable. Antonia forgot that she never told Rick or anyone about the lottery money winnings. Rick meant a lot to her but it felt different now, like she was letting him down, not living up to his expectations.

"Listen, Rick, I think I will be staying here in Italy for a while, maybe forever. Well, not forever, I am sure I will want to visit Texas again. I think, maybe…I don't know." Antonia began pacing choosing her words. "I can just sign the ranch over to you, Rick. If that is what you want or need. I should have done that after my parents died. I am sorry but I really have to go. Can we talk about this later?"

"You are telling me that this is not your home anymore? Antonia, no, I just can't accept that or the ranch, no. We will make do on the fences. I can get a barter or deal going. We don't need any illegal mafia money from Italy."

Forgetting that she hinted to Rick that Luca was in the family business, she changed the subject quickly. "Rick, my parents would want you to have it, they left me a little money. I am doing okay. I just can't sell it to a stranger. It is your home now, Rick. Please just think about it. We can talk more about it later or tomorrow, okay?"

"I won't let you do that, Antonia, unless I see your face. If you want to sign over your family ranch to me, then by goodness you have to come here and look me in the eye! Or hell, I will come there. I am not afraid of your new mafia man. Dang it, Antonia! You pull this on me now?" shouted Rick. "You told me you didn't feel Italy was forever. My heart is stuck on your heart forever. Do you know what forever even means, Antonia?"

"I know it sounds harsh but maybe you should – " Antonia struggled to finish the sentence.

"Are you telling me to move on? Never see you again? I can't do that. I tried," Rick said sarcastically. "I tried with Becky the bull rider. No one is you but you, Antonia. Only an idiot would give up on you and I am no idiot. I am at a loss for words. Call me tomorrow. Promise me?"

Antonia had no words of comfort for Rick's troubled heart. She felt it was all her fault that he couldn't move on properly. They made young promises to each other that were never fulfilled. She fell for Wade and followed him to Chicago without a thought of how it might effect Rick and now she was practically on the other side of the world and could only have hope the love fairy would make it all work out. Antonia craved stability and a new beginning and Luca could give her that. Rick could only share memories.

"Yes, I promise Rick I will call tomorrow. Now I really must go. I love you, I always will. I have to give my right now, right here situation, a try. I want to give a life in Italy, with Luca, my best effort. I feel obligated."

"Obligation is not love Antonia, and I love you too. Always will."

Why did I say obligated?

After a quick shower to wash away the smell of intimacy, she threw on a pair of jeans and long sleeve shirt and grabbed the gray sweater. Wrapping the sweater around her tightly, Antonia made her way from the villa to the main house, her long hair still wet. She could see the lights in the courtyard glowing in the sky and hear the laughter and high-spirited conversations. Darkness comes early in Italy this time of year and they did sleep in a little later than normal. When she saw the lights and heard the laughter, it made her heart feel warm.

"Maybe I can be at home here," she whispered. "I can have a family."

Antonia paused halfway to the main house to look up at the full moon beginning its nightly performance. The giant romantic moon lined up perfectly between the trees. It was radiant and so big she felt if she was on the hilltop in downtown Pico, she could touch it. The luminescence of the moon lit up the pathway to the main house. Antonia felt pleased with her decision to stay and marry Luca – at least for now.

Who wouldn't want to live in this romantic place?

Just as she was about to walk ahead, she heard the rustle of leaves as though someone was in the shadows. Looking around, she called out for Luca thinking he had come to see what was taking her so long. She stood still, listening but heard not another sound. Shrugging her shoulders, she continued on to the main house.

As she arrived, walking through the house to the courtyard everyone was all smiles. Carmella, Luca's mother, even came out of her writing nook. Armando, Luca's father brought out wine and paraded it around the room as he skipped. Luca joined Antonia and gave her a very protective side hug and kept his arm slung around her shoulder as they stood watching the family celebration. Aria was glowing as Nona rubbed her belly. Even Carmella was all smiles and clapping. It was an amazing feeling to belong to such a special close-knit family, a family Antonia always thought she wanted. Roberto, the youngest son, finally made his way around the room and embraced Luca, patting each other on the back and speaking in Italian. Next he stepped back holding out his arms while looking at Antonia. Luca introduced her just as Roberto scooped her up twirling her around in a circle.

"Welcome to *la famiglia*, Antonia!" shouted Roberto.

"Whoa, it is nice to finally meet you too, Roberto," laughed Antonia.

Roberto had the lightest and longest hair compared to the rest of the Vitalia family. He was tan with beautiful eyes and lips. He had a fresh clean school boy look with no facial hair besides a small stubble on his chin. Wearing a tight shirt and low cut corduroy pants he resembled a hippie from the 70s.

Antonia enjoyed Roberto's boisterous and happy attitude. He was like a rush of cool water from a spring that made you smile and suck in your breath at the same time. Antonia found herself laughing and watching as he made his way around the room. Soon Armando tapped a fork to a glass and got everyone's attention.

"This is a special night for the family," Armando began. "My youngest son has returned home. He left on his adventures as a boy and has returned as a grown man. But that is not all we celebrate tonight. Rico and Aria are having another baby, adding to *la famiglia* and Mateo and Rosa has set a date for the wedding! *Saluti!*"

Everyone clapped as Armando passed out glasses of wine. Roberto put on some music and everyone began to join in one by one. Nona disappeared into the house as everyone was dancing and celebrating. Antonia slipped away from Luca and followed her into the large kitchen.

"Is there anything I can help you with, Nona?" Antonia asked.

"I am making a simple pasta for dinner. I wasn't expecting a celebration but I am so glad to have everyone together. You can help me by slicing some of that Italian bread and putting it on my special tray. It was my mother's and she brought it out every festival or special occasion. We shall use it tonight. Go look on the top shelf of the pantry and be careful: it is delicate and old."

Antonia had never been inside the kitchen except to pass through. She felt special having been asked to retrieve such a family heirloom. Antonia stepped on a short wooden step stool to reach the top shelf. Bringing it down, she was captivated by the precious piece. The tray was a large oval pottery the shade of terra cotta. There were a few designs of olive leaf branches etched around the edge and in the middle was *FAMIGLIA*. It was beautiful and handmade. Antonia brought the tray into the kitchen and gently placed it on the large kitchen island. Nona handed her an apron and she quickly tied it on, finally feeling included.

"Place the bread on the tray, then in the middle we add a small bowl of olive oil infused with herbs like rosemary and garlic. I will teach you how while the pasta cooks," said Nona.

"Will we also be adding some fresh olives and tomatoes with mozzarella?" asked Antonia.

"Yes, dear, you are learning fast. I am glad Luca is bringing you into the family. I will teach you to cook many more things if you join me in the kitchen every day."

"I would love to, Nona. Well, not every day because I have been thinking about finishing college and becoming a doctor."

Nona snapped her head around looking at Antonia. "Have you and Luca discussed this already?" asked Nona.

Nona began pouring the olive oil from her special bottles that came from olives right here on the farm. Avoiding eye contact, she placed the rosemary and other herbs on a cutting board and gave them a rough chop.

"Now you smash the garlic and smooth it before adding to the olive oil," explained Nona.

"Don't you think having a doctor in the family would be a good thing, Nona? I mean since Luca does not want children, I can have a career, right?" asked Antonia.

Nona checked on her pasta turning her back to Antonia. She said nothing for a moment and Antonia decided it was best to leave the subject alone. She continued to crush the garlic and then added a few rosemary sprigs and basil to the olive oil. Fresh garlic and basil had to be the best smell and memory of Italian family dinners. Nona drained the large pot of pasta, steam filling the air, then added it to a large wooden bowl before placing it on the counter next to Antonia.

"I do understand, Antonia. My parents wanted me to be an accountant because I was good with my numbers in school. Before me, there were not many women with careers and they were so proud. My brother, Anthony, was to take over the olive farm and keep it in the family. We had a sister that died very young from fever. So our future was set. Anthony died from a tractor accident the first year in the groves. Leaving me, the only child to inherit the olive farm. Enrico and I fell in love but I could not leave the olives. My choice was made for me."

"Nona, do you miss your husband, Enrico? I wish I could have met him."

"I do miss him very much but I see little bits of memories everywhere I look. That bread platter was a gift for our wedding. It is why having family together is so important. I see parts of my Enrico in the faces of my children and grandchildren."

"I will never have that. I will never see Luca in our children. How did your husband die?"

"Enrico's father, Mario Vitalia, decided it was a good time to have all the family together to attend the festival in town. Mario had cancer but no one knew. He wanted one more gathering. The mafia had other plans. It was his first time in public in a long time and they took advantage of the situation by ambushing him. It was awful. There are still bullet holes in the stucco in town. So many family members and even friends were lost, including my handsome Enrico, God rest his soul," Nona sniffled.

Antonia felt bad for bring up bad memories so she wanted to give Nona reassurance.

"I just want you to know I love Luca. I love Italy. I love this olive farm and I definitely love this kitchen, Nona. I would love to learn how to cook in this kitchen," said Antonia.

"If you come over to the main house more often, I will show you how to make bread in this kitchen you love," laughed Nona. "For now, let us go feed the family."

Walking behind Nona carrying the bread platter made Antonia feel special as everyone turned to look. After placing the dishes of food on the table in the courtyard, there were audible gasps followed by clapping. Luca gave Antonia a wink and held up his glass to make a toast.

"To my *famiglia, buon appetito! Mangiamo,* let's eat."

Everyone began passing plates and wine around the table. Glasses were clinking with toast for a long life. The largest gathering Antonia ever remembered was a thanksgiving dinner on the ranch when momma invited all the ranch hands and their families to eat. Afterwards, momma complained about the stress of cooking such large quantities and washing up all the dishes but it was exciting.

Glancing around the large table at all the animated faces of Luca's family was exciting and hopeful. It felt right. Luca placed his arm around Antonia and gave her shoulder a squeeze. Then he whispered in her ear, "Nice apron. You think you can wear that to bed tonight?"

Chapter 23: Shoes and Wine

The next few days were filled with beautiful crisp weather and hectic wedding plans. The actual day was still kept secret but the planning was well under way. There were nights of endless pleasure with Luca and nights of sitting up sewing beads on the veil Rosa picked out. Rosa and Mateo wanted to have the wedding while Roberto was in town. No invitations were sent out but phone calls were made to extended special family. No one wanted to take a chance the actual date was leaked to the Family connections too soon. Messages were simple stating come for the weekend.

Isabella, Luca's sister, and her husband arrived on a Wednesday from Sicily hoping to get a little girl time with her sisters-in-law before the celebrations began. Isabella was a beauty, nearly a twin to Luca with her sea blue eyes. She had long dark hair to her waist that she wore down with a simple clip to keep it out of her face. It swayed as she moved, like angel wings. She was tall and stunning with perfectly smooth skin. Isabella was a dark, mysterious brooding beauty.

Appearing to be able to cut your throat at the same time she compliments your outfit. Isabella's husband, Lorenzo, was shorter than expected and a little older than her. His voice was grainy and was never seen without a cigar in his hand. Antonia's eyes caught the glimmer of the matching wedding bands that, if sold, could buy ten houses in

America: a huge diamond was surrounded by smaller ones on a thick gold band. The sparkle was blinding. Isabella was definitely in the category of the 'haves' and not the 'have-nots'.

Life must be very good in Sicily.

Antonia ventured over to the main house and met up with Nona in the kitchen before lunch. Nona was preparing food ahead for the upcoming wedding and for the large family dinner that night. She was very glad to see Antonia show up; her eyes sparkled as if Antonia was the one she had been waiting for. The kitchen smelled amazing as usual and Antonia took a deep breath to savor the aromas..

"Put on an apron and help with rolling the wedding cookies, Antonia, then we will start making a few loaves of bread for tonight and some berry tarts for the wedding."

Antonia went to the pantry where the aprons hung and giggled when she remembered not returning the last one she wore. This time she picked a bright yellow apron with grapes printed all over.

Returning to the kitchen island, Antonia took a seat on one of the high stools and watched as Nona rolled out a cookie ball in her hands then placed it on a baking sheet lined with parchment paper.

"There, you see how easy? Now you roll into balls. We will need at least two hundred cookies," said Nona, "we make some today and then on the final day, too."

"I will help with every thing I can, Nona, until the girls are ready to go shopping. Today I think we are picking out wedding shoes."

"Ah, yes, the high heel that will be embellished. I need to get some of the pearls from my dress to offer her. It is tradition. You will have fun today. I will not go because I need to get started on the dough for the tarts and make the meatballs for the wedding soup," replied Nona.

"Wedding soup. That sounds yummy."

"Yes, another tradition. You might want to learn some of our traditions for a wedding you and Luca might have one day, Antonia."

"I want to learn. What traditions?"

"Well, for one thing, you are making the cookies too big. This is Italy. Small wedding cookies but lots of them," Nona laughed. "Let's see now, one tradition is to never get married on a Friday; it is bad luck. Sunday is the luckiest day to marry. I think the most followed tradition is breaking a vase or glass. The newlyweds break a glass vase and the number of broken fragments symbolize how many happy years of marriage they have ahead of them. My Enrico, rest his soul, smashed my momma's vase into a thousand pieces. He wanted us to be together a long time."

"That sounds sweet. Hey, how am I doing on the cookies? There must be over a hundred here," said Antonia. "I can't wait to taste one."

Taking her time as if she was judging each individual cookie, Nona finally nodded and smiled giving the sign of approval. "That will do for now. I must get bread in the oven for the bruschetta. Everything is homemade for the wedding."

"When is the wedding, exactly? No one has said. I assumed it is this weekend since everyone is here and they are rushing the dress." Antonia observed.

Nona leaned back on her white porcelain sink and wiped her brow with a hand towel. She looked tired and weary. Behind her was the largest kitchen window Antonia had ever seen, overlooking the property and the valley leading to the olive groves making the kitchen very bright with natural light.

"Antonia, if you are to be married into my family, you must learn to not ask so many questions. It feels like an interrogation and it tires me. The wedding is soon. We don't talk too much about details, we just know. Now go with the women shopping and be back later to help with the pastry dough. I will let the bread dough rise and you can help with that too."

Antonia felt a little taken back. Luca told her basically the same thing about asking questions. Feeling a little embarrassed, Antonia wiped off her hands and slipped off the stool. She looked past Nona and pointed curiously at something outside the window never saying a word. When Nona turned to look, Antonia grabbed three cookies and stashed them in her apron pocket.

"I thought I saw a large bird. They do have birds in Italy, right? Okay off to shop. I will be back later Nona," said Antonia.

"Just a minute, young lady!" snarled Nona.

Thinking she had been caught sneaking cookies Antonia turned slowly to face Nona.

"Don't forget to put that apron back before you go. I seem to be missing the one you wore the other night while helping me with dinner."

"Yes ma'am."

Busted on the apron but I got the cookies!

Antonia was excited to hang out with the women of the family. She had shopped with her mother before but picking out cowboy boots and pearl button shirts was nothing compared to wedding attire. Antonia wanted to look sophisticated yet comfortable. Antonia chose to wear camel-colored slacks with a black and gold silk shirt that had butterfly sleeves.

While she was finishing up, she began to think about all the firsts she had experienced: life was an adventure with or without regrets for mistakes or taking the wrong fork in the road. Every place she had lived gave her unexpected life lessons and knowledge. She wanted to feel lucky she met Luca at the right time. After Wade, anything seemed grand but remembering to be humble was key. Luca knew her secret and still wanted to be with her; He sparkled with pride every time he saw her enter a room. She reminded herself that no one was obligated to buy a ticket to her circus called life.

Antonia heard a horn honk and grabbed her purse to rush out and meet up with the girls. Isabella was driving a beautiful Mercedes, Rosa was in the front passenger seat and Aria was in the back. Antonia hopped excitedly in the back seat next to Aria and settled back in the luxurious leather seats. Isabella gunned the engine and the four of them giggled loudly.

"It has been a while since I have driven myself anywhere. I usually have a driver, but I ditched him!" cackled Isabella as she turned down the driveway leaving a dirt cloud behind her.

"Everyone put on their seatbelts!" shouted Rosa laughing.

"You say that like you mean it!" laughed Isabella.

"We do mean it. Remember we have a pregnant lady in the back seat," said Aria.

Arriving in downtown Pico, Isabella parked the car so they could walk from store to store and specialty shops. Everywhere they went people stared, especially at Isabella. She had on a black short dress barely covering the important parts, with spaghetti straps and four inch heels that made a clicking sound on the cobblestones. Her fur coat was hanging low, exposing her beautiful shoulders. She had a sort of model strut and everyone gazed at her long, gorgeous, perfect legs. Men tipped their hat as she passed, grinning what could only be called a Christmas morning smile as the package all wrapped in pretty paper with bows was presented.

As they entered a shoe boutique, the proprietor stopped what he was doing and approached. It was obvious that he knew the family well and greeted Isabella with a kiss on the hand as if she was the queen.

"I am here to purchase many pairs of shoes, *signore*. Bring out all *il colore bianco*, the color white, and some other colors to fit the four ladies. Do you have wine for us while we try on shoes?" Isabella began. "This will be a *privata* fitting."

The shop owner snapped his fingers and his two employees began ushering others out of the shop and placing the closed sign on the door as they pulled the curtains. Soon a bottle of wine was brought out with four wine glasses and set on a nearby table near. Wine was poured as boxes of shoes were brought out for review. They were stacked all around the four ladies. Isabella finished her first glass of wine then motioned for Rosa to try on shoes first. As Rosa was parading back and forth in different pairs of heels, Isabella turned to Antonia.

"We are all to get new shoes today, Antonia. Feel free to try on any you like as long as they do not match Rosa. Be casual, look them all over, and pick a final choice."

"Thank you, Isabella. I have never owned a pair of Italian shoes before. I would love to try on a few pairs," Antonia said sheepishly.

Now I feel silly. I basically just said I was poor.

Pride and stubbornness share a fence. As soon as Antonia found a pair of shoes she liked she proceeded to take them to the cash register to pay. The owner stopped and looked at Isabella as if he needed her approval. Isabella stared blankly at Antonia. It was instantly obvious that Isabella loved to splash the cash and even the slightest opposition would not be tolerated.

"What are you doing, Antonia? We are not done and put away your money; the shoes are my treat. Consider them a birthday gift, please." said Isabella.

"Oh, it is fine. I will just put them on my card. It is all good. But I do appreciate the thought, and it is not my birthday," replied Antonia.

Rosa and Aria let out an audible gasp. Isabella set down her wine glass and stood up, straightening her dress. She turned to Rosa asking if they had made their decision on the shoes then pointed to the stack of boxes explaining that she would purchase them all. Walking toward Antonia, Isabella stopped and snapping her fingers, the host left the room.

"We need more wine and all the shoes wrapped in brown paper and brought to my car."

Antonia could sense Isabella staring a hole in the back of her head. She could also sense the coldness like she did something wrong and offended Isabella. As soon as Isabella got close enough to smell her perfume, Antonia turned sharply to face her with a lovely grin on her face.

"I know you were offering a kind gesture, I appreciate that, I really do. I didn't understand and I am sorry if I offended you in any way, Isabella. However, I am perfectly capable of buying my own shoes. If I made a mistake and flubbed up some kind of tradition, it is because I am American and didn't know the custom. Please don't let this come between us, I have had a lovely day with you ladies," pleaded Antonia.

Isabella crossed her arms and tapped her long fingernails on her purse. Her lips were puckered and her eyes serious. After a moment of silence, Isabella turned and motioned for Rosa and Aria to follow her to the car. Turning back to Antonia she put one hand on her hip.

"It is *perfecta*, perfect. If you wish to purchase your own shoes, it is fine. We will be waiting at the car for you," said Isabella.

Antonia stood flabbergasted at the way she was made to feel shame. *It is just shoes.*

As the two employees carried the boxes to the car the proprietor stood behind the counter and began ringing up the shoes for Antonia. He glanced up at her and smiled trying to be nice and ease the tension. He was a stout man with a long scar down one side of his face.

"So it is not your birthday, *signorina?*" the proprietor asked.

"No, the shoes are for a wedding, I think she was just trying to be nice," replied Antonia.

"A wedding at the olive farm?" he asked.

Immediately Antonia's eyes shot a look at the man, remembering Nona saying they don't talk about the date for safety reasons. Her neck and face began to flush. *How do I fix this?*

Turning back, she shook her head slightly, staring at him and not knowing what to say.

"You know the family, right? I mean you are friends with them, right?" Antonia asked calmly.

"*Si, si*. I know the family. I have been a shoemaker in Pico all my life."

"Okay good so you know them, right?" Antonia repeated. "Like maybe ignore what I said because I may marry into the family. I won't have children and I worry about the guns and danger, but hey, I will be okay right?" she rambled.

The shoemaker nodded his head and Antonia nodded her head as if she was agreeing with him. Turning to walk toward the door she stopped and gave a wave. "I am sorry I talk too much. It is the whole getting used to the family and their ways thing that makes me just ramble on sometimes. Just ignore what I said."

Antonia thought she noticed a wink from the shoemaker but she could be wrong. No harm can come if he winked right?

Antonia was quiet most of the ride home not knowing if she should say something to Isabella or let it go. After seeing the look on Isabella's face when she said she would buy her own shoes, Antonia felt real fear. Deciding to not say anything, Antonia took her new shoes to the villa, changed her clothes and headed to the main house to help Nona prepare for dinner.

As she entered the kitchen, she could see Luca in the courtyard talking to Isabella. It looked like a serious conversation. Luca looked up and seeing her through the kitchen window, he blew her a kiss which she pretended to catch. Nona appeared from the huge walk-in pantry carrying two large bowls and set them down on the island.

"Hello, Antonia! Was it a special day?" asked Nona.

"Oh, yes. Many pairs of shoes were purchased and a few pieces of jewelry, I think. So many stores. Fun times. What are we preparing for dinner? I am here to help," stammered Antonia.

"Antonia, Isabella is my granddaughter. I know her well. You do not have to explain anything. I see the look on your face. What helps me is try to remember that out there… out there in the world, we are mafia. The bad guys or *criminale*. But here on this farm, we are family. We love, eat and enjoy the family. No business here. Now, this is two bowls of dough. One for bread and one for pastry. Let us begin with the bread. Punching and kneading dough will take your mind off of everything."

"I hope so, Nona. I am ready to punch something."

"Slow down Antonia, baking is a personal and beautiful experience. Kneading the dough releases tension. Rolling, cutting and shaping the dough for cookies is artistic and precise."

"I just want to do something that will take my mind to another place if that is possible."

"Okay," began Nona, "keep it going. Use your knuckles."

Her instructions were simple and precise and after a few moments with her hands in the dough, Antonia forgot all about the shoemaker.

Sprinkling flour on the large butcher block island, the dough was dumped and Antonia was instructed to punch it down and begin to knead. The base of the island was painted a deep olive green with stools on two sides. Nona took a seat across from Antonia, laying out three baking sheets. Nona scooped out some solid shortening and generously greased the pans while Antonia continued to work out her arm muscles on the kneading. There was very little small talk aside from a few instructions.

Antonia watched with interest as Nona's hands seem to know just what to do to make the dough behave. Soon Nona broke off the dough dividing it into six pieces with a special tool. "Now you do one," said Nona. Nona brushed her hands together making a small cloud of flour that floated up. It made Antonia smile knowing she was making the bread with her own two hands. Nona allowed her to take over finishing the rest of the loaves. They were not perfect like Nona's but Antonia was proud of her effort.

"I have never made bread before. My mother wasn't big on baking or cooking for that matter, but she did make a delicious chocolate cake. I wish I had learned the recipe."

Nona took the sheet pans and placed them in her double ovens using her apron as hot pads. As she washed the flour from her hands, Nona became sullen and turned drying her hands to face Antonia. Her shoulders were slouched just a little as she avoided eye contact.

"This kitchen is my sanctuary, where I start my day making the rich hot coffee, and where I seek refuge after a busy day of cooking family meals. My mother taught me that cooking is making memories that will last a lifetime.

"'That beautiful pasta is something grandchildren will remember eating at their grandparents house,' she used to say." Pausing, Nona took a cleansing breath and walked over to the kitchen island and began wiping crumbs. "Baking establishes sacred traditions such as the berry tarts we will make for the wedding. Picking the right ingredients, using the memorized recipes handed down all written on bits of paper. Food brings happiness and family traditions. However, Antonia do you see any of my family here with me?"

"Well, I haven't been here long, but I am here now, Nona," replied Antonia.

"I have no daughters, just two sons. I have one daughter-in-law who stays with her nose in books. I have one granddaughter, Isabella. I have some granddaughters-in-law, Rosa and Aria, but they are not interested in learning to cook a family recipe."

"I assume it is something you either love or you don't, Nona. Don't feel bad, maybe one day they will be interested," replied Antonia.

Nona looked down as if trying to keep her composure then looked straight at Antonia with a slight sadness to her face and a noticeable tremble beginning on her lips.

"My biggest fear Antonia, is I will die, in this very kitchen, with flour in my hair and no one in my family will know the importance of basil or when to add the garlic in my momma's pasta sauce. All traditions will end with me. No one will carry on the traditions."

Nona looked at her hands and held them out in front of her as though she was watching them age before her eyes. She fiddled with the bits of dough still stuck under her fingernails. Antonia could feel the heaviness of Nona's heart. There would be no one to carry on any family traditions from her, not even her mother's famous chocolate cake. She could feel the loss just like Nona.

"This bread will be cut into thick slices and grilled," Nona continued breaking the silence. "Then it will be rubbed with soft baked garlic and drizzled with olive oil to make the bruschetta. That will be the day of the wedding. Now we must make the berry tarts that are filled with fresh fruits. Let's be happy we are together and create our own memories," said Nona. "Go ahead and sprinkle a generous amount of flour on your surface."

As Antonia sprinkled the surface area with flour, she began missing her own mother. She watched for signs of approval from Nona. Nona motioned for a little more then held her hand out to stop. As Antonia placed the bag of flour down Nona pinched a bit of flour and tossed it at Antonia. Antonia sputtered and stared back at Nona not knowing how to react.

"You have been baptized in flour" laughed Nona. "Now cheer up."

Chapter 24: Wedding Wine

After a little hot shower to rid herself of baptism flour and a little cuddle time with Luca, Antonia dressed and they both headed to the family dinner in the courtyard. As expected, everyone sat drinking wine as Nona brought out bowls of pasta and placed it on the table. Antonia stood to help when Luca grabbed her arm.

"Where are you going, love? I have barely seen you all day," asked Luca.

"I was simply going to help Nona bring out the food."

"You do not have to do that, Antonia. Just sit by me. Nona can handle it," Luca sneered.

Slowly Antonia sat down. She looked around the table at all the family talking, laughing and drinking wine. It was hard to relax as Nona made yet another trip from the kitchen. This time, she placed one of the loaves of bread that they had made together. Placing it on the table she made a big deal about how she and Antonia made the bread together. Antonia smiled remembering the softness of the dough: a creation she accomplished with her own hands.

Noticing the awkward silence, Luca stood and held up his glass of wine. "As usual, Nona has prepared another wonderful dinner for her family. Also it should be said that my soon-to-be-wife helped make the bread and I for one am very proud of her. Let's eat!"

As the dishes passed around the table, Antonia noticed Isabella had a frowning look on her face. As they made eye contact Isabella turned to her husband and whispered in his ear. Cupping her hand so no lip reading was possible. Her husband, Lorenzo, nodded at Isabella then turned to look at Antonia. Antonia felt her neck getting hot. She turned to Luca and whispered in his ear giving the impression that two can play this game.

"Did it embarrass you when Nona gushed that I made the bread?" whispered Antonia. Knowing this comment would make Luca frown then start whispering back, Antonia felt sure Isabella would think something was amiss or a secret was passed she was not privy to. As expected, Luca shook his head no, then put his arm around Antonia as he whispered in her ear. As Luca whispered his accolades and sweet support, Antonia turned to glance at Isabella with a perplexing grin.

I bet she wonders what I said to Luca, her brother, head of the mafia! This is fun.

The food arrived around the table just in time to change the focus. Antonia did not want to make Isabella an enemy, just let her know that she was not afraid. Antonia reached for the large fork and spoon and dished out a serving for Luca and one for herself. The *pollo piccata* smelled delicious and tasted like an Italian dream. The flavors of the chicken teased her taste buds and made her curious of the ingredients.

Antonia wondered if Nona would show her how to make such a wonderful dish one day.

"What are you so deep in thought about, Antonia? Did everything go alright shopping today?" Luca said in a quiet voice.

Antonia, feeling confident and a little giddy, squeezed Luca's thigh. "It was a wonderful day and I think I have made a decision. A temporary one, perhaps, but at least I have something to look forward to now. Something to occupy my mind."

"Really? This is interesting. So are you giving up on going to college or are we talking about something else?" Luca inquired.

"Something purposeful, something I can physically see and create. Something of my own heart and mind. I am going to learn to cook and bake. I want to know the ingredients, what makes a dish come to life. I want to study and discover the difference between basil and parsley. I might even write a family cookbook so all of Nona's recipes can be handed down to future generations. If Nona approves, of course, I am unsure about the rest of your family."

Luca looked at Antonia's face realizing she was serious. "Is that something you want to do to occupy your time while I am away on errands for the family business?"

Antonia gave Luca a playful nudge before she continued. "I am serious. I have to do something to contribute to the world and our life. I am not the type of woman who wants to lounge around in lavish clothes, shop or sip wine all day. I am not a princess, Luca. I am an intelligent woman with idle hands. Not a good combination. This will be a project of love that I can use my mind and develop knife skills. Not that I will ever need knife skills."

Antonia found herself in deep thought about how she should compartmentalize her life. She grew up on a ranch, had her heart broken by a terribly selfish man, and now she was living in Italy with a gorgeous man who loved her. College and being a surgeon wouldn't mix with the life she and Luca would share. Those dreams would be boxed away and she would love her life as it is.

Luca took Antonia's hand and gently kissed her on the cheek. "You are the perfect woman for me, Antonia. I did not choose you to make you a spoiled princess. I chose you because of your mind and your courage. Your beauty is not only physical, it is all of you as a whole. I will support this decision of yours. However, let's be careful with the knife skills."

With that being said, Antonia giggled then settled in to enjoy the food and the family conversations. Isabella's smug looks no longer concerned her. Luca had said he loved her mind and nothing else could make her more confident.

Antonia had a new quest to fulfill and hopefully it would occupy her time and keep her mind sharp. She had bonded with Nona. Aria would gladly let her be a special aunt to her children and Rosa would come around as soon as the wedding was over and Isabella returned to Sicily. For the first time, she was content that she could find fulfillment in her decision to stay in Italy with Luca even if she never returned to college to become a doctor.

When the meal was just about over, Antonia rose to assist Nona clearing the table. Luca looked up at her and smiled, knowing Antonia was trying to fit in and live her best life. He was proud of her. A few whispers and huffing began to be heard as she headed to the kitchen. The voices seemed to get louder. Antonia stopped and looked back at the table noticing, Aria had stood and was also helping to clear the dishes. Luca suddenly stood, banging his fork on his wine glass to get everyone's attention.

"Antonia is my future wife and my concern. Only mine. She is not one to sit idle sipping wine as she has just told me. She is made of a strong determination. I, for one, am very proud of her courage to find a purpose and not sit idle. She is not my puppet nor a princess. If you have nothing positive to say about her decision to learn what it takes to take care of the family, then say nothing. If you choose to challenge that order then bring it to me. Say nothing negative about

Antonia. Do I make myself clear? A disrespectful word about Antonia is disrespect for me."

No one said a word. The family that is usually so loud and boisterous was silent. Armando stood to speak next. Trying to change the mood. "I am the father of the groom and as usual when we have a wedding celebration in the family, we have wine. There is not enough cached in our cellar so the men folk will take a trip today to our family connections and gather the wedding wine for Rosa and Mateo!"

Mateo stood and agreed with his father then announced that the women should practice the *la Tarantella* and try on clothes. Then he dismissed the women. Once in the kitchen, Nona and Aria began chatting excitedly about *la Tarantella,* the dance guests perform to wish the newly married couple good luck.

Antonia decided to take a turn at washing because Aria's belly had gotten too big to stand at the sink. Nona and Aria began humming as they held hands showing Antonia the dance.

"… then we rotate clockwise as the music speeds up, then reverse directions. It is so fun Antonia. You will see," said Aria.

Antonia loved being in the big kitchen. She also loved watching Aria smile as she danced. Nona looked pleased as well. It was the one place Antonia felt comfortable and not judged. It kept her mind occupied with less time to feel disappointed in her career. She realized common sense and intelligence could be a gift or a punishment, especially if you have to deal with anyone who doesn't have it.

I must live my best life with no regrets.

When the dishes were all done, Aria put baby Ricky to bed and came back to put on the kettle. Nona, Antonia and Aria sat around the large butcher block island and poured a cup of tea. Aria talked about the new baby kicking so chamomile tea always settled everything down. Nona smiled with the girls surrounding her.

"Well, I have finished the meal planning for the wedding. I even ordered a box of Italian cookies from my cousin's bakery in town. I pick up the sausage for the wedding soup in the morning, then I am *finite*! I made an extra batch of *pollo piccata* pasta tonight, so we have some for the wedding," announced Nona. "Going to be simple but elegant."

"You did a great job on our wedding, Nona," said Aria.

"It sounds like tradition so, I guess you will be planning food for Luca and me someday," chimed in Antonia.

"You will want the same food, Antonia? No American dishes?" asked Nona.

"Well, if I want to include anything that reminds me of home, I guess it would be my mother's chocolate cake. But I don't even know how to make it," said Antonia, "I never learned."

"We will find a recipe or two and practice until we get it right. That I will promise you," said Nona. "I am sure you still remember how it tastes?"

Antonia jumped off her stool and gave Nona a big hug. Antonia remembered her mother but many memories she thought were tucked away for life seem to fade as time went by. As a young girl, she would come home from school and sit at the kitchen table doing her homework; when she finished her mother would cut her a thick slice of chocolate cake.

"How different is it living in America, Antonia? I always wondered," asked Aria interrupting her thoughts. "Is it all big cities and tall buildings?"

"America is so big and there are so many traditions that are important and different at the same time, depending on where you live. Our ranch is pretty flat with only a few trees."

"Is everyone a cowboy, riding horses?" asked Aria.

"No, sweetie, not at all. There are cowboys in Texas where I am from, more so out west and sprinkled throughout the country. There are cultures and subcultures throughout the nation. For example, there are areas in New York that are all Italian neighborhoods as well as the Irish," explained Antonia.

Tilting her head to the side, Aria wrinkled her nose. "That sounds amazing Antonia. I am not sure I will ever visit America but it does sound curious. Why did you come to Italy? Aria asked.

"I was on a journey. I was never one for jumping on the therapy train and I always wanted to visit Italy. I hoped with all that is in me, that setting my eyes on such beauty as the Italian countryside and special places would change me and give me a reset. A new look at life. It was taking a risk but I am so glad I did. Italy was the therapy I needed."

Aria continued to sip her tea and appeared deep in thought. "I have never thought about traveling anywhere. It seems brave to leave the country you were born in and travel."

"There are other countries I would love to visit as well." Looking down at her laced fingers then up again, Antonia continued, "I would love to visit Ireland. My mother's family was from there. She always talked of traveling there one day. Unfortunately, she died before she ever got the chance."

"It sounds so different. Are you sure this is where you want to be, or is it because you love Luca?" asked Aria. "He is the hottest brother in the family. Lucky you!" she giggled.

"Don't ask so many questions, Aria" scolded Nona.

Aria was only a few years younger than Antonia but the educational difference was obvious. Aria was almost child-like. She talked softly and always seemed to sway a little while rubbing her ever growing belly. Certainly with no cares in the world, Aria trusted her husband and the family she married into for all her needs. Never having to struggle, cook or pay any bills gave Aria a freedom to just be a wife and mother. An ideal life for some women.

It is obvious she never had an urge to murder someone.

Antonia felt her face flush as she struggled to find the right words. Her smile wavered as her lips pressed together in a grimace. "I do love Luca. Yes, it may be a little hard for me emotionally if I never return to where I am from. I will always miss it and Texas will hold a special place in my heart. There are still people there that I love and care about, Aria. To be honest, I am just living day to day loving Italy. I will make my home wherever Luca is."

As usual, talking about Texas and home created a nostalgic or wistful feeling for a former time or place in Antonia's heart. It was a simpler time when her parents were alive and before she met Wade at college. Feeling dewy-eyed, Antonia placed her tea cup in the sink, wiped away a single stray tear and excused herself. She gave a hug to Aria and Nona and vowed to be back in the kitchen early to help prepare meals.

"Don't expect the men to return until late. Going to collect the wedding wine can be translated into, we are having a bachelor party going from café to café and drinking wine while telling stories," joked Nona. "Lots of drinking and staying late noshing on antipasto."

"Duly noted," quipped Antonia.

Antonia left the main house and slowly walked to the villa enjoying the night air. The still glowing full moon filtered light through the branches of the trees lighting her path. There was a chill in the air as fall was beginning to end and winter begin in Pico Italy. Just reaching the door she paused and listened. Hearing the rustling in the leaves yet again, made her fearful. A feeling of imposing dread swept over her. Fear was derailing her efforts to settle into the life she had chosen.

"Is someone there?" she called out. Hearing nothing, Antonia shrugged her shoulders then proceeded into the villa. After turning on the two bedside lamps and shutting the curtains, she switched on the coffee pot. Sitting on the bed Antonia quietly listened to the low bubbling of the coffee maker. As the aroma filled the air, she stared at the unlocked door. They never locked the door because Luca said they were safe here. A gradual build up of worry and dread briefly entered her thoughts. Knowing Luca would not be back from the ceremonial gathering of the wedding wine until very late, Antonia got up and locked the door.

When confusing and uncertain thoughts come up, you phone a friend.

Antonia stripped down to her panties and settled in the bed. With the covers pulled up and her cup of hot coffee on the nightstand, Antonia called Rick. He answered just as she was taking her first sip of hot brew. It startled her and she splashed a tiny plop right on her bare chest.

"Hello," he said.

"Ouch!, Geez that is going to leave a mark on my tender boob!" Antonia squealed.

"Antonia? What is wrong and what is going to leave a mark? Hello?"

"Sorry Rick, I did not expect you to answer so quickly and it startled me. I spilled a dime size drip on my chest. It burned," Antonia explained. "I guess it is just a tender area."

"Now you are just teasing me."

"How is my pain teasing you?" asked Antonia.

"You call me late at night, obviously with very little clothing on, laying in bed and then talk about your tender breast. You are an animal," laughed Rick.

"Sorry, not sorry. Were you asleep?"

"No. Can't sleep, but I am laying on the bed with nothing but my boots on," said Rick.

"Now who is teasing who?" scoffed Antonia.

"Admit it: you were trying to picture it in your mind, weren't you?," Rick cackled.

"No, well… maybe," laughed Antonia. " Thanks for the laugh, I was feeling kind of down."

"What is it this time?" Rick asked.

Antonia took another sip of her coffee and set it on the bedside table. Leaning back on the pillows she pulled up the covers. "I was talking about Texas and my momma tonight with the ladies. It made me sad to think I may never see Texas again or visit my parents' grave. I am feeling disconnected. It seems unreal to me that I had an old life; it was genuine and happy. Then somehow I popped into a black hole and came out in a new country. If that makes any sense."

"It makes sense because you did have a life. You had plans here in Texas. You had a career and people who already loved you. Now you are confused. You are afraid to give one up and that is a sign that something just isn't right. You are having a tug-o-war in your emotions," said Rick.

"On top of all that, I keep feeling like someone is watching me or following me. It is probably nothing. Just the wind."

"Well I am glad you called me. I feel we still have a strong bond, so when you need to talk, you call me. You are never disconnected from me or the ranch. Maybe it is time you recognize the way you matter to other people. Choose your old life here with me," said Rick.

Antonia sat up in the bed holding her hand to her head and began to rock. Finding herself in love with two completely different men, in two different countries. One man is comfortable, familiar and protective who wants babies. The other man is exciting, mysterious, lustful and knows all her secrets.

There comes a day when you just have to turn the page.

I cannot choose.

"Rick, it is not that simple. There are things you don't know. Italy is sparkly in a way and yes, it has drawn me in. I am completely in love with Italy. There are a thousand reasons to stay or not and none of them are adequate. Italy is not the problem. It is me, I lack purpose here. Sometimes I feel lonely, too. Although I am learning to cook. There is a wedding here in a few days and I am preparing most of the food. That is exciting, right?" asked Antonia.

"If you say so. It is not close to being a doctor but I guess you compromise."

"I don't know how to explain it, Rick. I have a fear that when the dawn breaks one morning, the sparkly, mysterious and exciting Italy will eventually become a disappointing bucket of boredom. Being a good aunt to someone's children and redecorating a villa is all my future plans can muster up right now," said Antonia. "Will that be enough or will I get restless?"

"Actually I understand restless. My saddle is worn out but fits my ass just right. I love my old saddle. When we took the ranch to a rodeo in Fort Worth I bought a new saddle. I tried to break that flashy saddle in by oiling it and riding in it. However, I eventually put it on a rack in the barn. I love to look at it. I won't regret trying something new, but my old saddle is safe and reliable. You take your time, Antonia. When Italy loses its sparkle, and I know it will. *Then* come home to safe and reliable."

"You always come up with a story to make me feel good, Rick. You are my safe and reliable," said Antonia. "Even you will get tired of waiting one day."

Just as Antonia leaned back to relax again, she heard a noise. It sounded like the door handle. She turned off the lamp and sat in silence listening. The door handle jiggled again.

"I wish your safe and reliable ass was here right now," whispered Antonia.

"Are you all alone?" asked Rick.

"It is fine. Could be the wind. Luca is at a bachelor party for his brother tonight."

"So you call me when he is not around. I get it."

"It is so I can talk freely and openly."

"Are you saying you cannot talk openly to your Italian tour guide that turned into lover, what a shame."

"Don't tease me Rick. I mean that sadly, in my life you are the only one I can say anything to and talk openly with. You know me better than I know myself sometimes."

"You are a smart woman, you should recognize that as a sign Antonia."

Chapter 25: The Wine Blues

The rest of the night was dreadfully silent until the chill of the morning awakened Antonia. Without opening her eyes she stretched her arms to feel for Luca and he was not there. Grabbing the covers tight she opened one eye to peek out into the room. Luca was slumped asleep in the chair by the door. She had not heard him come in.

Sitting up she, stretched and yawned loudly. Luca didn't move. His face needed a shave, his suit coat was open and flopped out to each side exposing the inner pockets and his gun. His white shirt was unbuttoned and no longer tucked in his pants. His tie was stuffed in his pocket with the end flopping out. She had never seen Luca so disheveled. He was always groomed and dressed to the nines. The doctor in her found herself pausing to make sure he was breathing. As she slid her body to the side of the bed to sit up facing him, she noticed he only had on one shoe. One shiny Italian leather shoe was missing.

For the first time, she wondered if she could be good enough for Luca. He wanted a dutiful stay-at-home wife. Her previous relationship and trauma had left a wound that may not heal and she wondered if Luca could bring out the best in her or would she end up letting him down. Would she dread staying in Italy or regret leaving was the question on her mind.

Dread is a suffocating state brought on by gradual buildup of worry and melancholy. It results from refusing to acknowledge that there is a problem or thinking your troubles are exaggerated. The noises heard in the night and Luca looking so vulnerable actually gave Antonia a sense of dread. She shivered thinking there may come a day when Luca was the head of the family business and someone wanted to eliminate him.

Will I regret it all?

Antonia had a thought to tiptoe quietly and kiss Luca on the forehead to awaken him. Then she saw the gun. Not knowing what would be the best choice, she decided to make noise and let him react naturally. Antonia slipped off the bed and cleared her throat. Next, she coughed, pushing it a little too hard so early in the morning and released quite a loud passing of gas. Hoping the smell didn't linger in the room, Antonia went to the back windows and slung them open. As she turned around to check on Luca, he was smiling. Then he began to slowly clap.

"Good job, oh stinky one," laughed Luca"

"That is not funny, Luca. It was a frog outside the window!"

"Remind me to never ask you to spy on someone from the bushes. You wouldn't be able to keep it in quiet mode," Luca laughed.

"That is rude. Don't you know a gentleman pretends he heard nothing?"

Humiliated, Antonia covered her face with her hands then shrugged her shoulders. She had no time to have idle chatter about frogs with Luca, She needed to go to the main house and help in the kitchen. She knew Luca was only joking but Antonia was in a serious mode like the first day of class. Nona might be upset thinking Antonia was an unreliable sidewalk sally, so she grabbed her sweater and headed for the door. Luca grabbed her elbow, spinning her around for a deep good morning kiss.

Pushing him away, Antonia stepped back and gave Luca a sour look. "First of all, you can't talk with that lovely hangover breath. Secondly, speaking of bushes, I have heard rustling when walking home to the villa and felt like I was being watched," said Antonia.

"I think I will look around and come talk to you at the big house after I shower. Did you make coffee? I really need strong coffee."

"Yes."

"Good."

"Okay, now go brush your teeth, I have to go," snapped Antonia.

"Oh, I can tell you missed me. Don't pretend, Antonia," Luca chuckled.

As Antonia squeezed past Luca, he gave her a slap on the bum. She turned and flashed a smile. It stung a little but she sure loved the attention.

Antonia headed outside to walk to the main house to help Nona. The sun filtered through the trees highlighting the morning fog. The changes of seasons in Italy always brought on a different yet beautiful pattern of weather. After talking with Rick for hours last night, Antonia felt more aware of her surroundings and her choices. In her mind, Antonia was secretly making a mental pros and cons list. Beautiful weather and scenery gives a pro to Italy; Texas is mostly dry. This put a little skip in her step until she reached the courtyard. Mateo and Roberto, Luca's brothers, were both laying on the long wooden family table asleep. Nona peeked out of the kitchen door as she heard Antonia approaching. "No worries about them; they have the wedding wine blues!" said Nona.

"It must be hard work going around collecting wine from the family. It just wore them out, poor things. Couldn't even make it back to their own beds," laughed Antonia.

"Mateo better get cleaned up before his wife-to-be comes out and smells that strange perfume on his clothes. I tried to shake him. I will fetch the broom and start shooing them off," laughed Nona.

Antonia couldn't resist and leaned over Mateo taking a big sniff then shook her head.

Never underestimate the power of a good sniffer. Rosa will definitely know.

"I wonder how long women have been putting up with this caveman ritual of having a bachelor party, and getting drunk with loosey-goosey women?" asked Antonia as she entered the kitchen.

"Okay, enough about the bad behavior of men. We need cookies made. Roll the dough about the size of a pigeons egg. Then we start the soup," explained Nona as she grabbed her broom.

Ignoring Nona's foul mood, Antonia ran her hand across the well worn kitchen island. It was definitely a place to start finding a purpose. Putting her apron on, she dusted the butcher block with flour and pulled the large metal bowl of cookie dough from the refrigerator. She enjoyed being in the kitchen alone and was grateful Nona trusted her with the baking.

Meanwhile, Nona was outside sweeping the sleeping men from the courtyard and shouting orders for the placement of additional tables and chairs. "Armando and Roberto will string the lights while Mateo and Rico set up the chairs!" Nona shouted. "We have little time."

"Nona, my head hurts. I need a coffee first, please," said Rico complaining.

"You will get a coffee when you set up those chairs. Carmella has been working on the arch and she needs to know where to place it," replied Nona.

Luca appeared in the courtyard wearing sweat pants and a hoodie. "Nona, too loud. You go get the coffee and bring it out to us while we set up. We got this. We did it for Rico and Aria's wedding. Hand over the broom and go get us some coffee," said Luca firmly.

Nona looked at the boys then back at Luca. Giving up her broom was like giving up her sword. With a huff, Nona reluctantly handed over her broom and went to get some coffee, mumbling as she turned to leave. Nona herself was never involved in the family business but even she knew it was best to do as Luca told her to do.

Nona entered the kitchen still mumbling under her breath about the half drunk men cluttering up her courtyard. "Don't they know we have things to do?" she shouted as she poured the coffee. With the tray in hand, Nona set out to the courtyard.

While Nona took a tray of coffee out to the courtyard, Roberto popped in the kitchen from the side door. He was looking young and fresh, unlike the other men.

"Hey, Antonia, I just snuck in to get a few matches. Nona keeps them near the wood burning stove. I need a quick smoke. Would you like to join me?"

With all the ruckus from the bachelor party, drunk men laying all over, and the fear of not finishing the food in time, Antonia thought a quick smoke sounded good. She had never smoked a cigarette in her life except the time a ranch hand offered her one behind the barn. Roberto offered her the cig and Antonia took one look and remembered choking on that one single puff behind the barn.

"No thanks, Roberto. I just came outside for a break. My fingers are beginning to cramp after rolling all those cookies," said Antonia.

"Maybe I can help after I shower. Nona had me in the kitchen helping since I was five. I stood on a chair and helped knead bread," replied Roberto.

"That would be wonderful. I had the impression no one ever gave assistance in the kitchen. I took it all on as a project to learn how to cook and be productive somehow."

"Listen I make the best wedding soup. Escarole, kale and the little sausage meatballs. It is to die for and not just for weddings, by the way. It just feeds a large crowd. I started out cooking in all the family's cafés for some spending money. It will be fun to help you," said Roberto.

"You seem different than the rest of the family. You are the free spirit of the bunch."

"Thanks, but I know that is just a kind way of saying I am not stiff. I am more of the oddball and less rigid. It is fine, I take that as a compliment. I am different."

Antonia headed back into the kitchen hoping Roberto would be good on his word to shower and return to help. Voices were getting loud in the courtyard so Antonia went to the outer door to listen. Peeking her head out she saw Luca's mother on a ladder trying to adjust flowers on the wedding arch and all her boys screaming for her to get down. Antonia shook her head and strolled through the kitchen grabbing an apron.

Alone in the big beautiful kitchen, she took a minute to run her hand along the smooth surface of the butcher block table where all the magical cooking and prepping took place. She imagined how many times over the years loaves of bread were made right here in this spot. Touching the table was like touching the hands of many past generations. The faded yellow checked curtains on the window, the Italian tile backsplash and wood cabinetry gave her a feeling of comfort.

If only the walls of this kitchen could tell stories.

Nona came in the kitchen not looking too pleased. Slightly stomping her feet and mumbling under her breath in

Italian, Antonia sensed some stress. Roberto entered the kitchen and Nona turned about to snap, then recognized it was Roberto. She held out her arms to hug him. Roberto looked at Antonia mouthing the words, *"What happened?"* over Nona's shoulder. Antonia shrugged and rolled her eyes.

Roberto pushed away and held Nona at arms distance, then putting a finger under her chin, he stared into her eyes. "Nona, are you letting those naughty brothers of mine who are all having the too much wine blues get you upset on this glorious day?" asked Roberto. "They have been drinking all night. Just let them be and let's cook something fabulous!"

Antonia broke a smile and nodded at Roberto. It was at that moment she knew the stories about Roberto were not true. He was not chasing skirts all over Italy. Not at all. Not unless they were men in skirts.

Nona clapped her hands loudly and snapped in to action calling out instructions like a drill sergeant in a mess hall. Before long, Antonia and Roberto were rolling dough elbow to elbow as Nona stirred the wedding soup in the largest pot Antonia had ever seen on a stove. She chopped up cabbage, kale and grated parmesan cheese to add in the soup. The oven was full of loaves of bread and baked pasta. The aroma filled the air, making Antonia hungry. Around noon, Aria come into the kitchen and Nona sat them all around the kitchen table and served samples of the delicious wedding soup with hot fresh Italian bread right out of the oven.

Even if it was just the four of them, they were laughing and joking as they enjoyed good food as a family. A loving, close-knit, strong Italian family. Antonia felt truly blessed to be a part of it. Sitting back watching Roberto teasing Aria about her ever swelling belly while Nona let out a few big belly laughs, Antonia began to feel like she was finally where she belonged. She had found the happiness every soul searches for. Closing one door as another opens is a metaphor that in this case is pretty accurate. She finally let herself open up and accept the happy emotions, blocking out uncertain thoughts with optimism and gratitude. Roberto noticed the sparkle in her eyes and touched her shoulder.

"Hey, bestie future sister-in-law, what is on your mind making you look so pleased. Is it Nona's kitchen? It always makes me especially happy."

Antonia swallowed her last bite of food and wiped her hands on her apron. "I am smiling because I just realized that I have never been this happy. Love came softly and took me by surprise. Time gave me a second chance and I fought it. I questioned everything. Now I feel like I have confirmation. I am truly in love with a man and his family. I am right where I want to be," she said.

Roberto smiled, nodding while Antonia spoke. Warmth and kindness radiated from his body language. "We are going to get along just fine, me and you. I love to hang out in the kitchen with Nona and you like to hang out in the kitchen with Nona."

"Hey, I like hanging out in the kitchen with Nona! Include me in this group," laughed Aria.

Roberto reached over to touch Aria on the shoulder. "I am sure being pregnant and hungry has something to do with you hanging out in the kitchen but we will accept that."

Everyone laughed then Roberto got silent and put one finger to his lips. "I have something to say and since I am around my favorite people, I will give it a go. My father and brothers used to give me a hard time but they have mellowed some since two of the brothers are going to have babies and carry on the family name. I will never marry. Big Italian families put a lot of pressure on carrying on the family name and traditions. I, on the other hand have been traveling to research what I am called to do with my life. I think I am going to join the priesthood. What do you think?" asked Roberto.

He smiled and clasped his hands over his mouth briefly as though he just let out the secret of the century. Nona and Aria started clapping and hugging Roberto. Antonia patted him on the back and joined in the celebrating. Nona broke away wiping her eyes and pulled out some glasses to pour the wine.

"Roberto! That is wonderful news. Is this your official announcement? I mean, shouldn't you wait until the whole family is together?" asked Aria. "When will this happen?"

"I leave for seminary right after the wedding. Next time you see me, I will be a priest," said Roberto. "It is my life choice."

Nona put four wine glasses on the table and pulled the cork. As she began to pour each glass she cried a little more. "My parents always wanted one of us to become a priest or nun. I considered it until I met my husband and fell in love. May he rest in Peace. None of my children seemed interested but now, now I can proudly say my grandson will be the priest. I am so proud of you, Roberto," said Nona.

"Cheers to you Roberto. I am happy you found your happiness!" said Antonia as she raised her glass.

Aria raised her glass as well. "Here is to Roberto, who found his calling and here is to Antonia who has found her new family!"

"Let us also say here is to our loved ones past, present and future and also to Mateo and Rosa getting married today!" chimed in Nona.

As glasses clinked and hugs were shared, Antonia suddenly realized what Nona had said. Shocked, she looked around at the other three being so casual.

"The wedding is today?" she squealed."

"Yes, Father Christopher phoned and he will be here at six o'clock to perform the ceremony. Isabella and Rosa are already preparing. The food is ready so we should all go get cleaned up. It is a surprise wedding happening today," said Nona.

"So exciting!" shouted Aria.

Nona gulped her wine and placed the empty glass on the table. "We must hurry. Family is arriving soon and I must look good. My cousin who looks like she put on her makeup while on a trampoline will be bragging on her grandchildren. I must be prepared."

After a few final congratulatory hugs for Roberto, everyone broke away to their respective areas to prepare and dress for the wedding. Passing through the courtyard Antonia marveled at how the back courtyard had been miraculously turned into a fairy garden with twinkling lights and flowers everywhere, all while she was in the kitchen with Nona. She lingered for a moment taking it all in and soon Luca was at her side.

"Do you think it looks beautiful, Antonia?" asked Luca.

"Yes, it is beautiful and romantic and gorgeous! I have never seen anything like it."

"Really? Surely you have been to weddings before. Is this similar to weddings where you are from?" asked Luca.

Antonia turned to look into Luca's eyes. "Luca, sweetie, I am from Texas where most weddings are cowboy themed. At least the ones I have seen. I am sure some are in churches or gardens, just none I have ever seen."

"That is what I expected you to say but I am curious. Would you want a Texas wedding when we get married? I mean, I would look good in chaps and a ten-gallon hat, but I would miss having the twinkling lights," he laughed.

As they walked back to the villa arm in arm to begin dressing for the wedding, Antonia tried to picture in her mind what her and Luca's wedding would be like. "Listen, Luca, I am deep down all Texas. I am so Texas that my first bath was in a ten gallon hat; however, I want the twinkling fairy lights too. We can save the chaps and cowboy hat for role playing."

"I love it when you talk about role playing, Antonia," Luca whispered.

"I will race you to the villa and I will do more than talk," she whispered back.

Bursting into the villa like young teenage lovers, Antonia and Luca ripped off their clothes and fell laughing on the bed. Antonia stared into Luca's eyes and felt safe and warmth in return.

"I have had a surge of emotions today, Luca. I don't want to discourage any of your suave moves you are about to throw my way, but I just want to tell you I am happy. Happy here with you, your family and being your wife. I want to start planning our wedding as soon as Mateo and Rosa are wed. I am ready. Now let the lovemaking begin!" she said.

Luca put his hand on her lips. His eyebrows were deliberately raised giving him a smug look. "So it is safe to say you agree with my life choices, the conditions I have placed on being my wife, and you are totally ready to marry me?" asked Luca.

Pausing for affect, Antonia bit her lip and narrowed her eyes as though she was thinking hard on the subject. Immediately followed by a large grin and singing "Here comes the bride…"

Luca tilted his head, then in one swoop he moved Antonia placing her on top of his naked body. Antonia leaned down and kissed Luca hard, her hair falling gently on his chest. Luca placed his hands on her rump and squeezed. Teasing her further, he whispered in a gravely voice, I guess I better put a ring on your finger and make it official. You have agreed to obey me and my rules forever!"

In one fleeting second Antonia felt incomparable joy then a familiar feeling of disdain set in just as quickly. "I think *obey* is a poor choice of words, Luca…"

"I think it is the best choice of words Antonia. It is to keep you and the entire family safe. You will obey, there are no other choices."

Antonia became stiff as if she was paralyzed. She felt cold, her mouth like a dessert sand. Nothing could have prepared her for the sudden and intense trepidation she felt at that moment.

Chapter 26: Shattered Wine

When dark, confusing, and uncertain thoughts come up and fear imprints on your brain, it is not always easy to shake them away or push them back. Antonia straightened Luca's tie and smoothed the lapels that were trimmed in satin on his black tuxedo. The crisp white shirt stood out with its pearl buttons. His dark hair had been smoothed back. Holding his hands, Antonia stood back and looked at Luca.

"At this moment, you are the most incredibly handsome man I have ever laid eyes on, Luca Romeo Vitalia."

"Thank you so much, my love, but you need to finish up. I have to be there to keep my brother, Mateo, on task. Our father is giving away the bride since Rosa's parents could not attend at the last minute. Very strange… I wonder why they changed their mind," said Luca.

"It *is* strange. When I last talked to her, she said she was happy her parents were coming to the wedding. I hope she doesn't let it ruin her day. Maybe they just had other plans. You go ahead Luca. I will be right behind you. I just have to finish my makeup and run one little errand into town. I will be right back."

As Luca walked out the door, he turned, blowing a kiss to Antonia. She pretended to catch it when all of a sudden, she got a feeling of existential dread. She watched as the tails of his tuxedo flapped in the breeze of the door closing, and then he was gone. Antonia shook her head hoping to shake the feeling. She felt nauseous and held her hand over her stomach.

"It is just the season I am in right now. I am in Italy, attending a mafia wedding and considering to also marry a mafia man myself. I think I am just having normal emotions. Constantly looking over my shoulder will never be my future," she whispered aloud.

Having returned quickly from her errand, Antonia settled into getting dressed. She attempted to talk herself out of the strange mood she was in and prepare for the day's events.

Antonia knew Luca was intelligent, knowing the ways and unspoken rules of the family business. He would never take chances or put hers or anyone's life in danger and especially not women or children. Never on purpose. His family loved and trusted him. Here on the family's olive farm they were family, no business. It was their safe haven. Little flickers of seeing baby Ricky grow up only to be forced into the family business sent a chill up her spine. The illegal guns being smuggled in wine cases certainly was not her concern yet she doubted the integrity of the ones whose hands they were now in. Standing, she shook her head and fought back the implications that it must all be kept secret.

Antonia smoothed her hosiery and slipped on the high heels she purchased for the wedding then went to the mirror to touch up her mascara. Her dress was a pale burgundy sleeveless floor length gown. She chose it ironically because it was the color of cranberry wine. The bridesmaids were all wearing cobalt blue and she did not want to stand out or take away from the wedding party. This was their day to shine and she did not want to be mistaken for part of the wedding party. The dress amplified her tiny waist with a silk ribbon that made a bow in the back. The silver shoes she bought looked beautiful and finished the look.

Grabbing a small handbag, she took a deep breath and opened the door to the villa. As she made her way down the stone path toward the main house and courtyard she could hear violins playing softly. The wedding was about to begin, and it was exciting. Her phone call to Bethany earlier in the day went well with Bethany sending well wishes to the future of the family. It was a perfectly warm afternoon which gave Antonia some assurance.

When she reached the end of the walkway, she was startled to see the shoemaker standing near the house, next to the bushes. He was dressed in a light brown casual suit. He was a slightly round man and she could visibly see the sweat beading up on his brow.

"Hello, do you remember me?" asked Antonia.

Startled, the man turned to face her. He was holding his coat closed and Antonia detected something was wrong.

Perhaps he was not invited to the wedding and felt out of place. Surely he was where he was supposed to be.

"Is everything alright? You can accompany me to the seats; I think the wedding is about to start. Don't you want to be in the crowd with the guests?"

"Yes. Yes. Umm… the bride-to-be asked me to take pictures and I forgot my camera, so I am hiding here until my son brings it to me. Why don't you wait with me here. Yes, stay here with me please, American lady."

Antonia looked confused. She looked all around but could not see anyone from the family. She knew Luca would be busy with his brother so she was torn between waiting or just moving along and taking a seat so Luca would not worry.

"When I saw you in the shoe shop you did not speak good English. Were you pretending to not speak English? I mean, you let me ramble on and on. I don't understand," inquired Antonia. "I hear no Italian accent."

"The family reaches to the ends of the world. Hush now I need to prepare."

"I will just go casually and take my seat. Do you like my dress, it really stands out don't you think?"

The shoemaker turned to Antonia and grabbed her shoulders, startling her. "No more questions," he hissed, shaking her. "You must go back to your villa. Leave now."

"Stop! What are you doing touching me like that?" Antonia asked.

Looking embarrassed as the beads of sweat from his face were now running like a stream and making spots on his suit jacket, the shoemaker stood up straight. Taking a handkerchief from his pocket, he wiped his face.

"Okay, *mi scusi,* please. Listen, do you have a camera or phone that takes pictures? We don't have much time and you would not want the bride to have no pictures to remember this lovely occasion, am I right?" he pleaded.

"Okay… I feel a little scared and unsure but if it is for Rosa and Mateo, I could go back to the villa and grab my phone. I understand. I have a small camera I bought for traveling if I can find it. When will your son be here?" asked Antonia.

"Please, I need your assistance. Go back into the villa and get your camera. I don't think the wedding will start. Just go and don't hurry too much. It will be fine," he said.

Antonia had those uncertain feelings pop up again. She wanted to trust her intuition and run to find Luca but she didn't think the shoemaker would let her past him. Her love for Luca flared up making her want to run and find him, to warn him but slowly she just turned back toward the villa.

"I will be right back," she said.

Slowly, Antonia walked down the cobblestone path to the villa, occasionally glancing back at the sweaty shoemaker. She entered the villa remembering all the times she thought she heard someone in the bushes and shuddered. "Could it have been the shoemaker planning somthing all this time?" she thought. He appeared frightened or nervous. Perhaps it was just because he forgot the camera – or were her feelings of dread about to come true?

Antonia took one last look in the full length mirror. Taking her time, she smoothed her dress and grabbed her phone from the night stand. With her hand on the door handle, she paused. That is when she heard the first shots. Instinctively she sucked in a breath as her body stiffened. Her head up and eyes closed she felt her heart jump to her throat.

Perhaps it was champagne corks popping.

Then it got louder and continued rapidly. Antonia took a few steps down the stone path and stopped abruptly. In front of her at the end of the path was the shoemaker with a rifle aimed at the main house courtyard. The gunfire was now coming from all directions as she fell to her knees. She could hear screaming and yelling and she clasped her hands over her ears. Antonia squatted, frozen, afraid to move. She looked at the shoemaker again but he never glanced her way, he just continued to shoot into the crowd of people.

Antonia's mouth was open, but she could not hear her own screams from the massive gunfire.

After what seemed like hours, the sound stopped. Antonia looked up and saw the shoe maker turn to run. Stopping for a second, he gave Antonia a evil nod and a smirk then ran toward the front of the house and the road.

Antonia listened but her ears were still ringing. She could barely make out the sound of someone moaning. Crawling on her hands and knees, she rounded the corner from the pathway that led to the courtyard. Rising up to her knees she could see the beautiful archway where the wedding party stood was shot to pieces with flowers strewn on the ground. Under the now bare arch, Rosa was sitting on the ground with Mateo in her arms, blood staining her beautiful white wedding dress. The puffy sleeves and long veil were spread out like angel wings behind her.

Antonia looked around at the carnage. She could see the bridesmaids in their blue dresses all lying on the ground and assumed they were all hit by the gunfire, blood staining their beautiful gowns. It had been an indiscriminate and brutal slaughter of a wedding party. The entire family that came to witness the wedding bliss were now clustered on the blood-stained ground.

Antonia wiped her eyes straining to see. She stood up assuming the shooters had left, running away like cowards after a murder. Or were they brave for even making attempt of erasing a connected family? Was it a takeover or revenge for past indiscretions? Antonia heard faint crying and scanned the knocked-over chairs in the courtyard, spotting the small head of little Ricky. Next to him was his mother, Aria; her silver maternity dress was stained with blood. She was not moving; her eyes were closed and she slumped over. Her son was pulling on her, pleading for her to wake up. With her medical training trying to kick in she looked around hoping she could help someone but her legs would not move. She was in shock from witnessing a cold-blooded massacre. Her first concerns were for the entire family then she snapped her head around looking for Luca. Hoping he was spared.

"Luca! Luca!" she screamed as she began to step over the bodies. More family and friends had arrived while she and Luca were in the villa this afternoon and instead of being introduced to them all at the reception, she gazed at the well dressed bodies scattered on the ground. Blood splatter was everywhere, and faces were obliterated making some unrecognizable. White wooden chairs were knocked over and shot up with bullet holes and pieces of splintered wood flung everywhere. A large lady in a yellow dress lay on her back with a shard of wood lodged in her throat. The large wooden family table where wedding wine and food was set up was dripping with wine from the shattered bottles.

With her legs feeling weak, Antonia fell to her knees again with her dress soaking up blood from the scene. Her heart was racing and sending pounding throbs up into her throat. She felt like she was choking and it was getting harder to breathe when she heard another moan. Lifting her head, she again hollered out for Luca.

"Luca? Where are you?" she shouted.

Antonia paused and listened. Looking around searching for where the noise was coming from, she spotted the black tuxedo on the ground at the side of the courtyard close to the path that lead to the villa. With a glimmer of hope and running on adrenaline, she got to her feet and strained to see if it was Luca.

Stopping to listen again, she stood in silence. This time she was sure she heard someone faintly calling her name. It was Luca! She raced to him and fell on the ground reaching to cradle his head in her arms. Luca was covered in blood from his chest wounds. Antonia put pressure on the wound and leaned down kissing his forehead.

"Luca, I will get help. Please don't die. You are not supposed to die," she pleaded.

"Go home," Luca managed to whisper.

"Luca don't try to talk. I need you to stay awake and stay with me. I don't want to be all alone in Italy. Come to the States with me. Don't you dare die on me!"

Luca closed his eyes for a minute trying to muster up all the strength he had left. He looked up at Antonia, gasping for breath, a slight trickle of blood dripping from the corner of his mouth. His eyes were glassy and his skin was turning pale from loss of blood. His beautiful white shirt was now crimson red from his very own blood.

"Go home," he whispered.

Antonia leaned closer and stroked his face. "I am not leaving you, Luca. Please stay with me, I hear sirens. Help is coming," she begged. "Someone must have called for an ambulance."

Again Luca looked up at Antonia with pleading eyes and whispered. "Go home."

"I am not leaving you, dammit!" she said.

"Texas, go home. You are not safe," said Luca.

"No, how did this happen?" she cried.

"I forgive you," whispered Luca.

His body relaxed and went limp, his head turning to the side. Antonia closed his eyes and kissed his beautiful lips one last time. He looked peaceful. Antonia rocked Luca in her arms for a moment then gently laid him down in the grass, smoothing the lapel of his jacket.

"I will never say good-bye and I will always love you, Luca," she sobbed.

Her body trembling, she dared one last time to look around the courtyard at the slaughter of people. It was an aggressive cold-blooded massacre. Killing women and children was not off limits this time. She wanted to scoop up little Ricky but knew it would not go well and she didn't have the heart to force him away from his mother.

She wanted nothing to do with anything. Not Italy, not the gun smuggling and not being a mafia wife sitting at home. She didn't want to know the details of the family business. It was another ripple effect in her life that was not expected. Antonia got to her feet as she saw police and paramedics swarming the courtyard.

A paramedic approached her asking if she was injured. Antonia smoothed her dirty dress and looked him in the eye. "No, I am fine. Not injured. Please take care of the rest of the family. They mean a lot to me. Tell them I am sorry."

Antonia managed to walk to the villa unnoticed. Locking the door behind her, she sat on the bed briefly trying to catch her breath as her mind scrambled to choose her next move.

Did I start this ripple by running my mouth to the shoemaker?

Frightened the shoemaker would return or too many questions would be asked, she picked up her phone and called Bethany the travel agent.

"Bethany, get me out of here. I never want to see Italy again. I want to go home to Texas. I plan on taking one of the farm trucks and driving to the airport tonight.

"I will, do you have the keys to the truck?"

"Yes I got them this afternoon."

Are you sure?" asked Bethany.

"Yes, I am sure. Please hurry. I think I caused trouble. Unspeakable trouble. Women and children were not off limits. Never mind. Call Rick at the ranch and give him my flight information so he can pick me up at the airport in San Antonio."

"I will text you your flight information. You sound distraught. Did something happen? I have to ask Antonia, is Luca okay?"

"Bethany, Luca is dead!"

Antonia was devastated and numb as she found the keys under the mat where she left them earlier and cranked the old farm truck. Driving away from the family olive farm, she gained speed and gave one last glance at the wrinkled olive trees all planted in a row. They seemed to angrily look back at her. Nothing mattered now. Luca was gone. Wade, too, was gone and she felt responsible for it all.

Chapter 27: Memories of Wine

Three Years Later

I always enjoy the drive coming home from work after a long shift at the hospital, the dust trail rising up behind the Yellow Rose of Texas that car Rick had kept covered waiting for me in one of the barns. As I traveled the dirt road down Cranberry Lane to the ranch house, I gave Yellow Rose a pat on the dash for still purring along. It was getting slightly difficult to fit behind the wheel being in my third trimester.

As usual, Rick and our first child, Richard, were waiting for me by the cow pen. Richard loved feeding the cows some hay in the evening while waiting for mommy to come home. Rick had built a special pen closer to the house and kept one or two cows there at a time, just so Richard could go out in the evening and feed them. I admit it is cute but when the wind blows just right I wish the cows were much farther away. Smells bother me especially while I am pregnant.

As I pulled into the driveway, Rick and our son ran to greet me. Hugs and kisses all around and Richard always checked the pockets on my lab coat to see what I brought home for him. Some days it was a surgical mask or rubber gloves so he can play doctor. Today it was home-made chocolate chip cookies wrapped in a nice gift box from one of my patients. The family was very pleased that I caught their grandfather's ruptured appendix in time to save his life, so they brought in a sweet gift for me.

Rick kissed me hard then smiled as he greeted me. "Welcome home, Doctor Reynolds." Richard tugged on my scrubs to break us up. He always wrinkled his nose when we showed affection in front of him.

Richard just turned two and a half. He is very tall for his age with dark brown curly hair just like his father and has my green eyes. Rick rubbed my belly noticing how much the baby bump had grown as I removed my white lab coat and slung it over my arm. We stood there as a family watching the sun begin to set over the pastures. Sunsets at the ranch are astonishingly beautiful in the fall. The range of colors with bright orange and deep red are more visible here with no trees or mountains to block the view.

As Richard fed his special cows their hay, we noticed another dust trail was forming behind a car that turned on Cranberry Lane.

"Are you expecting anyone?" I asked Rick.

"No, it could be a delivery of those half million baby clothes you ordered, but it is sort of late in the evening for a delivery, don't you think?" asked Rick.

I gave Rick an elbow for teasing me. "It was not a half million but we are having our first girl and females need things."

"I understand that they need lots of pink. Pink clothes, pink curtains and anything pink," said Rick still teasing me for my spending.

"I suppose we will soon find out who it is, but I don't think it is a delivery. Perhaps someone wanting directions. What is for dinner by the way? I'm starving."

"I made a brisket stew with potatoes and carrots. You are going to love it," said Rick.

"Maybe I should head inside with Richard. I am dead on my feet. It was a long day with four planned surgeries and one emergency appendectomy."

"I love you, my hard-working surgeon wife."

"Don't tease, Rick. I love my job even if it is getting harder to fit in the surgical gowns."

"I will be in to rub your feet later," said Rick.

"You always know what to do to make me feel loved even when I am carrying around a basketball in my belly. You are my perfect cowboy."

Richard did not want to leave the cows and sunset so I turned to head to the ranch house by myself. As I turned to go in, I looked at the vehicle approaching. It was not a delivery van. For a short moment I felt panic even though my heart said it was not possible. I gently rubbed my hands on my baby bump and put one hand up to shield the setting sun from my eyes.

As the car got closer, I was curious and had to know who it was. It was a dark sedan with tinted windows. I looked over at Rick and he caught on quickly and walked to be by my side. I couldn't move and I could not possibly run being big and pregnant. As we stood there holding hands, the door to the car opened. A tall man in priest's clothing and a low-crowned hat emerged from the back seat. When he stood facing us, I recognized him right away.

"Roberto! Is it really you?" I shouted.

"It is, Antonia. I told you the next time you saw me I would be a priest."

I began to cry and my body shook. He had survived. As he walked closer, I held out my arms toward him. "Am I allowed to hug you?" I asked.

"Priests are allowed to hug, yes. Bring it in here. Although not too close as I see you are with child," said Roberto.

We hugged for a long cleansing hug then I stepped back and wiped my eyes. "Why are you here? I mean how did you know where to find me?"

"I will tell you everything, Antonia. Is there somewhere we can sit and talk? Maybe have a drink of something cool? It is hot in Texas and we have been traveling a long time."

"Yes, certainly. Let's go to the house and please invite your driver as well. This is my husband Rick and our son Richard. Let's all go in and find some refreshment. Can you stay for dinner? Rick has made a fantastic brisket stew."

I am unsure to why I was so excited to see a member of Luca's family alive. As soon as Rick picked me up from the airport three years ago I went straight to bed, fell into a deep depression and slept for two months. Rick was by my side the whole time getting me to eat and holding me when I cried uncontrollably. There was no pressure from Rick, just love and compassion.

I could not ignore that for too long. Rick was my first love, my childhood sweetheart who never ever gave up on me. He was steadfast in his love for me and protected my heart. I questioned everything. My sanity, my self-worth, and if I even deserved to live and feel happy again.

Jill, my old college roommate, came by telling me about her teaching job at the college and encouraged me to sign up for classes. She had found the love of her life at a youth club she was sponsoring. His name was Russell and they married just before I came home from Italy. Rick had invited them for dinner one night to cheer me up.

Gently, Rick convinced me to shower before they arrived. It had been almost three months without so much as a wipe down. I am sure it was a tactic to get me to shower, but it worked. I smelled pretty ripe, so I got in the bathtub to soak, excited to be seeing Jill again. Rick heard me crying and came in to wash my hair. I knew then that he would never give up on me. He would give up everything to make sure I was happy and had everything in life I wanted. I started looking at him differently from then on. Rick saved me. He also joked that the third time was a charm – which I did not think was funny.

Rick moved into the master bedroom with me and we lay awake long nights talking about everything that happened in my life that had brought me to this dark place. I told him about Wade and how I stabbed him with a steak knife and got away with it after stuffing my face with chocolate cake in Wade's hotel room. Rick never judged me or looked down on my choices. Because that is what they were: my choices. I chose wrong. It was all on me. I explained how Luca died in my arms and even Rick got tears in his eyes.

Slowly I started getting up in the morning and helping Rick with the chores. I didn't want to be alone, so I followed him around like a puppy dog. Rick made sure we started our day after a big breakfast of eggs, toast, hash browns and grits. He cooked for me and I didn't have to get dressed.

I made the coffee. Soon I could be alone longer and function a little better. It took some time and I had to forgive myself daily. The anxiety started to calm down as soon as I stopped having nightmares.

Rick started going to the barn alone and even went to town to buy horse feed and hay without me. One morning he saddled my horse, Julius, and insisted I ride with him to the far pasture. I had not ridden there since before I left for Chicago. The pastures were green with new hay planted for the season and it was the only pasture land that had a cluster of tall trees. Rick pointed out the tree he had carved our initials in to when we were teens. It was still there after all these years like some kind of prophecy of what was to be.

Being in nature, on my horse and with Rick by my side is when I made the decision to finish my medical training. I signed up that day. I was finally looking forward to becoming a surgeon, a dream that went unfulfilled for so long. It felt very freeing to make a decision about my life that I always wanted but had been discouraged from obtaining. I had healed from the ripple. I can have my dreams and share them with a loving man who only wanted the best for me.

I was in the first few months of internship when I discovered I was pregnant with a son. Jill's husband, Russell, married Rick and me on the ranch in front of the stone fireplace Daddy built. Jill made a small cake and the four of us hugged and cried celebrating my return and finally living the life I planned all those many years ago. My life had come full circle. I had the cowboy, children and I was becoming a surgeon -- three things I allowed myself to be denied for so long. Rick never denied me anything. I was free to be who I wanted to be.

The night Roberto arrived with his companion, we sat down and had a good meal. Rick is the best cook in this family, a grill master like no other. I usually make some side dishes and dessert, usually a chocolate cake. While searching through Momma's things, Rick found an old album and tucked neatly behind cellophane was mother's recipe for chocolate cake. I made it on my days off at least once a week. It was a way of telling my children about my mother and her love.

"I think we have a bottle of wine around here if my memory is correct. Would any of you like me to find it and pour you a glass? Otherwise, it is just sweet tea around here," said Rick.

"No, thank you, I have too many bad memories of wine. I will try your southern sweet tea," replied Roberto.

I had to agree with Roberto, I also had bad wine memories. That old bottle can sit on the shelf forever as far as I am concerned. The four of us had small talk at first because I didn't want to appear anxious about wanting to know what happened to the family after I fled Italy. I can only assume that is why Roberto is here and certainly it would be hard to talk about. It was his family, of course, but also the family that I left in Italy. The family I once considered my own. The family that no longer existed. I was curious if anyone suspected I caused the massacre by telling the shoemaker about the wedding. I still felt guilty that I may have caused so many deaths. I waited to let Roberto bring up the subject when he was ready.

"Rick that was a great meal. Thank you for you and Antonia being such wonderful hosts," said Roberto.

"It was my pleasure. Antonia has told me everything. We have no secrets. However, I am sure she has questions for you. Would you like to sit on the porch and talk while I put Richard to bed and make your companion a stronger drink? I have some good whiskey," said Rick.

I looked over at him and his handsome, understanding, compassionate face and mouthed the words, "*Thank you!*". Roberto and I left the table and headed for the huge wrap-around porch my mother insisted they had to have and sat in the rocking chairs. The night air was cool, being late in the fall. Crickets were singing and the stars were brighter than ever. I looked at Roberto as he sat comfortably in his chair next to me and I could feel the sting of tears starting.

"Was there a proper funeral?" I asked.

Roberto lit a cigarette and offered me one then laughed as I rubbed my belly. "I forgot. Forgive me. Yes, there were a few funerals. Rico, Aria and Mateo were buried together. Rosa insisted. She survived her wounds. She is now raising her nephew, little Ricky, and moved to be near her parents outside of Milan. They are still alive because they did not attend the wedding.

Our father and mother were both seriously injured. My father, Armando, lost an arm. It could not be saved. He still drives a tractor with one arm and does what he can on the olive farm. He hires workers every season and the surrounding families help out. My mother, Carmella, was in a coma for two years and finally passed away peacefully. Her book about the family was never published. She was shot in the head and body several times. When the shooting started, she ran to the archway to Mateo and Rosa. She threw her body over Mateo, but he had already been killed. They found eleven bullet wounds in him. Poor Aria was killed but she saved their son Ricky by shielding him with her body. The baby she was carrying was lost as well, of course. It was complete carnage in the courtyard. As for me, I was in the main house and I came down to check on Nona when I heard the gun shots. They had AK-47s, Antonia. They used the guns we were running against the family. I was not a part of that but I was privy to all the talk. My father and uncle thought I would surely join the family business so they talked freely around me. No secrets in the family."

Roberto took another drag off his cigarette and continued to rock facing straight forward. Never looking over at me. I knew it must be difficult to recall all the horrid details and I almost stopped him but he continued.

"Guests and cousins from out of town and other families that we had alliances with were all killed, murdered for just being associated with us. Some were the end of the blood line and no one came to claim their bodies. Nona paid to have them cremated with money she had saved in an old cookie jar and spread their ashes in the olive grove quietly and discreetly. It is now hallowed ground."

I stopped rocking and gasped, placing a hand on my chest. "Nona? She is alive?"

"Yes she is alive. She asked about you. She was getting something from the pantry when the shooting started. I came down stairs and shoved her and myself in, then closed the door. She was hugging a bread platter. The one that had 'Famiglia' on it. The one her grandmother made."

"Oh, my stars, I have worried about her and all of you. I cannot forget about the family. It has always been on my mind. I loved that bread platter. I told Nona it was special. I am better now but that horror will always haunt me in some way. I am so sorry, Roberto. I am rambling."

"It is nothing for you to be sorry about. Our uncle, Ricardo, was shot in the front yard. Right in front of the house. Nona says he was in the kitchen and got a phone call. He left out the front door thinking he was meeting family coming to the wedding. They shot him point blank in the head. He never had a chance."

"Roberto, you haven't said anything about Luca," I finally observed.

Roberto answered, "Luca was cremated. We did not want anyone to vandalize his grave. They were aiming for him. They came to seek revenge for what our grandfather did years ago and now again what Luca did. Mafia never forgets the sins of the father. Luca was the head of the family. It was a risk he took. The rest of the family did not deserve what happened to them. Neither did Luca. However, he was the gun-runner. Instead of importing booze or running a gambling casino, he chose to run guns to the bad people. The bad people used those guns to kill my family."

I put my head back to catch my breath while rocking. My lungs were being pushed up by the baby and being emotional did not help. "When Luca told me there were guns involved, I did not want to know any more. It scared me, Roberto. I just hate that these murders happened at all. Some were innocent and not involved in the business, but they were still killed. I felt as though they were my family, too," said Antonia. "I wonder often if eventually I would have been a victim of a horrible massacre."

We sat in silence for a while, then Roberto turned slightly to look at me. "I do have a question for you, Antonia, if you don't mind?"

"Sure, Roberto. Go ahead. I knew you would have questions."

"Where were you during the shooting?" he asked.

I felt my cheeks start to flush and my hands began to sweat as I recalled that day on the pathway. It never occurred to me that no one knew where I was. I just left. I got scared and I did the only thing I knew how to do, I ran.

I was not running now, so I explained to Roberto about seeing the shoemaker on the stone path from the villa and how he asked me to go back to the villa and get my phone. When I came out, the shooting had already started. I explained how I held Luca until the medics arrived then left that night, taking a farm truck. As the words came out of my mouth, it all sounded so cowardly but I also had to know if he held me responsible.

"Roberto, I am sorry if I made you worry. I was stunned. I didn't know what to do. I felt as though the shoemaker spared me by telling me to go back to the villa. Luca told me to go home. That is my only explanation. I was not going to be of any help if I stayed. Without Luca, there was no longer a reason to stay in Italy."

After another few awkward moments of silence, Roberto lit another cigarette. I was unsure if he believed my version but it was all I was willing to say. Less is best. Let the wounds heal.

"It would have been good if you stayed to check on Nona or long enough to tell us abut the shoemaker. I will relay the information, but you have no horse in this race. What happened to my family was because of guns and hate and murder. Poor choices for generations, not you buying a pair of shoes from town."

"What about Isabella and her husband?" I asked.

"Everyone is dead. I have no brothers or sister, no mother and a one-armed, hurting, angry, depressed father who hates that I am a priest and not an olive farmer. I left the week after the funerals to attend seminary in Rome. I still have more years of training and teaching. But I am at peace. I volunteered to train in the USA so I could look for you. Nona mentioned you were from Texas so I searched for you. I am happy. You are happy. Two children and a loving husband is better than mafia life and more than Luca was offering you. I could feel you wanted more out of life but, like me, you put your needs last. Be content ,Antonia. You are a remarkable woman and I am glad we got to know you. Your trip to Italy was not a waste. We loved you like family."

"Thank you for saying that and thank you for coming all this way, Roberto. I am happy you are following your heart and becoming a priest. Looks like we both finally got where we wanted to be all along. However, I do feel I need your forgiveness. Not just for what happened in Pico but for another crime I committed. Maybe this is my chance for confession."

"You have it, my forgiveness anyway. Whatever you have done in the past, I am sure you have paid for in suffering. The past is the past and the present is just that, the present. It is a gift, cherish it. I also have a gift for you from Nona. It is in the car. I will say my goodbyes and you can walk with me to the car."

"Will I ever see you again, Roberto?"

"Most likely we will never cross paths again, Antonia. I will return soon to Italy. That is where I belong. You belong here," Roberto said.

Talking to Roberto helped me feel like I could possibly put the past away and close the doors to the former life I fought so hard to make fit. I gave up my dreams to find love and tragedy occurred every time. My first choices ended up being the best. Occurrences that happened in between were because I did not stay true to myself. I tried to force the pieces of the puzzle and make myself a whole life.

Roberto and I walked back into the house and found Rick playing cards with Roberto's companion, Father Michael, his roommate from seminary. The four of us walked with them to their black sedan. Roberto opened the back door, pulled out a box wrapped in plain brown paper and handed it to me.

"I prefer you open it after I leave Antonia. I have been riddled with emotions all day, I have no more tears and I am sure there will be tears when you see what is in the package. I will tell Nona I gave it to you and that you asked about her. Please live your life knowing you are loved. A good life is the best revenge and also the secret to a long prosperous life."

Rick placed his arm around my waist and steadied me as we watched the dust trail from their car drive away down Cranberry Lane. The tears I had been holding back finally broke free and made snail trails down my face. The tears were cleansing and I did not mind them at all. I welcomed them. Rick offered to carry the package but I wouldn't let him. I knew it was something special.

"I got it, Rick. It is not heavy," I said.

"Okay, Antonia… This may sound inappropriate but have you considered the family may hold you responsible and the package is a bomb or a horse head?" asked Rick.

"I hope you are joking," I said.

"I saw the movie."

"Well, in the movie, the horse head was in the bed…""

"At least let me put Richard to bed first. If it is something notorious like a severed finger or ear, at least he will be in another room. By the way, why don't we call him Ricky for short instead of Richard?"

"No. His name is Richard," I snapped.

"He is named after me so why can't he be little Rick and I am big Rick?"

"Nope."

"I guess you spoke your mind, " said Rick.

"I am getting good at it, too," I snickered.

We both put Richard to bed and gave him a million kisses after Rick read his favorite bedtime story in his animated deep voice. He always acted out the characters and Richard listened with awe. I went to the living room, sitting on the worn leather couch in front of the fireplace while Rick brought me a slice of Momma's chocolate cake and a cup of caffeine-free coffee.

The box was sitting on the coffee table and I just stared at it for a while. I know when I open it, there might be heart rendering and stirring emotions but it will also be over. Like on Christmas morning when you open all the gifts and there are no more to open. It seems a little disappointing even though what you opened was absolutely thrilling and just what you wanted. I wanted to finish my cake and savor the moment. Putting down my fork after the last bite of cake, I looked over at Rick and squeezed his hand.

Slowly I untied the string and peeled off the tape, releasing the brown paper to reveal a box a little longer than a shoe box. Carefully I eased off the lid and reached inside. I almost immediately recognized the feel of the ceramic. Brushing off the white tissue paper it was wrapped in, I was amazed to be holding in my hand the platter made by Nona's grandmother. I ran my hands over the word *'Famiglia'* and hugged it to my chest.

"There is a note inside. Do you want me to read it to you?" asked Rick. Suddenly speechless, I nodded 'yes.'

"Ciao Antonia, I want you to have this platter my grandmother made. My Nona. I no longer have a family and no daughter to hand it down to. You loved the platter so much I want you to have it for your family. Grazie for showing me love in my kitchen. ~ Nona."

Chapter 28: Empty Glass

On the back of the note, Nona included her address in Italy. Nona and I became pen pals from that day on. I sent her pictures of my son, Richard, and wrote about life on the ranch and my job as a surgeon. She always wrote back keeping me updated on the olive farm and the festivals. She was the surrogate grandmother I never had. We talked about possibly visiting Italy one day in the future but deep down I knew I would never be comfortable visiting Italy or the family olive farm in Pico. My wine glass was empty having no more reasons to fear the future. I gave up olives for the smell of hay and exchanged Italy for the ranch and a career in medicine. I still had money left over from my lottery winnings, so I paid off my student loans and paid it forward making a scholarship at the university for up-and-coming female doctors.

I went into labor one afternoon while still on my shift at the hospital. Rick brought our son, Richard, and rushed to be by my side. I gave birth to a whopping 8-pound baby girl; we named her Isabella Gloria Reynolds. Isabella for Nona and Gloria after my mother. We call her Izzy for short. I was sure both grandmothers would be pleased. Her initials will be hard to make fun of when they are posted in her classroom. As for my son Richard, he will have to live with RRR for Richard Romeo Reynolds.

Rick fluffed pillows behind my back as I lounged on the leather couch in front of the fireplace after we returned home from the hospital. He has become the ideal loving husband just as I knew he would be. Taking Izzy from her car seat, Rick sat with Richard and Izzy on the floor. I reached for the camera to make a memory of our daughter's arrival. Both of my children had dark curly hair and beautiful eyes.

An unsolicited smile spread across my face. There is a new family in my life. My family. Rick looked up at me and smiled with a twinkle in his eye. He finally had the family he wanted as well. He looked back and forth at our two darlings sitting on each leg.

"How did you come up with our son's name again? Romeo does not run in my family."

"I told you, I love Shakespeare."

"Wasn't there a tragic ending in Shakespeare's Romeo?"

"There will be no more tragic endings. I am happy now," I said smiling.

The phone rang and I reached to answer it. I listened as the caller explained they were from the Chicago Bureau of Investigation. "Yes, that is me." I listened further while they explained the reason for the call. "Yes, I understand… Yes I will make arrangements… Thank you for calling. I will get in touch with a lawyer as soon as possible."

Hanging up the phone, I looked over at Rick curious with his eyes wide waiting for me to tell him about the call. I could see slight fear on his expression. Putting the babies down gently, Rick looked up at me.

"Whatever it is, we will face it together," he said.

"It is okay. They wanted to inform me that apparently Wade never had a chance to change his will before leaving for Italy. He left everything to me."

I have regrets. I also have hope. We are all one decision away from a totally different life. There are always well-made plans that end in disaster. Not all of them but some do. I could have come home to Texas after Wade left me by a dumpster. Do I regret that Marisa is in prison? It is just another weed in the garden. I didn't plant it there, so it is not my concern.

I do not regret going to Italy. Not at all. I made a choice to go to Italy. I didn't choose what happened there. Everyone has regrets. Do I regret not telling Roberto about secretly going into town and having a second conversation with the shoemaker? Not at all.

What about love? The fact that I fell in love is not something I regret. In my lifetime, I have loved three men. They all loved me differently, just as I loved them differently. Dread is a suffocating state brought on by gradual buildup of worry and melancholy. It results from refusing to acknowledge that there is a problem or thinking your troubles are exaggerated. I am no longer dreading the future.

I married the last and final one because he encouraged my dreams and challenged me until they came true. Rick was always my first choice. He didn't try to change me, he accepted me. He enhanced my life and never tried to take away my dreams. He is satisfied in his choices. The experience is similar to finding the right key to open the right door--it may take a few tries, but when you find the right one, it unlocks something special. I finally made the right choice.

I chose the cowboy.

Acknowledgements

Thank you to Amy @ prettysleepyart for her artwork used on the cover of several of my books, including this one.

Thank you to Author Michael Paul Hurd, owner of Lineage Independent Publishing, who was always there encouraging me to keep writing and suggesting edits. When I hit a roadblock he made me think and got me back on track. Thank you for sharing your knowledge with me.

Thank you to my family who never stopped believing in me. Thank you to my ladies Jenni and Rosemary who always listen, always encourage and support me without judging. Letting me run my crazy ideas by them has meant a lot to me. I really treasure the talks we have had in the past and the future.

Thank you to my mother in heaven. I did it, Mom!

Other books by Rebecca Conaty Bruce:

Esther Valentine Chronicles: *A clean crime series with occasional flirting, a little romance, and cold cases. Rated for teens and up.*

Book one – <u>Red Wood Fence</u>. Esther is hired to solve a cold case of a missing child in Amarillo Texas.

Book Two –<u>Blue Broken Glass</u>. Esther travels to Galveston, Texas to solve a cold case of a missing millionaire.

Book Three – <u>Gold Rosary Bead</u>. Esther is hired to solve a missing person case in Longview, Texas.

Book Four –<u>Silver Pocket Watch</u>. Esther solves a murder case gone cold in Austin, Texas.

Book Five – <u>White Snow Angel</u>. Esther is called to Canyon, Texas where a college student is found dead in the snow.

Book Six – <u>Green Paint Killer.</u> When Esther is a witness to a boat explosion, she is asked to solve the case.

Book Seven – Coming soon.

The Irish Bones Series – A two book Historical Fiction series following Lovina, whose father on his death bed tells her she has Irish Bones. Lovina reflects back on how she discovered her Irish Bones through the stories of her Irish Granddad. Book I captures you in the struggles of the past, Book II is her life after leaving Ireland. For readers 18 and up.

From Lineage Independent Publishing:

<u>Journey…the healer</u> (Young Adult Fantasy/fiction)
<u>Five Spirits in the Room</u>: A book about and for Angel moms and dads

Follow Me

<u>Facebook</u>: Facebook.com/Irishbonesbook1

<u>Twitter</u>: @Rebecca29971384

<u>Instagram</u>: Rebecca.a.bruce

<u>Email</u>: Irishbones310@gmail.com

Rebecca Conaty Bruce is also featured on Lineage Independent Publishing's web page, https://lineage-indypub.com

www.ingramcontent.com/pod-product-compliance
Lightning Source LLC
Chambersburg PA
CBHW030952190726
48285CB00004BB/1312